By Laura DeCosta

ALL OF SATAN'S SONS
The Chronicles of Lazarus

Published by Dreamspinner Press
www.dreamspinnerpress.com

THE CHRONICLES OF

Lazarus

LAURA DECOSTA

Published by

DREAMSPINNER PRESS

5032 Capital Circle SW, Suite 2, PMB# 279, Tallahassee, FL 32305-7886 USA
www.dreamspinnerpress.com

The Chronicles of Lazarus
© 2023 Laura DeCosta

Cover Art
© 2023 L.C. Chase
http://www.lcchase.com
Cover content is for illustrative purposes only and any person depicted on the cover is a model.

Trade Paperback ISBN: 978-1-64108-675-2
Digital ISBN: 978-1-64108-674-5
Trade Paperback published November 2023
v. 1.0

Printed in the United States of America
∞
This paper meets the requirements of
ANSI/NISO Z39.48-1992 (Permanence of Paper).

This book is dedicated to my Mom, who taught me kindness, and my Dad, who taught me strength. And to my sister, who taught me that I need both to live with love and understanding.

Acknowledgments

I want to start off by thanking my mom. She has always been so kind and so patient with everyone, even when we've made it hard for her. She's had to overcome more than most people ever have to deal with, and yet somehow she still manages to be so compassionate and understanding. I will forever be grateful that I was lucky enough to have her as my mother, and now that I'm grown, as my friend. I have a thick skull, but I like to think some of her warmth has rubbed off on me. If you're reading this, Mom, thank you for being you, and for putting up with all the times when I've been a little too much me.

I also have to thank my Dad. He and I are like night and day. Diametrically opposed in the ways we see the world and how we move through it. It took me awhile to understand him, and sometimes I still struggle, but he's always been there for me and I wouldn't be who I am today without him. When I told him I wanted to work on my writing, he was the first one to encourage me to start taking it seriously. He believed in me even when I didn't believe in myself. He taught me how to use my voice and stand up for what I believe in, even if this meant a headache for him a lot of times. And he's been so patient and supportive in helping me address the struggles from this last year in particular.

I owe a huge thanks to my senior editor at Dreamspinner Press. I had no idea how much work and editing went into this whole process. She's been so understanding and patient in explaining the process and discussing areas where I've felt conflicted or unsure. Also, her attention to detail is impeccable, and mine is horribly lacking. I've been very lucky to have her as the senior editor on my first book, and she's made what could've been a very stressful process a fun and enlightening experience.

Lastly, I want to thank all the friends from high school that I wrote my first stories with. They taught me how to use my imagination when I barely knew I had one and inspired many more stories to come. I discovered my love of writing through my friendships with them (you know who you are) and our love of storytelling, and the fact that this story exists is in large part because of them.

Chapter One:
All the World's a Stage

Eden

THIS WAS it.

The epitome of human existence. The bastard child of heaven and hell. Years of evolution and struggling to survive. Persevere. Become more than the sum of one's parts.

And *this* was it.

What a fucking shame.

It was the only thought that came to mind as Eden Zika looked down on the mass of sweaty, writhing bodies swaying back and forth to the bass bumping through Club Zero. Star athlete, college student, prostitute, drug addict. Some might clean up better than others, but they were all here for the same thing. Instant gratification, whether that came in the form of a quick fuck or a line of blow. Which meant, for the next few hours at least, he was God. Or the devil, depending on who you asked.

Shifting against the second-story railing, Eden's eyes skirted over the artificial rays of red, blue, green, and yellow from the strobe light overhead. Plumes of smoke danced lazily along the colorful rays, doing the devil's waltz. The stained-glass cathedral windows bordering either side of the dance floor vibrated with the bass, catching bursts of diluted color and throwing it back in shards of broken, fractured light.

It had been a church once, now a hotbed for drugs, prostitution, and any other deviant act a teeming metropolis like Denver attracted.

Apparently the club's owner had a sense of humor. Either that or the guy took some sort of sick, twisted pleasure spitting in the face of convention—a proverbial middle finger to the world. Tilting his head to the side, Eden lamented the fact that they'd never get a chance to meet. If they ever did, they'd probably get along swimmingly.

An imperceptible smirk tugged at Eden's lips. He shrugged off his leather jacket to reveal a black T-shirt with the words Fuck The Police in bold white print on either side. The white overlay was slightly crusted, the black backdrop now more of an ashen gray than the jet-black it had been when he'd bought it. One too many washes.

Because he was a creature of excess. In this, as in everything else.

It was early January, cold enough for the chilled winter breeze drifting through the archway to prick goose bumps along his skin. But he didn't pay it any mind. Club Zero always seemed cold. And erect nipples would only serve to further tonight's cause.

"Really?" Xavier Turner groused, gesturing to the bolded print on Eden's T-shirt as he joined him on the interior second-story balcony. "For fuck's sake. Why do you always insist on antagonizing them, Eden?"

The creaky metal railing groaned under their combined weight.

"Because it's fun. And I'm bored," Eden replied with a self-satisfied grin. He stretched his arms out to either side to make sure his statement piece was on full display. "It's not like they're going to stop following us if I wear something that says Jesus Loves You instead."

"That's not the point."

"Then what is?" He ran his hands along the rusted railing and watched the smoke trails curl in on themselves.

"They're already posted up in every corner of this shithole, jumping at the bit for the chance to catch us slipping. We don't need any more trouble. We haven't been able to sell shit for the past couple weeks."

"Exactly. So if we can't conduct business as usual, might as well have a little fun." Eden fished a cigarette and a lighter from his pocket, then lit the end and inhaled deeply before blowing a couple of O rings.

He adjusted his position against the railing so that he could continue tracking the tall blond to his right. Trev had said his name was Ross or Robert or some other fucking *R* name that didn't really matter. Rumor had it he'd spent the last two years working for Denver's small crimes unit and had been recently transferred to narcotics. Apparently he'd been assigned to be Eden's new babysitter.

Wonder who he pissed off, Eden mused with a snicker, reaching for his scotch.

In any case, All-American had become his second shadow for the last several weeks. It was a shame, really. He was tall with broad shoulders and size fourteen shoes. Thick, tussled dirty-blond hair stopped right below his ears. Long enough to pull if Eden hit it from behind. Maybe a little more clean-cut than what he usually preferred, but even so, he would've been almost fuckable if he weren't a cop. That and he dressed like a goddamn youth pastor. But what Eden wanted him for wouldn't involve much time with his clothes on anyway.

"Such a fucking waste," Eden muttered to himself. He shook his head and glanced out the window. The sky was dark. There were no stars out tonight. Just black and blue and miles of nothing.

"You know he's probably straight anyways. Most cops are." Xavier made a halfhearted attempt to deter what he already knew was inevitable.

"Come on, X. How long have you known me? You might as well save your breath."

"Eden."

Eden ignored the warning tone in his friend's voice. "Chill. I'm just going to have a little fun." He stubbed out what was left of his cigarette and picked up his scotch.

"You want me to tell Trev?"

"You want to wake up with another Betty White tattoo on your face?" Eden countered.

"Will it have a dick in its mouth again?" Xavier asked dryly. His tone made it clear he found the unsolicited body art considerably less amusing than his friend.

"Yes. With hearts. And this time it won't be semipermanent." Eden narrowed his eyes at Xavier to emphasize the seriousness of his threat, then disappeared into the crowd, heading in All-American's direction. He spotted him leaning against the wall, undoubtedly trying to appear inconspicuous as he cradled a drink in one hand and kept the other tucked into his pocket.

Ambling over, Eden added a slight stumble to his step as he passed, tipping his scotch down the front of blondie's untucked blue-and-white button-down.

"Oh shit," Eden muttered. He barely contained his smirk as he surveyed the damage.

"No, you're fi—" All-American did a double take as he looked up, recognition flashing in his glacial blue eyes.

"Hey, do I know you? I'm almost positive I've seen you before." Eden feigned innocence.

"Maybe." All-American's voice dropped an octave as he shifted his weight from one foot to the other. "Sometimes I come here."

Eden studied Captain America for half a pause.

Then he took a step into his space, ran his tongue along his lower lip and swallowed hard. All-American's eyes tracked his movements, drifting from his eyes to his lips and then down to his neck.

Bingo.

"Here, let me help." Eden reached for the stack of napkins on a nearby table, grabbed a couple, and began patting down the front of blondie's shirt.

Ostensibly to help, of course.

He could feel thick muscles and a simmering heat through the thin fabric. All-American's shoulders bunched when Eden's hands moved down, lingering at the waistband of his pants. With a single finger, he traced Captain America's belt buckle, right above his zipper.

Was he cut? Curved? Pale or pink? He definitely didn't have a Prince Albert. Wasn't the type. But Eden had a piercing gun back home. With a couple more shots of scotch, maybe he would be.

"No, it's fine. Really," All-American mumbled through gritted teeth, his words stumbling over one another. Clearing his throat, he pushed Eden's hands away.

"Yeah, you're right. Napkins probably won't do much," Eden replied, reveling in the other man's discomfort. Hell, he probably would've backed up if there wasn't a wall behind him. "I'd give you my shirt, but it's my favorite, so...."

The man's lips tightened into a thin line as his eyes skimmed across the Fuck The Police logo on Eden's shirt. His shoulders squared, and his brows furrowed. When he met Eden's gaze again, there was a hardness there. Something close to defiance, but not quite.

"That's okay. Probably wouldn't fit anyways. I'm bigger than you."

Eden raised a brow at the smug smile on the other man's lips.

Look who bites back.

This was going to be fun. A lot more fun than he'd initially anticipated, anyway.

"You don't like a tight fit?" Eden asked, his words laced with suggestion as he swiped his tongue along the inside of his cheek.

"You've got a pretty big opinion of yourself, don't you?"

Eden shrugged. He leaned a hand against the wall and drew closer to blondie. Close enough that when he spoke again, his breath brushed the soft stubble dotting All-American's jawline. "My therapist calls it a god complex. I just tell her it's proportional. Wanna step out back and find out?"

All-American coughed and broke eye contact. He adjusted himself against the wall and redirected his gaze elsewhere, polishing off his drink. Light beer, probably, or maybe even a nonalcoholic beverage. Eden could see no trace of redness in his eyes, and he was standing close enough to smell it on him if he'd been drinking anything harder.

What a fucking saint.

Eden drew in a deep breath, trying to catch blondie's scent over the smell of stale smoke and cheap perfume. It was slight, but it was there. Rich and earthy, like soil and pine-tree sap, with a hint of mint. What would his arousal smell like?

"Are you always this forward?"

"Pretty much. I'm Eden." Eden extended his hand.

"Ryan," the other man replied. He shook Eden's hand like it might be on fire, immediately pulling back. The electric touch was calloused and strong and way too brief.

"Ryan," Eden echoed, sampling the way the name tasted on his tongue. He rolled the *r* at the beginning and caught his tongue between his teeth. "What's that, Irish?"

"Yeah. Both my parents are Irish Catholic," Ryan responded, still refusing to meet his gaze. Well, that explained the youth pastor getup. "With a name like Eden, your parents must be religious too."

"Nah. A friend gave it to me. You wanna dance?" Eden asked, inclining his head toward the dance floor.

"I can't. I'm waiting for someone. Sorry." Ryan shook his head. The clipped tone of his voice implied it was a nonnegotiable. His eyes were focused on the dance floor below.

Laughing, Eden tried to remember the last time he'd been turned down so flatly. And with the oldest brush-off in the book at that. His eyes skirted across Ryan's face in an attempt to pinpoint how old he was. He couldn't have more than ten years on Eden, at most. Definitely not old enough for that line to be viable.

"Oh yeah? You got a hot date?"

"Something like that."

Eden smiled at Ryan's evasiveness. "A prostitute's cheaper if all you're looking to do is get laid. Between paying for drinks, roofies, and then a cab if they try to sleep over, that shit can run two hundred easy."

Ryan blinked at him, his expression incredulous. "You roofie your dates?"

"Only the prudes." Eden paused for half a beat and then snickered. "C'mon, Ryan. Keep up. The prostitutes are cheaper, remember?"

Ryan glanced down at the empty drink in his hand, then back up. "That line normally work for you?"

"Dunno. Never tried it before. Normally I just stick with 'Nice shoes, wanna fuck?' But you're wearing loafers, so...." Eden shrugged. Heat twined up his spine at the mixture of curiosity and disgust swirling around in Ryan's eyes.

"I think your friend's looking for you." The relief in Ryan's voice was almost palpable as he nodded at something behind Eden.

Turning, Eden cursed under his breath. Xavier was pushing his way through the crowd, intention clear.

"Eden, there you are." Xavier's words were laced with feigned concern as he slung his arm around Eden's shoulder and turned toward Ryan. "I'm sorry, is he giving you trouble? My boyfriend always gets a little loose-lipped when he drinks."

"No, it's fine." Ryan's eyes drifted between the two, his expression one of amusement. "Didn't realize you were taken."

"It's an open relationship," Eden responded hastily, shrugging Xavier's arm off and shooting him a mutinous glare.

"We only have the babysitter for another hour. If we stay out much longer, the kids are going to worry." Xavier pegged him with a hard look, nodding toward the exit.

"They're your kids. Not mine. You take care of them," Eden grumbled, detesting his friend for painting him into a corner with this assbackward version of reality.

"Don't be like that. You know they hate it when they wake up and you're not there." Xavier growled, grabbing his hand and pulling him toward the exit. Eden had barely enough time to slip a card into Ryan's breast pocket before he was hauled off into the crowd.

"You fucking cockblock. You know that Betty White tattoo? I'm adding a set of hairy balls to it now," Eden growled, making a futile attempt to yank his hand away.

"You'll thank me later." Xavier didn't bother to look back as he waved his hand dismissively, keeping the other tightly locked around Eden's wrist. He didn't let go till he'd ushered Eden into the passenger seat of his car. He activated the child safety locks to prevent Eden from escaping before sliding into the driver's seat.

"Seriously, X? Did you really have to do that?"

"Yes," Xavier answered without hesitation. "Check your phone."

Eden narrowed his eyes. He reached for his cigarettes and fished his phone from his pocket, skimmed over the only message that mattered. Eden cursed, glancing out the window before meeting Xavier's gaze.

"Did you tell him?"

"Of course I didn't, Eden. You know I never do."

"Bet it was Bobby. That fucking narc," Eden cursed, lighting his cigarette as Xavier pulled away from the curb. He had to remind himself to relax as his fingers reflexively curled into fists.

"Probably. He's been kissing Trev's ass trying to get back on his good side ever since he botched that handoff."

Both men were quiet for a moment. The hum of the engine filled the silence between them.

"I'll tell him you didn't know," Eden said. "Say I did it when you went out for a smoke or some shit."

"Eden—"

"No. It's fucking bullshit. He knows how I am. He shouldn't always be coming down on you too."

"And he also knows we're a team. So just stop, all right? I already told him I was there anyways."

"Damn it, X." Eden took a heavy drag from his cigarette and ran a hand through his hair. "Why the fuck do you always do this shit?"

Xavier glanced over at him. A small smile pulled at his lips. "Because you're a fucking idiot. And you're my friend. Now stop bitching and try to chill out. We're almost there."

Eden cursed but said nothing more as they pulled up in front of a rundown, nondescript apartment complex. Most of the windows were broken, the majority of the exterior covered in graffiti and crumbling brick. It was decrepit and dirty and as cold as the winter chill that nipped at Eden's skin through the folds of his leather jacket.

For a moment they simply sat there, neither man moving as they both delayed the inevitable. A crow flew low in the sky, doing its death dance. Gray clouds blotted out the moon overhead, turning the sky into an endless nothingness.

Slowly, Eden and Xavier made their way inside. They took the stairs to the second floor and knocked twice on the door at the end of the hall. After a couple of seconds, they were let into the room. Eden and

Xavier took their usual seats on the large black leather couch. The room was sparsely furnished, the only additions a low-lying glass table with metal legs, an oversized black leather chair near the window, and a large flat-screen TV attached to the wall opposite the couch.

There was already a man sitting in the chair opposite Eden. He knew from the text that the man wouldn't be happy.

"Look who finally decided to fucking show up. Heard you tried your luck tonight sticking your dick in a pig."

Eden ignored the sharp tone in Trevor Gills's voice as his boss regarded him and Xavier with a steely gaze. Most men would've flinched or at least offered an apology, but Eden was used to it by now. Had been for a while. Trevor was a mean son of a bitch with a gnarled, roguish face and severe bushy brows. He didn't mince words or pull punches. A great guy to have watching your back in a bar fight, but if you were unlucky enough to end up on his bad side, you'd better pray for a miracle, because mercy was definitely not in his vocabulary.

"C'mon, Trev. You know we can't sell tonight with the way twelve's been on us," Eden replied evenly, using the crew's shorthand for the District 6 police station on 12th Avenue. He curled his fingers into his palms to keep from fidgeting. Trevor always made him feel restless. Itchy, like a spot on his back he could never truly scratch.

"So, what, you thought you'd pick up a side gig as a sperm donor? You forget who the fuck you are? 'Cause if you need a reminder, I'd be happy to oblige. All these fucking ops dipping into my profits already has me on edge, Eden. I'd have laid you out already if I could afford it. You want to act like a dog, I'll treat you like one. And Xavier, you should know better. At least he has an excuse."

Eden pressed his lips into a thin line. His jaw tightened as he bit back his response. Trevor was clearly not amused.

"Fine. We're sorry," Xavier muttered, offering an apology.

"Sorry gonna pay my fucking bills? Didn't think so. Now get back to your post before I change my mind." Eden turned to follow Xavier out, but Trevor's voice stopped him.

"Not you. Can't keep your mouth shut or your dick in your pants, fine. Got a job for you that doesn't require either."

Chapter Two:
Nothing Will Come of Nothing

Ryan

"WHERE'S BREAKFAST? You look like shit."

Ryan didn't even bother to look up when his partner, Shawn Evans, greeted him with his usual version of good morning. Instead, he flipped off the general direction the voice had come from and continued to work on his report.

"Really? Not even a 'Fuck you too'? What crawled up your ass and died?"

Ryan sighed. A familiar hand reached out and snatched the paperwork from his desk. He made a halfhearted attempt to retrieve it, reaching across the long metal frame and swinging at him. Shawn had apparently anticipated as much, judging by the way he stepped back. He flashed Ryan a cheeky grin, holding the stack of papers just out of Ryan's reach.

"Needy bastard," Ryan muttered, sitting back down and meeting Shawn's triumphant gaze.

"What? You still mad at me over the shit that happened a couple weeks back? Cry me a fucking river. Since when did you turn into such a baby?"

Ryan groaned, glancing around for anything he could use to temporarily disarm his partner long enough to grab his report. The office area his unit occupied at the precinct was a wide-open space, poorly furnished with a few plastic floor plants and several heavy brown metal desks. Most of which were now vacant due to budget cutbacks. Cheap flimsy blinds hung on the northern wall. A couple of slats were bent, jutting out haphazardly. The other three walls were covered in a varying collage of framed newspaper clippings and heavy wooden plaques. Homage to the unit's former glory days.

How far the mighty have fallen, Ryan thought, shaking his head.

"No," Ryan finally relented. "But if I was, I'd have every right to be."

"I already apologized for that," Shawn muttered, rolling his eyes. "It was an accident, okay? Do you have to make such a big deal out of every little thing?"

"You shot me in the shoulder," Ryan deadpanned, making another grab for his paperwork.

"Not shot. Nicked," Shawn countered, once again stepping out of reach. "And you didn't even need stitches, so calm the fuck down."

"That's not the point." Shaking his head, Ryan marveled at how he'd survived this long having to rely on a guy like Shawn to watch his six. They'd been partners for the last two years and best friends for over a decade, a fact that all the scars on his body stood testament to, albeit unwillingly.

"Pretty sure it is. It was your fault anyways. Your shoulder got in the way."

Ryan resisted the urge to reenact the same argument they'd had two weeks ago. "Would you shut the fuck up? Please. I already have a headache. And I told you, it's not that." Ryan sunk back into his chair and rubbed his temples.

A desk phone rang on the other side of the room. The rhythmic click of footfalls echoed in from the hallway. Even the mechanical hum of the fax machine relegated to the far corner of the room made Ryan's head pulse.

"Then what is it?" Shawn asked, his tone accusatory as he helped himself to the Red Bull on Ryan's desk. "'Cause your shitty mood's really bringing down my vibe, and you know how McNeil is about team morale."

Ryan exhaled heavily. All the thoughts that kept him up the previous night came rushing back. Pulling the card Zika had slipped him from his pocket, Ryan slid it across his desk toward Shawn.

"Last night when I was running surveillance on Zika, he gave me his number."

"So? We already have his—" Shawn's eyes widened, a mixture of utter glee and disbelief contorting his features. "Wait. You mean he gave you his number as in, 'Hey, give me a call if you're ever in the mood for a quick fuck'?"

Ryan huffed. He grabbed the card and shoved it back into his pocket. "No. Not really. I think he was testing me, trying to feel out the waters. See how I'd react. I just don't know why."

"Maybe he just wanted to fuck you." Shawn mused with a smirk. "Word on the street is he has a thing for blonds."

Ryan rolled his eyes. Yeah, because nothing says let's get it on like roofies and a couple of thinly veiled jabs at his moral constitution. Either that or Zika was spectacularly socially incompetent. Not likely.

"No. He's not that stupid. He had me made for sure. But I can't figure out what his angle is."

He'd thought about it to exhaustion. Analyzed it from every possible angle. Eventually he'd narrowed it down to two possibilities. Neither of which he liked.

"It's possible he was simply trying to confirm his suspicions," a new voice suggested.

Turning, Ryan nodded in Kurtis's direction. He'd walked into the office with Alice, and he returned Ryan's greeting with a smile. They were also members of the narcotics unit, though Kurtis had only been with the precinct a couple months.

"No shit, Sherlock. You don't think we already fucking thought of that?" Shawn snickered.

"I was only trying to help—"

"You wanna help? Then shut your mouth and get me some coffee." Shawn shoved his half-empty coffee cup in Kurtis's direction.

"Don't." Alice put her hand out when Kurtis moved forward. "It'll only encourage him. He was walking on all fours up until a couple months ago, so he needs the practice anyways."

"Oh come on now, Ally, you calling me a dog?" Shawn grinned, blowing her a kiss from across the room.

"No," Alice replied coolly. "That would be an insult to the dogs. At least they don't shit where they sleep."

"That was a one-time thing, and I was fucking drunk, all right?" Shawn snapped, flushing.

Though it took him biting down on his tongue, Ryan barely resisted the urge to snicker.

"Should we really be talking about this sort of stuff in the office?" Kurtis shifted his weight from one foot to the other anxiously.

"Shut up, Mom. Didn't I tell you to go make me some coffee?"

"Shawn. Don't call him that," Ryan admonished. Ever since the kid had started several months back, his best friend had taken it upon himself to haze Kurtis. Thoroughly. Ryan had to hand it to the guy, he'd been dealing with Shawn's snide remarks for three months, and he still hadn't cracked. Ryan knew because Shawn had been marking the days on his calendar.

"What? He wants to act like my fucking mom, might as well address him accordingly—"

"Nice to see you all are putting Denver's taxpayer money to good use." McNeil's baritone voice boomed through the small room. The four detectives jumped to attention, Shawn slightly slower than the rest. Ryan's boss appraised the four with a disapproving glare.

"We were discussing some developments from last night's surveillance on Zika. Sir." Ryan cleared his throat.

"Yeah, you know, the one you wouldn't let me go on," Shawn added petulantly.

"Shut up, dipshit. If you hadn't shot your partner, I wouldn't have you on desk duty in the first place," McNeil barked, eliciting a nervous glance from Shawn.

"Why does everyone keep saying shot? It only grazed him."

"Did I ask for your fucking opinion, Evans? No. So sit down and get back to work. That stack of paperwork ain't gonna do itself." Motioning to Shawn's desk on the opposite end of the room, McNeil waited till Shawn took a seat before approaching Ryan's workspace.

"So, how'd it go?"

Ryan hesitated. "Honestly, sir, I don't know."

"You don't know?" McNeil parroted. "How's that? You were there, right?"

"Well, yeah, but…."

McNeil's eyes narrowed. "But what, Quinn? You have something you need to tell me?"

Ryan reluctantly pulled Zika's card from his pocket and slid it across the desk. McNeil was quiet for a moment. His brows arched slightly as he glanced at the white paper.

"He gave you his number?"

"Yeah. Don't know why yet. He has to already know I'm a cop. Maybe he was trying to see how much we have on him."

He'd been running surveillance on Zika for the past two weeks, part of the city's initiative to stunt the rising drug rates. Narcotics-related deaths had hit an unprecedented high in the last year. After some dirty coke left five kids at a college party dead, one of them the governor's nephew, his unit had received a direct order from the higher-ups that they needed to start producing results. And fast. As one of the leading drug dealers in Denver, Zika had made the top of their list.

Ryan had known Zika was gay from his file. And he'd expected the attitude. Most of the dope dealers he hauled in had a chip on their shoulder and a slick mouth. But Zika was dangerous in a way most of the others weren't.

He was charismatic, in an offensive, arrogant, fuckboy sort of way. He was also very clearly insane, a fact that Ryan attributed partly to all the cocaine Zika was rumored to snort and partly to an unfortunate oversight on God's part. Everyone has an off day, right? In any case, he'd already proven himself to be a worthy adversary.

McNeil chewed on the inside of his cheek for a moment, a pensive expression in his eyes. Finally he looked up at Ryan, sliding the card back to him.

"Well, this is the best lead we've got on the guy so far. I say we run with it. Even if he already knows you're a cop, doesn't mean we can't use the situation to our advantage."

Ryan recoiled. He felt like he'd been punched in the gut. He'd been afraid McNeil was going to say something like that.

"Define 'run with it.'"

"Don't play dumb with me, Quinn. Call him and set something up. Unlike your partner, you know how to play nice. Butter him up. See what you can get out of him. If you can get him to trust you, he might get comfortable. Let something slip."

"Sir. I know this is a sensitive situation, but...." The rest of Ryan's objection was lost on his lips as he met McNeil's unrelenting gaze.

He understood that McNeil needed to make something happen. That his boss had a boss to answer to. And he wasn't the greenest agent in his unit. But there were plenty of other detectives more qualified to take on Zika's case. Plenty of his coworkers that would be a much better fit.

"No buts, Quinn. I need you to take one for the team. Evans already has us in hot water with that last police brutality complaint."

A cackle erupted from across the room. Shawn grabbed his side, unable to contain his laughter. "Oh God, this is gonna be good. Can I watch? Please? I promise I'll behave."

Ryan groaned. There was no way Shawn was ever going to let him live this down.

"No," both Ryan and McNeil growled, glaring Shawn into submission from across the room.

"Listen, Quinn. I know this isn't ideal. But if you can land this guy, I promise you the boys up top are gonna be impressed. Might even consider you for a promotion. Zika's been a pain in our ass for years. Slippery as a fucking snake. But you've trained for this. You handle this, and I'll vouch for you." Glancing over at Shawn, McNeil lowered his voice. "I know you're not well versed on the gay shit. If you need a couple books—"

"No," Ryan muttered hurriedly. "I mean, I'm not. But my brother was gay. It's not something I haven't been around before."

Ryan resisted the urge to remind his boss that gay people weren't a different species. Nor were they all the same. Like reading an autobiography about one gay man's experience in America would speak for every gay man on God's green earth.

Especially Zika.

Nodding slowly, McNeil gave him a rough pat on the shoulder. "Good. You've got this. You have the experience, and you're good on your feet. Read through his file again if you need to. I'm counting on you."

Ryan swallowed past the tingling in his limbs as adrenaline spiked in his veins. This was everything he'd been working for. The chance to take down a top-tier member of a major narcotics ring was something most junior detectives dreamed of.

But he'd assumed it would come under different circumstances. And a couple of years down the road when the majority of his experience didn't consist of busting small-time street dealers who used as much product as they moved.

But opportunity was knocking. And even if he wasn't ready to open the door, McNeil had already busted it down for him.

Sighing, he waited till McNeil left to pull out his phone. "Take one for the team," Ryan muttered, his fingers hovering over his phone's keypad.

What the hell was he even supposed to say? *Hey, remember me from the club the other night? I know it seemed like I was completely repulsed by you, but I'm feeling frisky tonight. You dtf?* Flushing, Ryan shoved his phone into his pocket. He did his best to ignore the intermittent bursts of laughter coming from the other end of the room. Needing to clear his head, he left the squad room and ran a couple of laps around the precinct before trying again.

He retyped his message five times before finally deciding it was probably best to keep it simple.

Hey, It's Ryan. You free tonight?

He spent the rest of the day mulling over some unfinished reports, glancing back down at his phone from time to time. By five o'clock he'd almost given up on hearing back from Zika when his phone buzzed. The message was short and to the point.

4820 47th street. Be there at 10 tonight. Wear something comfortable.

Ryan took a deep breath. He got into his black 1967 Chevrolet Impala and headed for home. Something comfortable, huh?

Eden

PATIENCE IS a virtue.

Luckily, Eden was not a virtuous man. Rules, for him, were more like guidelines. Like the recommended serving size on the back of food labels—no one actually uses them.

Frowning, Eden lengthened his strides as he made his way down the sidewalk. Intent on expediting this little game of cat and mouse, he turned into the alleyway to his right. It was narrow, like a hangman's noose. The brick on either side had decayed, leaving gaping, hollow gashes along the walls. A dumpster covered in graffiti stood at the far end.

A good place for dumping a body. Or rotting away.

Hopefully the added privacy would give these fuckers the balls they needed to speed this shit up. He had an appointment to keep. His favorite underground fight club closed in a couple of hours, and depending on how this played out, he might need to have one or two bones set before his upcoming match.

Resting his hand on the gun at his hip, Eden stopped and turned to face his pursuers. The three men that had been following him for the last couple of blocks stepped out from the shadows. All three were wearing hoods and black ski masks and were armed with shiny sidepieces of their own. The tallest one in the middle stepped forward and gestured to the two flanking him. Eden didn't bother fighting as Mr. Tall's henchmen advanced and grabbed his arms.

"I trust you know why we're here," the apparent leader of the three growled. His voice was thick and gritty as he stepped forward and grabbed Eden by the chin.

"You guys get lost on your way to the whorehouse?" Eden offered with a smirk. "If you want, I can—"

Mr. Tall punched him hard across the face, cutting short whatever else Eden had to say. Eden tasted blood in his mouth, liquid metal on his tongue. The world spun around him as lights flashed in his vision's periphery.

"I'd blow your brains out right now if my boss wasn't afraid it'd start a turf war. All you new-age fucks ain't got no respect. Fucking punk. D sent me to give you a message. Stay out of our territory."

Eden laughed. His breath turned to white frost in the frigid winter air. "I would, but you see, there's only one problem with that. It's not your territory."

"It's ours," Xavier finished, stepping out from the shadows and pointing his gun at the back of Mr. Tall's head.

Cursing, Mr. Tall slowly put his hands up.

"Tell your men to stand down." Xavier's voice was cold as steel as he tugged Mr. Tall back by his jacket. Nodding, Mr. Tall and his cronies begrudgingly acquiesced.

Eden brushed himself off, righting his leather jacket. He spit the blood in his mouth onto the cold, gray asphalt before delivering a solid uppercut to Mr. Tall's jaw. "Now that we've gotten introductions out of the way, let's get a couple things straight. This here… this is our territory. Not yours. And sure as fuck not Dominick's."

Eden reached forward and pulled Mr. Tall's mask from his face. His gun gained the compliance of the other two as they followed suit. He took a moment to memorize their faces. "We're all intimately acquainted now. Know what that means? Next time we see you and your boys in our parts, we'll be sending you back to your boss in body bags. We clear?"

Mr. Tall nodded and stumbled toward the alleyway entrance with his lackeys following behind. Eden waited till the three men had disappeared from sight to stuff his gun back into his pants.

"Motherfuckers. I told Trev we need to do something before shit gets worse," Xavier growled. "Right now D's got us bent over like one of his two-dollar whores, fucking us farther and farther back into our own territory every day."

"And what do you want us to do? Pop a couple off just to prove a point when twelve's been breathing down our necks for the past week?"

"We've gotta do something. Nobody's going to trust us to move product if we can't even hold our own turf."

Eden sighed. "Chill, X. The only thing being trigger happy gets you out here is dead. There's a difference between lying down and lying in wait. You know that."

Xavier let out a frustrated breath beside him—his only response. They'd had this conversation every night for the past week, and it always ended the same.

Indeed, Eden was not a man of patience, much like his friend. But there were many other virtues he held sacred, even if he wasn't a virtuous man. Namely, being a man of his word.

Chapter Three:
Doubt Thou the Stars Are Fire

Ryan

ZIKA REALLY *knows how to pick 'em*, Ryan thought to himself dully. He scanned the crowd surrounding the makeshift boxing ring—if you could even call it that—in the center of the small room. In earnest, it was nothing more than four rounded wooden poles with a line of frayed rope surrounding the perimeter.

Not exactly high-end, even for an illegal underground fight club.

Ryan pushed his way through the crowd, searching for Zika's coal-black hair amid the sea of half-naked bodies and chest tattoos. The rowdy mass jostled him as one of the contenders in the ring landed a right hook.

Guttural shouts and jeers echoed off the crumbling concrete walls, so loud it was almost deafening as spectators cheered from the sidelines. The low vaulted ceiling amplified the thunderous roar.

Rolling his shoulders, Ryan took a seat against the wall. Zika probably wasn't even here yet. He tucked his hands into his pockets and drew in a deep breath. The combination of stale cigarette smoke and rank, raw body odor concentrated in the grayed-out, windowless space made his gut churn.

He recognized a couple of faces in the crowd. They were frequent flyers in Denver's world of underground narcotics trafficking. Thankfully, the recognition appeared one-sided. Not a surprise, given the fact that not only was he still relatively new to the narcotics department, but the wifebeater and sweats he'd donned for tonight's event were a far cry from what an on-duty detective would be seen in.

In fact he'd been worried about being underdressed. That was, of course, before he'd stepped inside and realized half the occupants hadn't bothered with shirts at all.

Zika had invited him here for a reason. Why, he was still puzzling out. Maybe to intimidate. Or maybe he simply felt more comfortable in his natural environment. Not that this motley bunch appeared to have much in common with Zika on the surface.

Giving the room another once-over, Ryan did a double take. He spotted Zika just as he entered the ring. Cursing under his breath, he suppressed the urge to scoff. He should've expected as much. Of course that egotistical blowhard wouldn't miss an opportunity to take center stage, even if it meant risking a couple of broken bones.

Zika's hands were covered in white, chalky wrappings, his bare chest on full display as he sized up his opponent on the other side of the ring. Swallowing hard, Ryan raised a brow, his gaze dropping to Zika's chest.

Well, this was unexpected.

Zika was fucking ripped. Long, sinewy muscles ran the length of his chest and abdomen. Veins chorded around his biceps and forearms, the blue webbing easily visible under the club's harsh fluorescent lighting. He would've looked like a well-trained swimmer if it weren't for the vast array of scars covering his upper body.

Ryan had already seen the single pigmented line across his right cheek when they'd first met. And he hated it. Mainly because it gave his already handsome pretty-boy features a rugged, edgy appeal.

His shoulders rolled as he walked, circling his opponent in the ring. His gait was confident. Focused. Like an apex predator stalking its prey. Every movement rippled with energy and tempered aggression. The ink on his upper chest only added to the lethal aura.

What it said, Ryan had no clue. And not only because it wasn't in English. Something else had caught his attention. Ryan's eyes were drawn to the two perfect flesh-pink pools on his chest. His nipples were hard, just like they'd been the other night. The perfect color for teasing.

He'd be hard-pressed to admit it, even under duress, but Zika looked good.

Really fucking good.

Forcing his eyes away, Ryan glanced at Zika's opponent on the other side of the ring. He had a couple of inches on Zika and at least fifty pounds. Apparently they didn't give a fuck about weight classes here. Not a surprise considering the fact that half its occupants had prison tattoos and poorly concealed illegal firearms. Judging by the noise the crowd was making, Zika was a fan favorite.

Part of him hoped it was unwarranted. Hoped Zika would get knocked flat on his ass, just to take him down a couple of notches. Nothing serious. No maiming or scarring. But enough to knock the chip off his shoulder. Put a chink in his otherwise pristine armor.

Ryan's adrenaline spiked as the bell chimed and the two men began circling one another in the ring. The other man was bigger and stronger, but as he watched Zika dodge one swing after another, he realized Zika had the distinct advantage. He was faster and smarter, tiring the larger man out and blocking the hits that he couldn't dodge. His movements were agile and calculated, almost like a dance.

When Zika finally went on the offensive, it only took a flurry of well-placed uppercuts to his opponent's jaw before the larger man went down. The crowd erupted. Several of the men patted Zika on the back as he made his way out of the ring. Even Ryan had to admit he was impressed. Zika had skill. Maybe not the mastery of a professional boxer, but he was good.

Ryan watched as Zika jumped over the rope and made a beeline straight for him. He braced himself for what would undoubtedly be another onslaught of inappropriate lack of censorship.

"Hey, you gonna get in the ring?" Zika was smiling, still dripping sweat, head cocked to the side.

"No, I'm good," Ryan replied. The words came out stiffer than he'd intended. Like gravel over glass. His eyes flickered from Zika's face to his chest. His pecs glistened, beads of sweat catching in the fine black hairs as his rib cage expanded and contracted rhythmically. He forced his eyes back up, chiding himself internally.

It wasn't that he minded fighting. In fact in a controlled environment, it was one of his favorite ways to blow off steam. But everything he knew about fighting had come from his police training. Any of the holds or maneuvers he'd use would out him instantly. Even if he was 95 percent sure Zika already knew he was a cop, he wasn't in a hurry to confirm it. Especially in front of this crowd.

"Too bad. Bet you shirtless is a pretty sight to see. How 'bout you just lose the wifebeater? You know, so we're even." Zika smirked, his gaze drifting downward with his usual lack of tact.

Ryan's frame went rigid as Zika's eyes ran the full length of his body.

"This isn't a game of 'I'll show you mine if you show me yours' on the playground."

Zika licked his lips, taking a step into his space. "Yeah. But if it were, bet mine would be bigger."

Ryan snickered. "You really think you can goad me into pulling out my dick? I'm not five, Eden." He forced some bass into his voice. He would not allow himself to be intimidated by some kid eight years his junior.

"Five inches?" A smug smile tugged at Zika's lips as he leaned his hand against the wall, blocking Ryan in. His eyes flared. His pupils dilated, the gray striations fading into black. "Got some bad news for you, Ryan. When I finally fuck you, I'm gonna give you a massive inferiority complex."

Ryan held Zika's gaze, forcing himself not to look away. "That's pretty fucking presumptuous of you." The words were right, but the sound was wrong. Scratchy. Strained. Almost hoarse.

"What?" Zika asked. "The five inches? You said it, not me."

Ryan resisted the urge to glance down and see if Zika was aroused. Instead he looked over Zika's shoulder, back out at the ring, focusing his eyes on the two new occupants.

"No. The other thing. If we ever did fuck—which is never going to happen, by the way—I'd be the one fucking you. Not the other way around."

To Ryan's immense satisfaction, Zika went still. He could feel Zika's eyes on him, staring at Ryan while Ryan stared out at the ring. He couldn't see the expression on Zika's face, but when he spoke again, the smirk was back, as thick in his words as heavy cream.

"You wouldn't even know where to stick it in."

Ryan shrugged, finally meeting Zika's gaze. "I could google it."

Slowly Zika's smirk gave way to a smile that stretched from ear to ear, a throaty laugh escaping his lips. The rich, full-bodied sound made Ryan feel more than a little smug. Not a snicker or a sneer, but a genuine laugh. A real laugh that lit up his eyes and soothed the worry lines between his brows. He realized then that this was the first time he'd ever heard Zika laugh. Ryan stood a bit straighter, crossing his arms casually in front of him.

"This where you take all your dates, Eden? If so, I can see why you have to roofie them to get laid."

"I don't do dates. I fuck."

"Right." Ryan chanced a glance at Zika's face. His features were striking. Beautiful even. Deep frost-gray eyes against spotless pale skin and plump nude lips.

He pondered why a guy like Zika would frequent the red-light district. Even if his main priority was being cost efficient—which Ryan highly doubted—Zika was hot. Hell, there were probably plenty of people willing to overlook his appalling personality and asinine smirk for that fact alone.

"You wanna take a picture? It'll last longer."

Ryan's eyes snapped back to the boxing ring. The chords in his neck tensed as he cleared his throat. "Sorry."

"Don't be," Zika replied easily, a self-satisfied smirk playing its way across his lips. "Unless all you plan to do is look." Stretching his forearms behind his back, Zika made a show of flexing his biceps and abdomen, ensuring he was on full display. God, he was ridiculous. Practically gloating.

And the worst part was, he had every right to be. The guy was drop-dead gorgeous.

"You're fucking shameless, you know that?" Ryan muttered.

"Yeah, it's one of my more charming features—shit, what the fuck happened to you?" Zika asked. He let out a low whistle and reached over to touch the area on Ryan's shoulder where Shawn's stray bullet had grazed him.

A jolt of electricity ran through Ryan at the unexpected touch. Zika's fingers lingered for a moment, the calloused tips surprisingly gentle as they brushed over the angry purple scar. "My pa—my best friend and I were messing around, and he got a little trigger happy."

"Oh yeah?" Zika asked, raising a brow. "No shit. Didn't realize you prim-and-proper types got down like that."

Ryan shrugged, kicking himself mentally for the near blunder. "Shawn's a little developmentally challenged I guess you could say."

"Your best friend's retarded?"

Ryan suppressed a laugh, wishing Shawn had been here for that bit. "Nah. Just a little half-cocked. We grew up together, and half the time our friendship consisted of me trying to talk him out of doing something stupid. In fact this place would probably be right up his alley—"

"Eden."

Ryan stiffened as Xavier Turner made his way over to them through the crowd. Well, wasn't this just fucking dandy. How the hell did this guy always manage to show up at the worst possible times.

"You done?" Turner asked, his words colored with disapproval as his eyes drifted between the two.

"Yeah, I'll be there in a sec," Zika said, turning slightly.

"Naw, I think you two have had long enough." Turner's tone was sharp as he pegged Zika with a hard look.

Zika's eyes flashed, something unspoken passing between the two.

"All right," Zika said slowly, pushing himself up off the wall. "I'll see you around, Ryan."

"Yeah, you too," Ryan muttered, watching as the two headed for the exit. What the hell was it between the two of them? They were friends and fuck buddies; he already knew that. And they sold dope together, which inevitably established some sort of camaraderie. But there seemed to be something more. He knew that line Turner had given him back at Club Zero about getting home to the kids was absolute bullshit. Neither of them had kids. And from what his file said, the two weren't exclusive.

Still.

Zika wasn't the type to let anyone rein him in like that. Ryan was missing something. He just didn't know what. Shaking his head, he cursed, realizing he was walking away tonight knowing nothing more about Zika's extracurriculars than he had before.

Eden

"I TOLD YOU. I warned you not to come back here." Eden spoke through gritted teeth as he held the chloroform-soaked rag over Stefan Nikolai's nose and mouth. The veins in his arms bulged at the strain as he held Nikolai in place behind the back-alley dumpster. He grunted when Nikolai delivered a couple of sharp blows to his midsection.

Of course he would fight. They always fought.

Regardless of the type of man, the reaction was always the same. Disbelief, fear, then, eventually, despair. They say the last thing a person loses in life is hope. As Nikolai's body finally went limp against him, Eden bit back a choked laugh. Maybe that was true for a lucky few.

But in his personal opinion, hope was an elusive bitch. The majority of people lose it long before death finally takes them. And some, the ones stupid enough not to see it coming, never did.

He was willing to bet Nikolai was the latter. He'd find out soon enough.

Eden waited till he spotted Xavier's car circling the block to drag the unconscious man toward the street. After shoving Nikolai into the back seat of the car, Eden slid into the passenger seat and huffed.

"The fuck is up with D's men and steroids? You see the size of this motherfucker?"

Xavier snickered, taking a couple of draws from his pipe. "Least this one didn't break your nose."

"Yeah. That's why he still has all his teeth." Eden leaned over the armrest and made a grab for the pipe. "Two hits and pass, you greedy motherfucker. Thought your momma taught you crackhead etiquette."

"You know what else she taught me? To finish your work before you play," Xavier said, motioning to the man in the back.

"You know I hate when you do this shit."

"What? Act like an adult?"

"Act like a fucking bootlicker." Eden rolled his eyes. He turned, contorting himself between the seats, and made quick work of tying Nikolai's hands and legs and gagging him with duct tape. "There. He's tagged and bagged. Now give me a hit."

"Eden."

"Fine." Eden blew out a frustrated breath. "But we're stopping by McDonalds on the way there."

"You're kidding, right?" Xavier's expression was incredulous.

"You know I can't go all Krueger on an empty stomach."

"And how the hell are we supposed to go through the drive-thru with this guy in the back?"

Eden shrugged. "We'll just throw a blanket over him. Tell them we're dropping off last night's mistake."

Nikolai moaned in the back, stirring slightly.

"And the sound?"

Eden turned in his seat and smacked Nikolai on the back of the head. "Shut the fuck up or I'll tase you. If I lose out on my McDouble because of you, I'm cutting off a finger."

"I'd listen to him." Xavier deadpanned. "He's not nice when he's hangry."

"Not my fault. The son of a bitch is, like, six four. Practically had to break his kneecaps just to fit him in the back seat. I deserve a cheeseburger."

"All right." Xavier relented. "But only because I'd have to listen to you mouth off for the next hour if I didn't."

"You know me so well."

Xavier nodded, stealing a glance in Eden's direction. "So what's the deal with you and Quinn?"

Eden grinned, licking his lips. "Think I found me a motherfucking unicorn."

"A what?"

"You know that shit I always say about white guys having tiny dicks. I think Ryan might be the exception."

Xavier shook his head. "I didn't ask you how big his dick was. I asked you what you're doing with him."

"Same thing."

"No, not really." Xavier's eyes narrowed. "That mean you're going out with him again?"

"Probably, yeah. And this time I'm not telling you where we're going. I'm tired of you pulling this mother hen shit."

"I wouldn't have to if you'd just stick with the prostitutes," Xavier stated matter-of-factly.

Eden smirked. "Caviar taste on a beer budget. I know."

"This isn't a joke, Eden."

"Chill. I'm just having fun. If I knock him up, I'll put a ring on it. Promise."

Xavier's brow's furrowed, a worry wrinkle forming between his eyes. "This could land you six feet under with Trev. You realize that, right?"

"'Course I do," Eden said, reclining his seat so far back it came down on Nikolai's head. He kicked his feet up on the dash. "That's why I wanna get *high*. Gotta balance that shit out. Maybe then I'll only end up in the third dimension of hell."

"I thought you didn't even believe in God."

"I don't. I was humoring you." Swiping the pipe from Xavier's hand, Eden lit the bowl and took a hit, a victorious grin spreading across his face. "See, I can be nice when I'm hangry too."

Xavier let out an exasperated sigh. "I give up. You're clearly beyond reasoning with."

"A gun to my head usually helps. But even then it's a fifty-fifty."

"Not funny," Xavier growled, shooting a glare in Eden's direction. By the time they'd stopped by McDonald's and made their way halfway across town, the sun was setting on the western horizon.

They pulled up in front of a metal warehouse on the south side of town. It was one of many safe houses Trevor had in the city. This location was used exclusively for holding their nonconsenting guests.

Eden and Xavier got out of the car and hauled Nikolai from the back seat, Eden gripping Nikolai's legs while Xavier grabbed his shoulders. After considerable effort and a stream of expletives, they managed to carry the semiconscious man through the back door of the warehouse and into the holding room. Once he'd dropped Nikolai onto the cold, hard concrete, Eden stretched, yawning.

Trev might bitch about the delay. But some risks were worth taking. Like stopping by McDonald's to combat the wave of nausea from knowing what was to come. Or throwing a couple of punches for the chance to impress his hot blond shadow with eyes like a spring thaw. Like chasing after a unicorn, even knowing they have horns.

Chapter Four:
One True Love

Eden

THE SMELL was always the worst part.

Stinging and pungent and slightly bitter, the scent of blood hung thick in the air. Vomit and piss were also present, notable but less prominent as they mingled together in the confines of the small windowless room. Eden felt suffocated by the familiar aroma, like it permeated everything it touched. Crept into his pores and sank straight through his skin right down to the bone. Staining. Maiming. Mutilating.

He should be used to it by now.

He'd grown accustomed to the screaming. The pleading and begging that came with the inevitable desperation right before a man breaks. But the smell of the blood always got to him. Maybe because it stirred up old memories. Or maybe he was just being a bitch. Blood in, blood out; it always smelled the same. The narrative might differ, but the eventual outcome only ever ended one of two ways. With a warning said recipient would never forget, or with death.

Bile stung the back of Eden's throat as he glanced up at the bloodied, barely conscious man handcuffed to a chair in the center of the room. Nikolai. The man that he'd chloroformed. He suppressed a wave of nausea as his hands curled into fists.

"You good?"

All Eden could do was nod as he made eye contact with Xavier. He didn't want to speak in case it encouraged his stomach to empty its contents out onto the cold concrete floor. Trevor would not like that. Not at all.

"You pathetic piece of shit." Trevor growled, bringing his fist down on Nikolai's face. Eden had lost count of how many times he'd hit him. Enough to where Trevor's knuckles were likely bruised and swollen. "Answer me! Where the fuck did you put them?"

Nikolai's head swung from one side to the other, blood dripping from his mouth and nose. Well past the point of being able to form a coherent response, all he could do was moan. His face was swollen, his features red and bloated from enduring hours of beatings. He was missing several teeth, his nose was broken, and both his eyes were red from the blood vessels bursting when they'd impacted with Trevor's fists.

Taking a deep breath, Eden took a single step forward. "Trev, I think he's out."

"Shut up, Eden. Unless you'd prefer to take his place."

Swallowing hard, Eden stepped back, falling silent. Trevor always insisted they watch this shit. Ostensibly for training purposes. Eden knew that was an excuse, that this little show was just as much an intimidation tactic to keep Trevor's men in line as it was a lesson in human depravity.

It was another hour before Nikolai stopped moving and Trevor finally dismissed them. In the bathroom, Eden splashed his face with cold water and ran a hand through his hair. It was only then that he realized he was shaking, beads of sweat giving his already pale skin a pasty, sickly appearance. Shaking himself, he bent his head and took a couple of hits from his dab pen.

After several inhales, his body tremored. The rush of adrenaline hit him like a semi. It was just a chemical reaction that bled the world black and blue, blurred Nikolai's face in his mind until it was just shapes and lines with a lopsided circle that meant absolutely nothing at all. His pleas became white noise with hints of static. Thoughts became disjointed segments. Flickers of something greater never truly realized.

Guilt would kill you faster than a bullet to your brain in this line of work. Luckily, Eden's extracurriculars left little room for his conscience.

After giving himself a quick once-over in the mirror to make sure he didn't look too far gone, he headed to his car. The unremarkable heap of rust and metal sat at the far corner of the lot, right where he'd left it when he'd met up with Xavier earlier in the day. He'd stop by the liquor store to buy a bottle of something hard on his way home, make sure he was able to sleep tonight.

Taking a deep breath, he sat in his car for a couple of minutes, not moving. The idling engine and the leaves rustling in the wind were the only sounds there to fill the silence, but Eden barely heard them. His ears were ringing. Whether that was from his high or the hours of screaming he'd borne witness to, he wasn't sure. That was the beauty of his one true love.

His chemical romance. It blurred everything together into nothingness. The good, the bad, and all the fucked-up shit in between. And even if only for an infinitesimal moment in eternity, none of it mattered.

None of it had any significance. Just an empty space to get lost in, somewhere between nowhere and oblivion.

Pulling onto the street, Eden turned on the car radio and glanced up at the sky. It was dark and empty and starless, so black it looked like it might engulf everything it touched. For a moment, he wished it would.

The chill of winter crept in through the vents, reminding him that this was real. That he could snort as much ice as he wanted, and sooner or later, he'd always come back down to the cold. Unless, of course, he never came back. But he couldn't. Not yet at least. He had things to do. People to take care of.

His little brother, Noah, was only fourteen. He needed someone there to cheer for him at his football games. Someone there to act like it mattered. Like he mattered. And his sister, Amelia, would have no one to pay her college tuition or listen to her vent about the latest asshole that had broken her heart. No one to remind her to study or tell her it was okay even when it wasn't.

And the two of them couldn't have afforded the small apartment they shared if Eden wasn't around to help with the rent.

So for now, he would stay and do what needed to be done. Because no one else would.

Selling dope paid five times what his day job did. Gave him what he needed to make sure he and his were taken care of. And even if it hadn't, he'd still be stuck doing this shit day in and day out. Life was like that. A fucked-up, senseless, never-ending cycle where people struggled to survive just for the sake of existing.

On nights like this, he wished he believed in God. Or anything at all. At least it would lend some meaning to a world that, in earnest, had none.

Ryan

"So where'd they get the coke?"

Ryan sighed, casting a sideways glare at Shawn beside him. To say interrogations were not Shawn's forte would've been an understatement.

They required a certain level of nuance and charisma, something that stood in stark contrast to Shawn's usual bullheaded approach.

"What he meant to say is, we're sorry for your loss, Rachel. It must've been very difficult for you," Ryan offered, affording the bereft eighteen-year-old girl sitting across from him an apologetic smile.

Rachel nodded, dabbing at her eyes with a tissue. "It was, thank you. I've never seen anyone overdose before. It was just so…."

"I know," Ryan reassured her, reaching across the table and squeezing her hand gently. "We have a couple grief counselors you can talk to after we're done here. They can help."

Shawn sighed loudly beside him, strumming his fingers on the metal table. "Rachel. I understand that you're going through some heavy stuff. And I'm sorry. Really. But we need to know where you and your friends got the dirty coke before someone else ODs."

Rachel sobbed, glaring at Shawn through teary eyes.

"Excuse us for a moment." Ryan dragged Shawn out of the interrogation room and gave him a shove.

"What the hell? What happened to easing our way into the interrogation? We're not going to get anything useful from her if you piss her off."

"Like I don't fucking know that. I read the file, same as you. It's not my fault her shithead friends couldn't tell the difference between dirty coke and the clean stuff."

"Yeah, but that doesn't mean you can act like an asshole either. She's grieving."

"So am I. You realize I haven't had sex in a month, right? And it's your fucking fault. All this guilt-tripping you've been hitting me with over what happened to your shoulder has been killing the mood." Shawn huffed. "Listen, I've got a lunch date with this girl I met at the club last night. You should see her. Fat ass, tits the size of bowling balls. Think she might even be down for a midday quickie. And if this shit goes on for much longer—"

"Just go." Ryan rolled his eyes, pushing Shawn toward the door. To be honest, he was grateful for the excuse to get rid of his best friend. He was driving this interrogation into the ground, and if he kept this up, Rachel might clam up and refuse to talk altogether.

"Thanks. I owe you," Shawn yelled over his shoulder, not skipping a beat.

"Yeah, right." Ryan muttered. He'd heard that line a million times and hadn't once received any reparations from Shawn's said debts. He pushed his way back into the interrogation room, and Rachel relaxed visibly when she saw that this time it was only him.

"I apologize for making you wait."

"No, it's fine." She sniffed, a small smile tugging at her lips.

"You'll have to forgive me for Detective Evans's behavior. He's having a difficult time of his own. Unfortunately there is some truth to what he said. As difficult as it may be for you to discuss, I do have to ask you about the coke. We're not looking to charge you. You were only a witness. We just want to identify where it's coming from so that we can prevent it from spreading. Were you there when your friends bought the coke?"

Rachel nodded.

"All right. I'm going to show you a series of pictures. I want you to tell me when you see one that looks like the guy you bought from." Ryan reached into his file and pulled out a couple of decoys before sliding Zika's picture across the table.

"I remember him," Rachel said, pointing to Zika's picture. "Scott wanted to buy from him, but he wouldn't sell to us."

Ryan paused and furrowed his brows. "Did he say why?"

"Yeah. He said something about not selling to kids. We told him we were eighteen, but I don't think he bought it," Rachel offered, shrugging.

Ryan frowned, running his tongue along the inside of his cheek. "You sure that's what he said?"

"Yes. Absolutely." Rachel blushed, looking down and wringing her hands nervously. "He turned us down, but he wasn't a dick about it. I remember thinking he was really nice for, you know…."

Ryan nodded, fighting back a smirk. Well, the rest definitely sounded like Zika, silver tongue and all. Apparently he'd made quite the impression.

"Did he say anything else?"

Rachel shook her head. "No. Scott was pretty pissed when he refused to do the deal, so he left after that and took us to see another guy we ended up buying from."

Ryan nodded, rifling through pictures of other well-known drug dealers in the city. When she failed to identify any of them as the man they'd purchased from, he thanked her for her time and led her out.

After making his way back to his desk, he rummaged through Zika's file, letting out a frustrated sigh. He'd left the interrogation with more questions than answers.

As he walked out to his car, Ryan kept replaying the conversation he'd had with Rachel. Zika could've sold to them. Would've made a good amount, too, with the amount of coke her friends were looking to purchase. But he hadn't. And that bothered Ryan. More than it should have.

Thirteen Years Ago

I MET HIM *on a summer day.*

The grass was green and the sky was blue and he looked like a Prince.

He had blond hair that glittered in the sun and blue eyes that reminded me of sapphires. And everything he said sounded like poetry.

He was different from the others. He spoke softly, and his touch was tender, and when he smiled it lit up his entire face. He smelled like honey and cinnamon.

After that he would come by often. Sometimes he would ask me about my day. Sometimes we would just sit together. He would tell me stories about kings and queens, heroes and villains. Love and death.

But he would always smile. And that would always make it all right, no matter how the story ended.

Sometimes I wouldn't know what to say. Because he was nice and kind and patient.

But he didn't care. Didn't call me stupid or slow for it. He would just smile like he always did and tell me another story.

One day he asked me my name. Like it mattered. I told him it was Jessie. He told me we could go for ice cream.

I picked strawberry cheesecake with sprinkles and gummy worms. And he laughed like it was the funniest thing he'd ever seen. I felt proud because I wasn't funny. And I wasn't smart. But somehow I'd made him laugh anyways.

We spent the rest of the day watching the sunset on a grassy hill. It was yellow and orange and pink and red. Trees blew in the breeze, and birds sung overhead, like a song made just for us. I told him the sunsets were better with him here. That it must be him that made the flowers bloom and the birds sing so softly and the ice cream taste so sweet. I asked him if he knew magic. He told me that he didn't.

That magic was a tricky thing. Hard for even a Prince like him. He told me he'd been a magician once. But someone had taken his powers away from him. So he'd searched and searched, trying to find what he'd lost. And that's how he'd met me.

He told me he'd never be the same as he was before, a great and powerful magician. But that it didn't matter anymore. Because he had me. And I was magic.

I blushed and looked down at my feet because he was a Prince and I wasn't.

I'd never felt special before. But in that moment, I did. I grinned so hard my cheeks hurt and my eyes stung, but I didn't care. Because I had him, and he had me, and maybe we weren't magicians, but we didn't need magic anymore. We had each other.

Chapter Five:
What is Past is Prologue

Eden

WELL, THIS should be fun. Or an absolute train wreck.

Shifting around uncomfortably, Eden reached for his cigarettes absentmindedly before redirecting his hands back to the small round table in front of him. Children prattled to one another in high-pitched voices all around him, accented by the occasional shrill scream when a baseball flew too close. The batting cage center Ryan had instructed him to meet him at was apparently a popular hot spot for families unfamiliar with the concept of birth control.

Visibly wincing as he glanced around the room, Eden pondered whether this was what it would feel like to be in an episode of *The Brady Bunch*. Or the fifth dimension of hell. The colossal headache he was going to have once this shit was over with was going to be worse than any hangover he'd ever suffered.

He doubted the parents here would appreciate it if he reeked of cigarettes and alcohol around their overly excited tweens. Which was also why he'd chosen to forgo his usual outfit, leaving his leather jacket and fingerless gloves at home. In earnest, they'd become like a second skin. He felt naked without them, but it was better than attracting the self-righteous disapproval of the PTA committee.

And he understood, to an extent. He never smoked around his little brother and sister. As much of a fucking buzzkill as it was, he could endure it for a couple hours. With plans to get completely shitfaced afterward to make up for lost time, of course. Life was all about balance, right?

"Hey."

Glancing up from the table, Eden's mood brightened considerably as he spotted Ryan making his way toward him from across the room. He was dressed in blue jeans and a simple tee. It had been a week since they'd last met up at the fight club, and even if Ryan was dressed like an uptight college jock at his first gay orgy, Eden had kinda missed his face.

"You're late," Eden replied with his usual patented smirk. "Thought you might've gotten cold feet."

"That a chink in your armor I see? Didn't realize you were humble enough to even contemplate the possibility of someone standing you up." Ryan snickered, sounding genuinely surprised.

"I'm not. It just means I think you have bad taste."

Raising a brow, Ryan stifled a laugh. "And here I thought you might actually have one redeeming quality."

"Yeah. I wouldn't hold your breath on that one. Thought we already established that's not really a thing for me."

Appraising him with a speculative glance, Ryan did a double take. "Nice polo. You have a job interview after this?"

"Shut up. I could've worn my shirt that says It's Not Going to Suck Itself with an arrow pointing to my dick, but I figured the soccer moms wouldn't be a big fan," Eden growled, gesturing to the parents in the room.

A loud gasp from a nearby parent reinforced Eden's point. She covered her child's ears with her hands and regarded him with wide-eyed shock.

"Do you mind? There are children here," she hissed, disgust drawing her lips into a thin line.

Eden paused, appraising the child she clearly felt had been scandalized. He looked to be about seventeen, maybe a little older. Child his ass. "Calm down, lady. This is free sex ed for him. He probably hears worse shit trading pornos with his friends in the school cafeteria. You know how it is. Kids grow up so fast these days."

"You're horrible," the woman muttered, pegging him with a disapproving gaze before rushing her child off in the opposite direction.

"Smooth," Ryan muttered, biting back a snicker as he motioned for Eden to follow, heading off to one of the empty batting cages. Following Ryan's lead as he retrieved a bat and then inserted a couple of baseballs into the metal machine on the other end of the batting cage, Eden took the opportunity to appreciate the view.

He hadn't had the pleasure of seeing Ryan from behind until now, at least not in the light. But, damn, did he have a nice ass. Firm and shapely, like two perfect globes in a tight little package. His broad shoulders painted a straight line across the horizon as he walked, framed by muscular arms on either side, which happened to be Eden's kryptonite. Body like Captain America, brain like Mother Theresa. What a fucking dick tease.

If there was a God, which he was almost sure there wasn't, the guy was definitely a sadist.

"So you like this sort of shit?" Eden asked, walking beside Ryan as they made their way to the front of the batting cage.

"Yeah. I grew up playing baseball with my brothers. Played all four years in high school too. I was never good enough to play professionally after I graduated, but if I had been, I probably would've."

"Shit, Ryan. You're so fucking white it hurts. Bet you were a Boy Scout too."

"Damn straight," Ryan replied proudly, grinning. "Worked all the way up to becoming an Eagle Scout. You ever get lost in the forest with just a compass and an axe, you know who to call."

"Oh yeah? Why? You gonna come to my rescue?" Eden scoffed.

"Why not? Having you owe me a favor might be fun. How do you feel about ass tattoos?"

Eden narrowed his eyes at Ryan, suppressing the desire to recoil. "I feel like they're only for two types of people. Fluffy, flamboyant twinks and drunks too fucking plastered to realize what's being done to them. I, clearly, am neither."

Ryan smirked. "You sure? 'Cause I'm not having any difficulty picturing it. A *My Little Princess* tattoo right across your asscheeks—"

"Don't even fucking think it," Eden growled menacingly. "Unless you fancy a slow and painful death."

"Might be worth it," Ryan said, executing a couple of practice swings with his bat. "That reminds me… earlier, when we first met, you said someone gave you the name Eden."

Eden's only response was a noncommittal nod.

"So what's your real name, then?"

"Jesus."

Ryan rolled his eyes.

"Did you really expect anything less?"

Ryan shrugged. For a second, Eden thought he would drop it. But then something in his expression changed.

"Okay, Jesus." He'd apparently decided to play along. "So you're Mexican."

"Half-Mexican, half-Russian."

Ryan chewed on the inside of his cheek. "Aren't most Mexicans Catholic?"

"Yup."

"But your parents weren't?"

"My mom was, right up until that last beating my pops gave her. I'm guessing she died an atheist." Eden noted the stutter in Ryan's movements as he turned away. It wasn't something he liked talking about, but Eden didn't want to spend the next hour dodging questions about how he'd ended up being so sacrilegious when his mother was clearly Catholic. Better to get it over with and out of the way.

"I'm sorry."

"Why?" Eden said with a shrug. "Everybody dies."

He could feel Ryan's eyes on him when he spoke. He didn't make eye contact, though. Didn't want to see in his eyes what he already heard in his voice. "Yeah, but still. That doesn't make it any easier. Especially when it happens like that."

Eden shifted from one foot to the other, finally forcing himself to meet Ryan's eyes. "Don't."

"Don't what?"

"Don't paint some sad sob story of whatever you think this is. It's not."

"Are you saying you don't care?"

"I'm saying where I come from, it was just another day," Eden responded, intentionally adding a bite to his words. "Now stop yapping and let's play. This place closes in two hours. If I wanted to talk shit all night, I would've gone down to the club instead."

Turning away from Ryan, Eden took a couple of practice swings.

"So you're actually excited to play? I've gotta say, I'm surprised. I thought this might be a little too tame for you." Ryan's voice sounded slightly strained from behind him.

"Why, you think all I do on my free time is fuck and fight?"

"Maybe," Ryan responded with a crooked smile, his tone implying that was exactly what he thought Eden did all day.

Eden feigned offense. "Would it earn me any brownie points if I told you I watch *The Golden Girls*? Or is that too risqué?"

Turning toward him, Ryan studied Eden's face for a moment, trying to figure out whether or not he was being serious. "You mean the show with the four old women, right?"

"Yup. You know Dorothy, the one who's tall as a tree, has shoulders like a linebacker, face always looks like she's taking a shit? She's my spirit animal."

Ryan burst out laughing, leaning on the bat he'd been holding for support.

"What the hell, Eden? What do you do on your free time?"

Eden shrugged, fighting back a smile. "Exfoliate. Sometimes I give myself manis and pedis. Tried my hand at gardening once, but I had to stop. Found out it was bad for my knees."

"Your knees?"

"Yeah. Gotta save 'em for prayer, after all. You know me, always an image of chaste purity," Eden replied with a wink. "That's how us Catholics do it, right? Get down on our knees and pray?"

"Fucking smartass."

"Fine. You caught me. I'm saving them for something else," he confirmed, a mischievous glint in his eyes. "In my personal opinion, if you're looking to be a humanitarian, there are a lot of other things you can do down on your knees to give back to your fellow man."

Ryan hoped the people around him would attribute the redness in his cheeks to how hard he'd been laughing a moment ago. "Thought you said you weren't into charity work, Eden."

"I'm not. S'why X always gives me kneepads and a banana on his birthday. Gotta practice that gag reflex," Eden replied, holding his hand up and sticking his tongue in his cheek to simulate a blowjob.

Ryan coughed and turned away before Eden could piece together his reaction.

"But yeah," Eden continued, "I'm looking forward to playing. I think I can make pretty good use of the opportunity."

After a couple more practice swings, he heard Ryan clear his throat. Right on cue.

"Umm... Eden. Have you ever played baseball before?"

Eden turned toward him, shrugging.

"Nah. But it can't be that hard. I mean you just swing the bat and hit the ball."

Ryan's expression was incredulous as he raised a brow in Eden's direction. "You're holding a bat, not repelling off a goddamn cliff. You've gotta loosen your grip and move your right hand up. Spread your legs too. They should be about a shoulder's width apart."

"Like this?" Eden asked, spreading his legs slightly and moving his left hand down.

"Oh, for Christ sake," Ryan mumbled, exhaling heavily. "No. Here." He laid down his bat and moved to stand behind Eden and placed his hands on top of Eden's, his chest pressed against Eden's back as he prompted him to move his right hand up. His grip was stiff, his calloused fingers warm and timid as Ryan slid his slightly larger hands on top of Eden's.

What a perfect fit, Eden mused, heat spreading from his chest to his groin as Ryan's breath brushed the back of his neck. He was so close Eden could feel every breath he took, the slight stutter as he inhaled, his chest expanding slowly, and then his exhale.

Eden waited patiently as Ryan moved his hands to his thighs, prompting him to spread his legs. Ryan's touch held the slightest tremor. How fucking adorable.

Eden had never been into the whole bashful routine, but for some reason on Ryan he found it pretty irresistible. Maybe it was because he hadn't expected it from a man who was six feet two inches of pure muscle with a face that looked more fit for the cover of *Glamour* than the streets. Not that Eden had any room to speak. It usually took the sexual prowess of a seasoned *Kama Sutra* expert just to get him hard. But with Ryan's hands on him, he had to bite down on his tongue to hold his train of thought. A couple more inches and Ryan would be groping his dick.

Then again, he'd never been the type to pass up a good opportunity. Smirking as he performed his best backward stumble, Eden white-knuckled the baseball bat to keep from groaning as he felt his ass rub against Ryan's dick.

Ryan made some sort of choking-coughing noise behind him. He probably would've jumped back immediately if it wouldn't have meant Eden falling flat on his ass.

"*Empujarlo más profundo,*" Eden remarked, rolling his *r* with extra flare as he looked back at Ryan.

"Since when the hell do you speak Spanish?" Ryan's words were strained and slightly distorted as he spoke through clenched teeth. His face was red, though whether it was from embarrassment or something else, Eden couldn't tell.

"Happens every time I get felt up. Sorry." Eden made his tone blatantly unapologetic. He contemplated the probability of getting away with another "stumble" versus the more likely alternative of Ryan letting him fall instead.

"*Mentiroso*," Ryan growled, pushing Eden forward onto his feet and pegging him with a hard glare.

"Well, aren't you just full of surprises." Eden lifted a brow, clearly pleased with himself.

"Fuck off."

"C'mon, Ryan. You really think I don't know how to play baseball? Really, it's your fault for falling for it."

Eden snickered as Ryan stepped forward and pushed him back a couple of steps. "I fucking hate you so much right now."

"Still worth it." Eden tried to suppress his laughter as Ryan snatched his own bat from the floor, turned away, and hit a couple of balls.

"You're lucky I don't have my gun on me," Ryan grumbled, shooting him a death glare over his shoulder.

"Even if you did, I wouldn't be too worried. It's pretty hard to aim with blue balls."

"Eden," Ryan warned, pointing his baseball bat in Eden's direction.

"Hey, can you blame me? This is our third date, and all I can do is ogle you. Normally I don't have to try this hard."

"You're a dog."

"Explains why I like your bone so much." Eden smirked, watching with a curious satisfaction as a flurry of emotions flickered across Ryan's handsome features. Ryan might hate him. Might even have taken a couple swings at him if Eden hadn't been careful to keep at least an arm's length between them. But Eden was also certain of one thing. In spite of what Ryan might think of him, his body clearly held a much different opinion.

Contrarians were, without a doubt, his absolute favorite.

Chapter Six:
The Better Part of Valor is Discretion

Ryan

PINCHING THE bridge of his nose between his thumb and his forefinger, Ryan closed his eyes, leaned back in his chair, and let out a heavy sigh. He'd spent the better half of the morning combing through Zika's file to the point of exhaustion. Their conversation last week had triggered something in the back of his mind. He'd never realized it before, but Zika's file contained nothing on his background. Nothing on him at all, in fact, before the age of thirteen when he'd been charged with his first case of narcotics distribution.

Ryan could find nothing on his mother, either. Not even her first name. All he'd been able to find on Zika's father was that the guy had apparently been a hard-core alcoholic. Several charges for public intoxication and assault before he'd eventually driven his car off a bridge in the midst of a drunken stupor about fifteen years back. Whether it was intentional or an accident, his file didn't specify.

Eden's little brother and sister had a different last name, so they were likely half-siblings. Their files showed the same conspicuous gaps in history throughout the first several years of their life. No medical records, no school reports, no birth certificates. Nothing until the ages of six and nine.

Shaking his head, Ryan made his way over to McNeil's office and knocked a couple of times before letting himself in. His boss was already occupied, glaring menacingly at the phone he'd set to speaker as he let loose a stream of expletives.

"Can I talk to you when you're done?" Ryan mouthed, not wanting to interrupt and potentially become the new target of his boss's apparent rage.

McNeil didn't bother answering, waving a hand in his direction dismissively as he continued his rant. In this office that was as good as a yes from the hot-tempered, no-nonsense Irishman. Nodding once, Ryan walked back to his desk, cursing internally as he spotted Shawn on his way in from lunch.

He'd managed to avoid most of Shawn's ribbing these last couple of weeks, largely on account of the fact that his partner been assigned to extra training as a result of the shooting incident. It seemed that his luck had finally run out, however, as Shawn made a beeline for his desk, a wicked grin on his face.

"Hey, Casanova, how's it going?"

"It's fine, you fucking cretin," Ryan responded, his voice clipped. "How's the compliance training? I see you've managed not to shoot any of your fingers off yet. I'm impressed."

"That's all right, talk that shit while you still can," Shawn countered, clearly undaunted. "Heard from a little birdie your dates with Zika are getting real steamy. You two do the down and dirty yet?"

"Fuck off, Shawn," Ryan growled, crossing his arms in front of him.

"Hey, I'm just saying, you've got a golden opportunity on your hands there. I was talking to Sanchez yesterday. He says crackheads give the best blowjobs. All the coke numbs out their throats so they don't have a gag reflex. Can you fucking imagine—"

"Shut the fuck up before I close your mouth for you." Chucking his stapler at Shawn, Ryan pondered how many years he'd get if he put a couple bullets in Shawn's kneecaps. It would likely be nonlethal, and he was almost positive McNeil would be more than willing to testify as a character witness against Shawn. "You wanna talk like a perp, then do us all a favor and lock your ass down in the cells with them too."

Shawn cackled, wincing as the stapler hit his shoulder. "You realize that's assault, right? You can't do that to me. They said so in compliance training."

"Yeah, and talking like that is sexual harassment. He might be a perp, but he's still a human being."

"And a dope dealer. And a crackhead. Since when did you get so fucking sensitive? You have a sex change and not tell me? 'Cause you're acting like you're on your fucking period."

Balling his hands into fists, Ryan decided it would most definitely be worth it to spend a couple of years in prison just to permanently incapacitate Shawn. Too bad he couldn't put a bullet through his mouth without blowing his brains out too—not that he had much of those to lose. "Moron, that's not how a fucking sex change works. I really hope stupid isn't contagious because if it is, this whole precinct is fucked." Running a hand through his hair, Ryan took a deep breath and tried to find his happy place. "Listen, there's a new episode of *Ozark* on tonight, so I'd really prefer not to have to shoot you and spend the night in jail—"

"Lovebirds, cut the crap," McNeil barked, his death glare enough to send Shawn scurrying back to his desk on the other side of the room. For once Ryan felt relieved that his boss's voice alone could strike the fear of God into any man with half a sense of self-preservation. "What did you want, Quinn?"

Ryan opened Zika's file again and splayed its contents over his desk. "Why don't we have anything here about Zika's background? We have nothing on him before the age of thirteen and nothing at all on his mother."

"Because it's not relevant." McNeil's answer was sharp and succinct.

"It isn't relevant?" Ryan echoed, his voice incredulous. "Are you serious? I mean, I'm not trying to say that it would ever justify what he does, because it wouldn't. But it is relevant. It helps us to understand his mindset and the connections he might be using to funnel drugs into the city. Did you even know his mother was Mexican? That could point to a link to the cartel—"

"His mother was an illegal. Didn't keep in contact with anyone after she emigrated, so if he does have a link to the cartel, it's not from anyone she knew."

Ryan narrowed his eyes, the hair standing up on the back of his neck. "If you know that, why isn't it in his file?"

"Because, like I said, it's not relevant. I've given you everything you need to do your job, Quinn. Stop wasting my time with bullshit questions."

Before Ryan could question him further, McNeil walked back to his office and slammed the door.

"What the hell is up with him?" Shawn whispered, raising a brow.

Shaking his head, Ryan glanced over at McNeil's office. He'd known McNeil for over two decades, first as a family friend when McNeil and his father had worked together on the force, and then as his boss. The guy had always been a straight shooter. He'd never been the type to hide anything, especially regarding an active case. So why the hell was he suddenly being evasive when it came to this? Chewing on his cheek, Ryan jolted slightly as a call came in over the police radar.

All available units respond. Two suspects traveling southbound on 23rd and Broadway in a high-speed car chase. Shots fired. One in a black Fiat Chrysler, the other on a black Kawasaki Ninja.

"Yippee-ki-yay!" Shawn whistled, jumping up from his desk and grabbing his gun. "Finally some fucking action. Let's go, partner."

Eden

EDEN'S ADRENALINE spiked as he weaved in and out of traffic on his motorcycle, nearly missing a semi. Car chases were usually his favorite part of this gig, assuming they didn't take place on the highway in the middle of rush-hour traffic. Today, it appeared, he'd have no such luck. He'd gotten back from his border run sooner than he'd anticipated, and the second he'd hit the city limits, Dominick's men had been on him.

Which he'd been expecting, considering the fact that he had over ten kilos of cocaine strapped to his back. But he hadn't planned for the back-to-back traffic or the fact that they'd shoot him instead of trying to run him off the road. If the packs he had on him were riddled with bullet holes, half of his product would be scattered along the highway before he made it back to Trevor, dead or alive.

Revving the engine on his black Ninja Kawasaki, or the Black Dahlia as he fondly referred to her, he cursed as he heard police sirens in the background. Just what he fucking needed. First Dominick's men and now twelve. Apparently he'd have to employ some evasive maneuvering if he wanted to get out of this clusterfuck in one piece. Eden braced himself as the car pursuing him on the shoulder of the highway rammed into the back of his motorcycle.

"Shit," he muttered through gritted teeth, white-knuckling the handlebars as his feet flew off the throttle. He could taste blood in his mouth from biting down on his tongue on impact. Swerving the motorcycle to the left, Eden cut into oncoming traffic, hoping to lose them that way. The Black Dahlia didn't do much for him in terms of protection from bullets, but what she lacked in defense, she more than made up for in her ability to maneuver through narrow spaces most cars were too large to follow.

Bullets whizzed past his ear, nicking his motorcycle helmet as the black car kept pace with him on the other side of the highway. Eden pulled onto the shoulder and slammed hard on the brakes, dropped back before turning and gunning it in the opposite direction. With how packed the highway was, there was no chance in hell Dominick's men would be able to pull a U-turn and double back in his direction.

Exhaling shakily, Eden turned his attention to the approaching police sirens. Cop cars appeared in his side mirror, heading in his direction. Two from what he could see, but more were undoubtedly on the way. He pushed his bike to its limit as he sped down the highway, the sights and sounds around him blurring together as he approached its max rate of speed. Spotting a nearby exit, he eased onto his brakes and made a hard right.

That was when it happened.

A popping sound erupted from his tires, and a second later he lost control of his bike. A horrible screeching sound filled the air as metal collided with pavement, the Black Dahlia turning over onto its side and skidding across the roadway.

For a moment, his vision blacked out, and he thought he might be dead. Blinking, he saw stars, millions of them, against the backdrop of a deep blue sky. A second later he found himself on his side, his flesh grinding against the concrete like a cheese grater as his body skidded down the roadway at over thirty-five miles per hour.

After finally coming to a stop fifty feet along, Eden limped to his feet, the entire right side of his body exploding with red-hot pain. That awful smell was back again. The stinging, pungent, slightly bitter aroma. But this time there was also hot oil and smoke. Burning flesh and rubber.

Ignoring the nausea rolling through his gut, he forced himself to think through the pain, his eyes darting around frantically for an escape route. He spotted it in the form of a nearby apartment building. He pushed his way into the main stairwell, then took the stairs two at a time, cursing as he heard heavy footsteps running behind him. He grabbed his phone and hit Speed Dial, then held the phone to the side of his helmet.

"Yeah?" came a muffled voice.

"I need you here. Now." His voice was shaky and out of breath as he spoke into the phone. It was cold enough that his breath fogged his visor on every exhale, but he didn't feel it. Not with all the adrenaline surging through him.

"Where are you?" X asked, his tone immediately alert as something rustled in the background.

"Some fucking apartment building near the exit of Broadway and 57th."

"Okay, I'm on my way."

Eden shoved his phone back into his pocket as he reached the top floor and scanned the area for an exit. His stomach dropped when he realized there was none—only a couple of apartments and then a dead end.

To his left, he saw a door and busted through it with his good shoulder, stumbling into an empty living room. He only made it a couple of steps before he heard the cock of a gun behind him.

"Freeze! Hands up! Don't fucking move!" Turning slowly, Eden put his hands up. He recognized the voice even before he made eye contact.

"Get down on the fucking ground!" Ryan yelled, his gun leveled directly at Eden's chest.

Fuck. Of all the cops that had to corner him, it would be him. Ryan might actually shoot him.

And for a moment Eden wished he would. Blow his brains out and splatter the walls with a million little pieces of what should've never been. Reduce his existence to a piece of metal smaller than a nickel. Too small to hold all the things that made him what he was and what he wasn't.

But a heart breaks, even when it shouldn't. Even just for the sake of what could've been. And he had people to take care of, he reminded himself. So giving up was not an option.

At least if it had been someone else, he could've reached for his gun and hoped for a bullet to the shoulder. He was out of options. It was either shoot or take the only exit left, four stories down. Lunging to the right, Eden smashed through the nearby window, plummeting forty feet.

He landed in an open garbage dumpster, the trash piled to the brim helping to break his fall. Even so he was sure he'd broken a couple of bones. As long as they weren't in his legs, he wasn't completely fucked yet. As he dragged himself out of the bin, Eden spotted Xavier's car at the end of the alley. It took everything he had left in him to limp over and slide in.

"Jesus, Eden, what the fuck happened?"

"I tripped," Eden muttered through gritted teeth, gripping his side tightly as Xavier pulled into traffic.

"I'm serious. What the hell happened?"

"Ran into a little trouble on my way back." Yanking his motorcycle helmet off, Eden glanced down at the right side of his body, surveying the damage. He wouldn't be able to tell how many bones he'd broken by looking, but he had a nasty case of road rash that stretched all the way from his lower calf to his shoulder.

"Did twelve see you?" The tension in Xavier's usually calm and collected voice let Eden know he'd fucked up. Bad.

"Nah, don't think so. I kept the helmet on. And the bike's unregistered, so they shouldn't be able to track it."

Releasing a shaky breath, Xavier shook his head. "For fuck's sake, Eden. Next time you need to have someone come with you. D's goons are getting more gutsy, pulling this shit in broad daylight."

Next time. Right.

Shrugging off his jacket, Eden winced. "You think it would've really changed anything if there were two of us? It's better this way. You wouldn't have been able to save my ass if you were caught in that shit too."

"How bad is it?"

"Just a scratch." Eden managed a tight smile as he pulled his jacket back on. He didn't need to worry Xavier. Eden knew he'd already stressed him out enough. Eden lit a cigarette from the lighter in the console and sank back into his seat, exhaling slowly.

That had been close. Too close. Worse than that, though, Eden knew there was no way Trevor was going to let this shit slide. He would take it as a direct threat, someone trying to steal right from his hand. And that, in his boss's book, was unforgivable.

Ryan

FROWNING AS he stared out the precinct window, Ryan ran a hand through his hair, rereading his text from Zika for the seventh time that night. He'd cancelled their date, ostensibly because he was sick.

Unfortunately Ryan wasn't the type of man who believed in coincidences. Especially when it came to Zika.

Replaying the day's events, he thought back to the man he'd leveled his gun at in the apartment. Well, he'd jumped out of the window of a four-story building, so he was definitely insane enough to be Zika. And he'd hesitated. Not that that proved anything. Most men hesitated when they had a gun leveled at them point-blank.

But he'd moved like Zika. Was the exact same height, and his jacket had been identical to the one Zika usually wore. Maybe if it had been just one anomaly, he would've been able to pass it off as a coincidence. But everything together led him to one irrefutable conclusion.

The man he'd almost shot back in the apartment had been Zika. Without a doubt.

A wave of nausea rolled through Ryan and settled in his gut as he finally accepted what he'd been trying to deny all night. He'd almost shot Zika. Christ.

Chapter Seven:
We Know What We Are,
but Not What We May Be

Eden

IT WAS going to be a long night.

Primarily due to the fact that Eden was still recovering from his little game of bumper cars with Dominick's men and the cops a few days back. Luckily, all of his injuries were nonlethal—a dislocated shoulder, a broken wrist, and a couple of cracked ribs. And the lovely road rash that made it look like he'd been mauled by a hoard of flesh-eating zombies, of course. Honestly, though, the biggest injury had been to his pride.

He'd lost the Black Dahlia and his favorite leather jacket dealing with this shit. It would cost him a good ten grand—at least—just to recoup his losses. Which was money he didn't have right now. And with his right wrist broken, his trigger hand was shot to shit for the time being. Which meant that if he did run into any trouble before it healed well enough for him to hold a gun, he was as good as dead.

So no. He was not in a good mood tonight.

Biting back the wave of irritation coursing through him, Eden tried to drown out the loud bass bumping from Club Zero's speakers and took a seat at one of the nearby tables. He usually preferred to stand, allowed for a faster response time in case shit went south. But in his current state, he'd be fucked either way, and his road rash was killing him. Everything about tonight made him want to put his head through a wall, and as he spotted Ryan pushing his way toward him through the crowd, he added yet another to the list.

"Hey, nice war paint. But last time I checked Halloween isn't for a while." A crooked smile tugged at Ryan's lips as he motioned to the bruised scratch on Eden's right cheek.

"Shut up or I'll cut you," Eden snapped. He could hide the majority of the injuries he'd sustained with clothes, but there was nothing he could do about the shit on his face.

"Cut and not shoot? Look who's feeling charitable tonight."

"Yeah, well, I left my kneepads at home. So if you're looking for a good time, don't hold your breath. Why are you here anyways? It's Sunday. Isn't there some line in the Bible about not getting shitfaced on Sabbath day?" He'd hoped to put off meeting up with Ryan for at least another week till he no longer looked like roadkill. But alas, here he was.

"That applies to every day, but yeah, there is. I'm not here to party anyways. And I don't think just walking into a club technically qualifies."

"So what, then? You got lost on your way home from church?"

"No. I came to see if you wanted to go for coffee," Ryan replied easily, taking a seat beside Eden at the small round table.

Eden frowned. "Coffee? At nine at night? What are you, a fucking hipster? You're lucky you're hot, Ryan, because your swag is all the way fucked-up."

"Figured you'd say that." Ryan reached into the paper bag at his side and produced a mug of what Eden could only surmise to be coffee.

Eden exhaled heavily. "Did you not hear me say that—"

"Calm down. I put some Vicodin in it."

Eden started at Ryan's words, wondering if maybe his irritation from the events of the last couple days had finally made his brain break. "Did I miss something? Because it really fucking feels like I did."

"Whatever you're thinking, you're wrong. I had a couple pills left from when Shawn 'nicked' me. Figured they might help with the road rash."

Eden narrowed his eyes. His entire body went rigid. Fuck. So Ryan had known it was him. A cold sweat ran down his back as Eden swallowed past the lump in his throat. Well, Ryan hadn't slapped handcuffs on him yet, so that was a promising sign.

"I get why you're worried," Ryan offered. "Here." Picking up the mug, he took a sip from the opaque cup first as if to prove he wasn't trying to roofie him with some sort of truth serum. Yeah. 'Cause that was really Eden's main concern after everything that had happened in the last several days. "I'm a cop, Eden. I'm not going to drug you."

Eden sat there for several useless seconds. The hairs on the back of his neck stood on end. Of course he'd known Ryan was a cop since the day he'd laid eyes on him almost a month ago. But to have him come out and say it of his own volition was something he'd never expected.

Eden pivoted in his seat. He surveyed the room for any undercovers he might be in cahoots with, quickly coming to the conclusion that he'd come alone. Maybe this was some sort of reverse psychology shit. A new police tactic he hadn't read up on yet.

Clearing his throat, Eden did his best to fight back the wave of paranoia gripping him. "So what prompted all this, then?"

"Do you really find it that hard to believe that I stopped by to check on you?" Ryan's eyes were filled with amusement as he held Eden's gaze.

"Considering the fact that you know me, yes. Absolutely."

"I'm not here on business. I swear. I got off shift a while ago. Check me for wires if you don't believe me."

Studying Ryan closely, Eden relaxed slowly, sinking back into his seat. Ryan might be a cop, but no matter what angle he approached it from, there was no way coming right out and revealing the fact would work out in Ryan's favor. As far as Ryan knew, this was news to Eden. And there was always the chance he could just call Trevor and resolve the predicament with a Glock. Ryan might be ignorant in some respects, but he definitely wasn't stupid. Or the gambling type.

Which left Eden with only one viable scenario. Aside from the possibility that Ryan had lost his mind, of course.

Maybe Ryan felt bad for almost shooting him. He was the fucking bleeding-heart type, after all. Coffee was typically how white preppy types talked out their issues, right? An olive branch of sorts.

Chancing a sip from the mug, Eden confirmed Ryan's words. He couldn't taste any extras in the drink, other than some atrociously strong coffee and a dash of sugar and cream. Even so, he was still on edge. He couldn't help it. His reality had suddenly been turned on its head, with no notable antecedent other than the fact that Ryan had almost shot him.

And in Eden's line of work, that was pretty much a daily occurrence. Not exactly a reason to suddenly have a coming to God moment and prompt an outpouring of truth and honesty.

"Hey, E, you got anything for me tonight?"

Eden frowned as one of his regulars approached their table. He remembered his name was Carl, a pushy motherfucker with a receding hairline and a handlebar mustache who went through ice like Tic Tacs.

He'd been pestering the shit out of Eden ever since they'd had to cut back on their sales. Apparently the guy was about as perceptive as a fucking sloth, approaching him to buy when Ryan was right there.

"Nah, I'm not doing business right now." Eden's jaw tightened slightly as he pegged Carl with a hard glare. "Come back in a couple hours."

"Man, please. I just need enough for a couple lines," Carl pleaded. "Just enough to get well. You know how this fucking shit is."

"I said come back in a while, Carl," Eden growled. The frantic, desperate look in Carl's eyes put him on edge. "I'm busy right now."

"Busy with what? For fuck's sake, man, don't make me beg. It'll just take a second." Carl stepped forward, grabbed hold of Eden's wrist, and pulled him to his feet.

"Hey, he said no." Eden almost flinched at the sharpness in Ryan's voice as he stood and placed himself between Eden and Carl. "Now I suggest you remove your hand, because I'd really hate to have to break it."

Carl's eyes drifted from Eden to Ryan. His gaze shifted toward something harder as he let go and stepped back. "And who the fuck are you? You got a bodyguard now, E?"

Stepping around Ryan, Eden rested his good hand on the knife concealed at his hip. "He's a friend," Eden stated evenly. "Now get the fuck out of here before I put you on Trev's blacklist."

Carl hesitated. After a moment's pause, he cursed and took a step back, clearly realizing his odds of winning this fight were next to none. He turned and stormed off without another word.

"You okay?" Ryan asked, moving toward Eden to gently examine his wrist. "You should really get this wrapped."

Eden stared at Ryan for a moment. A subtle warmth settled in his chest. Maybe almost getting shot and jumping through a four-story window hadn't been such a bad idea after all. If Ryan harbored any ill intentions, it definitely would've been in his best interest to sit back and watch this little situation play out.

The car-chase clusterfuck was a bit of a gray area.

Technically, the police had no proof Eden had done anything wrong, other than speeding and going the wrong way on the highway. And evading arrest. And fleeing the scene of an accident of course. Even with that, those weren't charges that carried any real weight. But what this could've been—witnessing a drug deal, even if it was only for a couple of lines—was all Ryan would need to lock him up. And it would give him probable cause to seize everything Eden owned, which is what would really get him in hot water.

"Not really an option," Eden muttered, acutely aware of the way Ryan's calloused fingers brushed carefully over his wrist. "If I go to the hospital, they'll wanna know how it happened. Staff could call your buddies in blue."

"You have fifteen minutes?" Ryan asked, looking up and inclining his head toward the entrance.

"Yeah. Why?"

"Come with me."

Nodding, Eden followed Ryan out to his car. "I can't leave. Still have to finish my shift."

"We're not leaving. Just get in and you'll see."

Eden's curiosity got the better of him, and he raised a brow as he joined Ryan in the car. Watching silently as Ryan reached into his dashboard and pulled out a travel-size first aid kit, Eden flushed.

"You don't have to—"

"I know. Now shut up and sit still." A soft smile tugged at Ryan's lips as he gently took hold of Eden's wrist and began wrapping it with white bandages. "It won't be as good as what a doctor or nurse would do, but it's better than nothing."

Eden didn't move a muscle. He sat there in silence for several minutes, watching as Ryan made quick work of wrapping his wrist. The winter winds whipped around, dancing gleefully through the narrow street. They brought with them a pure white frost. He could hear Ryan's breath, slow and steady, interspersed by the occasional muffled purr of nearby cars as they passed.

Eden smiled, and for a second everything felt right.

Like the promise of something more. Something tender and gentle and merciful, though his hands could never hold it. If such a thing did exist, even if he couldn't reach out and grasp it, somehow it made him happy. Happy for just the chance to be aware of its presence.

Swallowing past the tingling sensation radiating from his wrist through his body all the way down to his toes, Eden looked up at the sky. The stars were out. But tonight they looked different somehow, and for a moment, Eden couldn't tear his eyes away.

"You like the stars, Ryan?"

Eden felt Ryan's eyes on him as his movements paused.

"Yeah, I guess. Why?"

When Eden spoke again, he didn't recognize his own voice. It sounded empty, lacking it's usually blasé charm. "When I was a kid, someone told me most of them are already dead. Their light takes thousands of years to reach the earth, which is why to you and everyone else, they look alive. Vibrant. Beautiful even, if you're into that sort of shit."

Eden turned back toward Ryan and smiled faintly. Ryan's expression was serious, pensive, like he was trying to follow Eden's sudden change of topic.

"You sure you're okay?"

"You should relax your shoulders when you walk. At least when you're undercover."

Ryan shook his head, clearly confused. "What?"

"When you square your shoulders like you usually do, it makes you look like you're walking with a sense of purpose, like you've got something you take pride in. There are only two types of people that walk like that. Soldiers and police officers. Your hair's too long for you to be in the military. S'how I knew you were a cop."

Ryan blinked at him. Clearing his throat, he smiled slowly, and for a moment, Eden thought it might be the most beautiful thing he'd ever seen.

Which seemed impossible in a world where nothing was ever beautiful.

"I should go," Eden muttered, tearing his eyes away and looking back out the window. "Get back before Trev starts bitching about me leaving my post."

"You want me to stay?"

"Nah. You should get home. Get some sleep. Work's got you up at the asscrack of dawn, don't they?"

Ryan nodded. "Eight in the morning."

"Thought so." As he reached for the car door, Eden did his best to flash Ryan a parting smirk. "Thanks for setting my hand. If you're ever looking to change careers, you'd make a pretty good nurse."

"Oh, but not a doctor, huh?" Ryan joked.

Eden shook his head as he stepped out of the car. "No. Doctors are only in it for the money. And you're a fucking bleeding heart. Wouldn't suit you. See you around, detective." Closing the car door, Eden walked back into the club and took a seat at the same table.

He didn't feel the pain from his road rash or his broken wrist. He didn't feel irritation at the fact the Black Dahlia was gone and his leather jacket was ripped to shreds. He didn't feel frustration at the knowledge Carl would probably be back bitching for his next hit within the hour when Eden had told him two.

Glancing down at his right wrist, Eden traced the folds of the bandages with his good hand and felt something he hadn't felt in years. Hope.

Thirteen Years Ago

SOMETIMES THE Prince would take me to hotels. I liked it, because they had TV and hot showers and clean sheets and room service where I could order whatever I wanted to eat.

My favorite was bacon and macaroni.

Sometimes, when I couldn't sleep, he would tell me stories.

He had lots of them, but my favorites were always the ones with heroes.

Men and women with swords and bows that would fight to protect the people they loved. They made me feel strong, like maybe I could be a hero too one day. I asked him once if he thought that I could. He told me I already was.

He told me that heroes aren't always good, and villains aren't always bad. I didn't understand.

He told me about Romeo and Juliet, that they were heroes to each other. But that to everyone else, they were villains. Selfish and foolish kids.

He told me about Hamlet, and how he missed his dead father so much that he'd killed his uncle.

He told me about Othello, and how his heart was broken. How he was in so much pain. And so desperate to stay with the one he loved most in the world that he killed her and then himself so that they could be together in another world.

He told me that that one was his favorite.

He told me that people were never just good or bad. That they were always both. That one could not exist without the other.

I told him that was a lie, because he was always good. He smiled then, but it wasn't like all his other smiles. It was sad, and I wanted to ask why, but I was afraid it would make him sadder.

So instead I made up a story that I thought would make him happy. About a beggar and a prince that had fallen in love over sunsets and ice cream. He smiled for real then, and so did I.

Chapter Eight:
Uneasy Lies the Head
That Wears the Crown

Ryan

GOD, HE needed this.

Finishing up their last song of the night, Ryan let his hands move automatically over the chords of his guitar. He met up with a couple of his friends from high school once or twice a month to play at a small dive bar whenever they all had the time. That was less and less often nowadays, with all of them holding down full-time jobs and a couple of the guys starting families.

They'd had a band in high school, had tried to make it big like most teenage boys with a vague interest in music and stars in their eyes. But reality had bitch-slapped them within a couple of months of their pursuit of stardom, and they'd focused their efforts on more realistic endeavors.

Tonight had been a nice, albeit temporary, distraction from the fact that he was so very clearly fucked.

He was withholding knowledge related to an active shooting. Not that Zika had been the one doing any of the shooting, but still. And last week he'd almost sat there and watched while Zika sold cocaine to a random junkie. Or at least he would've if that fucker hadn't gotten so handsy. He was technically supposed to be observing and reporting everything he saw back to McNeil. But as things stood currently, his report on the case was nothing more than a blank white page with his name and badge number at the top.

The illusion that what he did as a cop actually made a difference in the world had ended within his first year of taking the job. For every dope dealer and illegal arms distributor he took off the streets, there would always be three more waiting to replace them. He was just another cog in the machine, grinding his way through the monotony that was life with the same lackluster enthusiasm most cops eventually adopted.

But he'd always been able to stand by one thing. The fact that no matter how the reality of the situation played out, he had chosen to do the right thing. Even if the bad guys did win in the end, he'd been one of the good ones—for whatever it was worth.

The right thing to do would be to turn Zika in. To tell McNeil everything he knew and walk away from what was becoming an exceedingly complicated situation. So why the hell did the very thought of doing that feel so wrong?

Letting out a frustrated sigh, he waved goodbye to his ex-band members and headed to the bar for a much-needed drink.

"Hey, you guys were really good up there."

Turning, Ryan registered the fact that the young girl was talking to him, with more annoyance than was warranted. She looked slightly familiar, but he couldn't place from where. Maybe she came here often and he'd seen her in the crowd before.

"Thanks," he offered, hoping to end the conversation there.

"My little brother's always wanted to learn how to play guitar. We never had money for lessons, but I've heard some people are self-taught. Is that how you learned—"

"Amelia."

Ryan knew who it was before he even turned. How could he not? He'd been replaying the last words Eden had said to him over and over again for the last week. Ryan did his best to maintain a neutral expression as Zika came to stand next to Amelia.

Zika was dressed in yet another polo that highlighted his broad shoulders and muscular arms perfectly, this time with product in his hair and a fresh shave. And sweet Jesus, he looked hot. Ryan could smell cologne on him. Zika's expression was uncharacteristically unsure as he fidgeted nervously from one foot to the other.

Wait. Were they on a date?

Ryan's jaw tightened as he regarded the pair hesitantly, waiting for one of them to continue. Maybe Zika wasn't strictly dickly after all. Judging by Zika's posture, she was definitely something to him. But she didn't look like any of the prostitutes he'd claimed to frequent.

So what the hell was this?

Amelia was the first one to speak, her eyes drifting between the two men with a curiosity that mirrored his own.

"Calm down, Eden. We were only talking. Do you always have to get like this every time I talk to a guy?"

"It's my job. I'm your brother." His answer was matter-of-fact, his tone lacking its usual sharpness as he regarded her with an unapologetic gaze.

"Last time I checked, your job was to work on cars, not make it your life's mission to make sure that I never reproduce. And besides, it's not like that. We were just talking. I was asking him for some pointers for Noah since he's so good at playing guitar—which you would've seen for yourself if you weren't always late." She turned toward her brother with a cursory glance. "What's with the look? Do you two know each other or something?"

Zika's eyes wavered as he glanced over at Ryan. "Kind of."

"Kind of? How do you kind of know someone?" Amelia challenged, looking almost amused by Zika's evasiveness.

"We know each other from work," Ryan offered, extending his hand to Amelia. "Sorry for not introducing myself earlier. I'm Ryan."

"Work," Amelia repeated, appraising Ryan as she shook his hand. "Really now? You don't look like a mechanic."

"No, I don't work on cars. I know your brother 'cause he worked on mine," Ryan answered easily. He knew from reading Zika's file that by day he worked as a mechanic at Joe's Autos.

"Oh." Amelia nodded. "You should stay, have a couple drinks with us. I never get to meet any of my brother's friends."

"Amelia, stop being so nosy," Zika muttered. "He already told you how we know each other from work. That should be enough."

"Oh come on, Eden. You really think I'm buying that? Or are you really trying to tell me you remember everyone that comes in and out of Joe's?" Amelia pegged Zika with an accusatory look, then turned her attention back to Ryan.

"Please, join us. As I'm sure you're already aware, my brother's people skills are more than a little lacking. He could really use the practice," she teased, eliciting a flush from Zika as he looked down at his feet.

Holy shit. Zika was actually blushing. Ryan nodded and all the tension drained from his frame. He was suddenly finding the conversation a lot more interesting.

"Yeah, okay, sure. I was about to grab a drink anyways."

The three of them found a table near the back of the bar and snagged a waitress to bring Ryan a scotch. Thankfully, Amelia did most of the talking. Ryan realized only five minutes into the conversation that Amelia was definitely the antithesis to her brother. If Zika was sarcastic, sharp-tongued, and arrogant, Amelia was warm, personable, and open.

"So how'd you learn to play the guitar?" Amelia asked, smiling.

"I took lessons when I was a kid. You know how it is, every teenage boy dreams of being a rock star."

"Yeah. Eden's been trying to learn so he can teach our little brother. He's still at the stage where everything he plays sounds like a dying cat."

Ryan laughed, glancing over at Zika, whose only response was to sink lower into his seat, the red on his face spreading from his cheeks down to his neck. How very unlike Zika, Ryan mused to himself, grinning widely. It sort of reminded him of the way a porcupine might blush if it were able to. Undeniably charming, almost to the point of endearing, but ready to lash out and draw blood the moment anyone around him pointed it out.

He'd never thought Zika was the type to get embarrassed. Figured it simply wasn't in his genetic makeup. How incredibly wrong he'd been.

"That's to be expected. It always sounds like that when you first start. He'll get better with time," Ryan offered, enjoying the fact that for once, Zika was the one on the receiving end of the teasing.

"Yeah, I guess. Maybe you could give him a couple pointers. God knows he needs it."

"Don't go roping people into things just because you can't stand my playing," Zika chided.

"I'm not roping him into anything. I'm just saying it would be a good idea." She shrugged innocently.

Ryan couldn't help but smile at the dynamic between the two. In a room full of dope dealers and police, Zika made no attempt to censor himself, often even going out of his way to provoke those around him. Yet here, sitting next to a girl of eighteen or so who looked about as harmless as a bunny with three legs, he seemed embarrassed. Nervous, even.

"Anyways, Ryan, you said you're not a mechanic, right? What do you do for work?"

Ryan took a sip of his scotch, unsure how to answer. He didn't want to cause any problems between Zika and his sister. And he wasn't sure exactly how much she knew about Zika's extracurriculars.

"He's a detective," Zika muttered, shooting a murderous glare at Amelia as he nursed his own drink.

"A detective?" Amelia repeated, sounding impressed. "Well, isn't that something. My brother and a cop. I'm surprised, Eden. Normally the only guys you bring home have face tattoos and ankle bracelets."

Ryan choked on his next sip of scotch as the implication of her words hit him.

"Amelia, for Christ's sake. He's right there," Zika hissed. He focused on his drink like it had suddenly become the most fascinating thing in the world.

"And since when are you so shy," Amelia replied, grinning like a Cheshire cat. "Anyways, I think it's great that you're a detective. Hopefully you can keep this one out of trouble." Motioning to her brother, she lowered her voice in a conspiratorial tone, leaning in slightly. "He's trying to turn over a new leaf now with the whole mechanic gig. But believe it or not, back in the day he was a real handful. Running the streets, picking fights with anyone who looked at him the wrong way."

"You don't say?" Ryan raised a brow, stealing a glance in Zika's direction. He was fidgeting in his chair, with something close to worry in his eyes. "I would've never guessed," Ryan said slowly. "Glad he's changed his ways, especially seeing as you two are so close."

Amelia laughed, nudging Zika playfully. "Yeah. He'd never admit it, but he's a real teddy bear when you get to know him. Even reads Shakespeare—"

"Amelia, please—"

"What? Someone's gotta say it. You never talk about yourself, not even with Xavier, and you two have known each other forever." Rolling her eyes, Amelia continued, pivoting back to Ryan. "My brother has his faults, as I'm sure you're well aware, but he's always been there for Noah and me, even when things were rough. He's a good guy, just has a hard time showing it."

"Yeah, I'm sure he is."

Zika turned toward Ryan, an unreadable look on his face. It was so unlike the cocky, arrogant expression he usually wore that for a second,

Ryan stared back. At that moment Zika looked younger, almost fragile, his black hair and gray eyes casting soft shadows across his pale skin.

Breaking eye contact, Ryan looked away and downed the rest of his scotch. The last thing he needed was to be having inappropriate fantasies about Zika while his baby sister was sitting right there, practically encouraging it.

When he looked back up, Zika's expression had hardened, his eyes focused on something across the bar. Following his gaze, Ryan cursed silently when he realized why. He recognized the two guys glaring at Zika as a couple of members of a rival narcotics gang his unit was on a first-name basis with. And judging by the frowns on their faces, they were definitely looking for trouble.

Setting his drink down, Zika looked over at Amelia apologetically. "Hey, Amelia, not that I haven't been enjoying this nice little chat, but I've gotta get back to the shop. Joe has a car that he needs finished by tomorrow."

"This late? Oh come on, Eden, can't you tell him you'll work on it in the morning? This is the most you've talked all night, and it's to say you have to leave."

"I'm sorry, Amelia. I can't. I'll make it up to you next time I see you, okay? We can go and see that movie you've been talking about, the one with the guy and the girl."

Amelia huffed, looking unimpressed. "You realize that describes pretty much ninety-five percent of all movies, right?"

"Please, Amelia. Later, okay?" Zika stood, placing a rushed kiss on Amelia's forehead to signal the end to their conversation.

"You want me to come with?" Ryan asked, exchanging a knowing look with Zika. He wasn't sure if the guys across the bar were packing tonight, but at least two against two would even the playing field.

"Nah. I'm good. You've still got that problem with your shoulder, remember? Can you make sure Amelia gets home safe, though?"

Ryan nodded slowly, even as Amelia began to protest. "I'm nineteen now, Eden. I don't need an escort—"

"Bye, Amelia. Thanks, Ryan. I owe you one," he said, brushing off his sister's complaints and heading out the door. Ryan watched as the two men across the bar followed, unsure of what to do. He didn't want to leave Amelia by herself, but he couldn't just sit by while a couple of gang members jumped Zika in some back alley.

"Listen, Amelia. I need to ask your brother a quick question. Stay here, okay? I'll be right back." Not waiting for an answer, Ryan rushed out the door after them. By the time he'd made it outside, they were already gone. Their footsteps in the snow came to a stop right in front of the road.

They'd gotten into a car. Shit.

Picking up his phone, Ryan called Zika. No answer. He called three more times before he finally got a text response.

Everything's good. X and I are taking care of it. Plz make sure Amelia gets home safe.

How do I know this is you? Ryan texted back, pacing around in front of the bar.

It was a couple of minutes before he got a response.

The fuck if I know. Ask me something that proves it.

His thoughts racing, Ryan typed the first thing that popped into his head. *What's your favorite show?*

The next response was almost immediate.

The Golden Girls. *By the way, if you tell anyone else that, I will kill you. Thnx again.*

Ryan smiled, exhaling a sigh of relief as he went back into the bar.

"Everything okay?" Amelia asked, appraising him with a curious gaze as Ryan sat back down.

"Yeah. Sorry. I needed clarification from your brother on something."

"I hate when he does that," she muttered, rolling her eyes.

"Does what?"

"Just leaves. It happens a lot, and I barely get to see him as it is. I know he's busy but… sometimes I think he still has a couple bad habits."

Ryan pursed his lips, mulling over her words. "Maybe. But everyone has one or two bad habits. Most of the time we grow out of them."

Amelia shrugged. The tension in her face eased slightly. "Yeah, that's true. Sometimes I forget that he's only twenty-two. He always acts like such an old man around me."

"Yeah, sometimes I forget too." He'd probably read it somewhere in Zika's file, but his smart mouth and the hard expression he always wore made him seem so much older. Zika was barely old enough to drink, only five years older than Ryan's brother had been.

"He really likes you, you know."

"I don't know about that," Ryan said. He looked down at his glass, wishing he had more scotch. He wasn't sure where he and Zika stood to be honest. They weren't friends—not exactly. But they weren't more than that either. For all of Zika's come-ons, they'd never even kissed. Regardless, it certainly wasn't something he wanted to discuss with Zika's little sister.

"Trust me, I know. It's hard to read him if you haven't known him for a while, but he does. He's just horrible at showing it."

Laughing, Ryan nodded toward the door. "Let's get you home. It's getting late. I don't want your brother kicking my butt for breaking your curfew."

Amelia snorted but didn't fight him. After making their way out to his car, she gave him directions to her place and continued to make small talk during the twenty-minute drive. He waited till she was safely inside to pull off. Replaying the night's events, Ryan found his thoughts drifting back to Zika.

He thought about checking on him, driving by his place to see if the lights were on, before realizing that even if things had gone well, Zika probably wouldn't be heading home till much later. And he thought about how different Zika had been tonight. The way he'd flushed at practically everything Amelia said.

A part of him wished he could make Zika blush like that. Maybe he was like that around Turner when they were alone.

Fucking Turner. That guy annoyed the ever-loving shit out of him. He always showed up at the most inconvenient times—aside from tonight of course. But Ryan could've handled it. He could've helped. And a part of Ryan wished he had. That he'd been the one to come to Zika's rescue instead of fucking Turner. They clearly had some sort of sick, codependent, fucked-up relationship, and until Zika chose to share more about it with him, all he could do was wait.

Cursing, Ryan hung his head, letting it rest on the steering wheel.

What the hell was he even thinking? Getting angry that Turner had been the one to help when only hours ago he'd been unsure whether or not he was going to tell McNeil everything he knew. He was the worst type of hypocrite. And even more damning, the realization did nothing to quell the entitled, jealous anger rolling in his gut.

Chapter Nine:
God Gives You One Face, and
You Make Yourself Another

Ryan

RYAN WAS definitely going to hell.

At least if McNeil had anything to do with it. With any luck his boss and God weren't on good terms, seeing that half the words that left his mouth on a daily basis consisted of fuck, shit, hell, and sometimes dipshit when he was feeling particularly inspired.

"Where the fuck is that report, Quinn? It's been weeks since you met up with that sorry son of a bitch. Why don't you have anything for me?"

"I'm working on it."

"You're working on it?" McNeil parroted, pegging Ryan with a hard stare. "What the fuck else do you have to do? I haven't assigned you to a new case. All I need is a summary of what you two said and did. That should take you all of thirty fucking minutes to type."

"I'm sorry. I've been distracted. Just some personal stuff." Ryan winced internally. That was almost as bad as the classic "my dog ate my homework" excuse. And McNeil was definitely a lot sharper than most of Ryan's grade-school teachers had been.

"Anything you wanna tell me, Quinn?" His boss watched him carefully, clearly not buying it. "If you need some time off, you should've said something."

"I don't need any time off. I just… give me a week or two and I'll have it finished, all right?"

McNeil nodded slowly, not appearing fully convinced but letting the matter drop. "Fine, Quinn. You've got one more week. No excuses."

"Yes, sir." Nodding, Ryan exhaled heavily. He grabbed his keys, stepped out of the precinct, and began to drive in the direction of his parents' house. With work keeping him busy, he didn't get the chance to see them often. But McNeil had agreed to let him off early today so that he could make it to the weekly family dinner his mother held every Monday.

Once he reached his parents' house, Ryan quickly made his way inside the quaint brick two-story. The smell of corned beef and cabbage wafted in from the kitchen as he greeted Shawn and his father in the living room. The house was an older model on the outskirts of town, with wooden paneling that creaked when you walked and arched windows on every exterior wall. Family pictures and landscape portraits decorated the walls, interspersed with the occasional cross or scripture. The house had an old, antiquated feel to it, like it had been frozen in time all the way back in the 1980s when his father had first bought it. He'd grown up here with his two brothers, and as he glanced around the room fondly, he was glad his mother hadn't changed it much.

"So how's work? McNeil still riding your ass?" his father asked from his seat on the recliner.

"Yeah, you know him. If he wasn't he wouldn't know what to do with himself," Ryan replied, joining Shawn on the couch.

"Son of a bitch hasn't changed a bit," his father remarked with a small smile. He and McNeil had worked together before his father had retired. Thirty-five years on the force had made the two thick as thieves, and even when they'd stopped being coworkers, they still stayed in touch.

"What are our numbers looking like this year?"

"You know how it is. More arrests than we have cells for, yet the narcotics rate's gone up by at least five percent since last year. Not to mention they keep cutting funding to our unit. This same time last year we used to have twice the number of men we do now," Ryan replied with a shrug.

"Welcome to being a cop in downtown Denver, son," his father replied, repeating his favorite phrase. Even though Ryan had spent several years as a cop, his father still liked to talk like he was brand-new to the unit. "Always less of us and more of them. Those bastards get craftier every year. Give it fifteen more years, and then you'll really have something to bitch about."

"Would help if McNeil didn't have us riding a desk half the time," Shawn muttered, clearly still pissed over his week's worth of compliance training.

"Well, word has it you did a bang-up job on the last one. Maybe if you actually learned how to use your fucking gun instead of always running your goddamn mouth, he'd trust you to do more than paperwork," Ryan's father shot back, casting a disapproving gaze in Shawn's direction. Shawn bit back whatever response had been on his lips, sinking further down into the couch.

"Language, Ronnie!" Ryan's mother's sharp voice called out from the kitchen.

Ryan's father's brows drew together in annoyance as he glanced toward Harry, Ryan's nephew, who'd taken a seat on the couch between Ryan and Shawn. "Oh c'mon, Marie. The boy's old enough. You think he doesn't hear it at school?"

"I don't care! Watch your mouth unless you want your dinner ending up in the trash."

"That mean it's almost done?" his father grumbled, glancing at the clock. He was to his very core a man of routine. For the last forty years, he'd woken up at five in the morning every day, gone down to the local diner for his morning coffee, and hit the gym for an hour after work before heading home and taking his dinner at six sharp. He did not like deviations to his schedule, which had made retiring all the more difficult for him to adjust to these last couple of years.

"Yes, come on in, boys." Ryan's mother called from the kitchen.

The four moved from the living room into the kitchen, taking a seat at the dining table as Ryan's mother began to serve the food.

"So, Ryan, how you and Julia doing?" Shawn asked, a mischievous glint in his eyes as he glanced at Ryan from across the table. Ryan delivered a solid kick in reply, glaring at him. Of course that son of a bitch would bring it up now. Julia had been his on-again off-again girlfriend for the last four years. He'd broken up with her about five months ago. The fact that he hadn't told his family was more a matter of convenience than anything else.

They liked Julia. And he did too. Just not quite as much as they did. Hence the problem.

"We're fine," Ryan muttered through gritted teeth.

"That's good, honey," Ryan's mother cooed. "So when are you two getting married?"

They'd been having this conversation religiously every time there was a family dinner, starting three months into his and Julia's relationship. And Shawn always made it a point to be the first one to bring it up. Wishing he could jump across the table and throttle Shawn, Ryan made a mental note to ask Zika what other sick and twisted shit he had up his sleeve next time they ran into each other. 'Cause Shawn was long overdue to get back what he was putting out.

"Not anytime soon," Ryan responded, affording his mother an apologetic smile. "We're still trying to figure things out."

"Nah." Shawn snickered. "All you've gotta do is bat those pretty blue eyes at her and lay on some of that Quinn charm, and I'm sure she'll be down on her knees before you can—"

"Shawn!" Ryan's mother swatted him with a dish towel.

"Sorry, Mrs. Quinn," Shawn replied. He did his best to look sincere in spite of his grin.

"Would you give it a rest, Marie?" Ryan's father muttered, shaking his head. "The boys work their asses off dealing with these street thugs every day. You can't expect them to come back home and talk like fucking saints."

"God help me, Ronald, if you swear at this dinner table one more time, I'm dumping your dinner in the trash and making you sleep on the couch tonight."

"Here we go again," Adam, Ryan's brother, observed flatly, announcing his presence as he took a seat at the dinner table.

"Anyways," Shawn interjected, "I think we were talking about something important. That's right, Ryan and Julia getting married. You know I've heard spring weddings are good luck."

"Yes, dear. You two have been dating for quite a while, you know. Four years is a long time to ask a woman to wait," Ryan's mother said.

"Lots of couples wait a lot longer than that. And most of that time has been more off than on," Ryan muttered, picking at the food on his plate to avoid meeting his mother's gaze.

"Ryan, you know your father and I are getting a lot older. Who knows how long we have left. Even if you two were to get married tomorrow, it could take you years before Julia gets pregnant—"

Ryan choked on the food he'd been chewing, earning a hearty backslap from Shawn.

"Mom, please, lay off the baby talk, all right?" Adam interjected. "If he's not ready, he's not ready. The fact that he's choosing to wait is a sign of maturity."

"I'm sorry, how old were you when you knocked Christine up?" Shawn smirked, feigning ignorance. "Sixteen, right—oww!" Shawn winced as he received a prompt slap to the back of the head, courtesy of Adam.

"Not while he's sitting right here," Adam growled, motioning to Harry.

"Relax, he's barely old enough to add."

"Unlike you, my son isn't an idiot. Just because you didn't learn addition until you were eleven doesn't mean everyone else is a halfwit too." Adam shook his head, motioning for Harry to follow him into the living room. Presumably to finish eating in peace, away from Shawn.

"So, dear, are you free around this time next month?" Ryan's mother asked, turning to him. "I was thinking of holding a vigil for your brother this year—"

"Marie. I already said no." Ryan's father's voice was rough as he pegged his wife with a hard stare.

"I'm tired of you forcing the rest of us to act like he never existed, Ronald. He deserves to be remembered—"

"I said no." Ryan's father slammed his fist down on the table. Everyone fell silent.

Clearing his throat, Ryan put a hand on his father's shoulder. "Dad, please."

"We don't talk about Luca," Ryan's father barked. "We've already been over this. We're not holding a fucking vigil." His father stood and left the room.

Shifting in his seat, Ryan cast a sympathetic look in his mother's direction. It had been like this ever since Luca had passed. His father refused to talk about it. And refused, by extension, to allow anyone else in the family to do so either. "Maybe the rest of us can do something. You, me, Shawn, and Adam."

Ryan's mother smiled tightly, shaking her head. "That's all right, dear. You know how your father will get if he finds out. You just finish your dinner and focus on your work."

Seemingly unconcerned, Shawn turned toward Ryan. "So I met this chick the other night. Really hot piece of ass. Kinky as fuck too—"

"That's it. Out!" Marie demanded, removing Shawn's plate from the dinner table.

"But I'm not finished!"

"Too bad," Marie admonished. "You should have thought about that before you decided to talk like that at my dinner table."

With a crestfallen expression, Shawn motioned for Ryan to follow as he headed for the back door.

"I'm not finished either. And I didn't get kicked out," Ryan stated smugly.

"It'll only take a second."

After a couple of bites, Ryan relented, realizing he wouldn't be able to finish eating in peace until he did.

"Anyways, I met this real hot chick. She said she wants to go out tomorrow night, but she doesn't want it to be just the two of us. I dunno, some bullshit about not wanting to be alone with me on the first date. Anyways, the only way she'll agree is if I can find another couple for a double date. Can you come?"

"And did you ever stop to wonder why she doesn't want to be alone with you, Shawn?" Ryan asked incredulously.

"That's not the point, Ryan. Will you come or not? It's gonna be at, well, it's sort of like a masquerade ball."

"All right, well, in order for it to be a double date, that would require me to have a girlfriend. Which you're well aware that I don't," Ryan growled.

"Don't worry about it. I've got you covered. My date said she can bring one of her girlfriends. You know how they are. Always wanna travel in twos."

Ryan frowned, realizing the easiest solution to this conversation was to say yes.

"Come on, don't make me beg. I haven't gotten laid in five days. I need this. Please."

Sighing, Ryan relented. "Fine."

It would only be for a couple of hours, and afterward he could make up some excuse to work if her friend asked him out again. Besides, even if Shawn was an ass, he'd have to reel his behavior in to at least a tolerable level if he hoped to get laid. How bad could it be?

Chapter Ten:
Some Cupids Kill with Arrows,
Some with Traps

Ryan

SHAWN—IN ALL his acts of moral deficiency and depravity throughout the years—had officially hit an all-time low.

In the time that Ryan and Shawn had been friends, the conniving, dim-witted son of a bitch had put him through a lot. He'd pantsed him in PE class in front of his high school crush, slipped him laxatives the day before he was due to give his graduation speech, had even stolen his clothes after baseball practice and made him walk the entire five miles back home in only a bath towel and shower sandals. Which, in a staunchly religious Irish Catholic neighborhood, was not something you lived down easily.

But even for him, this was a new low.

"A BDSM club? You invited us out to a fucking BDSM club?" Ryan could barely contain his anger as he pulled Shawn off to the side, leaving Shawn's date alone at the rounded table.

"Why do you think I told you to wear a mask?" Shawn shrugged.

"You told me it was a fucking masquerade ball!"

"No, I told you it was *like* a masquerade ball."

"Oh for Christ's sake." Ryan exhaled a frustrated breath, turning away from him. "My date already fucking left, you realize that?"

"Listen, if you wanna bitch to me about your little predicament tomorrow, be my guest. But I'm trying to get laid right now, and my date is really feeling the vibe. If I leave her by herself much longer one of these whips and chains guys is going to swoop her up. So stop cock-blocking and I'll talk to you tomorrow. You'll get over it. You always do." Shawn turned away from him with a dismissive wave and headed back to his date.

Channeling all of his willpower into resisting the urge to strangle his best friend in a room full of witnesses, Ryan stalked through the hallway, trying to find the exit. He'd been so pissed—and shocked— earlier that he hadn't paid attention to where they'd come in. Reaching the end of the corridor, he turned the corner, only to find himself standing in a small room filled with BDSM toys on one side and a table with two men sitting across from each other on the other.

He was about to turn and try the other direction when something caught his eye. He recognized the tattoo on one of the men's chests. Zika was seated at a rounded table across from another man, dressed in leather pants and a mask that covered the upper portion of his face. Ryan only needed one guess as to who the other man was. Of course Zika would be here with that fucking prick.

The two were engaged in a heated argument, so much so that they didn't seem to notice Ryan as he stood in the doorway.

"C'mon, Eden, we've gotta go." Turner's voice was harsh and pleading, tinted with irritation.

"No, you go. I'm staying," Zika replied, the words heavily slurred and equally irritated.

"Eden."

"What?"

"You know you can't just not show up. He said he wants us to be there in thirty."

"Fine, then, you go. And when you do, you can tell him to suck my fucking dick. I'm not going. I'm done taking orders from that stupid fucking cocksucker." Lowering his head, Zika brought his hand to his nose and snorted a line of blow from the table.

"For fuck's sake, Eden. You've had enough. Now come on—"

"I'm not fucking going!" Zika's tone was hoarse as he slammed his fist down on the table.

"And what about Noah and Amelia, huh? What happens to them, then?"

Leaning back in his chair, Zika closed his eyes and let his head rest against the wall behind him. He muttered his response. Ryan couldn't hear his answer from halfway across the room.

"You need to get your shit together, you understand me, Eden? I'm covering for you this time, but you know Trev's not going to keep letting this slide. Call me if you need me." Shaking his head, Turner stormed out, leaving barely enough time for Ryan to step back into the shadows as he stalked off.

Swallowing hard, Ryan stood there for a couple of seconds, frozen in place. Taking a deep breath, he slowly walked into the room and took a seat at the table across from Zika.

Now that he was closer, he could see several lines of coke laid out on the table. Zika's head was still tilted back, eyes closed with white powder dotting the tip of his nose. He reeked of alcohol and was sweating profusely, strands of silky black hair slicked to his forehead.

Ryan cleared his throat to announce his presence. When that didn't work, he reached out and shook Zika lightly.

"Mmm…," Zika mumbled, slowly righting himself and meeting Ryan's gaze through half-lidded eyes.

A cold shiver ran through him as Ryan locked eyes with Zika. For a second, he felt haunted, trapped in that familiar gaze. He'd seen it before. Could never forget it despite how hard he'd tried, not even twelve years later. And he still saw it every time he closed his eyes. That lost, forlorn look, full of everything and nothing all at once.

Blinking, Ryan tightened his grip on the table in front of him, as if to try and force himself awake. His next few breaths came out strained and stuttered. He thought that when he buried his brother, he would never have to see it again. That thousand-mile stare that terrified him, not because of what he saw there, but because of all the things he didn't see. And how each and every time, there wasn't a damn thing he could do to change it. To fill it with something—anything—that didn't feel as if it would break the second he looked away.

"And who the fuck are you?" Eden asked. A lopsided smile tugged at his lips as his body slouched to one side.

Eden didn't recognize him, clearly. Whether it was because Ryan had a mask on, or Eden was just that fucked-up, Ryan wasn't sure.

"You want a ride home?" Ryan asked, the words hoarse on his lips.

"Naw. Not going home. You wanna play?" Eden asked, motioning gracelessly to the array of whips, chains, and toys affixed to the wall.

Ryan shook his head, not trusting himself to speak.

"Mmm, that's too bad. You're probably straight, huh?" Eden mused, his words garbled as he bent his head and snorted another line. "You sure? Promise I'll make it worth your time." He pulled three crumpled hundred-dollar bills from his pocket and held them out. "I'll give you this much to whip me."

Ryan's eyes drifted from the bills in Eden's hand back to his face. And his chest ached. A pain that radiated outward from his center all the way to his fingertips till he felt it in his bones. He couldn't think, couldn't articulate a response. Like his brain was short-circuiting, rejecting whatever twisted version of reality he'd accidentally stumbled upon.

So instead, he leaned forward, lifted his hand to Eden's cheek, and placed his lips on his.

It was barely a touch, his lips brushing against Eden's tentatively, sampling the soft warmth. After a moment's pause, he could feel Eden's lips move against his own. Urgent. Willing. Their mouths molded together, leaving no space in between, a slight tremor in the velvety smooth heat. Eden's tongue slid across his lips, seeking entrance. The sensation sent an electric shock jolting through Ryan, straight to his groin. Opening to him, Ryan leaned farther forward, cradling Eden's cheek in his hand. Drawing him closer.

Ryan's tongue slid along the wet warmth of Eden's mouth, tasting him. Their hot breaths mingled together, and for a moment time stopped. Sliding his chair forward, Ryan slipped his other hand behind Eden's head. Eden moaned into his mouth, biting down on Ryan's lower lip, and Ryan almost lost it. His lips moved against Eden's with more force, his breaths coming in disjointed stutters as his tongue explored. Fisting the front of Eden's shirt, Ryan's body demanded more. Much more.

More of him. More of this. More than what a kiss could offer.

When Ryan finally pulled back, he was breathless. His face was hot, and his lips felt swollen, tingling from the loss of sensation. Eden had a slight blush on his cheeks, and his lidded eyes lingering on Ryan's lips.

It wasn't anything like he'd imagined. Wasn't greedy or controlling or demanding like he'd expected Eden would be.

"Why'd you stop?" Eden asked, his words breathless.

"Not here." Ryan inclined his head toward the door. "Let me take you home."

This time Eden nodded, and the relief Ryan felt was immediate as he offered him his shoulder. At first Eden pushed him away, but after stumbling a couple of times, he allowed him to help as they made their way out to Ryan's car. The two sat silently as Ryan drove to Eden's apartment, and by the time they arrived, Eden was out cold.

It took a substantial amount of effort for Ryan to shoulder Eden's dead weight and carry him up to his apartment. He fished Eden's keys from his pocket, unlocked the door, located the bedroom, and eased Eden down onto his bed.

The apartment was bare of personal touches. A couch, a flat-screen TV, and a black wooden coffee table out in the living room. Two bookcases on either side of the TV, a black rug against white carpet in the center, with a mirror and a couple of framed black-and-white abstracts on the walls. The bedroom had the same black-and-white theme, a black plush comforter draped across the bed and another abstract painting above. A small dream catcher hung overhead, swaying slightly as the air in the room shifted.

For a moment Ryan just stood there, standing over Eden in silence and watching him sleep. He looked peaceful, more peaceful than he ever had before. The tension lines that typically creased his forehead were gone, his mouth relaxed into a small smile.

Eden probably wouldn't remember any of this with how fucked-up he'd been. And Ryan knew it was for the better, that it would keep things simple. Less complicated. But a part of him wished he would. A part of him wished Eden had known it was him he'd kissed. That he'd let him do it again. That reality wasn't what was, and the idea that somehow, somewhere, this could be something more....

"Sweet dreams, Eden." Touching his hand to the dream catcher for a moment, Ryan ran his hands along the felt ring.

Ryan left Eden's keys on the counter and closed the door quietly behind him. He stood there for a moment, his feet rooted in place. He looked down and realized his hands were balled into fists, shaking slightly. Sliding down the door, Ryan closed his eyes and took a deep breath, unclenching his hands. He waited like that, not moving a muscle. He wasn't sure for how long. Only after he heard movement in the apartment—proof that Eden was alive and well—did he make his way down to his car.

He'd been right. He was so clearly fucked. And not just because of everything he was withholding. Up until tonight, he hadn't been sure of what he was going to do. Initially, he'd felt obligated to check up on Eden and make sure he was in one piece after he'd almost shot him.

But this was different.

He knew now what he had to do. And he knew, after this, there would be no turning back.

Thirteen Years Ago

THE PRINCE *and I never argued. But that day we did.*

He told me he wanted me to sell stardust instead, that he loved me too much. That he couldn't take it anymore. That thinking about it was making him lose his mind, and he wasn't sure how much longer he could take it. I'd never seen him beg before, but that day he did.

And it hurt my chest, because he was a Prince. And he shouldn't ever have to beg, especially not to me. I hugged him and asked him to stop crying. I didn't know what to say to make him happy. I wanted to say yes, but I wasn't sure if I could. And he knew it.

I think that's what made him cry more than anything else.

He got down on his knees and held my hands and made me look into his eyes. He asked me to promise to try my hardest, and I said I would. But I was scared that it wouldn't be enough. That I would fail him, and he'd never stop crying.

I told him that I loved him, and he said he loved me too. I asked him why he was still sad, if he loved me and I loved him.

He said it was because he loved me that he was sad. But I still didn't understand. I asked him if it would be better if we didn't love each other. If our love made him sad, how could it be a good thing? He shook his head and told me that it didn't matter. That it was too late. We were already in love, and there was no going back.

I told him I was sorry, and he told me that it wasn't my fault.

He said I love you. I hate this, but I love you.

He said they won't understand you. I understand you. They don't love you like I do.

He said you're everything. You make me real. I don't exist without you.

Chapter Eleven:
Beware the Ides of March

Eden

TODAY WAS a bad day.

March 15th always was. Each and every year.

Usually Eden spent it alternating between lines of blow and shots of liquor till he passed out, but alas, tonight he had to work. And he had no desire to hear Ryan's bitching followed by a game of twenty questions as to why he was so wasted he could barely stand. Especially since Ryan had started showing up religiously at Club Zero every Friday night for the past two months—ostensibly to make sure Carl didn't pull the same shit he had before—which had eventually become Saturdays and then Sundays too.

Ryan's presence at Club Zero had become a staple of Eden's weekends. Why Ryan had suddenly felt compelled to put in overtime on his days off, Eden had no clue. But he'd never been the type to look a gift horse in the mouth. Especially one that was buying him free drinks and, on occasion, something deep-fried and soaked in grease. So it wasn't exactly out of the realm of possibilities to think he'd be by tonight. Although given the fact that it was a Monday, he highly doubted it.

Nursing the scotch in his hand, Eden scanned the dance floor from Club Zero's second-floor balcony. He spotted a familiar blond head weaving through the crowd and proceeded to take the stairs two at a time until he met Ryan halfway… and stopped dead in his tracks.

Ryan reeked of hard liquor. His eyes were bloodshot and glazed, his movements clumsy as he greeted Eden with a lazy smile.

"Hey."

"Hey. Rough night?"

"Something like that," Ryan muttered, glancing around. "Your fuckbuddy here tonight?"

"Who? You mean X?" Eden asked, raising a brow.

"Yeah. That's what I said."

"Nah." Eden snickered. "Trev's been sending him to the Mansion. Wants to increase profits. Divide and conquer, all that bullshit."

He nodded, tilting his head to the side. "Good. That's real good…. You looking for a substitute?"

Pausing, Eden studied Ryan for a moment. "Never thought you'd wanna try your hand hustling narcotics, detective. Don't think your boss would like that too much."

Ryan laughed huskily, stepping into Eden's space. His hair was damp, a couple of snowflakes caught in the golden strands. His eyes flashed as they drifted down Eden's body. "You know that's not what I'm talking about, Eden."

Ryan smelled like petrichor and vodka, a dizzying combination that went straight to Eden's dick. Eden's mouth watered as he imagined running his hands through Ryan's silky blond hair and pulling hard as he fucked him from behind. He wondered idly whether or not he was a moaner. If there was a God, he sure as fuck was.

"If I'd known all it took to get you in the mood was a couple shots of vodka, I would've tipped the bartender to slip some extras into your drinks, Ryan."

"Stop deflecting. And no, you wouldn't. I've spent every weekend with you for the last month, and you haven't tried to do shit with me." Ryan's voice was low and deep with just the slightest hint of hoarseness.

"Well, you're a cop. So yeah, I haven't. Don't mistake me covering my ass for some misplaced sense of chivalry."

Running his tongue along the inside of his cheek, Ryan half smiled. "You think I don't see what you're doing every time you say shit like that. But I do. I see you, Eden. Even when you don't want me to."

"You're shitfaced, Ryan." Eden cleared his throat, a sense of foreboding clawing at his chest. Maybe it was just a coincidence, his peculiar choice of wording.

"Yeah, and you're high most of the time. What's your point?"

Eden looked down, then away, lowering his voice. "Let me give you a ride back to your place. I get off shift in five. We'll talk after you sleep it off."

"Naw. Not going home. You wanna play?"

A shiver ran down Eden's spine at the familiar words. It had been Ryan. At the BDSM club that night. He'd wondered, then dismissed it. Because how could it be? But now he knew for sure. Eden turned and pushed his way through the crowd into the alley out back. He felt suffocated by the club, which had suddenly become too small. And Ryan's words that had suddenly become too large.

Eden heard Ryan call his name behind him, but he didn't stop. He needed to get out of here. Away from this. Whatever this was. He only made it a couple of steps before he felt a strong hand wrap around his arm.

"Get off me," Eden growled, his hands balling into fists.

Ryan spun him around, forcing Eden to face him. "Why? You'll let some fucking stranger touch you, but you won't let me?"

"That's different."

"How? How the fuck is it different?"

"Because."

"Because why, Eden? For once, give me a straight answer instead of hiding behind all your bullshit bravado."

The words were too much. And as he glared at Ryan, for a moment he hated him. Hated him for making him face this. Fisting the front of Ryan's shirt, Eden slammed him against the brick wall. "Because that's not all I fucking want from you, all right?"

"Then let me be more." Ryan's words were soft as he wrapped his hands around Eden's wrists.

Eden shook his head. Ryan didn't understand. He couldn't. He was probably just drunk. "You don't know what you're saying."

Looping one hand inside Eden's belt buckle, Ryan slipped the other behind Eden's head and pulled him into a kiss. Eden tried to push away. Pull back. But Ryan's grip was firm, unyielding, as the soft warmth of his lips consumed him. Groaning, Eden responded in spite of himself. His body moved without thought, leaning him into the kiss. His hands roved up Ryan's chest, hungry for the warmth rolling off of him. Ryan shivered under his touch as he pulled Eden closer.

Ryan's hand at Eden's waist slipped inside his jeans, past his boxers, and stroked his erection. Eden choked on his next breath, the raw, guttural sound echoing in the narrow alleyway. His head tilted back, his knees shaking as he grabbed at Ryan's shoulders to steady himself.

"Look at me." Ryan's deep, gravelly voice was barely enough to keep him grounded as Eden met his gaze. Ryan's eyes were a piercing blue, desperate and focused with a single-minded intensity that made Eden's blood run hot.

Bowing his head, Ryan bit down on his neck, sucking hard on the tender flesh. Eden moaned, digging his fingernails into Ryan's shoulders. The tender sensation was so intense it almost hurt as Ryan's lips moved against his skin.

"I like you, Eden. I like you a lot. And I'm not talking about this bullshit act you put on. I like *you*. I don't know why you hide. But you don't have to. Not with me. Because I've already seen you. So please, just—"

Eden cut Ryan off as his mouth found his. He fastened his hands in Ryan's hair and forced his head up. He could feel Ryan's erection pushing against his groin as Ryan rubbed against him, his movements eager and demanding. Eden bit down on Ryan's lower lip, and Ryan moaned into his mouth, slipping his hand behind Eden's back and pulling him forward so there was no space left between them. His skin burned everywhere it touched Ryan. His body shook. Begging for more. Breathless, Eden pulled back, grabbed Ryan's hand, and pulled him toward his loaner bike.

It was snowing. Pure white snowflakes dotted the horizon as snow crunched beneath his feet. Everything about this moment felt special. Untainted. Like the pages of a book he'd forgotten long ago. Or a letter that held all the secrets of the world.

"You sober enough to ride?" Eden asked, his voice hoarse.

"Yeah." Ryan nodded, shivering slightly.

"Good. We're going to my place." Once he'd jumped onto his bike, Eden found he could barely steady his hands enough to make it the short ride home. The second they were inside his apartment, Ryan pushed Eden against the wall, pulled his shirt off, and licked a hot, wet trail up his chest. Heat rushed to Eden's groin as his head rolled back and hit the wall behind him. He looked down as Ryan's movements suddenly halted, bereft at the loss of sensation.

"What's wrong?" Eden asked, his voice scratchy.

"When did you get these?" Ryan motioned to Eden's nipple piercings.

Eden took a deep breath, trying to clear his head long enough to form a coherent response. "I don't know. A couple weeks ago. For fuck's sake, Ryan, why does it matter now?"

Ryan shook his head, muttering to himself. "I thought... how did I miss it?"

Before Eden could ask him what he meant, Ryan wrapped his hands around the back of Eden's thighs, lifted him up, and carried him to the bed. Eden pulled off Ryan's shirt and ran his hands along the firm warmth of his chest before pushing off Ryan's pants. Sliding halfway down the bed, Eden lifted his head and—

"No. I want you on top."

"Ok." Eden didn't give a fuck what position he was in. He'd take him any way he could get him.

In one fluid motion, Ryan flipped him over so that Eden was straddling him. He cradled Eden's head and slipped a hand through his silky black hair. Eden's chest tightened in anticipation as his eyes drifted down the vast expanse of naked skin, to the tuft of blond hair right above Ryan's dick. He was already fully erect. The head of his cock was a rosy pink, slightly darker than his shaft, and even more glorious than Eden had imagined. Long and thick with a slight curve that made the head bob against his stomach every time his arousal twitched.

Eden licked his lips and slid down Ryan's body. He lowered his head and took Ryan into his mouth, moaning as the taste of Ryan's precum mixed with the tang of his sweat. He'd wondered what Ryan's arousal would smell like, taste like, ever since the first night they'd spoken back at Club Zero. And fuck if finally knowing didn't make every nerve ending in his body short circuit with white-hot lust. The salty, bitter musk was a perfect balance to the way Ryan's body was splayed out before him, sweet and willing.

Eden grinned and slid his tongue along the vein that ran the length of Ryan's cock, lapping at the heated flesh. He hummed in approval when Ryan's dick pulsed in his throat. The vibration of it was like a visceral thing that started at his tongue and echoed through his chest. Ryan groaned, and his free hand fisted the bedsheets. He rolled his hips, cursing, and his dick hit the back of Eden's throat.

As he slid his tongue along the slick heat of Ryan's arousal, Eden massaged his balls with his free hand, his eyes focused intently on Ryan's. His blue irises, usually so clear and focused, were swimming, like they couldn't decide whether they wanted to focus on Eden's lips around his dick or the way Eden's hips were rutting against the mattress as he sought relief from his own erection. Ryan let out a choked breath. His lips were drawn tight, slightly. His entire body was rigid beneath Eden, hips slanted at an angle, like he was caught between trying to keep them from bucking up to chase the wet friction of Eden's mouth and letting Eden come to him.

Eden's pulse roared in his ears as he watched Ryan writhe beneath him through half-lidded eyes. He pulled up slightly and swirled his tongue along the swollen head of Ryan's dick before taking him back inside his mouth. Usually he'd be tempted to reach down and jerk himself off. Borrow some friction from his right hand to make it to the finish line. But seeing Ryan like this was so much better than anything he could do with his hands.

"Fuck, Eden," Ryan groaned. His hips rocked back and forth, shaky and disjointed, against Eden's lips. What had once been a hungry rhythm broke off, and a violent tremor gripped Ryan's body. Eden tightened his throat around Ryan's dick in response. Ryan's head snapped back into the pillow, and his orgasm shot into Eden's throat. Eden watched him through heated eyes, sucking him dry till Ryan's body went limp.

Finally lifting off of him, Eden grinned, a self-satisfied smirk on his face as he licked his lips. He took a moment to admire Ryan's body, his thick pink dick and his heavily muscled chest, glistening with sweat.

"Holy shit, Ryan muttered breathlessly, lifting his head and looking up at Eden through glossy sky-blue eyes. He shifted enough to lock his hands behind Eden's knees, then pulled him forward on the bed, clearly intent on returning the favor.

But Eden swung off of him, shaking his head, and fished his cigarettes from the pocket of his pants.

"Nah, I'm good. Thanks, though."

Ryan's brows drew together. He blinked at Eden for several useless seconds, clearly confused, as his breath came in strained stutters. "What? Why?"

"I'm a giver, not a taker." Eden winked and took a deep drag from his cigarette as he lay next to Ryan on the bed.

"Since when?" Ryan snorted, propping himself up on his elbows. "What if I wanna make you feel good too?"

Eden glanced over at him. "You already do. Trust me."

Sitting up fully, Ryan reached over and began unzipping Eden's jeans. "Then at least let me see you. Let me watch."

Eden raised a brow, smirking. "Never thought you were the voyeuristic type."

"Neither did I," Ryan muttered, his eyes roving over Eden's body hungrily.

Eden kicked his pants the rest of the way off and straddled Ryan, still holding his cigarette between his lips as he began stroking himself. The way Ryan's eyes roved over him felt better than his own hand. His heated gaze sent a jolt of electricity down Eden's spine. As Ryan watched Eden touch himself, his dick grew hard again, and he palmed his erection and let out a choked laugh.

Eden drew out his impending orgasm, stroking himself slowly. The thrill of the way Ryan's eyes fixated on him was a heady high, better than any other drug. Like he was something worth watching. Eden tipped his head toward the ceiling and bit back a moan. The cigarette in his mouth almost slipped from between his lips when he came all over Ryan's chest. Ryan let out a low, gravelly groan, swiping his hand across his chest and lifting his cum-covered fingers to his mouth.

"Wait." Eden's words were sharp as he grabbed Ryan's hand. "Don't."

"Why?" Ryan asked, his eyes drifting hungrily from his hands to Eden's face.

"Just don't. Okay?"

Ryan nodded slowly, lowering his hand.

The tension drained from Eden's body as he slumped down next to Ryan.

Glancing over at him, Ryan rubbed the cum into his skin instead. "You wanna fuck?"

The words caught Eden off guard. His eyes widened slightly as he returned Ryan's stare. "Nah. I mean, yeah. Fuck yes. But not tonight."

Ryan raised a brow at him, clearly intent on a more in-depth explanation.

"'Cause you're drunk," Eden explained, his eyes drifting to the dream catcher above as he exhaled a slow stream of smoke. "Your first time with a guy shouldn't be when you're fucked-up."

He could feel Ryan still beside him. "You're a fucking lie, you know that? You talk about roofying people and fucking the cheapest bidder. But then when it actually comes down to it, you pull this white-knight shit."

Eden snickered. He wanted to tell Ryan there were no such things as white knights. Romeos and Juliets. Heroes and villains. But he didn't. Because for all he knew, Ryan still believed in all that shit. And he didn't have it in him to shatter his rosy version of reality. Instead he shook his head.

"I think the word you're looking for is hypocrite."

"Stop hiding."

"Then stop calling me out."

A heavy silence fell between them as Eden finished the rest of his cigarette. Before he could slip out of bed like he usually did, Ryan's arms came around him, pulling Eden's back to his chest.

"What are you doing?" Eden asked, his entire body tensing.

"Holding you. Sometimes people do that after sex," Ryan responded, his voice tinted with amusement.

"I don't cuddle."

"Well, too bad, 'cause I do. Deal with it."

Gradually, Eden relaxed into Ryan's arms, the slow rise and fall of Ryan's chest against his back like a silent lullaby. He usually hated this shit, but for some reason, tonight he found it tolerable. Pleasant, even.

It reminded him of summer days. Of strawberry cheesecake and burning sunsets. Back when nowhere and everywhere was his home. Back when special had a name and a face and a sound.

Ryan

WHEN RYAN awoke, it was still dark outside. The bed was cold next to him, and as he looked around the black-and-white bedroom, it took him a second to remember where he was. The small dream catcher hanging above swayed back and forth, listing gently. Turning over on his side, he saw the silhouette of a figure through the curtains leading to the balcony. He slid off the bed and slipped his pants on before joining Eden on the terrace.

He was smoking a cigarette, his eyes turned toward the sky.

"Can't sleep?" Ryan asked, following Eden's gaze as he looked up at the stars.

"Nah."

"That happen often?"

Eden shrugged. He had a distant look in his eyes as he took a hard drag on his cigarette.

Ryan was silent for a moment, leaning his forearms against the railing as he took a deep breath. "My little brother used to have bad dreams. Had trouble sleeping. He tried sleeping pills, natural supplements, counseling. But none of it worked."

Eden turned toward him, his words deep and low when he spoke. "You ever find anything that helped?"

Ryan laughed darkly, though it sounded more like a choke. "Yeah. He died." He could feel Eden's eyes on him as Ryan's gaze swept aimlessly over the sky.

"I'm sorry."

"Don't be. Like you said, people die. He was really... unhappy near the end. Went through some rough stuff when he was younger. Sometimes when he'd have trouble sleeping, I'd sit by his bed or outside his door. I thought maybe it would help him, knowing there was someone there watching over him."

"Did it?"

Ryan shrugged, finally looking over at Eden with a sad smile. "I like to think so, but honestly, I don't really know. I tried to help him, did what I could, but I didn't always know the right things to say or the right things to do. How to help, you know?"

Eden nodded wordlessly, moving close to Ryan so their shoulders brushed together. "Life's like that sometimes. Gives you fucked-up situations you're not ready for, some you'll never be ready for. Sometimes all we can do is be there and try. Your brother was lucky to have you."

Ryan cleared his throat, blinking back the wetness in his eyes. "Thanks," he muttered hoarsely, managing a strained smile, "for saying that."

"Not just saying it. I mean it." Eden slid his hand up Ryan's back and around his shoulder. The motion was awkward, like Eden wasn't used to it. But the thought that he was trying anyway warmed Ryan. "And I'm sure he'd be proud of who you are today."

Shaking his head, Ryan swallowed past the lump in his throat. "How can you be so sure?"

"'Cause, you'd have to be damn near deaf and blind not to be. Or a complete fuckhead."

Ryan made a laughing, pained sound, leaning his head against Eden's. He needed his warmth. Needed his touch when everything else felt so cold. Clearing his throat, he smiled slowly. "You say the sweetest shit when you're not trying to be an asshole. You know that?"

Eden shrugged, smiling. "Your fault. Someone told me once that bleeding hearts are contagious." Stubbing the rest of his cigarette out against the railing, Eden inclined his head toward the door. "C'mon. Let's try that trick. See if we can get some sleep."

Ryan smiled, following Eden inside and joining him on the bed. After about half an hour, he could feel Eden relax beside him, his chest rising and falling slowly. Reaching over, Ryan gently brushed a lock of hair from his face. His chest tightened for a moment as his eyes drifted to the scar on Eden's cheek. "I'm sorry. I'm sorry you have bad dreams."

Ryan stayed up till the sun shone through the curtains, gentle rays of pale yellow and white streaming through. When Eden yawned next to him, he smiled softly, biting back a laugh at his groggy expression as he opened his eyes. His black hair stuck out in a haphazard jumble atop his head as his eyes crinkled to block out the sunlight. Rubbing at his face, Eden turned toward him, a smile slowly spreading across his face.

"You stayed up."

"Of course I did." Ryan laughed, raising a brow. "What, you thought I wouldn't?"

"Nah, it's just…. Thanks," Eden muttered awkwardly, flushing as he looked down at his feet. "For trying to help. For caring enough to."

The subtle warmth that spread through his chest lit up Ryan's face in a wide grin. "It helped me too. Knowing that it helped you. Makes me feel like I wasn't as off base as I felt sometimes." He slid off the bed and slipped on his clothes. "I've gotta get going. Work in an hour."

Eden reached into his nightstand and produced a piece of paper and a pen. He scribbled something onto the paper before handing it to Ryan. "Here."

"What's this?" Ryan asked, looking down at the number on the paper. "I already have your number, remember."

"Not my burner phone." Eden's eyes glinted mischievously as he smirked up at him. "Figured it might be nice to text without your boss being able to read all our shit."

Ryan blinked, glancing down at the paper and then back at Eden. Then he blushed and grinned so wide his cheeks hurt.

Eden was crass and rude and offensive. He did shit Ryan would never agree with no matter how much time they spent with each other. But he was also sweet and caring and adorably awkward. Ryan saved the number in his phone before slipping the note into his wallet. He planned on keeping the paper there till the numbers wore off and the paper frayed at the edges, leaving nothing more than a crinkled shred.

Chapter Twelve:
What's Done Can't Be Undone

Ryan

"HOLY SHIT. Look who finally got laid."

Shawn's surprisingly astute observation wasn't quite on the mark but close enough. His voice carried the full length of the small office, apparently intent on making a PSA on the newest development in Ryan's sex life to all his coworkers. Well, there went any chance of his fellow cops ever taking him seriously. At least on a professional level. If he ever got a promotion, he was definitely going to have to transfer precincts.

"I don't know what you're talking about," Ryan grumbled, training his eyes on the newspaper in front of him.

"Don't play dumb, Quinn," Alice said wryly. "Actually, I'd like to congratulate you. Evans and I were worried that if you didn't get some soon, you might forget how to use it. And speaking on behalf of all women in the world, that would've been an absolute shame."

Kurtis cleared his throat from his desk in the far corner. "You guys realize this is sexual harassment, right?"

Shawn glanced over, rolling his eyes. "Shut up, virgin. You don't get to have an opinion until you've actually popped your cherry."

"Be nice," Ryan warned, casting a sympathetic look in Kurtis's direction. He was like a lamb in a den full of wolves. Why McNeil had thought it was a good idea to hire him, Ryan had no clue. Maybe he wanted him as a decoy target for Shawn, who usually caused a good five-hundred-dollars' worth of damage to office property every month.

"It's his fault," Shawn snapped. "Mom should know to keep his mouth shut when the big boys are talking."

"Anyways," Alice cut in, "who was it? That new blond secretary who started working on the third floor a few weeks back?"

"I'd fuck her," Shawn offered his approval.

"You'd fuck anything that said yes. Or maybe," Alice countered.

"Not Mom." Shawn snickered, gesturing to Kurtis.

"Would you please stop calling me that?"

Ryan winced. Kurtis was never going to get anywhere with Shawn if he thought using the word please would actually elicit a favorable response.

Shawn grinned, his eyes glinting mischievously. "Only if you beg. On your knees."

Ryan shot Shawn a disapproving glare, then turned back to Alice. "They don't work here, so just drop it."

"You know that's not going to happen," Shawn said. "So you might as well tell us now—"

"Quinn, in my office. Now." McNeil's voice boomed through the small office, causing everyone to jolt slightly.

Shawn glanced over at him, raising a brow. "What the fuck did you do? Cum in his coffee?"

"Shut up. Before you get me in even more trouble," Ryan snapped, standing and making his way over to McNeil's office. He had a feeling he knew what this was about. He closed the door behind him and took a seat in the chair opposite McNeil.

"What the fuck is this?" McNeil growled, throwing Ryan's report onto the desk in front of him.

"The report on Zika," Ryan answered evenly, forcing himself not to fidget as he met McNeil's steely gaze.

"Exactly. You've spent months with that little shit, and all you've got is some shit about ass tattoos and his baby sister. Five fucking pages of bullshit. What the fuck are you doing out there? Girl Scouting with him?"

"No, I... he's a hard guy to get to know, all right?" At least he could be honest about that much.

"Do I need to send Evans in on this shit—"

"No," Ryan snapped, his jaw squaring at the mere thought. "I'll handle it. Just give me more time."

"You've been saying that a lot lately, Quinn." McNeil's eyes were pensive as he studied Ryan from across his desk.

Ryan sat up a little straighter, forcing his tone to remain steady. "We knew this was going to be a hard sell with him, especially with Zika knowing I'm a cop. You can't expect him to spill his guts to me about his entire operation in a few months, sir. I know you want to see results, but this is going to take time."

McNeil was quiet for a moment, running his hand through his beard. "Fine. But when all this shit's done, you better have something for me that I can actually fucking use."

"I will," Ryan reassured him. "Thank you, sir."

Ryan made his way back to his desk before letting out a heavy sigh. What the hell was he going to do? He couldn't keep bullshitting McNeil forever. Running a hand through his hair, he glanced down at his phone and did a double take. He couldn't help but smile as Eden's name popped up on his notifications. He opened the text with a couple of swipes of his finger.

Morning, detective, how's the hangover? -E

I'm feeling pretty good overall. Has nothing to do with the hangover though. -A

Oh yeah? And why's that? -E

Finally got some action from this fine piece of ass I've been chasing around for the past month. Turns out he blows like a dream. -A

What a coincidence. Me too. Dick was so big I could barely fit it all in. -E

Ryan choked on the coffee he'd been drinking and coughed hard.

"Sexting already?" Shawn snickered, raising a brow at him from across the room. "That's my boy. Sounds like your new chick's a real fucking freak. My type of woman. She send you a pic? If she did, I call dibs."

"I'm going on break." Ryan stood before Shawn could make a grab for his phone and headed out the precinct doors, doing a couple laps around the building till his body no longer felt like a sauna.

You can't say shit like that to me while I'm at work. Otherwise I'm gonna be walking around the office all day with blue balls. -A

That's kinda the point :) -E

Sadist. -A

Don't act like you didn't already know that when you let me suck you off. -E

Looking up from his phone, Ryan cursed, adjusting himself in his pants. This was going to be one hell of a long day.

You free tonight? -A

I can be. You wanna come over? -E

Yeah. You want me to bring pizza? -A

I make some mean enchiladas if you're not a bitch about spicy food. Was gonna cook a batch for Noah and Amelia anyways. And if you say something smart about me cooking, I will put rat poison in your food. -E

Truer words of endearment were never spoken. See you tonight, Chef Ramsey. -A

Slipping his phone back into his pocket, Ryan promised himself he wouldn't text Eden again till he got off shift. For his dick's sake. He only made it about half an hour.

Ryan

DEVOURING THE last of his enchilada, Ryan stared at the flat-screen TV in front of him. His mouth hung open slightly as he glanced over at Eden on the other end of the couch with a mixture of disbelief and morbid curiosity.

"What the hell is this?"

"*Maury.*"

"I know what it is. But why in the world do you watch it?"

"They're my people," Eden answered with a smirk. "Makes me feel at home. Kinda like a kindred spirit."

Ryan shook his head. "Eden. What the hell do you have in common with a white woman who's had eight kids by seven different men? Besides maybe drugs. I mean, the only reason she even cares who the baby daddy is, is so she can collect the money for her triple-D boob job."

Eden snickered, amusement flashing in his eyes. "Not her. Maury. The man's a fucking genius. Think about it. His business model takes people's bad life decisions, which are always in ample supply, and turns it into a feel-good flick. People watch this shit, and regardless of whatever they have going on in their lives, they feel better afterwards. The thank-God-it's-not-me phenomenon.

"I guarantee you before he got this talk show, that man hustled hard on the streets. Probably not drugs. He's too soft for that. More likely something involving copyright infringement, like burned CDs or videos. Or rip-off designer bags."

Ryan laughed, raising a brow. "You think?"

"I know," Eden answered confidently. "Bet he has some baby mama living out the back of a trailer with three of his bastard children.

Tell you what, though. Triple-D can't be much good in bed if her batting odds are one out of eight return customers. Either that or she's a fucking champ at giving head. Maybe you should call in and give her some pointers."

"I haven't even jerked you off yet. How do you know I'm any good in bed?"

"Because the suppressed, uptight types always are. Gotta have an outlet for all that pent-up sexual frustration."

"I am not suppressed."

Eden raised a brow, snickering. "Do you even own a dildo?"

"Not owning a dildo doesn't make someone suppressed."

"Oh, so you're a masochist, then?"

Ryan rolled his eyes. "I've just never had the need for one."

"See, that's the shit I'm talking about. You have a dick and a G-spot. You can't say you've never had a need for one." Inclining his head toward the door at the far end of the hall, Eden smirked. "Want me to show you how to use one?"

Ryan's face flushed. "On you? Or on me?" Not that it mattered. Because the answer to both was definitely a resounding yes. But he needed to set his expectations accordingly.

"Depends." Eden licked his lips. "You in the mood for a ride or a show—"

The deafening roar of shattered glass erupted in the living room. A million shards of white fell like an avalanche from the wall-sized window to Ryan's right. A second later, he hit the ground hard, Eden's body pinning his against the carpet. Blinking, Ryan shook himself, trying to clear the ringing in his ears. A spray of bullets whizzed overhead like firecrackers as his brain tried to catch up with the cacophony of sound and motion around him. He vaguely registered Eden dragging him over to the nearby hallway.

Shaking himself mentally, Ryan kneeled behind the hall wall, glancing over at Eden.

"You shot?" Eden had to yell to be heard over the shattering of glass and the violent screech of metal against metal.

"No, I'm fine," Ryan yelled, reaching for the gun he always carried at his waist. "You?"

"I'm good. Stay here."

"Wait."

Eden was already darting down the hall before Ryan could get the words out. Cursing, Ryan kept his body low to the ground and followed after him. He reached the bedroom doorway just in time to see Eden retrieve a pistol from his nightstand. Returning to his side, Eden motioned to the front door.

"Get to your car. I'll cover you."

"What the hell's going on?" Ryan yelled, flinching as another round of bullets shot through the living room window to his left.

"Dominick's men."

Ryan cursed, gripping his gun a little tighter. He was familiar with the name. Most members of the narcotics unit were. He was another major player in the world of narcotics distribution. An up-and-coming drug lord who had a history of run-ins between his men and Trevor's.

"You go first and I'll cover you," Ryan said, gesturing toward the door.

"Not coming. Gotta finish this."

Ryan's gut rolled, a cold shiver running down his spine. He'd been afraid Eden would say something like that.

"No. We go together. Or I can call backup, and we'll wait till they arrive."

"We don't have time for this shit. If you stay you'll just get in my way," Eden growled.

Ryan shook his head adamantly. "I've got a gun. I can help."

"That's not the point. I don't want you involved."

Before Ryan could respond, he spotted movement out of the corner of his eye. His reaction was instinctual, honed by years of police training. Stepping in front of Eden, Ryan leveled his gun at the masked man. Before he could pull the trigger, a thunderous bang reverberated through the small room. Falling back, Ryan gasped, clutching at his chest as he tried to breathe past the pain. He could hear Eden return fire from behind him, the figure in front of him crumpling to the ground a second later.

"Fuck!" Eden's words were fragmented and frantic as he leaned over him. Ripping open Ryan's shirt, Eden's eyes roved over his chest, searching for the bullet wound. Relaxing above him, Eden exhaled heavily, running his fingers along the badge that hung from Ryan's neck. "Your badge. It got caught on your badge—"

"Hands up!" Police officers stormed the room, guns aimed at both of them. Cursing under his breath, Eden slowly lifted his hands. Ryan did the same as he struggled to sit up.

Eight hours later, Ryan had explained the majority of the situation to the officers, leaving out any details that could incriminate Eden. The bullet wound the intruder sustained had been nonlethal, thankfully, so they were treating it as a botched assassination attempt instead of a homicide. Aside from the bruise he'd received from where the bullet impacted his badge, Ryan had come out of the incident with just a few scratches.

Luck had been on their side. At least for now.

He'd tried to talk Eden into getting checked out by the paramedics on site, but he'd refused vehemently. Other than that, he'd been uncharacteristically quiet. Which made sense, considering what they'd both just been through and the fact that almost a dozen cops were suddenly standing in his living room. As the last of the officers cleared out, Ryan spotted Eden slipping into his bedroom. He'd give Eden some time alone to process everything. He wasn't sure how Eden reacted to things like this, but he didn't want to crowd him.

Not that he had any intentions of leaving him by himself. Not with the window wide open like it was. He'd give Eden a good hour and then broach the subject of Eden staying over at his place till the repairs could be made. The thought of what might've happened to Eden if he hadn't been there left him shaking long after the adrenaline had cleared his system. He needed to be sure there'd be no more hired hits. For both their sake.

Eden

EDEN PACED back and forth in his bathroom, running a hand through his hair. He'd snorted a couple of lines to try and center himself, but his nerves were still frayed to shit. Those fuckers had shot Ryan. He was so angry he was shaking. But he could hardly go after them now, not when the cops were involved. He'd have to wait. Bide his time till the heat died down a bit.

He splashed his face with cold water, then slapped his cheeks a couple of times.

"It's fine, Eden muttered to himself. "He's fine. Everything's fine."

Pausing as he bent over the sink, Eden's eyes drifted to the ink peeking up from his chest.

All black. Like the bottom of a closet where he'd whispered "It's ok" and "He doesn't mean it" and "He's just drunk." Like his mother's bruises. Like his father's eyes. Always black. Always seeking. Searching for something he'd never quite been able to find.

Black like all the parts Eden always tried to hide.

How could he forget? Had he? Even with the tattoo as a constant reminder, had he really forgotten? Would it always be like this?

Anger, thick and violent and ugly, scorched his veins. It numbed him out till all he saw was red. Red like the day the sun had gone away, leaving a black sky and a silent earth. Nothing but dirt and asphalt and a body buried underneath, beside a broken crown. Eden thought about taking a razor and scraping the tattoo from his chest. He couldn't take the sight of it. But that had been the point, hadn't it?

"Eden."

Eden jolted at the sound of Ryan's voice on the other side of the door. He wasn't sure how long he'd been in there. Maybe a couple of minutes. Maybe a couple of hours.

"Hey. I need a minute," Eden called back.

"You've been in there for three hours."

Cursing, Eden drew in a shaky breath. He needed a cigarette anyway. Might as well face the firing squad. He pushed open the door and flashed Ryan a tight smile. He knew his pupils were blown, but if he—

"What were you doing in there?" Ryan asked, stepping in front of him.

"Thinking." Looking away, Eden fidgeted.

"You're bleeding."

Eden followed Ryan's gaze to the shards of glass that had lodged in his forearm when the window had shattered. "Oh. Have you seen my cigarettes?"

"We should get that taken care of first."

"It's fine," Eden muttered, sidestepping Ryan and heading to his nightstand. He rifled through its contents until he found what he was looking for near the bottom of the drawer. Turning, he almost ran into Ryan, who stood in front of him, blocking his way.

"Sit," Ryan demanded, motioning to the bed. He had some disinfectant and a pair of tweezers in his hand.

"I said I'm fine."

"You say a lot of things that aren't true. Now sit down and let me help."

"I don't need your help. Didn't need it earlier either," Eden growled, lighting his cigarette and looking away.

"Sure as hell looks like you do," Ryan countered, motioning to Eden's arm.

"Oh fuck off already, would you." Pushing past him, Eden walked into the living room. He grabbed a broom from the closet and began sweeping up the shards of glass. He could feel Ryan's eyes burning a hole in the back of his head as he did.

"You're this mad at me for staying?"

"No. I'm mad at you for getting shot. If something bad happened to you, it would be my fault. I already have enough shit on my conscience."

Ryan crossed his arms and leaned against the wall. "It wouldn't have been your fault. It would've been because of a choice I made, Eden."

Eden laughed bitterly, glancing over at Ryan and raising a brow. "Yeah, 'cause you were really left with a lot of decent fucking choices back there, weren't you?"

Pushing himself up off the wall, Ryan stepped forward and took the broom from Eden's hand. "I'm a cop, Eden. It's my job to protect people."

"Yeah, people, Ryan. Not dope dealers."

"Dope dealers are people too. So are addicts. And thieves and everyone else I lock up. My job isn't only to lock people up. It's to help those people too." Ryan's tone was soft.

"So you're just doing your job, then?"

Ryan let out a frustrated breath. "Christ, Eden. Is it that hard for you to let me help you?"

"Yes."

"Why?"

"Because bad things happen to good people. You're a good person, Ryan. You shouldn't be risking your fucking life for someone like me," Eden snapped angrily.

"I happen to think you're a pretty good person too."

"Yeah, well you're an idiot." Eden tried to yank the broom back from Ryan, but he wouldn't let go.

"Eden, listen to me. You make me feel good. Better than I have in... a very long time. Doesn't that count for anything?"

"Not if it fucking kills you." Eden's lips drew into a thin line as he glared at Ryan, willing him to understand.

Ryan tilted his head to the side. "But isn't that the whole point of all this? Finding something that makes you happy?"

"The point...," Eden repeated the words, like they didn't make sense.

"In fact, if you think about it that way, I really did it for myself, not you. So be mad at me if that's what you need right now," Ryan offered. "But stop fucking blaming yourself."

Eden flinched at his words. He was close. Too close. "Never said I blamed myself."

"You did, just not in words," Ryan countered, nodding to the glass in his arm. "Do you believe in forgiveness, Eden?"

"What type of fucking question is that?"

"You forgave me when I pointed a gun at you and made you jump through a four-story window."

"So?"

Ryan stepped toward him, placing a hand on his shoulder. "So why can't you forgive yourself?"

The question hit Eden like a brick wall, and he stepped back. He pushed his next few breaths through gritted teeth, past the tightness in his chest. He would tell Ryan the truth. Some of it anyway. Maybe it would be enough to make him leave. Not that he wanted Ryan to. But it would be better. For Ryan's sake.

"What if... what if I told you I hurt someone I loved. Hurt them bad."

"Then I'd tell you that if they loved you back, I'm sure they'd forgive you. And if they didn't, then they never deserved you in the first place."

Eden shook his head, laughing darkly. It was easy for Ryan to say that, not knowing what he'd done. If he did, his words would undoubtedly be different. "And what if I don't deserve to be forgiven?"

Something flashed in Ryan's eyes, and Eden looked down before he could decipher what exactly it was. Why the hell were they even having this stupid conversation? It wouldn't change anything. Nothing would.

"Eden," Ryan said softly, "everyone deserves forgiveness, even if you don't think so. Life is short. Don't spend it torturing yourself over ghosts of the past, things you can't change. Trust me, I know how it feels. And that's no way to live. What's done is done. I don't know who you were back then or what you did, but I know the person you are now. And he doesn't deserve this."

Reaching into his back pocket, Ryan pulled out his wallet and withdrew a silver chain with a cross. It was simple but elegant, with words engraved into either side.

"Here. I want you to have this."

"What is it?"

"The Serenity Prayer. My mother gave it to me after my brother died. Read it."

Eden held the necklace carefully in his hands, sliding the smooth metal between his fingers as he read the words engraved on its sides.

God

Grant me the serenity to accept the things I cannot change

The courage to change the things I can

And the wisdom to know the difference.

Eden reread the engraving three times before he looked back up. When he did, his eyes were wet and his hands were shaking.

"You know I don't believe in this shit." The words were gruff as he fisted the necklace in his hands.

Ryan placed his hand on top of Eden's, closing his fingers around the necklace. "Humor me. How about this. You hold on to it for me till you don't need it anymore. Then you can give it back."

Eden blinked, his eyes drifting down to the necklace, then back to Ryan. He stood there for a moment, taking in the sights and the sounds. The leaves rustling in the wind outside and glass crunching beneath his feet as he steadied himself. Everything around him was broken, except for Ryan. Ryan, standing in front of him with his gentle smile and kind eyes. For the first time in ten years, Eden felt real.

Real and true and here. Not just some fleeting spark of a shadow waiting to fade away.

Eden leaned forward and wrapped his arms around Ryan awkwardly before pulling back. When he did, Ryan's eyes were wide with surprise.

"Sorry," Eden mumbled, blushing as he looked down at his feet. "I'm not good at the whole... hugging thing. It's just... sometimes I don't always know the right words either."

Before Eden could look back up, a pair of strong arms wrapped around him. He stiffened, tensing at first, before relaxing into the hug.

"No," Ryan whispered into Eden's hair. "I liked it. I didn't expect it, but I liked it a lot. Especially from you."

Eden held his breath, not daring to move an inch. If he did, he was scared the moment would shatter. He wanted to stay like this for as long as he could, soaking up the warmth of Ryan's embrace. Breathing in his scent and feeling the way his chest slowly rose and fell against his own. It was a foreign gesture, and it scared him, but only because he couldn't bear the thought of having to go without it.

Finally Ryan stepped back, smiling sheepishly. His face was slightly flushed, his eyes a vibrant blue. And he looked like a fucking king. "C'mon. Let's go take care of that arm."

Chapter Thirteen:
Cowards Die Many Deaths, the
Valiant Never Taste of Death but Once

Ryan

"HE'S OUT on bail already?" Ryan shook his head, cursing. "How the hell is someone who's in for attempted murder already out? He was there. I saw him do it."

Shawn glanced over at him disinterestedly. "Probably paid off the judge. You know how these guys operate. Dirty money makes the world go round."

Ryan threw Kristoff Vladimir's file onto his desk, raked a hand through his hair, and stared out the precinct window. He wasn't worried for himself. He could handle Vladimir now that he knew what to watch out for. The man was a drunk. And clearly not thorough with his work. Ryan was living proof of it.

But he was out to kill Eden. One botched attempt wouldn't likely be the end of it. And the fact that he was one of Dominick's men meant he would probably just send someone else if Kristoff refused or failed again.

Ryan made his way to McNeil's office, knocking a couple of times before letting himself in.

"What?" McNeil barked unceremoniously, not bothering to look up from the stack of paperwork splayed out on his desk.

"Kristoff Vladimir, the man responsible for the assassination attempt on Eden—I mean Zika. Why the hell is he already out?"

McNeil glanced over his desk at him. "The hell if I know. You know I don't make the rules, Quinn. I just follow them."

"This is bullshit.... He attempted to assassinate someone in front of a cop, and he's already back out walking the streets."

"He'll have his day in court, just like everyone else. Your job isn't to rewrite the law. It's to enforce it."

"I understand that, sir. But—"

"No but's, Quinn. I've got a ton of fucking paperwork to do thanks to your partner's latest stunt. So get the hell out of my office and bitch at him if you insist on throwing a conniption fit."

Ryan let out a frustrated breath. He'd always known the system was broken, but this was insane.

"Fine," Ryan growled, "I'm taking the rest of the day off."

"For what?"

"To make sure Zika doesn't end up on the other end of a bullet again. You and the rest of this precinct are apparently content with sitting here and letting the cards fall where they may. But he's my case. My responsibility. Perp or not, I don't intend on letting him end up in a body bag."

With that, Ryan left. He might not be able to fix the system, but he'd be damned if he allowed something to happen to Eden just because the rest of his unit couldn't be bothered to give a fuck.

Eden

HIS NAME was Kristoff Vladimir. And he was going to die tonight.

As he loaded the bullets into his gun one at a time, Eden stared out the car window, calmed by the resounding click of metal against metal. The sky was an inky, depthless black. A static silence hung heavy in the small car. Even the wind was still and lifeless, as if nature itself was paying tribute to the blood that would soon be spilled. It was always like this on the way there. Eden focused on how the cold, heavy metal felt in his hand, steeling himself against what he knew he had to do.

Most of the time the violence he carried out on Trevor's behalf was simply a matter of business. But tonight was different. This was personal.

Trevor had gotten the name of the man behind the shooting from an inside source. Who exactly, Eden didn't care. He wasn't here to get intel. He was here to get even.

Or execute a threat, rather.

He might have considered roughing up the guy if it had only been him in the apartment. But that son of a bitch had shot Ryan. And it would've been lethal if the bullet hadn't gotten stuck in his badge.

That was unforgivable. And Eden was a firm believer in the eye-for-an-eye philosophy. To those who said that left the whole world blind—the world was an ugly place anyway. Should one be so lucky to be blind to its horrors, that was a blessing. Not a curse.

"Everyone ready?"

Eden turned and made eye contact with Xavier. They nodded silently to each other before Eden looked back at Trevor and nodded.

"Yeah. We're ready."

The three men got out of the car and walked several blocks till they reached their destination. Eden snickered as his eyes roved across the sprawling two-story—white picket fence, cream paneling with wooden shutters on every window, green manicured lawn with a pool around back. Even a fucking Welcome Home mat. The place looked like something right out of Mulberry Lane. Too bad they were about to turn it into *A Nightmare on Elm Street*.

Trevor lifted his hand, sending Eden and Xavier in opposite directions as they jumped the fence and made their way around the perimeter of the house. Locating the power box, Eden retrieved the knife from his pocket and cut the power. Xavier was fifteen feet away, setting up a device their tech guy had designed that temporarily disabled phone service within a half-mile radius.

Vladimir wouldn't be calling the cops. Not with over fifty kilos of coke stashed in various hidey holes around his house. But that didn't mean he wouldn't try and call for backup if he saw them coming.

The three men reconvened near the back door of the house. Trevor inclined his head toward the door, and a moment later Eden was on his knees, picking the lock. It took only a few moments for him to crack the rudimentary device, an imperceptible click the only indication that the door had been breached as Eden pushed his shoulder against it and slid the door open soundlessly.

The interior was just as sickeningly picturesque as the outside had been: granite island counter in the kitchen, imitation van Gogh's on the walls, fireplace in the living room, a coat rack in the foyer. Eden wondered idly how many people he'd sucked off for this shit. Couldn't be from his job—the guy was only half competent as a hit man and clearly an amateur, aiming for the chest instead of the head.

No bodyguards, Eden noted with a smirk. Either all the alcohol Vladimir drank had made the wannabe hit man slack on his security measures, or the drunken idiot was just that confident.

The three men moved with a practiced focus through the house, easily locating Vladimir's bedroom. They knew where it would be from studying the floor layout of similar houses being sold in the area.

Standing over his bedside, Eden paused for a moment to admire the soft smile on Vladimir's face as he slept. It would be the last time he ever smiled. And he would be one of the last people to see it.

Silently, he retrieved the needle from his pack and injected the sleeping Vladimir. The concoction was designed to immobilize him while still allowing him to remain conscious. He would feel everything being done to him, but he wouldn't be able to move a muscle. Eden waited a couple of seconds for the drug to take effect before duct taping Vladimir's mouth and yanking him up roughly.

"Remember me," Eden growled, throwing him into a chair and watching with grim satisfaction as Xavier tied him to the metal frame. Spitting on the man, Eden punched him twice across the face before Trevor raised his hand.

"Me first," Trevor demanded, cracking his knuckles. "Then you can have your fun."

Hesitantly, Eden stepped back. Adrenaline shot up his spine, his skin tingling with a restless itching as he inhaled sharply. The only thing that kept him from jumping on the man and beating him to within an inch of his life was the knowledge that he'd have the opportunity to do just that once Trevor was finished with him.

"Find the coke. Take any other valuables he has," Trevor said, turning to Xavier. Nodding, Xavier left the room, leaving just the three of them.

It had taken Vladimir a couple seconds to gain his bearings, but now that he was fully awake, his eyes darted frantically between the two men. They flashed with a raw, wild terror as he tried to move his body, to no avail.

"We gave you a little something to make sure we wouldn't have any problems," Trevor explained, nodding to the needle prick in Vladimir's wrist. "Now that we have your attention, let's get this shit started." Trevor reached forward, grabbed Vladimir by the hair, and slammed his head down against the table in front of him. "You wanna fuck with my money? You clearly don't know who I am. But you're about to."

Retrieving a pair of shears from his pack, Trevor grinned at the horror in Vladimir's eyes. All he could do was moan as Trevor lifted his right hand. "You shot at my man. One of my best, actually. Makes me a lot of money. Would've been a fucking shame to lose such a valuable asset…. Do you know the origin of the word decimate, Kristoff? It comes from an antiquated Roman military strategy. Whenever the Roman army lost a battle, the generals would have their surviving soldiers draw from a bag filled with stones, one black for every nine white. And do you know what would happen to the men that drew the black stones? They would be beaten to death by their own comrades. A form of discipline to discourage the surviving soldiers from losing again." Trevor leaned forward so that he and Vladimir were nose-to-nose. "Unfortunately for you, I'm not as merciful as they were."

Trevor's words were cold and calculated as he regarded Vladimir with the same expression a hunter might have for a wounded animal caught in a trap. "You have ten fingers. The Romans would only take a decimal. One. But me? I pride myself on being a bit more thorough than those half-assed fuckers."

Lifting the shears, Trevor began the bloody work of removing the fingers on Vladimir's right hand one by one while Eden watched silently beside him. For a moment, Eden wondered if he might be dreaming. Caught in some gruesome nightmare of his own making.

Swallowing back a wave of nausea, Eden ignored the slight tremor in his legs as the stinging, pungent, slightly bitter scent engulfed the room. For once, he was grateful for Trevor's penchant for cruelty. Eden had never had it in him to stomach all the blood and gore. To blunt his horror at what a man like Vladimir, a cold-blooded killer, probably deserved. But Trevor? He had it in him, all right. And he had it in spades. As much as a part of Eden wanted to be anywhere but here—in this room, watching Trevor work—Eden had to see this through. For Ryan. And for himself.

Vladimir sweated profusely, and his eyes began to flutter after the first couple fingers. Trevor didn't stop, though. He kept cutting till Vladimir's right hand was nothing more than a bloody stub.

Finally, once Trevor had finished, Eden stepped forward, cocking his gun. Trevor reached his hand out and pushed Eden's Glock to the side.

"No." Trevor's words were sharp as he pegged Eden with a hard glare. "We're here to send a message to Dominick, not get the feds back on our asses."

Eden squared his jaw, his shoulders stiffening. He understood what Trevor was getting at, but Vladimir had earned this. He deserved to die after almost killing Ryan. Swallowing hard, Eden paused, something shiny catching his eyes in the nearby mirror. Looking down, he cursed, slowly running his fingers along the serenity prayer necklace Ryan had given him.

This wasn't what Ryan would want. That fucking bleeding heart. He wouldn't want Eden to kill Vladimir, even after almost being killed by the bastard himself. Cursing, Eden shoved his gun back into his pants.

"Fine," he growled, turning away. "Give me a sec alone with him. I won't shoot him."

Trevor raised a brow but said nothing. Eden was counting on Trevor's conviction that Eden never went back on his word. To his relief, Trevor nodded once and left the bedroom.

Eden made his way into Vladimir's bathroom, retrieved an ice-cold glass of water, and threw it in Vladimir's face to rouse the now half-conscious man. Vladimir jolted, his eyes flickering open. They were glazed over, unfocused, but it was enough.

Placing his hand on Vladimir's chest, Eden pushed down hard, his gloved finger digging into the half-healed bullet wound he'd given him. Vladimir howled, whimpering as Eden curled his finger and twisted.

"Not my best handiwork," Eden observed flatly. "But I was a little off that day. For obvious reasons."

Bending down, Eden dropped his voice to nothing more than a whisper and spoke into Vladimir's ear.

"I came here today with five bullets in my pocket. You wanna know why? Sure you do, 'cause all you've got right now is fucking time. Not much, though, based on those bleeders hanging off your hand. I want you to listen, and listen closely, because I'm only going to say this once.

"If you so much as look at him the wrong way again, when I find out, this first bullet, that'll be for your mother. The second one will be for your pops, the third for your pretty little wife, and the last two for your little girls. And unlike your little fuckup back at my place, I won't leave the job unfinished. I aim for the head.

"You're lucky, Vladimir. Lucky the guy you shot is a good man. But see, the thing is, I'm not. So understand this. For me, it's not about the money or the power or the motherfucking coke. Growing up, I never had nice things. Had to fight for what little I did have. But every dog has its day. And mine finally came. After a lifetime of shit, I finally got mine. Found something nice. And I'll burn this entire world to the ground before I let you take it from me."

Cutting the ropes around Vladimir's body, Eden watched as the disfigured man slumped to the ground, crumbling into a bloodied heap. He walked out without another word.

"We ready?" Eden asked, finding both Xavier and Trevor waiting by the back door. The two men nodded, and they left the same way they'd come in. In silence.

No one spoke till they made it back to their car three blocks down.

Eden could feel Xavier's eyes on him as he removed his gloves and rubbed at his eyes.

"What's that?"

Eden turned toward him, raising a brow. "This?" he asked, pointing to his neck. "What the fuck does it look like? It's a necklace."

"No shit." Xavier's lips stretched into a thin line. "But you never wear shit like that."

Eden sighed heavily. They'd have to have the conversation at some point, seeing as he had no plans of removing it anytime soon. Might as well get it out of the way. Lowering his voice, Eden glanced over at Trevor in the back seat. He was occupied, rifling through the duffel bag filled with their take from Vladimir's.

"It was a gift," Eden muttered, his words barely above a whisper.

"From him?"

"Stop asking questions you already know the answers to."

Xavier cursed under his breath.

"For fuck's sake, Eden—"

"Don't," Eden growled, turning away from him and redirecting his gaze out the window. They'd had this conversation multiple times. He already knew how Xavier felt about his relationship with Ryan, and to be honest, he didn't give a fuck.

Xavier was quiet beside him, white-knuckling the steering wheel as he looked straight ahead. "You're getting too close to him."

"Not in front of Trev."

They made the rest of the car ride back to Trevor's in silence. Eden hated how strained things had gotten between him and Xavier lately. They were best friends, and if there was anyone Eden trusted to watch his back, it was him. But Xavier didn't have the right to interfere in every aspect of his life. Especially this one.

They were friends and occasional fuck buddies, but they'd never made any commitments to each other. Nor did he plan to. He loved Xavier. But only as a friend. Maybe it was because they'd known each other since they were kids, but he'd always been like more of a brother to him.

Eden cleared his throat as they pulled up in front of Trevor's apartment, waiting for Trevor to get out of the car before turning to Xavier.

"Listen, X, I appreciate you having my back. Really. But this is one of those things I need you to trust me on. Okay?"

Xavier was quiet for a moment, not moving a muscle. The tension in the small space was almost tangible, Xavier's jaw set in a straight line as he hissed through his teeth, "I heard what you said back there. At Vlad's. You wanted to kill him."

Eden swallowed hard, nodding silently.

"Was it for him?"

"No," Eden answered easily. Because it wasn't. It was for himself. Because he wanted to keep Ryan safe, wanted the reassurance of knowing Vladimir wouldn't be able to come back and finish what he'd started. Not killing him, that had been for Ryan. Not the other way around.

Slowly, Xavier nodded his head, the tension easing from his frame. "All right. That's all I needed to know."

Eden

TILTING HIS head back and closing his eyes, Eden turned the heat up to high with the shower handle. It burned, would scorch his skin an angry red, but that was how he liked it on nights like tonight. It reminded him that he was still real, even if he didn't feel it.

Steam filled the small public shower area as he scrubbed his skin with bar soap. He'd stopped by a small community pool and slipped into the shower area to clean up. He couldn't go home to Ryan yet. Not like this, covered in blood.

Shaking himself, Eden drew in a deep breath and scrubbed at the skin on his hands till it was red and raw. He knew it was pointless, but he couldn't help it. His skin always crawled after shit like this. He'd never truly be able to get clean. But that didn't quell the wanting. The need to try. After the shooting, Trevor had officially declared a turf war. Which meant nights like tonight would be one of many to come.

He felt disgusted. Repulsed. And yet if he'd been given the same choices, he knew he wouldn't do anything differently.

He wanted to be someone Ryan deserved. Someone he could stand next to in public without feeling shame or embarrassment. Even if they never became anything official. He wanted to be that for him because Ryan deserved it. Ryan deserved everything.

Yet all he had to offer were a couple of sick jokes and the occasional good time. Leaning his head against the tile wall in front of him, Eden cursed. He was so completely and utterly screwed. And in more ways than one.

Maintaining his habit was getting harder and harder with all the time he'd been spending with Ryan. He'd cut back substantially, but he hadn't been able to quit completely.

Eden had never been a coward. Had always faced every challenge life had presented him head-on. But he wanted to run from this. From the look in Ryan's eyes. And the fact that no matter how hard he tried to mask it, Ryan could tell whenever he was high. The shame was eating him alive, corroding his insides and hollowing out the hole in his chest.

But fuck, he wanted to use so bad right now. From the prickling, incessant itch eating away at his skin to the throbbing, searing ache in his bones. He longed for it. Yearned to return to that nothingness. To the only true home he'd ever had. The cravings kept him up at night. And when they didn't, the dreams were so much worse. So fucking vivid he preferred the lack of sleep.

But it was one of the only things of any real value he had to offer. His sobriety. Or at least his futile attempts at it.

Cutting back on his habit wouldn't wash away his sins. Wouldn't change what he was or everything he'd done. But after much prodding, he'd accepted Ryan's offer to stay at his place while the repairs were being made to his apartment. And he couldn't be excusing himself every hour to get high in Ryan's bathroom.

At least not if he didn't want Ryan looking at him like he was just some strung-out crackhead. Even if he was.

He didn't believe in God. Probably never would. But he believed in Ryan. His opinion mattered. And in a world where nothing had any meaning, the fact that it did was nothing short of a miracle.

Chapter Fourteen:
Conscience Doth Make
Cowards of Us All

Eden

"EDEN, WHAT the hell did you do to my bathroom?"

The ceiling bent, shadows dancing across the cream-pebbled surface. Eden's shirt clung to his chest, his body drenched in sweat. Blinking, he held on to Ryan's voice. The deep, rich baritone kept him grounded as his mind splintered.

He hadn't slept in three days. Couldn't. Not without blow. His bones ached from exhaustion, and nausea rolled through his gut on each inhale. But every time he closed his eyes, the anxiety of what might happen if he fell asleep kept him awake. Ate away at him till he'd finally given up on any semblance of rest.

It was always like this when he tried to quit. Sleepless nights. Nausea. Cold sweats. Usually he could just curl up in a ball in the comfort of his own bed and wait for it to pass. Not that the guest bed wasn't comfortable. But if he spent the entire day lying in bed, Ryan would know something was going on.

Eden propped himself up as Ryan yelled to him from the other room, sounding nearly distraught as he repeated his previous question. They'd only been living with each other for a couple of days while he waited for the repairs to be made to his apartment. Eden had anticipated the lack of entertainment, living with a cop who was about as straight-laced as a choirboy. Surprisingly, he was finding quite a few ways to keep himself entertained.

Unfortunately for his new roommate.

"Why is my toilet shooting water up my ass?" Ryan demanded, storming into the living room with a bereft expression.

"Because I wired it to," Eden answered simply, forcing his expression to remain neutral as he stretched out on the couch.

"You broke it."

"I upgraded it. It's called a bidet. They're the future. You should really get with the times."

Ryan's face flushed as he raked a hand through his hair. "Change it back," he demanded.

"Can't do that." Eden shook his head, a tight smirk pulling at his lips. "You don't want me catching pinkeye, do you?"

"What the hell does this have to do with you catching pinkeye?"

"Everything. I'm a purist. Don't like croutons with my salad."

"What?"

Eden bit back a grin. Ryan was so fucking easy it was almost criminal. "When I rim you out, I wanna make sure I'm tasting you. Not yesterday's beef and broccoli."

Ryan's cheeks turned bright red. "You're a fucking deviant. You know that?"

"Only around you." Progress. At least now Ryan wasn't insistent on denying the inevitable. "Besides, that's what bidets were designed for. Keeping your ass clean. Don't you want to have a clean ass, Ryan?"

"Stop."

"I'm serious. Most people would be thanking me right now. How many other people do you know who are this concerned with making sure your hole stays primed?" Otherwise known as fuckable. But if he used the f-word, Ryan might resort to removing the bidet with his bare hands. Eden had already hidden the tools.

"Oh for fuck's sake," Ryan groaned, the flush on his cheeks spreading to his neck.

"I always do it for the sake of fucking. Besides, I'm the one with the perpetual hard-on. Just be grateful I have the willpower of a fucking god."

Ryan shook his head, a begrudging smile tugging at his lips as he rolled his eyes and walked back into his bathroom. Eden licked his lips, watching the way Ryan's denim clung to his ass. At least he had some hot fantasies to provide a reprieve from the barrage of bad dreams.

Not that he normally didn't have bad dreams. They usually weren't this vivid, though.

He probably should've abstained from playing handyman, given the fact Ryan could easily kick him out the second he got tired of his shit. But

Ryan's ass was fucking gorgeous. And it deserved to be worshipped. As a self-respecting gay man, Eden had a duty—no, an ethical obligation—to all gay men to do just that. Lord knows Ryan never would.

Glancing around, Eden scratched at his skin, looking for something else to occupy him. The apartment was small, meant to be a bachelor pad, but luckily Ryan had been able to turn the study into a makeshift guest room—albeit not exactly one with five-star decor, though he'd tried his best.

The living room was slightly more presentable. A brick fireplace was built into the right corner, with large open windows framed by tawny curtains bordering either wall. He'd stuck with earthy tones—a tan suede couch, a deep crimson rug, and a circular glass coffee table. A bonsai tree stood at the other end of the room, with a huge flat-screen TV affixed to the wall on the left. The wooden floor was a deep, rich brown, with a couple of framed landscape paintings to occupy the empty spaces in between.

Hell, the place looked like something right out of *Better Homes: Gay Minimalist* edition. A buzzing at his hip jolted Eden from his musings. He stood to more easily retrieve his phone and then raised a brow at the caller ID.

"Hello."

"Hey, what's up?" Amelia's tone was chipper on the other line, a slight lilt to her words.

"Not much. Just chilling."

"Good. Now is the perfect time for me to stop by, then."

"Amelia, I told you there was a little accident at my place, so I'm staying at Ryan's."

"Exactly. I miss him. It would be nice if we could all talk some more." Eden sighed internally at his sister's words. Once Amelia had her mind set on something, deterring her was like finding a virgin in a whorehouse.

"You miss him? You've only talked to him once."

"So? I can still miss him. He's a very likable guy. But I'm sure you already know that."

"You're not coming over."

"Why not? You just told me all you're doing is lying around on your laurels."

"Because I said so."

"That's not a real answer."

"From me it is—"

Eden jolted as his phone disappeared from his hand. Spinning on his heels, he glared at Ryan, a mischievous glint in his blue eyes as he spoke into Eden's phone.

"Hey, Amelia," Ryan responded easily, a self-satisfied smirk on his face as he glanced over at Eden.

"Hey!" Amelia's tone was shrill on the other line. "We were just talking about you. Thank you so much for letting my brother stay at your place. I know he can be a real pain in the butt sometimes."

"Yeah, of course. What else are friends for, right?"

"Right. Hey, listen, I have some free time tonight, and I was hoping I could come over. I haven't seen Eden in so long, and you know how hard it is getting ahold of him sometimes."

"Give it back," Eden mouthed, lunging for his phone. Ryan spun around, keeping it just out of reach.

"Yeah, of course. Stop by whenever. I'll cook up some burgers, and we can make a night of it."

"Okay, sounds great. I'll be on my way soon. You mind if I bring Noah too? He's really been wanting to meet you."

"Yeah, sure. The more the merrier. See you soon."

Ending the call, Ryan raised a brow at Eden. "So you've been talking me up, have you?"

"Don't know what you're talking about," Eden grumbled, grabbing his phone and shoving it back into his pocket. "Why'd you invite them over?"

"Revenge for what you did to my bathroom."

"I did you a service."

"And now I'm doing you one. Family time is very important, you know."

Eden glared mutinously at Ryan. Apparently his new roommate was a quick study. Looks like he'd have to develop some countermeasures to avoid future sabotage.

"Now I'm gonna have to fucking change," he muttered, gesturing to his Orgasm Donor shirt.

"Good. Now you know how it feels." Ryan smiled smugly.

Eden couldn't help but smirk as he raised a brow. Looks like he'd finally met his match.

The breeze through the open window ruffled the fringe on Eden's leather jacket, the cool spring chill prickling goose bumps along his sweat-slicked skin. He smiled as Ryan held his gaze, a triumphant grin on his lips. Gentle sunlight trickled in from the open window, playing across Ryan's skin, illuminating his eyes a glacial blue. Usually the cold got to him, made him yearn for the artificial warmth of a heady buzz.

But Ryan was standing so close to him, Eden could feel his warm breath on his neck.

And Eden felt real.

Lately, he'd been noticing things he hadn't noticed in years. Like the cold, hard wood beneath his feet and the way one spot in the living room creaked slightly every time you walked across it, or the small pebble lodged in his sock. Like the way the food truck that was always parked out in front of Ryan's apartment smelled like grease and sriracha, even from here, or how the A on the Jose's Taco's sign in the van's front window flickered on and off sporadically.

Like the way Ryan draped his arm around him, casual and relaxed, or how he pulled him a little closer as a gust drifted in through the open window, seeking out his warmth. Or the way Ryan's touch lingered as he pulled back, his eyes skirting across Eden's frame for a moment before he turned away.

They were small things. Little things that made him feel so fucking big his lungs felt like they might burst through his rib cage.

Things that made him feel real and alive and truly here. Like maybe the last fourteen years of his life had been a bad dream he was finally waking up from.

Living hurt. Sobriety hurt. Remembering hurt most of all. But if it meant being able to remember this—if he needed to go through the discomfort and pain in order to hold on to these moments—he would.

In a fucking heartbeat.

Ryan

"RYAN! IT'S so nice to see you again!" Amelia pulled Ryan into a hug like they'd known each other forever as he greeted her at the door. A smaller boy, maybe around the age of fourteen, stood behind her, looking almost as disgruntled to be here as Eden. He had wiry, curly black hair and familiar gray eyes.

"You too. How's school?"

"Same as always. I've got finals coming up, so I won't have much free time these next couple weeks. Figured I'd make use of the weekend before I buckle down," she chimed, winking at Eden over his shoulder.

"You're a smart girl. I'm sure you'll do fine," Ryan reassured her. "Is this Noah?"

"It is," she confirmed, stepping to the side and pushing Noah forward. Ryan extended his hand, which was met with a flat stare and a grunt as Noah looked up at him like he'd offered to shank him.

"Be nice." Eden's firm voice startled Ryan as Eden approached from behind, pegging his little brother with a hard stare.

"Fine," Noah muttered, shaking Ryan's hand quickly before stepping back.

"He's just shy," Amelia offered, elbowing him in the ribs. "Has about as much social skill as Eden, minus all the vulgar language."

"No, I get it. My little brother was the same way when he was younger. Why don't you two come in, and I'll show you around."

"Wait!" Amelia exclaimed, reaching into her purse. "I brought you two a housewarming gift."

Ryan flushed, accented by the choked cough from Eden to his right. The words "housewarming gift" implied a lot of things he and Eden hadn't even begun to discuss.

"Oh for Christ sake," Eden grumbled, glaring at the wrapped present Amelia was holding like it might be filled with snakes.

"Thank you. That was very thoughtful of you," Ryan offered, doing his best to hide his surprise as he took the present and unwrapped it. Pulling the top off the box, Ryan froze.

"What the hell are you doing with these?" Eden barked, grabbing the box filled with condoms and lube from Ryan and thrusting them out of sight.

"Calm down, Eden. They're not for me. They're for you two."

Eden turned beet red, matching the blush on Ryan's cheeks and neck as he cleared his throat and glanced between the two.

"Yeah, but how the hell do you even know what they're used for?"

"How do I know?" Amelia echoed incredulously. "Eden, c'mon. You realize I'm not twelve anymore, right?"

Eden cursed under his breath, frantically combing a hand through his hair while Noah snickered in the background.

"Who gave them to you? You didn't tell me you were dating anyone."

"I'm not," Amelia replied calmly, clearly used to her brother's overprotective attitude. "I bought them myself. You know, the appropriate response when someone buys you a housewarming gift is to say thanks. I put a lot of thought and effort into that. The lube's cherry flavored—your favorite. And the condoms are ribbed—"

"Amelia, Ryan and I did not buy a house together," Eden said, speaking slowly as if it would somehow help drive his point across. "This is his apartment. I'm only staying here till the repairs are made to mine. And we're not—we don't need those."

"How many times have I told you it's dangerous to go bareback—"

"You know what," Ryan interjected, laughing nervously. "I think you two need better boundaries. You know, certain topics that are off-limits." As in boundaries at all. About the only one they seemed to have was not discussing Eden's night job.

"It's a little too late for that. Not after he tried castrating my first boyfriend when he found out I'd lost my virginity."

"He was a convict," Eden stated matter-of-factly.

"So are you," Amelia countered.

"Yeah, and I wouldn't want you dating someone like me either."

"Don't be too hard on him. It's an older brother thing," Ryan offered, attempting to play mediator.

"Oh no, not you too," Amelia groaned.

"Sorry, but I probably would've done the same thing. I was bad enough with my little brother, and we were only one year apart. I can't imagine what I would've been like with a younger sister." Motioning everyone inside, Ryan began dishing out the burgers and fries as his guests took a seat at the dinner table. At least they wouldn't be able to argue if their mouths were full.

He noted Eden speaking to Noah in a hushed tone as he finished serving everyone and took a seat beside him.

"You still having trouble sleeping?"

Noah shrugged, glancing over at Eden. "Yeah."

"You remember what I told you?"

Noah nodded. "Yeah, but it's hard to remember it when I'm—"

"I know." Eden reached over and squeezed his brother's shoulder gently. "All you have to do is pinch yourself. If you don't feel pain, it's a dream. Dreams are about fear, not pain."

Noah chewed on the inside of his cheek, scooting a little closer to his brother.

"No need for the condoms, huh?" Amelia called out to her brother from across the table, holding up the instructions for installing the bidet Eden had apparently forgotten to get rid of.

"Mind your business," Eden growled, snatching the papers from her and shoving them under his chair.

"Kinky," Amelia observed, raising a brow.

"N-no," Ryan stuttered, shooting a sideways glare in Eden's direction. "Your brother was just playing a prank."

"I figured. That's just his definition of foreplay. He used to do stuff like that to Xavier all the time back when we were kids."

Ryan's lip twitched as he tensed in his seat. So Amelia knew Turner pretty well. Maybe they'd been more serious than he'd initially thought.

"Oh yeah? Guess I shouldn't take it too personally, then." Laughing stiffly, Ryan shoved a fry into his mouth.

"Don't worry, that's old news. They tried the whole couples thing a while ago, but they really weren't a good match."

"Why's that?" Ryan stole a glance in Eden's direction, wondering if this was another subject that was off-limits. He didn't appear to have noticed, having picked up where he'd left off in his conversation with Noah.

Amelia flashed him a lopsided grin from across the table. "Too similar. That and Xavier's a realist. My brother needs someone a little more idealistic. A dreamer, I guess you could say."

Ryan tilted his head to the side, intrigued by her explanation. "Why do you say that?"

"Because your other half should be, in essence, what you aren't. Of course you two have to have some things in common, but the best pairings typically balance each other out. One's strength is the other's weakness. That sort of thing."

"And I strike you as the idealistic type?"

"Well, you are a cop."

Ryan chuckled, surprised by her bluntness. He was finally beginning to see the family relation.

"I didn't mean that in a rude way," Amelia added hurriedly. "In fact, I think it's great. Like I said, the best pairings are all about balance. Noah wants to be a cop when he graduates."

Ryan raised a brow, glancing over at Noah. Apparently Eden had the "do as I say, not as I do" approach to big brothering these two. "That true? If you want, I could give you a tour of the precinct sometime, let you ride around in my squad car."

Noah's eyes lit up, a small smile playing across his face. "You're a cop? That's awesome. I bet you have some badass stories."

"Language," Eden admonished, looking quite pleased with Noah's change in demeanor despite his chiding.

"'Course I do." Ryan smiled warmly as he began regaling them with some of the more adrenaline-inducing experiences he'd had as a cop, adding a few embellished details to keep Noah interested. He'd never used his status as a cop to impress anyone, let alone a fourteen-year-old boy. But as he glanced over at the beaming smile on Eden's face, he couldn't resist.

Eden's siblings were clearly important to him. And the fact that Noah wanted to become a cop spoke volumes to the type of environment Eden strove to create for them. Being a part of that was a lot more meaningful than his usual day-to-day grind. The handsome dimples peeking out as Eden grinned widely didn't hurt either. In fact, Ryan was almost certain he'd never seen anything more endearing.

After a couple of hours, everyone was full and splayed out in different areas of the living room, laughing as Ryan recounted how Shawn had "nicked" him during their last drug raid. Noah had opened up considerably after a few slightly exaggerated cop stories. He still wasn't exactly talkative, but he'd stopped looking at Ryan like he was the Antichrist.

Eden appeared equally relaxed. His relationship with Noah stood in stark contrast to the way he interacted with his sister. Maybe it was the age difference, but the boy seemed to look at him more as a father figure than a big brother. Which was cute, if not slightly unusual.

"Hey, Ryan. I'll help you with the mess." Inclining her head toward the kitchen, Amelia winked at him conspiratorially.

"Sure." Standing from the couch, Ryan picked up as many plates and glasses as he could carry before following Amelia into the kitchen.

"I'll do the washing if you do the drying," Amelia offered, tossing him a dish towel. Ryan chuckled at how at home Amelia seemed after only being there a couple of hours. Another unexpected similarity between her and her brother.

"Sounds like I'm getting the good end of the deal here," Ryan joked.

"No, I wouldn't say that." Filling the sink with dishwater, Amelia lowered her voice slightly, glancing over at him. "Thank you."

"Grilling is about the only form of cooking I can do. So honestly it wasn't as much work as you'd think."

"No, not that. For him. He looks good. A lot better than he has in a while."

Ryan paused, running his tongue along the inside of his cheek as he contemplated Amelia's words. He'd noticed it too. The healthy color across Eden's cheeks, the way his eyes seemed to shine with a brightness that hadn't been there before. He knew Eden had cut back on the coke. Recognized the symptoms—the excess sweating, the restlessness, the change in his appetite. And he was proud of him for it. More than proud. He was impressed. He knew how hard it was to quit, or even just cut back. Not from direct experience, but he'd seen it firsthand. And the fact that Eden was making an effort at all made his chest swell.

But he wasn't sure if Amelia knew the why's of his subtle change in appearance. And he had no intention of confirming it if she simply had her suspicions.

"Yeah, he does. Doesn't he?" Ryan responded carefully, keeping his eyes on the plate in his hand.

"It's been a while since he's cut back like this. I've asked him to quit plenty of times, but he's only ever managed to stop using a couple days at most."

Swallowing hard, Ryan stole a glance in Amelia's direction. Apparently she wasn't as ignorant to Eden's double life as he'd initially assumed.

"He's smart. And strong. But he's also young. Give him time."

Amelia chuckled. "I don't think time is what he needs. In fact I think he has everything he needs right here."

Ryan flushed, clearing his throat. "Don't know about that. Addiction is complicated. Layered. Just because you meet someone you enjoy being with, it doesn't solve whatever led that person to use in the first place."

Chewing on her cheek, Amelia nodded, something flashing in her eyes. "You're right of course. Maybe it's just wishful thinking. It's just… he's happy. Finally. I haven't seen him happy in so long."

"That isn't necessarily because of me, you know."

"It is. Otherwise he wouldn't be so miserable when you're not around."

Ryan blinked, stilling. He was happy of course. Happy that he could even have that effect on Eden. That he could make him happy at all. But something tugged at his chest as he thought of Eden miserable when they weren't together. Miserable like he'd been the night of the shooting.

"How long has he...?" He couldn't spit out the words. They were on the tip of his tongue. And he wasn't asking to be nosy. He wanted to help Eden. And part of that involved knowing what they were up against. Even so it felt wrong to ask. Like he was prying into a part of Eden's life Eden might not want him in.

"I don't know exactly when it started, to be honest. He started when we were kids. I guess he would've been nine or ten. But it didn't get bad till he was around twelve."

Ryan didn't respond. Didn't say anything at all. Because he couldn't speak past the hot, tight coil that had wrapped its way around his chest. It wasn't until the plate he'd been holding cracked under his grip that he realized he was shaking.

"Ten?" Ryan repeated, his voice thick with anger. "How the hell does a ten-year-old get hooked on coke?"

Amelia placed a hand on his shoulder, clearly trying to console him. The gesture only made him angrier. It took every bit of self-control he had not to shrug her off and slam the plate in his hand against the wall. It wasn't her fault. He knew it wasn't. He knew she would've likely done everything she could to prevent it. Hell, he didn't even know the details of how and why.

But still. She'd been there. And he couldn't help but resent her for not doing more. Taking a deep breath, Ryan set the plate down on the counter and turned to her.

"Where the hell were his—your—parents."

"They were dead."

Ryan cursed under his breath, looking down and raking a hand through his hair. "Shit. I'm sorry. I—"

"Don't be. It means you care," Amelia replied softly.

"How did he... at ten, how the hell did he get his hands on coke?"

Amelia pursed her lips. "That... I think that's a story for another time. You're already upset. Eden would kill me if he knew how much I've told you as it is."

He wanted to push. To demand that she tell him. So that he could make it right. Fix it. Even when he knew it was too late for that. Instead he bit back his protests and nodded. This wasn't her story to tell. It was Eden's. And one day, when he'd proven he was worthy of keeping his secrets, he would ask Eden.

Whether or not he'd be able to handle his answer was a different story entirely.

At ten, Eden hadn't had a chance. Hell, even Ryan's little brother, Luca, had been a teenager before he'd experimented with that shit. Ryan had always believed in the power of choice. That everyone *has* a choice, and therefore is responsible for wherever their life takes them. That people are in control of their own fates. God can help to steer them in the right direction, but the individual has to be the one to make the right decisions.

But at ten? At ten Ryan had been playing baseball and watching cartoons, not snorting coke and doing God knows what else. How the hell was anyone supposed to have a chance when that was their foundation? Their standard for normalcy? For life?

Ryan laughed to himself bitterly, shaking his head.

They didn't of course. They didn't stand a chance.

Eden

EDEN WALKED alongside Ryan through the graveled back alley. The side street was dimly lit, with only the moonlight to distinguish road from rock. But it was a shortcut, and all the drinks he'd downed earlier that night had given him a case of lazy limbs.

He smiled, the alcohol from earlier relaxing his gait as his arm brushed against Ryan's. They'd spent the night at Eden's favorite bar on the south side of town. And by favorite, he meant the only place in the city with cheap food, no drink limit, and a clientele that normally ended the night either passed out on the bar counter or in a stranger's bed. Four beers and two servings of nachos later, they were on their way back to Ryan's apartment, stumbling slightly as they traded jokes.

They could've taken a cab, but Eden liked the idea of a boisterous and slightly inebriated Ryan all alone with him in the dark. The night was still young, and the liquid courage coursing through Ryan's veins might be good news for the partial woody he was sporting.

"Hey, can I ask you something?"

Eden raised a brow, surprised by the unexpectedly serious note in Ryan's voice.

"Yeah, sure. Shoot. I'm all yours."

Ryan flushed, a lopsided grin tugging at his lips. "Have you always liked guys?"

Eden laughed. "You've got me drunk and all to yourself and that's the fucking question you ask?"

"It's important."

"Why?"

"Because. I haven't. I mean, I don't. Other than you…." Ryan cleared his throat, his words trailing off.

Before Eden could respond, he spotted three silhouettes turning into the other end of the alley. Their movements were purposeful, and Eden knew before they'd gotten close enough for him to see the ski masks what they were here for.

The masked figures didn't bother with formalities, simply surrounded them and blocked off both exits. Each had a knife in hand, something easily concealed. Something that wouldn't make a sound if anyone happened to walk by the alley.

Ryan exchanged a knowing look with Eden and reached for the gun at his waist. The man on the right lunged for him, stabbing forward with a sudden flick of the wrist. With a quick glance, Eden saw Ryan pivot to the side, barely avoiding the sharp metal. He brought his arm down and pistol-whipped the man.

By then the two other men were coming at Eden from both sides. He cursed and stumbled back, wishing he hadn't had quite as much to drink. He had just enough time to reach for his own knife before a blade plunged toward his chest. Metal clashed against metal, shattering the silence in the small back alley. Eden blocked the knife with his own and shifted his weight forward. He had the strength to keep the man at bay, but not enough leverage in the close quarters to gain the distance he'd need to reach for his gun. Cursing, Eden tightened his grip on the knife and kicked the man back.

The other masked assailant was on him before he could catch his breath, slashing at his abdomen. Lifting his arm as he pivoted to the left, Eden brought his elbow down, catching the other man's knife-bearing hand between his arm and his rib cage. He delivered a series of uppercuts to the man's face, releasing his arm just far enough to break his wrist when he tried to pull back. The man cried out and dropped to his knees, cradling his broken wrist to his chest.

Eden tried to track Ryan in the corner of his eye as he parried his initial attacker. Ryan only had one man on him, but the other guy moved with skill. Moved with the prowess of a practiced fighter.

Anxiety spiked in Eden's chest. The split-second distraction was all it took for his attacker to land a blow with the knife, slashing his right arm. It was barely a cut, the angry red line dripping blood as Eden forced himself to refocus on the man in front of him. He wouldn't be able to protect Ryan if he let himself get shredded first. Eden stepped forward and plunged his knife into the man's hand. The sharp metal impaled skin and bone like softened butter.

A shrill scream echoed in the alleyway as the man stumbled back, dropped his knife, and gripped his skewered palm.

Eden turned back toward Ryan. The third man had Ryan on the ground, knife pulled back as he prepared to deliver a lethal blow. Eden lunged forward and tackled the man, and the two stumbled to the ground, wrestling for control of the knife.

Ryan pushed himself onto his feet and lurched forward to grab the remaining man from behind. He wrapped his forearm around the man's neck, cutting off his airway while Eden struggled to keep the hand with the knife at bay. It took both of his own hands just to hold him off, his arms straining under the force. Finally, the man's body went limp above him, the knife dropping from his hand as his eyes fluttered shut.

Ryan rolled the man off of Eden and helped him to his feet and gave him a thorough once-over. "Your arm."

"Later." Eden nodded toward the end of the alley. "We need to get out of here before they send reinforcements."

"I can call for backup—"

"No, you can't." Eden shook his head. "It's just going to be the same as last time, Ryan. They'll lock them up for a couple days before they post bail. All it'll do is piss Dominick off. Now come on." Grabbing Ryan's arm, Eden began tugging him toward the exit till he was following.

It was pointless. Because there wasn't really anything the cops could do. Not when Dominick would simply send more of his cronies. More than that, though, it put Ryan in their crosshairs.

And Eden didn't want Ryan any more involved than he already was. If they kept it off the record, Dominick would only come after Eden. Or at least that's what he told himself.

Ryan

YOU OWE us Trevor's errand boy. Hand him over and stay out of our way unless you want another bullet to the chest.

Ryan skimmed over the note he'd found taped to his front door. His hair stood on end as he yanked the paper from the door and surveyed the area. He didn't doubt the authenticity of the threat. Which was why he'd taken to wearing his bulletproof vest, even in his apartment. He'd brought one home from work for Eden as well, though he was quite sure getting him to wear it was going to be a hard sell, if not impossible.

But it was all he could do to keep him safe, aside from sticking a tracker up his ass. There was no way McNeil would assign a patrol to the area. Not when he still looked at Eden as more of a perp than a victim.

Letting himself into his apartment, Ryan made a mental note to take a picture of the paper later. He might need it as evidence if they ever followed through on the threat. But for now he needed to find somewhere to hide it where Eden wouldn't be tempted to look. He didn't want him worrying. Ryan had no desire to see a replay of the other night, when Eden had all but shut down and blocked him out.

No. He would keep this a secret. For the sake of Eden's sanity. And his own.

Chapter Fifteen:
All Things Are Ready,
if Our Minds Be So

Ryan

SOMETIMES EDEN had bad dreams.

Ryan had heard it the first night that Eden had slept in the guest bedroom. Normally it wasn't anything more than a muffled sound. A whimper or a sob as he tossed and turned in the night. It reminded him of his little brother, Luca, the way he would toss and turn, making those same noises as he tried to escape the darkness in his mind.

Sometimes he wondered what Eden dreamed about. Sometimes he even thought to ask him. But he couldn't. Maybe he was a coward for not bringing it up. But the mere thought of what he might say paralyzed him. Seized him with a nameless terror, like necrotic acid through his veins. Even more than the fear and hopelessness he'd felt trying to help Luca through all those sleepless nights. And he wasn't sure why.

Maybe because back then, he'd been able to convince himself that what Luca had been going through would heal eventually. That time would heal his wounds when the counseling and the medication and all the talks they had about life and religion and forgiveness never did.

Now he knew better. Understood that some wounds never heal. People just get used to the pain.

But not Luca. He never had, and it had driven him to such a dark place that no matter what Ryan and the rest of his family did, they weren't able to pull him back.

Eden was strong. Stronger than Luca had been. Ryan felt like a horrible brother for thinking it, but it was true. And it was the only thing that gave him comfort on those nights when Eden would toss and turn and sob in his sleep. Whenever he did, Ryan would go in and sit by his bedside, like he had with Luca. He would touch Eden's arm or his shoulder or his face, just enough to let him know he was there. And he would sit by his bed till the sun came up. Most of the time it helped. But not always.

The next morning they would never talk about it. Because Ryan didn't know the right words. And part of him knew there weren't any. That sometimes life gives you fucked-up situations you're not ready for. Some that you'll never be ready for.

And even if he was ready, he suspected Eden never would be.

"MY BET'S on the big guy with the Hitler 'stache." Eden's tone was emphatic as he nodded toward the man on the right side of the flat-screen TV. "Built like Harambe, has the reach of a goddamn crane. Easy win."

Ryan laughed, his eyes drifting from the boxing match on TV to Eden. His gaze lingered for a moment, tracking the way Eden's muscles strained against the tight-fitting I'm Here for the Gang(bang) tee he was wearing. "Who's Harambe?" he asked, a slight rasp to his words.

"You don't know who Harambe is?" Eden deadpanned.

"Should I?" Amusement flashing in Ryan's eyes as he raised a brow. It was rare he was ever able to truly shock Eden. Even if it was at his own expense, he found himself grinning.

"The huge-ass ape they shot down when that little shit jumped into its cage at the zoo. Looked like King Kong's firstborn—motherfucker was massive. You ask me, they should've let him eat the kid. S'why we have so many fucking idiots running around nowadays. All these human rights activists interfere with natural selection's way of weeding out the morons."

"I take it you're not a kid person." Ryan snickered, his eyes dropping to the perfect curve of Eden's lips. He pondered whether Eden had ever considered a career modeling lip moisturizer. Because his lips were fucking perfect. Shapely, with just the slightest hint of plumpness.

"I am. If it had been a grown man, I would've shot him myself. Someone stupid enough to jump into a gorilla cage shouldn't be allowed to reproduce and spread that shit. Stupidity is the worst STD out there."

"Dunno. AIDS is pretty bad too." So were blue balls. Especially when Eden sat like that, his dick outlined perfectly against the formfitting denim of his blue jeans.

"Yeah, but AIDS only hurts the person who has it. Being stupid is worse. The people who have it walk around thinking they're some gift from God while everyone else feels the pain of their existence."

"Point taken," Ryan acceded. Eden's worldview might be fifty shades of psycho, but apparently Ryan had some sort of latent Sweeney Todd meets Hannibal Lecter fetish. And he did have a point. Shawn was living proof. His best friend never had a care in the world while everyone else suffered the burden of his existence.

"God, I wish you had Dish. Maybe I can reroute your wires so we can piggyback off your neighbor's service."

That had been Eden's chief complaint ever since he'd started staying over at Ryan's place. Of all the things he could've found to bitch about—the kitchen with the old-fashioned coil stove, the sparsely furnished guest room, or the heat that had stopped working months ago—his main gripe had been the lack of satellite TV.

"No." Ryan shot Eden a warning glance. "I'm a cop, remember. No illegal stuff in the apartment."

"Fine. Fine," Eden groaned. Yawning widely, he stretched out on the couch, extending his hands above him. Ryan's eyes drifted to Eden's midsection as his shirt rode up above his belly button.

Eden's main complaint about their new living arrangements might be the lack of Dish TV, but Ryan's was of an entirely different nature. They'd been spending every free moment they had together. And yet Eden still hadn't made a move to fuck him. Or to let Ryan fuck him. At this point, Ryan didn't really care who fucked who. He'd take him any way he could get him.

He just wanted him. And his dick. They could figure out the rest once they were both naked.

Maybe the Dish TV idea wasn't that bad after all. Anything was better than ruminating on the pent-up sexual frustration driving Ryan up the wall. He'd been to the gym almost every day. Jacked off till he'd given his right hand carpal tunnel. Hell, even his dick had a friction burn. The neighbors living below his bedroom probably thought he was secretly harboring some breed of large cat in heat. He couldn't seem to find any relief. Like an itch he couldn't scratch.

Ryan disappeared into his bedroom and came out a moment later with two pairs of swimming trunks. He cleared his throat.

"We're going swimming," he informed Eden, tossing him a pair of trunks.

"Ryan, it's thirty-five degrees out." Eden raised a brow.

"I know. My apartment complex has a hot tub right outside the gym area."

Eden smirked. "All right, I'm game. But if I get frostbite from this shit and end up losing my fingers, I'm giving you jack-off duty."

"Deal," Ryan agreed easily. If Eden only knew how many times he'd fantasized about doing that—and then some—he wouldn't have said that. Made the prospect of getting frostbite a little too appealing.

Eden only took a couple minutes to change into the swim trunks and reemerge from the bathroom. Ryan was already waiting for him at the door. He made a point to walk in front of Eden so he wouldn't be tempted to ogle. God knows he'd already done more than enough of that this past week.

Leading the way, Ryan winced at the cold, the chill of the winter wind biting at his bare skin. The entire complex was blanketed in a thick layer of snow, draping everything in pale crystals of pure white.

By the time they made it down to the hot tub, they were both freezing, complete with chattering teeth and goose bumps.

"Shit, it's cold," Eden hissed, running his hands up and down his arms as Ryan pulled back the cover on the hot tub.

"You'll be a lot warmer in a few," Ryan reassured him, setting the heat to high before they both jumped in. It took a couple of minutes for the water to warm up, during which time Eden filled the silence with a stream of expletives.

Chuckling, Ryan raised a brow. "You don't deal with the cold very well, do you?"

"Nah. Wrong state to live in for this shit, right? When I retire, I'm buying a shack somewhere on a beach in Jamaica. Gonna spend the rest of my days smoking reefer on a hammock under the stars." Even in thirty-degree weather, Eden lit up, having already parked his cigarettes and lighter at the side of the hot tub.

Ryan paused. He studied Eden for a moment and smiled. This was the first time he'd heard Eden talk about the future in a positive light. Or any future at all, really. Ryan's eyes drifted to the silver chain around Eden's neck. A subtle warmth tugged at his chest. He hadn't taken it off since the day Ryan had given it to him. Ryan hoped he never would.

"Well, I'm still cold. So c'mere." Ryan pulled Eden into his lap, his chest pressed to Eden's back.

"Cold, huh?" Eden laughed against him. "About time. Was wondering how long it would take you to make a move."

Ryan chuckled, wrapping his arms tightly around Eden's chest. "You could've made your own move if you were waiting this whole time."

"Nah." Eden shook his head, a lilt in his voice. "It'd be bad manners. I'm a guest here, remember?"

Snorting, Ryan raised a brow. "And since when have you cared about manners?"

Eden shrugged. "Had to be sure last time wasn't a case of liquid courage."

Ryan paused for a moment, surprised. "You have nothing to worry about. Trust me. I've been walking around with perpetual blue balls for the past week. Never had this problem with anyone else. Drunk or sober." Ryan pressed a kiss to the side of Eden's neck, running his tongue along the soft skin. He dragged his teeth along the pebbled flesh, sucking hungrily. Eden shivered, leaning his head to the side to give Ryan better access. Inhaling deeply, Ryan breathed in his scent as he licked at his skin. His other hand slid up Eden's wet chest, gently tweaking his pierced nipples.

"Who gave them to you?" Ryan whispered between kisses.

"What? The piercings?"

"Yeah."

"Some guy at the club."

"Club Zero?"

"No. The other club."

Something tight and suffocating coiled around Ryan's chest as he thought of another man putting his hands on Eden. Especially like that. It took all his willpower to keep his body from going rigid as Eden relaxed against him.

"Do you like that sort of stuff?" It was just a whisper against his skin, but Ryan felt like he was standing at the edge of a cliff. Fear pulsed through him like an electric shock, mingling with his arousal.

"Sure."

Sure. Ryan flinched, his gut twisting. He didn't understand a lot about that world. But he understood enough about it, and about Eden, that his answer made bile rise in the back of his throat. Ryan lowered one hand and palmed Eden's arousal.

Eden tensed against him, his hand reaching out to still Ryan's wrist. "Wait."

"Wait?" Ryan echoed, confusion coloring his words.

"Let me get you off instead." Pushing Ryan's hands away, Eden tried to turn around in his lap. Ryan kept him where he was, though, holding him there by the hips.

"Eden."

"Yeah?"

"Why won't you let me get you off?"

"There's more than one way to get someone off. You've been watching too much of that fucking vanilla porn. That shit's all the same," Eden joked. Despite his blasé comment, his spine was stick straight, and he was shaking slightly. Whether that was from the cold, anticipation, or something else completely, Ryan wasn't sure.

"Well, it's definitely not because you aren't in the mood," Ryan muttered, motioning to the bulge in Eden's swimming trunks. "And I'm not going to just sit here and let you do all the work again. Listen, I know I'm not exactly an expert at this yet, but if you tell me what to do, I can make it at least half decent for you—"

"No… it's not that. Shit." Eden sighed heavily and took a hard drag from his cigarette.

"Is it because of Turner?"

"No. I told you X and I aren't like that." Eden was quiet for a moment. Every muscle in Ryan's body tensed. He felt it. Felt something. Like somehow he was standing on the precipice of a knife's edge. "Just trust me when I tell you that if you knew, you wouldn't want to anymore."

"I already know you sell dope. And that there's probably a lot of other illegal stuff that goes along with it."

"No. Not that. Other things." A frustrated breath left Eden's lips, and for a moment Ryan thought he was going to pull away. He didn't, though. "I can do other shit with you. Whatever you want, I can do it. Just not if it involves that."

Ryan paused, searching for the right words. It would help if he knew what the problem was. But he had a feeling that if he pushed any harder, Eden would tell him to forget it altogether. "What if I told you I don't care. Whatever it is, it wouldn't change what I want. From you. Or for us."

"You can't say that, not without knowing."

"Can't I? Your past is your past. It doesn't define who you are. Everyone has things about themselves they'd rather other people not know. Even I have stuff in my past that would probably make you look at me differently if you knew."

"Like what?" Eden challenged, his voice laced with disbelief. "Did you litter once when you were five?"

The quiet of winter seeped into Ryan's bones, the mechanical hum of the hot tub drifting in and out of focus. He thought back to the conversation he'd had with Amelia the night she and Noah came over. Of how much courage it must've taken Eden to cut back on a habit he'd relied on for over half his life. If he could face that, Ryan could face this.

"My little brother. Before he died, he made some bad decisions. Running around at all hours of the night, drinking, stealing from my parents to fund his bad habits, shit like that. Got to the point where they were threatening to kick him out if he didn't stop. I should've been there for him. Should've tried to be more understanding, but I wasn't. I judged him for it. Told him he needed to clean his act up instead of trying to run from everything. I told him he was a coward. I told him he was sick. That he needed to stop fucking guys. That maybe that was the reason his life was so fucked-up. God punishing him, or some stupid shit like that," Ryan choked out the words.

He'd never told anyone else this. Not a soul. Because he hated himself for it. Hated what he'd said. He'd been desperate, willing to say anything to try and get Luca to change. He'd never had a problem with gays. But both his parents were traditional Catholics, and to them, being gay was a sin. Nothing else had worked. He'd thought that maybe fear would.

Fear of God.

Fuck, he was such an idiot. And an asshole.

He forced the next words out, needing to finish. Needing Eden to know. Even if Eden hated him for it afterward.

"I was stupid. It was stupid. I should've never said that. But I did. And that was the last conversation I had with him. Sometimes I think he'd still be alive if I'd been more understanding. More supportive. I preach all this bullshit about God and forgiveness, about acceptance and understanding, but that night all I did was reflect all the negative things he felt about himself back at him."

Eden was still for a moment before leaning back into him and sliding his hands on top of Ryan's, pulling him closer.

"You were only trying to do what you thought was best. That's all anyone can do. You were scared. And so was he. People don't think when they're scared. They just act. I'm sure a part of your brother understood that."

Ryan nodded. He rested his face against the back of Eden's head and closed his eyes. For a moment, he just held him, his arms wrapped so tightly around Eden that Ryan could barely breathe.

Eden hadn't run. Hadn't told him he was a horrible person or a bigoted hypocrite for wanting what he wanted from him after what he'd said to his brother. It was only then that he realized he'd needed to tell him. Needed Eden to know that part of him. The ugly, angry, unfair part that he'd never been brave enough to show anyone else.

Ryan ran his hands up and down Eden's chest, needing to feel him. Needing him closer. "Trust me. Please, Eden. Not with everything, but with this. Trust me to make you feel good. I won't ask anything more than that. I promise."

Ryan could feel Eden hesitate as he tensed in his arms. Like he wanted to, but a part of him just couldn't.

"What if it hurts. To feel like that."

"Then I'll make it better. What I do won't hurt. And if it does, I'll stop."

There was a long silence that seemed to stretch on forever before Eden finally spoke.

"Ok," Eden said slowly, nodding. His response warmed Ryan to the core, fought back the chill that threatened to engulf him whole.

Taking a deep breath, Ryan reached in front of him and removed the cigarette from Eden's lips, stubbing it out on the side of the hot tub.

"Just close your eyes and relax," Ryan whispered, pressing soothing kisses to the back of Eden's neck.

"Wait. I need to see you. When we…. I need to know it's you."

Ryan nodded and loosened his grip around Eden's chest. His hands shook as he slid Eden's swim trunks off and then removed his own. The frothy water sloshed around them when Eden turned and lowered himself into Ryan's lap, twining his legs around Ryan's. Dipping his hands beneath the water, where Eden couldn't see, Ryan flexed his fingers once, twice, to try and steady the shaking. Had he ever been this excited to touch someone before? This nervous and eager all at once. If Ryan had, he couldn't remember.

But something told him he'd have no trouble remembering this.

Eden lifted his hands to Ryan's neck, nails biting into Ryan's skin as he traced a slick line of goose bumps from his collarbone to his nape. Sighing, Ryan pressed his lips to Eden's. He could taste the nicotine on Eden's lips, eager breaths precipitating to frost on the chilled winter air.

"Better?"

Eden hummed and licked at him hungrily. Urgently. Like he was searching for something to hold on to. Like the death grip he had on Ryan's neck wasn't nearly enough. Ryan dropped his hands to Eden's ass, his fingers melting into the soft, tender flesh. Groaning, Ryan closed the space between them, hoisting Eden farther up his lap. His dick throbbed as he felt Eden's erection rub against his thigh. It was finally happening. So many nights spent fantasizing about what it would be like—how it would feel—and Eden was finally letting Ryan touch him in earnest. The thought of that alone was enough to turn Ryan's desire into desperation.

Ryan took a deep breath to steady himself and slid his hands from Eden's ass to his knees. His fingertips trailed across the pebbled skin till they reached the bends of Eden's knees. Slowly, he brushed his hands along the inside of Eden's thighs. He could feel it when Eden's breath caught in his throat. When his skin puckered under Ryan's touch and his toes curled against the back of Ryan's calves. Pulling back slightly, Eden bowed his head, his swollen lips resting right above Ryan's collarbone.

Eden was still tense. Ryan could feel it in the way he clung to him. In the way Eden's lips moved against his neck, speaking words into his skin that would never reach his ears.

Ryan drew back and nipped at Eden's ear. His tongue drew wet, lazy circles along the slanted lobes. Sliding his hands up and down Eden's thighs, Ryan ignored the painful ache of his own erection. Instead, he continued to caress the inside of Eden's thighs till Eden's frame went slack against his chest, his hot breaths slow against the crook of Ryan's neck.

Drawing in a raspy breath, Ryan placed one hand on Eden's arousal. His chest tightened at the feel of the smooth, rippled skin, hot and heavy in his palm. Eden knotted his hands in Ryan's hair and braced himself. Groaning, Ryan began to stroke Eden's dick, his own arousal throbbing painfully.

He was trying to take it slow. God knew he was. Ryan was using every single ounce of willpower he had to hold himself back and focus on what Eden needed. But the feel of Eden's erection in his hand—physical proof that Eden was aroused and it was because of *him*—was almost too much.

Ryan lifted his other hand to Eden's slick chest, needing to feel more of him. His arms trembled as he held Eden to him, Eden's heartbeat a frantic cadence beneath his palm. Stilling, Ryan tried to memorize the rapid pitter-patter. He wanted to lick and suck and touch him everywhere. Leave red and purple hickeys all over his body for everyone to see. Mark him as his. And only his. But this wasn't about that. Not yet.

"Let me see you." Ryan's words were hoarse as he pulled back and dropped his gaze between them. His eyes fluttered at the way his pale fingers looked sliding over the dark pink of Eden's arousal. His dick ached painfully, and heat surged to his groin.

After a couple of strokes, Eden moaned, and a shudder rolled through his body. His hips flexed back and forth as he began humping Ryan's hand. Spurred on, Ryan tightened his grip around him till he could feel Eden's dick throb under his touch.

"God, you're so fucking hot," Ryan breathed, watching through half-lidded eyes as Eden fucked his hand.

Eden placed his hand on top of Ryan's and tightened his hold. Demanding more. His touch burned, every nerve ending in Ryan's body seeking out the smooth, searing sensation of Eden's skin on his. Ryan's eyes flickered up from the sight of Eden's hand wrapped around his to the expression on Eden's face. His lips were red and swollen, his pupils blown, his cheeks red and flushed. Shivering, Eden dug his fingers into Ryan's thigh and lifted up onto his heels. The sensation of Eden's ass rubbing against his erection while Ryan palmed his dick was almost too much. Groaning, Ryan flexed his hips into the curve of Eden's ass. The wet friction was slick and hot and not nearly enough.

Exhaling a ragged breath, Ryan used his free hand to still Eden's movements. He eased him back till their arousals were side by side. Reaching between them, Ryan pressed his dick against Eden's and thrust both of them roughly into his hand. The velvet heat of Eden's cock against his left Ryan breathless.

Ryan's eyes drifted from the silver chain around Eden's neck to the smoky gray of his glossy gaze. His cheeks were flushed a light pink, his expression relaxed and blissed-out all at once, and for a moment Ryan couldn't breathe. A second later his orgasm hit him hard, his body exploding in a series of tremors. Eden followed him over the edge, his eyes never leaving Ryan's, shuddering fiercely before going slack in Ryan's arms.

Ryan smiled at him, caressing Eden's cheek before pressing a slow kiss to Eden's lips.

"You want to—"

Ryan's question was interrupted by the familiar buzz of Eden's phone.

"Fuck," Eden muttered, glancing over at it mutinously. "I'm sorry."

"No, it's fine." Offering him a reassuring smile, Ryan reluctantly removed his hands. He watched in silence as Eden waded to the other side of the hot tub and grabbed his burner phone.

Ryan was familiar with the drill at this point. He knew from listening in on previous conversations that these calls were usually related to his extracurriculars. Eden had explained at some point that he was obligated to answer, even though most of the time he looked like he'd rather smash the phone into a million little pieces.

If it was his boss or Turner and he ignored it, there would be serious ramifications. That much Ryan had understood without an explanation from Eden. He never asked what they talked about, and usually Eden would go into another room for the majority of the conversation. Just like Ryan never asked when Eden would slip out of the apartment at midnight and return at four in the morning, smelling like soap and cigarettes. It kept things simple for both of them. But the more time he spent around Eden, the more he wanted to ask.

"What?" Eden barked. "No, I'm busy right now … Then ask Bobby. All he does is sit on his ass anyways … It's none of your fucking business what I'm doing, X. Do I ask you what you're doing every time I have to call you about business? … We've had this conversation. Not in the mood to have it again."

Ryan's hands curled into fists at the mention of Turner's name. Of course it would be him, that fucking bastard. Ending the call, Eden turned toward him.

"Sorry."

"You have to leave?"

"Nah. They can figure something else out," Eden growled, his brows creased together in annoyance as he drifted back to Ryan's side.

"Why is he always the one who calls you?"

"Who, X?"

"Yeah."

"'Cause Trev knows I'll just tell everyone else to fuck off." Eden snickered bitterly.

Ryan frowned. He hated Turner. Hated the influence he had on Eden. How every time he called, it was always some bullshit about needing him to do something dangerous. And he knew it was. Otherwise Eden wouldn't always leave the room. "I don't like him. He's a fucking punk. Always sticking his nose in everything you do, like he has a right to every part of your life. Then when you actually need him, he bails like a fucking coward."

Eden raised a brow at him questioningly.

"At the club." Ryan's tone was clipped as he tried to bite back his disgust for Turner. "He shouldn't have left you. Not when you were like that."

Flushing, Eden looked away. "I was... being difficult that night. If he had stayed, he would've been in hot water too. And then I wouldn't have had anyone to cover my ass."

Ryan shook his head, clearly unmoved. "I don't give a fuck. I know he's your friend, but that was wrong. He should've at least made sure you got home safe before running to kiss your boss's ass. Thought drug dealers were supposed to have more balls than that."

Eden snickered. "He's a good friend. I promise. Most guys would've given up on me a long time ago."

"I wouldn't have. And I wouldn't have left you there either."

Eden smiled softly, brushing his shoulders against Ryan's. "I know. But you're not like most people."

Ryan grinned, slipping his arm around Eden's shoulder. He could take better care of Eden than Turner ever could. And he would. He couldn't explain why, but he wanted Eden to know that. And he wanted Turner to know that.

Eden didn't belong to Turner. Even if neither of them knew it yet. They would soon enough.

Thirteen Years Ago

HE TOLD *me I couldn't see the Prince anymore.*

And I hated HIM for it. Hated it more than his big hands and his angry voice and his hard eyes. I hated it so much I couldn't stop shaking. I didn't know how to tell the Prince.

So I didn't. Not at first.

The Prince was hurt. His sapphire eyes were dark and stormy when he pulled me into the alleyway.

He asked me why I was avoiding him. I told him I couldn't see him anymore, that HE had told me not to. The Prince told me it didn't matter what HE said. That I didn't have to listen to HIM. That he would protect me. Protect us.

I shook my head. Because I knew that he couldn't. Nowhere was safe from HIM.

The Prince grabbed me and shook me. Like he was trying to make me understand. The sky was black and the earth was silent. There was only dirt and asphalt.

He said, "Don't you see? He's just trying to keep us apart. He's jealous of us. Of what we have. I won't let him take you from me."

He said, "That fucking bastard. I'll kill him. I will. I'll kill him, and then you'll never have to be afraid again."

He said, "Please, don't do this. I need you. I can't exist without you. You chase away my darkness. You're the only thing that does. Don't leave me alone in the dark."

My chest hurt. I wanted to say I was sorry. But I knew it wouldn't matter, knew it wasn't what he wanted to hear.

I was hurting him. And I didn't know how to stop. So I told him maybe he was wrong. Maybe I was bad for him. Maybe we were bad for each other.

And he shook. And he screamed. And he cried and said, "Don't you fucking say that. Don't you dare fucking say that. This isn't you. This is him. I know you would never say that. Because you love me. And I love you. Never forget that. Never."

Chapter Sixteen:
There Is Nothing Either Good or
Bad, but Thinking Makes It So

Eden

EDEN HATED cop bars. And not just because they were filled with fucking cops. The bartender was typically some stick in the mud that bitched the second any of the patrons started getting loud. Or drunk. Who the hell bitches over a free show? Watching the drunks dance on top of the bars—and hopefully fall off—was half the fun of going out. And if he just so happened to be one of them, that was a marked sign of a good night.

Or if you happened to be in a cop bar, drunk and disorderly conduct.

But alas, life is all about compromise. Or some shit like that, Eden thought dully, glancing around the dimly lit dive bar. The décor wasn't all that bad at least. The place had a '90s feel to it, with high-tops and Martens lining the ledge behind the bar. Nirvana and Pearl Jam posters covered the majority of the walls, interspersed with the occasional Nintendo 64 ad. Warm yellow lights were strung along the ceiling beside a couple of flat-screen TVs angled toward the center of the room.

Shifting anxiously in his seat, Eden glanced around, his eyes scanning the room for the umpteenth time that night. He didn't have any active warrants, at least none that he was aware of. But he'd pissed off more than his fair share of men in blue. So his diligence was more than warranted.

"You okay?"

Jolting slightly in his chair, Eden's eyes snapped back to Ryan. He flashed him a reassuring smile from across the table. "Yeah, sorry, just… taking in the scenery."

Ryan chuckled. "Sorry, I figured this place would be right up your alley, what with the whole '90s grunge vibe."

"No, it's cool. Really. Just an adjustment." Only half a lie at least.

"My little brother used to love it here. He was obsessed with the '90s, loved almost every song by Kurt Cobain."

"Oh yeah? He dream of being a rock star too?"

"Nah, they just had the same fatalistic view of the world. I think he felt understood when he listened to Cobain's music. Less lonely, I guess."

Eden paused for a moment. His eyes flickered over Ryan pensively. "Did your brother do drugs?"

Ryan's eyebrows lifted in surprise. "Why?"

"Have you met Cobain's fan club? The only people who *really* like Kurt Cobain like that are angsty teenagers and druggies. As a member of the latter group, I suppose you could call it intuition."

Ryan was silent for a moment. He nodded slowly. "You know, it's too bad I didn't know you back then."

"Back when?"

"Back when he was alive. You guys probably would've gotten along pretty well. If he'd had someone like you, maybe he wouldn't have felt so alone."

Eden shook his head, his expression softening. "Nah. People don't feel alone because of others. People feel alone because of themselves. Because of things inside of them that they feel are broken or missing. That's why lonely people do drugs instead of prostitutes."

"And what about people who do both?"

"Your brother frequented the red-light district?" he asked.

"I don't know for sure. But if I had to guess, I'd say yeah. He probably did."

Eden was quiet for a moment, chewing on his cheek as he mulled over Ryan's words. Normally he'd brush questions like this off with a crude joke or a simple change of subject. But he couldn't, not when Ryan looked at him like he was searching for the world.

"People like that... they're looking for everything. And nothing at all."

"What do you mean?"

"I mean they're lost. Some of them might not even know what they're looking for, just something to fill the hollowness. Others might know what they're looking for, but for whatever reason believe they'll never truly find it for themselves.

"Take my father, for example. He was the former. Always had this hole in his heart he was looking to fill with anything and everything. Don't know what it was from. But it was there. Funny thing is he never did quite find anything that ever made him feel whole. I think that's why he decided to drive his car off that bridge. Not because that fucker felt bad about what he'd done to my mom, but because he finally realized that, for him, this was all there was.

"Knowing why won't make it any easier, Ryan. I get why you want to understand your brother and why he made the decisions that he did. But any answers you find will only bring you more pain."

"How can you be so sure? Without knowing him—"

"Because. That's what it's about for everyone. Finding a way to ease the pain. Some people choose drugs, others choose pussy or religion. And some people choose a career in law enforcement." Eden stared at Ryan, flashing him a soft smile. "What's important, more than anything else, is that your brother would want you to be happy."

He leaned forward and patted Ryan on the shoulder, his touch lingering for a moment. He wished he could hug him again, but a bar full of likely homophobes with guns and batons wasn't the place for that.

Ryan nodded, swallowing hard. "Do you ever miss him?"

"Who?"

"Your father."

Eden shifted in his seat and took a long drink of his scotch before he responded. "Yeah. Yeah, sometimes. People are funny like that. Someone can make decisions you hate, throw their life away like it's not shit. Like it doesn't matter how much you love them. They can hurt you so bad you swear to yourself you'll never forgive them. But then they're gone, and you do. And you miss them and all the fucked-up bullshit they put you through. Because even if you hated it, it was a part of them...."

He never talked about his father because he didn't see the point. What was done was done. Same with his mother. But maybe in a weird way, it might help Ryan—being able to share that sense of loss with someone. "My father, he used to teach me how to work on cars. Would call me over to sit with him and explain what each tool was used for. Sometimes he'd even let me do the work myself. I miss that. I miss him, even after what he did to her. Even when I shouldn't."

Eden focused on his drink, absorbed in the sight of the ice twirling around, the cubes clinking against the cold glass, as he stirred. Ryan reached forward and placed a hand on Eden's. The gesture startled him, his eyes snapping up to Ryan's as his movements stilled.

"You were a good son, to miss him after everything he did. Better than that asshole deserved. And you were a good son to your mother too. If she was a Catholic, like you said, she wouldn't want you to hold on to the anger. The hate. She would want you to forgive."

"Thanks." A smile played across Eden's lips, the warmth of Ryan's touch calming him.

"Your father, was he a mechanic?"

"Nah. He was a truck driver. Working on cars was about the only hobby that stupid fucker had. Besides drinking of course."

"And your mom?"

The smile on Eden's face widened. Not because of the change of topic, but due to the question itself. Ryan was actually curious about him. It was cute in a way that made Eden's heart beat a little faster. Made him smile stupidly, like some love-struck teenager, even though it was totally inappropriate given the grim nature of their conversation. God, he had it bad.

"Mom worked in the red-light district. She was a crackhead before anything else, had her own demons to deal with. And she was here illegally, so she didn't have a whole lot of job prospects. Guess you could say I take after her." Eden snickered darkly. "Better her than my father, in any case. The two were a fucking match made in hell."

Ryan's eyes softened. He still hadn't let go of Eden's hand. "I'm sorry. That must've been really difficult growing up."

Eden shrugged, flushing at the prolonged contact. "Made me an advocate for sterilization. Learned a lot about life. And people. After they died, Trev really stepped up. Was more of a father to me and my brother and sister than my own pops had ever been. So it wasn't all bad."

Ryan blinked at him, his brows creasing. "Trev as in your boss, Trevor?"

"Yeah—"

"Well, ain't this some shit." Ryan visibly flinched as a man with short brown hair and mirthful hazel eyes approached their table. "Don't you two look fucking cozy. Ryan, you didn't tell me you had a hot date. I'm hurt. Friends don't keep secrets from friends."

Ryan sighed heavily, a worry wrinkle forming between his brows. "Not now, Shawn."

Eden ran his tongue along the inside of his cheek, glancing over at the man. So this was Ryan's best friend. Made sense, judging by the man's *Miami Vice* getup and the ridiculous grin plastered across his face. He reeked of hard liquor and hot sauce, apparently not quite as dedicated to his Catholic religion as his hot blond counterpart.

"What's wrong?" Shawn snickered, his eyes drifting between the two. "Trouble in paradise? Or did I interrupt a little game of footsie…." His words drifted off, his eyes narrowing as they locked on to the necklace around Eden's neck. Something in his expression shifted and his hands balled into fists at his sides. When he spoke again, his tone was sharp, almost accusatory. "Why the fuck is he wearing that?" he demanded, turning to Ryan.

Ryan stood slowly, holding out his hands like he was trying to placate him. "Shawn, just listen to me, all right—"

"You dirty fucking Mex!" Shawn growled, lunging at Eden. Ryan barely caught him in time, holding Shawn back as his face turned a curious shade of red.

Well, this was interesting.

Eden didn't bother to stand as he observed the scene unfolding before him. There was no point. Now that he'd seen Shawn, he was more than confident in his ability to put him down if need be. He was clearly someone important to Ryan, so Eden had no intention of making mincemeat of him. But even a bull mastiff bites back if a Chihuahua nips at its heels for long enough. And he had a feeling this man's capacity for bitching was otherworldly.

"Stop. Fucking stop," Ryan growled, his words labored as he held Shawn back.

"Why does he have that on? That fucking dirty greaser!"

"I gave it to him," Ryan barked, giving Shawn a hard shove back. "So just stop. It was mine to give."

Shawn froze, his eyes narrowing as his gaze shifted from Eden to Ryan. "No. No way. No motherfucking way." His words were laced with a mixture of disbelief and denial as he shook his head.

"You heard me, Shawn."

Shawn laughed, the sound half-crazed as other people in the pub began to look over at the spectacle. "No. This isn't you. I know you. This is Zika. He's gotten to you. Crawled inside your mind somehow and fucked with your head—"

Eden cleared his throat. They were attracting too much attention. If Shawn intended to continue his bitch fit, they needed to wrap this up outside. "Ryan—"

"Shut the fuck up, you cocksucking piece of shit! You're trash, you hear me, faggot? What the hell did you do to my friend?"

Eden breathed in slowly, flexing his fingers as he forced himself to remain calm. Attacking a mentally handicapped man in front of a room full of cops was not a good look.

"Shut your fucking mouth, Shawn. We'll talk about this later." Ryan pushed Shawn again, clearly trying to reel his friend in.

"No. No! We're talking about this now!" Shawn yelled, his eyes flashing.

"Listen for one fucking second, all right. I understand why you're upset, I do. But you need to calm down."

"Me?" Shawn bit back incredulously. "I need to calm down? Are you fucking kidding me? If it weren't for scum like him, your brother would still be alive! He's a fucking waste of space, and that crackhead's wearing Luca's necklace!"

Eden's breath caught in his throat. He gripped the table, his fingernails digging into the glazed wood. He wanted to stand up and put himself between them. Drag Ryan away. He didn't want him hearing this.

But how could he when nothing Shawn had said had technically been a lie. He was a crackhead. And a fag. And a waste of fucking space. What he did for a living hurt people, whether he wanted it to or not. People like Ryan's brother who were just lost and looking for a safe place to hide.

Standing, Eden turned and headed for the door. This wasn't a fight he could win. Not in the way that really mattered.

"Eden, wait," Ryan said.

"Nah, it's good. I should give you two some time. Not like he said anything that wasn't true." Eden turned and left, the bitterness in his words leaving a bad taste in his mouth. He hadn't meant to say that.

But it was only a matter of time.

Eventually Shawn's words were going to get through to Ryan. Not because Ryan lacked conviction. But because it was the truth. And because Ryan loved his brother. And when they did, he didn't want to be there for the moment Ryan looked at him with the same hate and disgust everyone else did.

He'd run like a fucking coward. But the alternative had been putting Shawn's head through a wall to shut him up. Which would've been just as bad when it came down to it. Running from the truth of who he was, what he was, pacing around the alley out back, Eden paused and punched the wall a couple of times before reaching for his phone. "Hey, I need a ride."

Ryan

"WHAT THE fuck is wrong with you?" Ryan was shaking, almost as livid as Shawn as he pushed his friend back into the wall. "You have a problem, you take it up with me, not him."

"My problem isn't with you, it's with Zika." The anger in Shawn's voice had ebbed slightly, but his face was still red.

"No it's not, Shawn. I gave Eden the necklace. And I asked him to come here. Where the hell do you get off talking to him like that? Did you forget how Luca was near the end, huh? He did dope. And probably a lot of other bad shit. But that doesn't change the fact that he was still a good kid." Ryan stared Shawn down, daring him to say otherwise.

"This is different, and you fucking know it. Do you even hear yourself?" Shawn's words were tinted with disbelief as he stared back at Ryan. "How the hell can you even compare Luca to that lowlife street scum?"

"He's not street scum," Ryan snarled, taking a step forward so he and Shawn were nose-to-nose. "He's a good guy. You wanna talk like you're defending Luca's honor, but in case you forgot, my brother was gay too. He'd be rolling in his grave if he heard the shit you just said."

"Oh my fucking God. Don't pull the gay card with me when you're the one that's totally lost it. Zika is not Luca, all right? And if Luca wouldn't have had access to the dope—because of people like fucking Zika—he would've lived long enough to turn his life around."

Ryan shook his head, his lips curling in disgust. "And if he hadn't, then what? Are you saying his life would've been worthless then? That it would've been okay to just lock him up and throw away the key like what you want to do with Eden?"

"Why the fuck do you keep calling him Eden?"

"Because that's his fucking name, Shawn. I like him, all right. I like Eden. There's a lot more to him than you think. And I swear to God, if you ever talk about him like that again, I will lay you out. Do you understand me?"

Shawn swallowed hard, taking a step back and running his hands through his hair. His face was no longer red, now a clammy pale hue. "Christ, Ryan… this is so fucked-up. I think I'm gonna be sick."

"Fine. You do what you need to do, and then when you're calm enough to act like a half-decent excuse for a human being, we can talk. Till then, I've got shit to do." Ryan turned and stormed out. Headed straight to his car, then hit the highway going ninety and made it to his destination halfway across town in ten minutes.

Chapter Seventeen:
Let Me Be That I Am
and Seek Not to Alter Me

Ryan

HE NEVER thought he'd be back here again. Or at least not so soon.

Taking a deep breath, Ryan got out of his car and approached the large black building he'd parked in front of. It was the only one on the block with no sign out front and no windows. He was stopped at the door by a gargantuan man with a bald head and a nasty scar across his brow.

"Hey, we've got a dress code here." Mr. Clean's voice was sharp and clipped as he held out his hand, blocking Ryan from entering.

"Yeah, well, so do I," Ryan bit back, moving his jacket to the side and flashing his badge. "Unless you want me and my guys to come back later for a shakedown—which I can't imagine would do much for business, considering how private most of your clientele is—I suggest you get the fuck out of my way." He was in no mood to be diplomatic. If Mr. Clean kept giving him issues, he'd throw handcuffs on him and charge him with obstructing the police. He didn't have time for this shit.

Narrowing his eyes, Mr. Clean nodded once and stepped back. Pushing past him, Ryan entered the foyer. Whips and chains greeted him, its occupants in various shades of undress as they surveyed him with curious stares. Metal music blared overheard, smoke and strobe lights distorting his gaze as he tried to remember which way he'd taken last time. Hopefully they'd be in the same room as before. It took him a couple wrong turns before he found it. Stepping inside, he froze, red-hot anger rooting him in place.

Eden was handcuffed to the wall, hands spread up and apart on either side with a blindfold around his eyes. Turner was standing in front of him. His expression was one of annoyance as he turned and met Ryan's gaze. Before he could speak, Ryan had him up against the wall, his hands around his collar as he slammed him against the black brick.

"You piece of shit," he growled through gritted teeth. Ryan kept his voice low enough that only Turner could hear him above the blare of music in the background. "Stay the fuck away from him. If I need to break every bone in your body to keep you from bringing him here, I will."

"What? You're mad just because I'm not some self-deprecating evangelist afraid of his own dick? If my boy wanted to see you, he would've called you instead of me. So get your fucking hands off me." Turner clawed at Ryan's wrists, trying to break his hold. Ryan laughed darkly. Thank God he didn't have his gun on him. Because right now putting a bullet through Turner was looking pretty fucking tempting.

"He's not your boy. And if he needs some space from me, fine. But I want to hear it from him, not you. That is between Eden and me, so stay the fuck out of it. And just so we're clear, if you ever bring him here again, I'm putting a bullet between your eyes. With your record, it won't be much of a stretch to pass it off as self-defense."

Turner raised a brow at him, looking impressed instead of scared. "Look who finally grew some balls. Well then, cop, maybe it's about fucking time you understand something too. If it involves Eden, it involves me."

"Cut the fucking umbilical cord, Turner. Last time I checked, you're not his parent. Or his husband. You have no right to dictate who he does and doesn't see."

"You'll always bleed blue, not red. So you'd never understand, even if you tried. I don't expect you to get it. But I sure as hell expect you to listen."

Ryan's hands shook as he dragged Turner out of the room. "Don't talk like you know shit about what Eden and I have. Even if he does want you, you don't deserve him. You fucking left him here last time when he could barely even stand."

Turner scoffed, his eyes cold as steel as he glared back at Ryan. "Thought that might've been you. What are you, stalking him now too?"

"No. But if I was, I'd still be better for him than you. If you were any sort of real friend to him, you'd be trying to keep him away from this shit—the drugs and this fucking place—instead of constantly pulling him back in."

Something flashed in Turner's eyes, and for a moment, Ryan thought he might swing on him. He hoped he would. That would give him the excuse he needed to beat him to within an inch of his pathetic life and put him behind bars. Keep him away from Eden.

"You should really stop running your mouth about shit you could never begin to understand," Turner snarled. "Just because you've spent some time with Eden doesn't mean you know shit about our world."

"You're right. I don't understand your fucked-up world. And I don't want to. Not if that's how you justify treating someone you claim to care about like this. Eden deserves better, regardless of whatever fucked-up rule book you choose to live by."

"Better? And by that, you mean you?"

Ryan swallowed hard. "Yeah, maybe. If he wants to. At least with me he'll be taken care of. He doesn't fucking belong to you."

Turner snickered. "Say what you want about me and the shit we do. But at least when he fucks me, he doesn't have to worry about waking up in a jail cell the next day."

Ryan's fist hit Turner's face before he could even finish his sentence. Stumbling back, Turner dodged his next few punches, spitting the blood from his mouth as he swung Ryan around and pinned him against the wall.

"You're lucky, Ryan. I'd put you down right here and now if I didn't think Eden would never forgive me for it. Next time you touch me, I'm not holding back."

Releasing his grip, Turner stepped back as Ryan spun around. Glaring, Ryan stood between Turner and the doorway. He didn't give a fuck what it took. He wasn't letting Turner back inside.

Shaking his head, Turner left, mumbling something under his breath. Ryan stood there for a couple of seconds, his shoulders heaving up and down as he breathed in heavily. He'd meant what he said. Didn't care what it took. Next time he caught Turner here with Eden, he was shooting him on sight. Cop or no cop.

Until then he was putting an end to this the only way he knew how. Ryan walked back inside, grabbed a chair from the table, and jammed the door by the handle. He wasn't going to allow any interruptions. Not for this.

Ryan turned toward Eden and stood there for a moment. He stepped forward slowly, his footfalls echoing off of the black walls. When he reached Eden, Ryan lifted his hand and caressed Eden's cheek with just his fingertips. Eden jolted at the touch, rearing back and hitting his head against the brick in a hollow thud.

"So you thought you could get rid of me that easily, huh?" The words were husky and raw as they left Ryan's lips.

Eden paused for a moment, swallowing hard. "What are you doing here? Where's X?"

"Turner's where he should be. So am I."

Eden shook his head, tugging at the handcuffs. "No. I wanna go. Let me out."

Ryan's shoulders tensed at the slight panic in his voice. He wanted to take him away from this place more than anything. But he couldn't, not yet. The next words were more choked than the steady calm he'd been hoping for. "So this is what you like, huh? Being tied up, whips and chains? You like pain, Eden?"

Eden tuned his head away and to the side, even though he couldn't see. His body trembled slightly, and his lips stretched into a thin line as he yanked at the handcuffs again. The clank of metal against brick sunk into Ryan's skin. His hands curled into fists so tight his fingernails broke skin and he bit down on his lip till he tasted blood.

In that moment he hated the world. Hated everyone and everything. A murderous rage rolled through him, every muscle in his body going rigid. It was the type of blind rage that made him wonder if he was all that different from the people he locked up. He'd only felt this way one other time in his life. When his brother had died. Back then he'd promised himself he would kill whoever had done this to Luca. And if Eden ever told him why—who had made him this way—he knew he would do the same.

With shaking hands, Ryan reached down and unzipped Eden's pants and pushed them to the floor along with his boxers. Stepping forward so they were almost chest-to-chest, he lowered his head and drew wet, lazy circles with his tongue along the hickeys he'd left on Eden's neck earlier. The taste of sweat on Eden's skin mingled with his scent as Ryan inhaled deeply.

They were his. Eden was his. And nothing he could ever say was going to change that.

"Stop," Eden muttered, his voice barely above a whisper. In spite of his protests, Eden bent his head back, leaning into the wet, tingling sensation. His body shuddered against Ryan's clothed chest when Ryan nipped at his neck. Even through the thin fabric, Ryan could feel the heat rolling off of him. Like rage. Like fire.

Ryan's hand dropped to Eden's dick slid his fingers over the smooth velvet skin as he stroked it from base to head. Eden groaned slightly, his hips rolling as he pumped into Ryan's grip, trapped between his hand and the wall. The sound sent a surge of heat straight to Ryan's groin. His eyes roved over Eden's naked form, taking in the flex of each and every muscle. A thin sheen of sweat coated his skin, accenting the hard lines of his body. Ryan pulled back for a second and tugged off his own shirt before continuing. He needed to feel more of him. Needed to feel him without anything between.

Pressing his chest against Eden's, Ryan's skin burned, every point of slick contact a feverish caress as he pinned Eden to the wall behind him. The sensation of Eden's cold metal piercings against the warmth of his sweat-slicked chest sent a thrill up Ryan's spine. He could feel Eden's breath on his neck, hot and disjointed as Eden rutted his hips against him, blindly seeking any sort of relief.

"You like this?" Ryan whispered, drawing back and licking hungrily at Eden's chest. When Eden didn't respond, he stopped, holding Eden in place by the hips. "Answer me, Eden."

"Yes," Eden responded hoarsely.

"Good." Spitting into his hand, Ryan continued stroking Eden, his pace slightly faster. Chest-to-chest, he slid his other hand behind Eden, his fingers gripping the soft swell of his ass. Ryan sighed harshly against Eden's neck, his dick aching. He could feel his pulse beneath his lips, beating frantically. His own heartbeat roared in his ears as he braced one hand against the wall, drawing on the cold, hard surface for focus. "Tell me why."

"Why what?" Eden rasped, his tone pleading and hungry with wanting.

"Why you like it."

"Because."

"Because what?" Ryan tightened his grip on Eden's arousal. Not enough for it to hurt. Just enough pressure to let him know he needed to answer for him to continue.

"Because it feels good."

"And why does it feel good?"

Eden exhaled heavily, cursing under his breath. "Please, Ryan. For fuck's sake. Would you just—"

Ryan covered Eden's lips with his own, forced his tongue inside. Licking hungrily at the warm wetness, Ryan kissed him hard. Shaky and breathless, Eden sighed into his mouth. Ryan's body trembled as he bit down on Eden's lower lip, leaving the pink flesh red and swollen.

"Answer me, Eden. Why does it feel good?"

"Because it hurts," Eden relented, his dick throbbing in Ryan's hand. His body expressed his need as he writhed against Ryan, seeking more friction. "Because I hurt. Because I don't hurt when it hurts."

Ryan's breath caught in his throat, generating a choked, guttural sound. "I could hurt you if I wanted to. Tied up like this, I could do anything I want to you."

A violent shiver rolled through Eden's body. He held his breath, waiting.

"Do you know what I want to do?"

Eden shook his head, licking his lips.

Ryan removed Eden's blindfold, dropped to his knees, and took Eden into his mouth, sliding his tongue along the hot flesh. The taste was new on his tongue, a tangy, salty flavor that made his dick throb in his jeans. He gripped the back of Eden's ass, holding him in place as Eden tried to pull away.

He gagged when he tried to fit all of Eden's cock into his mouth, the head hitting the back of his throat. He didn't pull off, though. Instead he lifted up on his knees and tried taking him down at a different angle. Eden shook violently above him, unsteady on his legs as he shifted his weight to the handcuffs holding him to the wall for support. Sweat dripped from his chest and slicked his hair to his forehead. Ryan kept his eyes on Eden, reveling in the blush on Eden's cheeks and the way his chest heaved every time he took him down.

Once he was sure Eden would no longer pull away, Ryan began stroking Eden's base with one hand, massaging his balls with the other. He sucked hard on the head, hollowing his cheeks out and running his tongue along the rounded tip. Above him, Eden choked out a labored breath. His body shuddering as his orgasm hit him. Ryan moaned around his head, tasting him on his tongue, salty and tangy.

He'd wanted this for so long. Had wanted to share this with Eden. And have Eden give it to him. Sighing around his dick, Ryan finally pulled off and stood shakily.

"You don't get off on pain," Ryan said, reaching up and twining his hands with Eden's handcuffed ones. "You just think you deserve it. But you don't. You say that everything Shawn said was true, but it's not. Everyone does bad things sometimes, Eden.

"Because people are fallible. Sometimes all we can do is try our best, and sometimes even our best ends up hurting others—and ourselves. You told me so yourself, remember? Life isn't black and white. People are beautiful and complicated and sometimes contradictory. Sometimes our scars change the way we see the world. And that's not our fault. But it can make us blind to all the good still left in the world. And ourselves."

Ryan kissed Eden slowly. Gently. Whether it was for Eden's sake or to quell the ache in his own chest, he wasn't sure.

"I'm sorry for everything Shawn said. He's an idiot. And what he said was bullshit. No one else has the right to look at you and judge. They haven't seen what you've seen, not the way you've seen it. And they haven't felt what you've felt. If someone looks at you and tells you you're less than, it's because there's something broken in them. Not because there's something broken in you."

"But what if there is? What if they're just seeing what's there, Ryan?" Eden's words were raw and throaty as he shook his head.

"Eden. The most important parts of a person aren't seen, they're felt. And I've felt you. You're a lot of things, but broken isn't one of them. If it were, you wouldn't be able to make me feel so utterly whole when nobody and nothing else has."

Eden cried then. He cried, and he looked away. Ryan kissed the tears on the side of his face and wrapped his arms around him. He didn't let go till Eden had stopped shaking and his eyes were dry. He didn't say anything, just covered Eden's face with warm kisses and slid his hands up and down his back.

Sometimes people are funny. They hide behind words and actions that put up a wall between themselves and the rest of the world. Because they're hurt. And because they're scared. Sometimes people deny themselves what they need the most, like doing so will make them stronger. More deserving somehow.

Eden was funny. Funny and stubborn and so many other things Ryan didn't have words for. Sometimes when he looked at him, he was reminded of Luca. And sometimes when he looked at him, he was reminded of so much more than what he'd felt for his brother. So much more than he'd ever felt for anyone.

Thirteen Years Ago

THE PRINCE told me he was sick.

Sick from not seeing me. Sick from not having his stardust.

That I was the only one he would get it from. Because I was that special to him. Because everyone else made him sick.

He had purple shadows under his eyes and he looked like a skeleton, all skin and bones. I asked him if he was eating. He told me he couldn't. Not without me.

I tried to get him to eat, but all he wanted was stardust.

One day, his eyes rolled back in his head, and his body went limp, and I thought he had died. He hadn't. But he'd come close.

I told him I wouldn't sell to him anymore. That it scared me. That we couldn't see each other, not even for that.

He got down on his knees. He begged me. He slapped me. He scared me.

But I still told him no.

I told him, "You're doing too much. It's going to kill you."

I told him, "You're sick. I'm scared something bad's going to happen."

I told him, "I think you need to stop doing stardust."

He told me, "Stardust doesn't make me sick. Being without you makes me sick. If you want me to get better, all you have to do is stay."

I told him, "No."

Chapter Eighteen:
One May Smile and Smile,
and Be a Villain

Ryan

RYAN FLIPPED through the channels on his flat-screen TV, picking at the leftover burger on his plate. Exhaling heavily, he set aside his half-eaten dinner and paced back and forth inside his apartment. The stillness nipped away at him like a dog at his heels. Eden had insisted on going home today, now that the repairs to his apartment were finished. Ryan had offered to let him stay. He'd even tried bribing him with an offer to spend the day watching *Maury*, despite the fact that he was quite sure a couple of his brain cells died a slow and agonizing death every time he did.

But Eden had declined, insisting that he needed to get back to work, whatever the hell that meant. Ryan had never found his apartment to be particularly quiet before. Had always found something to occupy his time. Now, it seemed vacant. Dull. Lackluster even.

Ryan jumped to his feet at the sound of the doorbell—maybe Eden had changed his mind after all—and was at the door within a couple of long strides. The person that greeted him on the other end, however, was not who he'd been hoping for.

"So you're him. Can see why he can't keep his dick in his pants. You're a pretty little fucker."

Ryan's shoulder's tensed, his hand moving to the gun concealed at his waist as he met Trevor's stony gaze. Listless brown eyes stared back at him, crinkled in amusement as Trevor stroked his thick salt-and-pepper beard.

At six foot four and over two hundred pounds, Trevor was a force to be reckoned with. But it wasn't the two inches he had on Ryan that immediately put him on edge. The man radiated danger. Like a predator in its natural environment, he moved with an unabashed confidence. Almost as if he knew, regardless of what he encountered, he was top dog on the food chain.

"What do you want?"

Ryan didn't bother with formalities. Trevor clearly knew who he was already. Or at the very least, had deduced that he and Eden were more than friends. The man was a sociopath, not an idiot. Ryan wasn't sure how much Eden had told him, but even if he hadn't disclosed what he did for a living, Trevor could have figured out as much on his own. A simple tail would tell him where Ryan worked if he hadn't already recognized him from the surveillance he'd run on Eden several months back.

"A straight shooter. I like that. Cuts through all the bullshit. One of the very few things no amount of fucking money can buy."

"That your way of telling me you're here to buy me off? Because if you are, the answer is no." Ryan moved to shut the door. Trevor stopped him from doing so, the gaudy gold rings on his right hand clanking against wood as he held his hand out.

"If that's how you think I operate, you're in for one hell of a rude awakening, blondie. You and I both know there are things more valuable in this world than money. At least to a man like you."

Ryan stilled, his eyes narrowing as he allowed Trevor to push the door open again.

"That's better." A wicked grin spread across Trevor's pitted face. "It's come to my attention that you've taken quite a liking to one of my boys. One of my favorites in fact."

Ryan's lip curled in disgust, his fingers forming fists at his sides. The hair on the back of his neck stood on end as a sinking feeling settled in the pit of his stomach.

"I'm not a selfish man, Ryan. I don't mind sharing. But I am a business man. I'm here to broker a deal."

"He's not yours to share." Ryan's words were clipped, his nostrils flaring as he glared Trevor down. "And if you do anything to him, I'll see to it personally that you spend the rest of your life in a four-by-four cell."

Trevor laughed, cocking one brow. "What a reaction. Always knew my boy had game. Never thought he'd reel in a big fish like you, though. My condolences for your brother, by the way. It's a real shame what happened to him."

Ryan froze, his entire body going rigid. Blood roared in his ears, red-hot anger coursing through his veins. "What the fuck do you know about my brother?" he growled through gritted teeth.

"You think you're the only one with a couple tricks up his sleeve." Trevor laughed. "Kids gotta be careful these days. All it takes is one dirty hit and it's game over. Would be a shame if Eden went down the same path as Luca."

The vein in Ryan's neck bulged. Digging his fingernails into his palms, he willed himself to stay calm. "Yeah, it would be a shame. Especially for you. As you said, you're a businessman. So I highly doubt you'd take out one of your highest-grossing dope dealers just to get back at me. But if you are that stupid, if you fuck with me or Eden, I promise you, I'll have every cop in this fucking city after you. And I won't need proof to lock down your operation. Just enough eyes on you to put you out of business."

Trevor tilted his head to the side, intrigued. "And what makes you think Eden isn't just doing what I tell him to?"

This time, Ryan was the one to smile. "Because if he'd wanted to use me for whatever the hell you've got going on, he would've done it by now." It was a concern that had genuinely crossed his mind in the beginning. But Eden had spent the last week living in his apartment. If he'd wanted to use him to get backdoor information, that would've been the perfect time to do it. He'd had access to Ryan's computers, his phone line, even his cell phone. Yet he'd been more interested in "upgrading" his toilet than hacking into anything that would potentially lend him an advantage.

That and Eden had never actually tried to seduce him. He'd flirted, sure, but when it came down to it, he'd never tried to manipulate Ryan in a way that would play to his favor. He'd been crass and brutally honest to the point of offensive. And on the few chances that had presented themselves for them to take things to the next level, Ryan had ended up needing to be the one to push for more. Not Eden.

Not exactly the hallmark of someone trying to pry information by establishing a romantic relationship.

"That's too bad. Was hoping you'd be a bit more fucking reasonable." A humorless smile stretched Trevor's gnarled features taut as he leaned in slightly. "See, the thing is, I'm not like you. And to a man like me, money is the most important thing. Every minute Eden spends with you is a minute he could be working his corner. My rule is, if you can't get down, then get the fuck out. You don't want to take me up on my offer, fine. Then you don't need to be fucking with my boy at all."

"I already told you, Eden doesn't belong to you. He's not your boy. So I'll speak to him whenever I damn well please. Now get the fuck off my doorstep before I lock you up for trespassing."

Ryan slammed the door, locked the dead bolt, and took a couple of steps back, glaring at the deep brown barrier. After Luca had lost it, his brother had changed. Stayed out late drinking, drugging, and doing God knows what else. It was possible he'd purchased dope from Trevor at some point. Still, the fact that he'd brought Ryan's brother up sent a chill down his spine.

Whatever his angle was, he'd clearly done his research.

Reaching for his phone, Ryan shot Eden a quick text.

Hey, you okay? -R

Yeah, why? Did something happen? -E

No, just making sure. -R

Sounds like you're getting separation anxiety. -E

You'd love that, wouldn't you? -R

Want me to get you a blow up doll to keep you company? -E

Are you talking about a sex doll? -R

Yup. -E

Shut up. -R

You don't want one? -E

Of course not. The only people who use those are creeps with a necrophilia fetish. -R

I have one. -E

You're kidding. -R

Nope. Like to stick its dick in X's mouth when he's sleeping. Funniest shit I've ever seen. -E

Ryan set his phone down and shook his head, then picked it up again when it announced a new message with a ding.

Just kidding. -E

Are you really? -R

Dunno. -E

Eden. -R

It worked though, didn't it? -E

Didn't what work? -R

You're not anxious anymore. -E

Blinking, Ryan realized he was smiling.

Nope. Still miserable. You must be losing your touch. -R

You're right. I'm touching myself right now, and it's not working. You wanna come over tomorrow night and show me how? -E

Ryan flushed, heat rushing to his groin as he imagined what Eden had described.

What was the point of you moving back into your place if we're just gonna hang out every night anyways? -R

We're not hanging out every night. -E

Pretty much. -R

Don't you think you'd get in trouble if your boss found out I was staying with you? -E

Ryan stilled. Eden was right. Even if he managed to come up with some sort of legitimate excuse as to why he'd invited Eden to live in his apartment, McNeil wouldn't be happy that he hadn't asked for clearance first.

You're right. Thanks. -R

Sure. Gotta go, duty calls. -E

Ryan chewed on the inside of his cheek as he set his phone down. Eden did have a point, but he had a feeling that his choice to go back home had as much to do with Eden's boss as it did his own.

Ryan

"GET READY to breach!"

The order came through Ryan's earpiece, followed by the shattering of glass and a piercing screech as a smoke grenade exploded to his right. Kicking open the door in front of him, Ryan said a small prayer as he leveled his gun and made entry. He took cover behind a large wooden crate, flinching as bullets whizzed by. The shrill shriek of metal against metal offset his equilibrium as he strained through the smoke, trying to make out the figures darting back and forth in the darkness.

Fuck, this was bad.

The order for the drug raid had been handed down last minute. Too soon for him to send Eden anything more than a short text telling him to stay away from the warehouse on Broadway and 67th. They'd identified it as one of Trevor's safe houses. Judging by the bullets ricocheting off the jagged metal walls of the warehouse, it had definitely been occupied when they'd made entry.

Glancing over, he made sure Shawn was close enough to hear him before proceeding. They hadn't spoken since their blowup back at the bar. But they had to communicate here if either of them wanted to make it out alive. And as his partner, it would be on him if he let Shawn get shot. As tempting as the prospect was.

"Cover me," Ryan ordered, nodding in Shawn's direction before making a run for the next wooden crate several feet ahead. He flinched as the box he'd taken cover behind splintered, jagged shards of wood spraying in all directions.

"Fuck," he muttered, lifting his head to return fire. He only got off a couple of shots before a barrage of bullets had him pinned down again.

"What the hell is this?" Shawn growled, slamming himself up against the wooden crate as he crouched down next to him. "Don't they have anything in this bitch that's not made of wood?"

Scanning the perimeter, Ryan spotted a metal counter lining the far end of the room.

"There." He had to yell over the howl of bullets to be heard. Not waiting for a response, Ryan ran to the left. A sharp pain shot through his left leg as he dove behind the counter, cursing loudly. The searing heat of the wound blurred his vision. He bit down on his tongue, pushing past the pain.

He needed to focus.

Peering over the counter, he spotted several figures in the direction of the gunfire. There was still too much smoke to make out anything more than vague shapes. He needed to return fire. Needed to gain some leverage.

But all he could think about was whether or not one of them might be Eden.

"Cover me!" Shawn yelled.

Nodding to Shawn, Ryan sprayed a couple of bullets in the direction of the gunfire, enough to keep their attackers pinned down but nothing close enough to hit. A second later Shawn was beside him.

"These fuckers aren't kidding around," Shawn groaned, cursing loudly.

To his right, Ryan saw something move in the darkness. He immediately leveled his gun at the figure. But he didn't shoot. He couldn't. Not without knowing for sure.

It was tall enough to be Eden. Had just the same build. But he couldn't make out the face yet. Couldn't be certain.

"What the fuck are you doing?" Shawn yelled, leveling his own gun at the figure.

"No!" Ryan yelled, tackling Shawn to the ground. A burst of gunfire exploded to his left. Ryan watched in horror as Alice shot down the figure, the silhouette crumpling to the floor.

Panic shot through him, terror freezing him in place for a moment before he lunged forward. It only lasted a couple of seconds, but the time it took him to reach the body on the ground felt like forever. He exhaled a sigh of relief when he didn't recognize the bloodied face staring back at him.

He let himself be pulled backward as Shawn dragged him behind the counter.

"What the hell's wrong with you?"

Ryan shook his head. He was so relieved he didn't even have it in him to form a coherent response. Ryan watched silently as their backup flooded through the rear door. He knew he should be covering their entry. Shooting back. But he couldn't bring himself to pull the trigger. Not after what had just happened.

He watched mutely as the other officers flooded the compound, vaguely aware of Shawn's eyes on him. He wasn't saying anything. Ryan didn't care.

It hadn't been Eden. It hadn't been him. Thank God.

He didn't move, even after he heard the all clear, his hands shaking as he sat on the cold concrete floor. It was only later when the medics began assessing his leg that he remembered to breathe again. The bullet had just nicked him. A flesh wound.

The pain in his leg paled in comparison to the ache in his chest. At least that one had a finite end.

Ryan

RYAN SAT across from McNeil, staring his boss down as the Irishman met his glare with cool ambivalence. He wanted to deck him. Jump across McNeil's desk and shake him till he saw things Ryan's way. But he knew there'd be no point. Even if he beat him till he was black and blue, his answer wasn't going to change.

"This isn't optional, Quinn," McNeil stated flatly.

"You're really going to take his side over mine?" Ryan spat incredulously, leaning forward in his chair.

"It's not about that, and you know it. Evans told me what happened back at the warehouse. You're too close to this. You need some distance. Time to regain your perspective."

"I told you I'm fine."

McNeil paused, his eyes narrowing. Shaking his head, he let out a heavy sigh. "Ryan, I watched you grow up. I've known you for over twenty fucking years. You really think I'm going to believe that? You're not fucking fine. Normally you'd have a file filled to the brim with shit on this guy after five months. Yet you haven't given me a single piece of information I can use. And now you're tackling your own men in the middle of a gunfight because you're worried about that piece of shit.... That's not you. That's not fine."

Ryan's fingers curled, his nails digging into the chair as he willed himself not to respond. Arguing with McNeil about the way he'd referred to Eden would only reinforce his boss's point.

"Please, sir. Just give me another chance—"

"Already did that. I'm done arguing with you over this shit, Ryan. You hear me? This is what's gonna happen if you want to keep your fucking badge. You're taking two weeks off. Nonnegotiable."

"You're putting me on suspension?"

"No. Fucking listen to me. I said time off. You're going to take that time to clear your head, and when you get back, we'll reevaluate whether or not to put you on another case."

Anger made his entire body stiffen as the realization of what McNeil meant by that hit him. "You're handing my case off to someone else? Who, Shawn?"

"Fuck no. You think I've lost my fucking mind? Alice and Kurtis will be working on it while you're out."

Ryan exhaled a sigh of relief, the tension in his shoulders easing slightly. They were better than Shawn, but still. The thought of any of his coworkers going after Eden made his blood boil. "This is my case, sir. My guy. You can't just hand it off to someone else—"

"You want to fucking bet?" McNeil barked, raising a brow. "He's not your guy. He's our perp. And if this were anyone else, your ass would've been canned. So stop acting like I'm punishing you and get your shit together."

Closing his eyes, Ryan forced a deep breath. His knee-jerk reaction was to tell both McNeil and Shawn to fuck off. To tell them they didn't understand. Didn't know Eden like he did. That he couldn't just stand by and watch while the rest of his coworkers went after a good man.

While they went after *his* man.

But the weight of the badge around his neck stopped him. Had it always felt this heavy? He used to welcome the burden. Feel a sense of pride in upholding the responsibilities that came with his position.

And now? Now the metal band around his neck felt more like a noose than anything else.

"Fine," Ryan growled. He pushed himself up from the chair and headed for the door.

"One last thing, Quinn. When you get back, you better act like you give a fuck about this goddamn job. Because as of late, you could've fucking fooled me."

Ryan burst out of McNeil's office and made a beeline for Shawn's desk. Shawn flinched when Ryan slammed his fists down on his desk, leaning in till they were nose-to-nose and lowering his voice.

"I swear to God, Shawn, if anything happens to him because of you...."

Turning, Ryan walked out before he could finish. Not because he didn't mean it. But because he did. Meant every single fucking word of what he'd said. If something happened to Eden just because Shawn had been in his feelings about their little spat earlier, Ryan was holding him personally responsible.

RYAN PUSHED open the door to his apartment and slammed his keys onto the counter. A high-pitched whine sounded to the right. He grabbed his Glock and leveled it at the foreign noise.

A laugh escaped his lips when he identified the source. A large rottweiler stared back at him from inside a crate, the name Butch on the collar around its neck. It was black and brown, with big brown eyes and a mouth that made it look like it was always smirking. Even when it wasn't.

A simple note lay on top of the crate. Ryan picked it up, his eyes skimming over the short message: *For your separation anxiety.*

Chapter Nineteen:
Give Sorrow Words; the Grief That Does Not Speak, Breaks

Ryan

WHY DIDN'T you tell me? -E

Ryan paused, his fingers hovering over his phone. That could mean so many things. About Trevor. About the little nick on his leg. Or about his suspension.

The answer to all three was the same.

I didn't want to worry you. -R

You thought I wouldn't fucking find out? -E

Was that a trick question? Ryan's leg went numb as he idly scratched Butch behind the ear. In spite of the dog's enormous size, Butch insisted on being a lap dog, splayed out across Ryan's legs like a small feline as he sat on the couch.

It's not a big deal. -R

Not a big deal? You don't understand. Once Trev sees something he likes, he never lets go. -E

I'm a cop, Eden. He's not stupid enough to try anything with me. -R

You don't know Trevor. We need to stop seeing each other. -E

Ryan reread Eden's last message three times. He had to be joking.

What? Temporarily? -R

No. Permanently. -E

Ryan's hand shook. Inhaling sharply, he quickly typed his reply.

We need to talk about this. In person. -R

There's nothing to talk about. -E

I'm coming over. -R

Not home anyways. -E

Then tell me where you are. -R

Ryan waited for five minutes before he realized Eden wasn't going to reply. He threw on his jacket, headed down to Club Zero. If Eden wasn't at home, that's where he had to be.

THE CHRONICLES OF LAZARUS

As he pushed his way through the large glass doors, Ryan scanned the dance floor. He spotted Eden near the back of the club, engaged in what looked like a heated conversation with several other men the narcotics unit was on a first-name basis with.

Before he could begin making his way across the room, a fight erupted between Eden and the other men. Cursing, Ryan began pushing his way toward them through the crowd. Eden was a good fighter, but he was outnumbered. One to six were odds not even Mike Tyson could beat. Within a matter of seconds, the men had Eden on the ground, the clear leader of the group leaning over Eden with a gun pointed to his head.

The teeming club erupted in chaos, inebriated onlookers scattering for cover. Screams sounded above the backdrop of techno music, the frantic occupants jostling Ryan as they trampled one another to get to an exit.

For every step he took forward, the crowd pushed him two steps back. He wasn't moving fast enough—wasn't going to make it there in time. The terror of the moment washed over him like a tidal wave. Fear coursed through his veins like an electric shock.

Horror turned to panic as he shoved frantically at the bodies blocking his way. He drew his gun with shaking hands. He was too far from the group. Even if he pulled the trigger, he didn't have a clear shot.

"Stop! Police!" Ryan yelled, his voice lost in the cacophony of screams and toppling chairs.

Eden, however, looked perfectly calm. Staring down the barrel of the gun, he smirked, taunting the man leaning over him, then spit in his face. Ryan's stomach dropped as the man leaning over Eden pulled the trigger. The sound of a gunshot never came, though, and a moment later club security was on them, pulling the men apart.

The gun had jammed. Thank God.

Ryan exhaled a sigh of relief, the tension in his frame ebbing slightly. But the realization did nothing to ease the ice-cold vise grip constricting his chest. Shaking off the man who had pulled him up, Eden stalked out the back door.

Eden

EDEN STOOD in the narrow alleyway, a cigarette between his lips, his eyes staring at nothing in particular as he wiped the blood from his nose. He'd been itching for a fight. Craving it. But security had broken it up before the fun had even started. Stupid fuckers.

He pulled a syringe from his pocket and tightened the tourniquet he'd placed on his left arm earlier. He flexed his left hand into a fist a couple of times before spotting a vein and injecting the contents of the hypodermic into his arm.

His ears rang as he slumped back against the wall, the cigarette almost falling from his lips. His head dropped back as he took a couple of labored breaths, his eyes upturned toward the sky.

Cursing, he let the needle drop from his hand and kicked at the dumpster to his left. Fuck the stars and fuck the sky and fuck him for acting like a goddamn child, still wanting to believe in fairy tales when he already knew how each and every one of them would end. At least for him.

The door to his right grated open. Ryan appeared in the alleyway a moment later. Fucking great. Just what he needed.

Charging toward him, Ryan didn't stop till they were nose-to-nose. He was fuming, his chest heaving, his eyes flashing with anger as he fisted his hands at his sides.

"What the hell was that?" Ryan growled, the words sounding strange and frayed, like a raw nerve ending. Like the edge of a knife.

"A fight. They happen in clubs sometimes—"

"Bullshit." Ryan grabbed the cigarette from Eden's lips and stomped it out. "You send me that stupid fucking text, and then you almost get yourself shot. What the fuck is wrong with you?"

"That's really more of a question for my shrink."

Ryan grabbed Eden by the collar, pinning him against the brick wall behind him. "You think this is a fucking game, Eden? You think I'm joking?"

Eden laughed, a raw, broken sound that echoed in the silence off the narrow alleyway. Mocking him. Reminding him.

"Have you ever watched someone die, Ryan?" Tilting his head to the side, Eden flashed Ryan a smile that didn't quite reach his eyes.

Ryan's breath stilled.

"I have. I've watched someone bleed out. Standing over him. Knowing he didn't deserve it. I've watched innocent men die. And I'd do it again if I had to."

Ryan didn't let go, but the anger in his expression wavered, the crease between his brows easing slightly.

"If you had to kill someone you knew was innocent, could you?" Eden asked. "If it was either you or him, could you really do it? I don't think you could."

"What does that have to do with anything?"

"Because, Ryan, that's my world. And it always will be. A world where you don't belong. A world you couldn't survive in. You're a good person. Good people don't live very long in my world."

"So what, then? You expect me to just walk away?" Ryan's words were incredulous as he shook his head.

"That's exactly what I fucking expect," Eden snapped, grabbing on to Ryan's hands and trying to free himself. "I can't always be there to protect you."

"I'm not asking you to protect me."

"You don't have to. I brought you into this shit. Now I'm showing you the door." Eden's voice cracked as he choked out a laugh. "You told me once that I'm not broken. Even if you believe that, even if it's true, that doesn't mean I can't break you."

He knew this was unfair to Ryan. That this was his fault for forgetting the most important rule. People like him didn't have nice things for a reason. Because they broke them. But it wasn't too late. He could fix this. He could get him out before he was in too deep.

"You really think I'm buying that shit?"

"You don't have to."

"I'm not letting you do this."

"I'm not asking for your permission." Eden shoved Ryan hard, sending him stumbling back a couple steps. He needed to get the fuck out of here. Before he lost his resolve.

Ryan stood in front of him, blocking the alleyway exit. "If this is about Trevor, I can handle him. I've dealt with assholes like him before—"

"No, you haven't. If you had, you'd be dead."

Ryan shook his head, running a hand through his hair. "This isn't just your decision to make."

"Too bad. I'm making it anyways. Now get the fuck out of my way."

Ryan stood his ground, staring him down.

"Move, Ryan."

"No."

"Move!" Eden stepped into his space until they were nose-to-nose.

"Or what, Eden? You'll lay me out? Fine, go ahead. Hit me. It would be less fucking painful than this shit."

Something in Eden broke. Split right down the middle, and he pushed Ryan to the ground. Straddling him, he fisted the front of Ryan's shirt and pulled him up so they were face-to-face.

"Don't." His voice shook, every nerve ending in his body screaming. "Don't fucking do that when you know I can't be what you need."

"If this is what you think I need, then you don't know me at all."

"You need to be safe—"

"No, *you* need me to be safe. What I need is you. I need you, Eden. So don't fucking do this. Don't leave me like Luca did." Ryan's eyes were pleading, desperate. A breathtaking, vibrant blue Eden wanted to drown in.

Guilt clawed at his chest as he looked down at Ryan through wet eyes. "I'm not leaving you. I'm trying to keep you safe."

"Yes, you are."

Eden hung his head, every ounce of strength he had centered on his grip on Ryan. "You're going to get hurt. He's going to hurt you, and it'll be my fault."

"Don't give me that shit. Stop blaming yourself for everything. This was my decision too. And it still is. You can't push me away, Eden. You can try. But I'm not going anywhere. Not unless it's with you."

An anguished breath escaped Eden's lips. Bending down, he wrapped his arms around Ryan. He could feel Ryan grip the back of his shirt as he held him to his chest, closing the distance between them. "I'm sorry. I'm sorry," he choked out.

Eden didn't understand this. Didn't understand what was happening. But he couldn't see Ryan hurt like this and not do anything. And he'd be damned if he let it be because of him.

A sound to his right made him pull his gun, peering into the darkness.

"It's just me. Put that fucking thing away." Xavier stepped into sight, walking toward them. "Robby called me. Said you might need backup."

Ryan was up from under Eden in a matter of seconds, glaring Xavier down as he stepped between him and Eden. "Stay the fuck back."

Eden put a hand on Ryan's shoulder. "It's okay—"

"No it isn't."

Nodding slowly, Eden turned toward Xavier. "I'm fine. Ryan had my back. We just need some time to finish talking."

"Didn't look like you two were just talking—"

"He said get the hell out of here, Turner. Or you want me to make good on my promise from the other day?" Ryan flexed his fists. Apparently Eden wasn't the only one itching for a fight.

"Just give us some time." Eden put some bass in his voice to make it clear he and Xavier were done talking. Nodding slowly, Xavier turned and left. Eden exhaled slowly and fished his cigarettes from his pocket.

"Do you love him?"

The question almost made Eden drop his lighter as he lit his cancer stick. Blinking, he took a hard drag from his cigarette and stared at Ryan for a moment. He could say yes. Could make this simple for both of them. Finally give Ryan an excuse he'd accept to walk away. But if he did, he'd be lying. And Ryan deserved better than that. Hell, Ryan deserved better than him. Better than what he could offer on his best day, let alone his worst.

When he'd first met Ryan, he'd wondered why the hell someone like him would ever even give him a second glance. Eden was broken. Knew he was in spite of everything Ryan said. And Ryan was so fucking perfect it hurt. Two halves that, by design, would inherently never fit together.

He still didn't understand why Ryan wanted this. Wanted him, with all that he'd never be able to offer. But at some point, he'd started believing that he did. That for whatever impossible reason, he did make Ryan happy. The same way Ryan made him happy.

And it had scared the shit out of him. The same way Ryan's question now scared him. Because it was so close to something real, it wouldn't just break him if he lost it. Or if he was wrong. It would ruin him.

Eden lifted his head and held Ryan's gaze. "You don't see me losing my shit over him talking to Trevor, do you?"

Ryan studied him for a moment, a broad smile that lit up his eyes slowly stretching across his face.

Eden flushed, looking down and kicking at the ground before nodding toward the alley exit. "C'mon, let's go back to your place. I need to talk to Butch, make sure he's been taking good care of you."

Ryan snorted, sliding his arm around Eden's shoulder as the two headed for the exit. "Him taking care of me? Not to be a snitch, but it's definitely been the other way around. That dog is eating me out of house and home. And he shits like a horse."

Eden snickered. "Yeah, I kinda figured that'd be your favorite part. Used to just let him shit in my neighbor's yard so I wouldn't have to deal with it."

"You're horrible."

"And you still like me anyways."

Ryan laughed, raising a brow. "I have bad taste. Remember? Oh. And for the record, if you ever pull any shit like that again, I'm kicking your fucking ass."

Eden nodded, laughing. Maybe he was an idiot for letting this happen. For allowing himself to think that somehow, someway, they'd be able to make this work. But he was already in too deep. He couldn't bring himself to push Ryan away. Not when Ryan made him feel everything he'd been searching for in oblivion.

In a world where nothing was beautiful, Ryan held all the stars. Lit up the night sky so bright that all the broken shards looked alive. Vibrant. Like maybe one day they might still form a whole.

Like they used to.

Thirteen Years Ago

THE WORLD *ended.*

The stars went away, and the sky shuttered, bending till big, wet tears fell on the concrete. I was wet, dripping wet. But that's not why I felt cold.

The Prince was dead. They said it was the stardust. I thought it might be me.

He'd looked so sad. So impossibly sad the last time I saw him. He barely spoke. And when he smiled, it looked like he might cry. But he didn't.

He told me to be good. To remember him when I had sunsets and ice cream.

He told me he was tired. Tired of struggling. Tired of wanting. Tired of begging.

He told me he was sorry. Sorry for everything he'd put me through. Sorry for loving me.

I asked him why he would be sorry for that.

He told me that love isn't always good. That sometimes love is deep and dark. That sometimes it becomes an ugly thing that consumes everything it touches.

He told me he'd thought about killing me. Killing us. That he'd wondered if maybe it was the only way we could be together. He'd thought of different ways to do it. That taking stardust would be easiest. Less painful than cutting our wrists or drowning.

I told him I was scared.

He said he knew I would be. That he knew if he did what he wanted to, I would hate him forever. So there would be no point. Even if we were together in another life, I wouldn't love him anymore. And nothing could be worse than that.

He made me promise to never stop loving him. He made me promise not to be sad. He made me promise to never forget him.

And the next day he was dead.

I stared up at the sky, the starless sky. And I screamed till my throat burned. Till my lungs gave out, and all I could do was sob and wheeze. I screamed for them to give him back. I begged for them to give him back.

I went to his grave and sat there for days. Willing him to come back for me.

And eventually, I left.

I hated him for leaving me. For taking the stars away. I hated him for choosing that. For choosing stardust over everything else. Mostly, though, I hated him for not taking me with him.

Chapter Twenty:
Expectation is the
Root of All Heartache

Ryan

"I'M MOVING in." Eden pushed past Ryan, dropping his bag in the living room and plopping down on the couch. Stretching his arms out, he reached for the remote and changed the channel from *Cops* to *Maury*.

"What prompted this?" Amusement flashed in Ryan's eyes as he picked up Eden's bag and carried it to the guest room.

"I missed Butch," Eden called from the living room. "Don't worry, it's not permanent. Just till we're done with this shit with Trevor." A second later, eighty pounds of fur and muscle rushed past him, almost knocking Ryan flat off his feet. He heard a muffled grunt from the living room and then a stream of expletives.

Returning from the bedroom, Ryan chuckled at the sight that awaited him. Butch was on top of Eden, his paws on Eden's chest as he licked at his face happily.

"For fuck's sake," Eden grunted, pushing Butch off and glaring at the dog before sighing heavily and petting his head. "What the fuck have you been feeding him? Baby gorillas?"

"What? No, why?" Ryan snorted, joining Eden on the couch.

"You've only had him for a week, and he's already getting fat."

Ryan balked, reaching over and covering Butch's ears with both hands. "Shhh. You're going to hurt his feelings. He's very sensitive."

Eden snickered, raising a brow. "I hate to break it to you, Ryan, but Butch is probably more hard-core than you. I've seen him rip out a man's heart with his own bare teeth."

Ryan raised a brow in disbelief. "Butch? No way. If that was true, then he would've attacked me when we first met."

Eden grinned. "Nah, I trained him not to."

"How? He'd never even met me."

Eden shrugged. "Threw some of your clothes into his crate a couple days before I dropped him off so he could get used to your smell."

Ryan blinked, clearly impressed. Who would've thought snarly little Eden would be the next dog whisperer. "Wait. When did you take some of my clothes?"

A roguish grin played across Eden's face. "The last time I broke into your apartment."

"The last time?" Ryan echoed. He had noticed a couple of things had been moved, but he'd assumed he'd done it and simply not remembered.

"Yeah. Which reminds me, we really need to talk about upgrading your security around here."

Ryan wasn't sure whether he should be impressed or genuinely concerned. His environmental awareness was definitely slipping if Eden had managed all that without him even noticing. Good thing he hadn't been slacking on laundry day.

"You do realize you could get into trouble if someone sees you, right?" Even as a cop, it would be hard for him to explain away a well-known drug dealer breaking into his apartment, even if he did volunteer that Eden was, for all intents and purposes, his informant on Trevor's case.

"Nah." Eden stood and made his way into the kitchen to rifle through Ryan's refrigerator. "Your neighbors already know me. Most of them, anyways. I ran into Ms. Anderson on my way in last time. She's baking me a pie."

"Ms. Anderson? The grumpy old woman next door who demanded I arrest a group of eight-year-olds for writing on the sidewalk with chalk?"

Eden nodded, popping the cap off a bottle of Bud Light and throwing one of his Lean Cuisines into the microwave. "Yup. That one."

Ryan shook his head, gawking. He'd been trying to get on Ms. Anderson's good side for the last year. Had offered to take out her trash, drive her down to the farmer's market, had even invited her to Sunday church. And she still called him "boy" every time they ran into each other in the hallway.

"So, what's with the decor?"

"Huh?" Ryan started, distracted from his moping.

"I mean, why don't you have any pictures of your family up? Catholics are normally pretty gung-ho about that sort of shit, aren't they?"

Ryan stilled, surprised that Eden had noticed. "Yeah. All the pictures I used to have had my little brother in them, so I had to take them down."

"Why? You don't like seeing him?"

Ryan shook his head. "No. Actually, I'd prefer to have a couple of him up. But my father is... a little weird about it?"

"Weird?" Eden turned to face him.

Ryan chewed on the inside of his cheek, his chest heaving slightly. It always hurt to talk about Luca. And it probably always would. But in a way, it was nice to be able to talk about him with someone. To be able to acknowledge his loss instead of pretending like he'd never existed.

"Yeah. Ever since my brother died, my father's refused to talk about him. Got rid of all of his things, any pictures he was in. I guess it was easier for him that way. To pretend like he'd never existed versus having to deal with his loss."

"And you? How do you feel about it?"

Ryan's shoulders stiffened as he attempted a nonchalant shrug. "It is what it is. He's gone. That's all that really matters. Sometimes it feels wrong, like we should be honoring his memory instead of getting rid of every trace of him. But everyone's grieving process is different, and my father's never been very good with emotions."

Eden popped the top off another Bud Light and passed it to him, leaning against the counter. "Was he a cop too?"

"Oh yeah." Ryan laughed. As if his father would ever let them forget. It was practically his middle name, the way he worked it into almost every conversation he had with friends and strangers alike. "He was old-school. The type of man that believes everything is black and white. Right is right and wrong is wrong. He grew up in a different generation. Things were simpler back then."

Eden stared at Ryan for a moment, a pensive look in his eyes. "Bet he wouldn't be too happy to hear his golden child is shacking up with a convicted felon."

Ryan ran his tongue along the inside of his cheek. It wasn't something he'd ever contemplated, primarily because whenever he saw his family, it was always at his parents' house. Aside from the situation with Julie, he'd always kept his personal life separate from his family.

They were good people, but they were traditional. And the fact that Eden had a criminal record wasn't the only objection they'd have to this little arrangement.

Letting out a heavy sigh, Ryan shrugged. "Probably not. But I live my life with them, not for them. They're my family, and I love them. But they don't have the right to dictate what I do in my personal life." Just like they hadn't when it came to Luca.

Something flashed in Eden's eyes. Something he couldn't quite put his finger on. Smirking, he slung his arm around Ryan's shoulder and led them toward the living room. "Glad you have a mind of your own. Wouldn't want to be sharing that headspace with your parents when I fuck your brains out."

"And when's that gonna be?"

"Impatient much?" Eden snickered, his expression one of utter self-satisfaction.

"You're the one making empty promises."

"Don't worry, they won't be empty for long. Got something coming in the mail."

Ryan's brows creased in confusion. "You know they sell lube at the local grocery store, right?"

"It's not lube. And no, I'm not telling you. But I did get a new set of kneepads that need breaking in."

Ryan grinned. The prospect of Eden's lips around his dick was almost enough to temper his restlessness. Almost.

Eden's oral skills were the best he'd ever had. But he needed more than that. He wanted all of Eden, even if he had to bottom to get it. Not that the sex was a prerequisite to whatever it was between them. He enjoyed Eden's stupid jokes. His borderline psychotic worldview added color to all of Ryan's gray.

So much color that sometimes it left him a little blind.

It was easy to forget that Eden was a drug dealer. Or that Ryan himself was a cop. Sometimes, he found himself wishing he wasn't a cop. And that Eden wasn't a drug dealer. That they were just two men enjoying each other's company. Sometimes he found himself imagining what it would be like if they were living together just because.

Because they wanted to share the simple, small moments with each other. Because they missed each other when they were apart. And all those simple, small moments became fragments of something greater when they were shared. Something special and precious that made his heart beat a little faster and his blood hum in his veins like he'd found something so incredible he never wanted to be parted from it. Something impossible.

Eden

"AGAIN."

Eden stepped to the side, easily countering Ryan's swing. Wrapping an arm around his abdomen, he delivered a sharp kick to the back of his knees and brought him down easily. Smirking, Eden stood over him, offering him a hand up.

"Damn it," Ryan cursed, wiping at the sweat on his brow as he took Eden's hand. His body bore the marks of his previous attempts, deep purple bruises scattered along his arms and legs. Eden had tried to take him down as gently as possible, but he couldn't go easy on him. Because when shit inevitably went south, the people coming for him—for them— wouldn't either.

He needed to prepare Ryan for the real thing. For all eventualities.

"You're getting better."

"Yeah, right," Ryan grumbled. "We've been training for a week, and I still haven't managed to land a hit on you."

"You've got good technique. And the strength to back it up."

"Then why haven't I landed a single hit?"

Eden grinned, tossing Ryan a bottle of water. "Because you're predictable. Anyone who's studied up on those shitty training videos they show you in the police academy knows how you'll react. Which puts you at a distinct disadvantage."

Ryan sighed, running a hand through his sweat-soaked hair. "So what, then? I just need to wing it?"

Eden shook his head. "That's not what I'm saying either. You're treating it like a game of chess when you need to be thinking of it more like a dance. Technique is important, but you need to trust your instincts more. Fighting isn't just about executing the right moves. It's about catching your opponent off guard. Figuring out how they think, their weak spots, and then taking advantage of them." Eden dabbed at his brow with the back of his hand. "C'mon. Let's go again. This time focus on improvisation."

Ryan nodded, setting his water bottle down and joining Eden on the small blue mat laid out in his living room. Eden waited till Ryan had resumed a fighting stance to move forward. This time, when Eden swung at Ryan's chest, Ryan parried his punch and hit him on his left side. It wasn't a full-contact hit, but it was enough to knock the wind out of Eden. Groaning, he grinned, clapping Ryan on the shoulder.

"Good. Much better." Eden smirked at the grin on Ryan's face. He was practically beaming, his eyes flashing with renewed determination. "Told you you've got this. You only need a little practice fighting without a rule book. Let's go one more time, and we'll call it a day."

Acquiescing, Ryan took his position opposite Eden on the mat. Eden blocked the first several punches he threw but left his left side open again. When Ryan swung at his weak spot, Eden slid his leg out, catching Ryan's foot on his own and sending him tumbling to the ground. Ryan hit with a hard thud, cursing as he pushed himself onto his knees. Before he could get to his feet, Eden pinned him down, his knees on the back of Ryan's legs and his hands on top of Ryan's.

Ryan was strong. Stronger than Eden had anticipated. He had to use his full weight to keep Ryan down, his chest straining against the long, sinewy muscles of Ryan's back as he strained to throw him off. Eden bore down on him. It took every ounce of strength he had to keep Ryan from gaining the leverage to break free. After a couple of moments of struggling, Ryan finally went slack beneath Eden—a silent surrender as the tension drained from Ryan's frame and he sank down onto his stomach.

Breathing heavily, Eden stilled, acutely aware of his half-hard dick nestled in the crevice of Ryan's ass. The smell of Ryan's earthy petrichor shampoo filled Eden's nostrils. Sweat-slicked strands of his silky blond hair stuck to Eden's cheek. He could feel every breath Ryan took, could feel the slight stutter in Ryan's breathing as his rib cage expanded and contracted against Eden's chest.

Eden's cheeks flushed, his dick twitching. Fuck. He'd fantasized about this exact position so many times in the last month. But the reality of it felt so much fucking better than anything he'd imagined. He was half tempted to keep Ryan pinned, tear his shorts off, and fuck him till he went cross-eyed.

But, of course, there was the problem of consent. Last time he'd checked, not saying no wasn't exactly the same thing as a yes. Though that was, admittedly, a minor issue compared to the real reason he hadn't tried fucking Ryan till neither one of them could walk.

Eden moved to stand and pushed himself up onto his elbows. Before he could fully lift off, Ryan's hand slid to his ass, pulling Eden back against him. The soft halves of Ryan's ass tightened around his dick.

Eden groaned as heat gathered in his groin.

"Don't fucking tease. I'm barely holding back as it is," Eden said huskily through gritted teeth.

"It's only teasing if I'm not willing to give what I'm offering. Take it. I want you to."

Ryan's grip on his ass tightened. His fingers sank into the tender flesh and he began rutting against Eden's erection. Eden's back arched, hands forming fists against the mat. He rolled his hips, humping Ryan's ass, chasing the heated friction. Ryan's arms shook as he lifted up onto his elbows and let out a strangled breath. The adjusted angle allowed him to rock his hips in time with Eden's thrusts.

"Fuck," Eden cursed. He should pull back. Or at the very least rely on more than just a sheer piece of fabric to separate himself from Ryan's perfect ass. He was already skirting the precipice between his waning willpower and taking the very thing he'd dreamt of for months. Instead, he shifted his weight to his knees and leaned forward.

And when Ryan brought Eden's hand to his mouth and sucked hungrily on Eden's fingers, any thoughts of backing off completely disappeared.

The tension lines that ran the length of Ryan's back told Eden he already knew what was coming. That he was ready and willing. Eden slid down Ryan's body, tugged off Ryan's shorts, and massaged his ass. His fingers dug into the soft swells. Trembling, Ryan propped himself up on his hands and knees and pushed back into Eden's grip.

Half of him wanted to skip the formalities and fuck the ever-loving shit out of him here and now. His veins sang at the sheer thought. Blood roared in his ears as he took in the sight of Ryan splayed out doggy style in front of him, his blond head bowed, his back arched with his knees parted slightly.

Instead he slid one arm under Ryan, stroking the silky heat of his arousal. The other stayed on his ass, pushing the flesh to the side as he lowered his head and slid his wet tongue along the crease of Ryan's ass.

"Yes," Ryan moaned and rocked back and forth, trapped between Eden's tongue and his hand.

Eden let out a throaty hum of approval. He licked a wet line from Ryan's ass up his lower back, the smell of Ryan's arousal thick in the small enclosure. He could feel Ryan shiver beneath his touch, utterly responsive to every touch and stroke.

Eden grinned against his ass, finally content that Ryan was thoroughly primed. Ignoring the tight throbbing of his own erection, Eden pushed his face against the shuddering heat of Ryan's ass and began tonguing his asshole. Ryan inhaled sharply, and Eden had to slide his other hand to Ryan's belly to keep him propped upright.

Dropping down to his elbows, Ryan cursed. His knees dug into the carpet as he fisted the thin mat cover beneath him. Sweat prickled on his skin. His chest heaved, his breaths ragged and labored as he leaned back onto Eden's tongue.

"Fuck, Eden. Stop. I'm going to come." Ryan choked the words out, his voice hoarse from the tension in his neck. Eden pulled back. His eyes were on fire as he flipped Ryan over once more and slid his hands up and down Ryan's shaking thighs.

Eden reached into the bag he'd placed beside the mat before the start of their training session and pulled out several different dildos, ranging in size and color.

"We'll start with something small," Eden explained hoarsely. "Get you used to it first. It won't be exactly like the real thing, but it's close enough to get you off—"

Ryan's brows creased, his lips drawing into a thin line. "No."

Eden stilled. "Okay," he said slowly, putting the toys back in his bag. "You want me to blow you, then?"

Ryan propped himself up on his elbows, shaking his head. "No, Eden. I don't want that dildo. And I don't want you to blow me. I want you to fuck me."

Eden swallowed hard, breaking eye contact and rolling off of Ryan. "I can't do that. I already told you."

"When?"

"When I told you I could do everything except shit involving that."

Ryan exhaled a frustrated breath, yanking his shorts back on. "I don't understand. What's the fucking difference between me blowing you and you fucking me?"

"You only blew me that one time. And I wouldn't have let you. Not if it was up to me."

Ryan glanced over at him, his expression incredulous. "You're fucking kidding, right?"

Eden shook his head, not meeting his gaze. Ryan was upset, understandably so. But he didn't understand.

"Eden, we've been fucking around for almost a month. We've literally done every other thing possible that doesn't involve your dick in me or mine in you. If I'm missing something, then fucking tell me. Because this shit doesn't make any fucking sense."

"I already told you, Ryan. I can't do that. Not with you."

"But you can fuck Turner?" Ryan's jaw tightened, his shoulders squared as he spit the words out.

"That's different."

Ryan looked like he'd been slapped, blinking a couple of times as he looked away and ran a hand through his hair. When he spoke again, he was yelling.

"How? How is it fucking different? What? Because you've known him for longer? Like that makes him any more fucking trustworthy!"

"It's not that."

"Then what? Is it the fact that you two do dope together? The fact that I'm a fucking cop? Does he turn you on more than I do?"

"No. Why can't you just fucking trust me when I tell you that it's complicated?"

Ryan shook his head. "Because it's not about trust, Eden. It's about understanding. You'll fuck Turner and half the fucking prostitutes in this town, but you won't fuck me. What do they have that I don't?"

Eden ran a hand through his hair and looked away. "I stopped fucking X the night you and I hooked up at the club. It's not about that. And it's not what you don't have that's the problem. It's the other way around."

Ryan's eyes narrowed, frustration drawing his features taut. "What? Is it my badge? The fact that I'm a cop—"

"No. You're...."

"I'm what?"

Eden stood, reaching for his cigarettes. "Never mind. Just fucking forget it." He headed out the front door before Ryan could respond. A hot, ugly gnawing settled in his gut as he made his way down the sidewalk, nearly running.

Always running.

He wasn't running from it. Not really. He'd come to terms with everything a long time ago. But he was running. Because Ryan kept pushing. And if Ryan ever found what he was looking for, it would change the way he saw Eden. Change it to the point where Ryan might not want to touch him or look at him ever again.

Because in a world where nothing was beautiful, there were great and horrible things.

Things so horrible they kept you up at night, making monsters out of shadows. Things that never washed off. Left you sick inside. Made you wonder if you even deserved to reach for more. Or if life was just a pipe dream, filled with dead stars and shades of oblivion.

Eden

LATER THAT night, Eden stared up at the ceiling, unable to sleep. For once it wasn't because of a nightmare. After he'd returned from his three-hour walk, he'd slipped into Ryan's apartment and retired to the guest bedroom. Just as he'd resigned himself to another night of what-if's, he spotted it.

A dream catcher hung over his bed, listing gently in the breeze.

Unlike his black-and-white one at home, this dream catcher was red and gold. Slightly bigger than the one he had above his bed. It looked handmade. Sliding his fingers along the outer rim, he caressed the soft leather. Ryan had made it. Even when he hadn't deserved it. Even when he never would.

A calm like he'd never felt before washed over him as he stared at the small treasure. Like he'd stepped into a cool spring stream. Something that would wash away all the grime and dirt that had been his life for almost as long as he could remember.

He'd probably still have bad dreams because he always did. But this dream catcher was different. Special. It stood as a reminder that, for once, he actually had something worth waking up for.

There was no way to avoid the darkness, no way to escape it entirely. But he could hold on to these moments of light. Save them for the nights when the sky was starless and the silence was deafening.

Drawing in a deep breath, Eden lay there for a couple of minutes before slipping out of his bed. He pushed open the door to Ryan's bedroom, careful not to wake him as he closed the door behind him. Pausing, Eden stood over him, his eyes skirting over Ryan's face. Moonlight shone through the nearby window, illuminating the soft gold of Ryan's hair. He looked beautiful, almost noble, his sun-kissed skin draped in soft shadows.

Some treasures, like the dream catcher, he could hold. Keep close to his heart even when he was away. But others were so precious it scared him to even try. Like everything Eden was might bleed through. Stain something that was never meant for him to touch.

A wretch begets a wretch. And broken people were only truly good at one thing. Breaking what was whole.

But even broken people had dreams.

Eden slid under the covers beside Ryan and slipped his arms around Ryan's chest, closing the space between them. He could feel by the rise and fall of his chest that Ryan was still awake, but he didn't say anything. And neither did Eden. Instead, Ryan placed his hands on top of Eden's and pulled him tighter against him.

Sometimes people dreamed of things they had no right to. And sometimes people didn't always know the right things to say. But that was okay because the most important things weren't said, or even dreamed. They were felt.

And Eden fucking felt it. So much it hurt down to his bone marrow. It was a good hurt. A pain that made him feel alive. Feel real and cared for. Like all his broken bones had finally found a place to sleep.

Chapter Twenty-One:
One Touch of Nature Makes the Whole World Kin

Ryan

RYAN RUBBED at his eyes.

His gut churned. His skin burned as he stared up at ceiling. He spent an hour staring into nothingness before he finally found the energy to pull himself out of bed.

Two hours later, he was showered and shaved. Not that his attempts at proper hygiene did much to hide the bags under his eyes. Pulling up in front of the precinct, he took the stairs two at a time. Once he'd reached his desk, he began combing through Eden's file.

"Damn, look who's back from the dead." Glancing up from his file, Ryan nodded to Alice and Shawn as they walked into the office, trailed by Kurtis.

"Yeah. Been busy."

Alice raised a brow at him, flashing Ryan a rueful smile. "Busy with the new boo? It's been what, almost two months now, right?"

"You marking it on your fucking calendar?" Shawn snickered. "Didn't realize you were that desperate for the D. You should've said something earlier, Ally. You know I'd never leave a woman in need."

"Yes, a girl has needs. Doesn't mean I'm desperate enough to share STDs with you and the harem of whores you cycle through. The CDC should be using your little black book as a watch list for gonorrhea and chlamydia carriers."

"I'm flattered you'd assume my sexual conquests are that extensive. Nice to see you finally giving me the recognition I deserve," Shawn replied, puffing his chest out.

"I don't think that was a compliment," Kurtis offered, looking more than a little disturbed.

"You wouldn't, fucking ankle biter," Shawn snapped, casting a glare over his shoulder at Kurtis.

"Better be careful what you say to him, Evans," Alice chided. "I heard McNeil might be retiring soon. At the rate he's going, he's on track to be your new boss in a couple months."

Shawn flinched. "Over my dead fucking body. The day I start taking orders from that beta is the day I turn in my fucking badge."

"If you want anyone in this office to buy that alpha bullshit, you might want to start by being a little less melodramatic," Alice muttered, rolling her eyes.

"It's called flair," Shawn responded indignantly, making his way over to Ryan's desk. "Hey, you have a sec to talk outside?"

Ryan glanced up from his file, his eyes wavering. "Yeah. That's fine," he responded stiffly. He set the file down and followed Shawn outside.

Ryan waited patiently as Shawn kicked at the sidewalk, hands crossed in front of him. "About what happened back at the bar…. I don't like Zika. And I probably never will. I'm not going to apologize for that. But I shouldn't have taken it as far as I did. With the faggot stuff. And the shit about him being a fucking Mex—I mean, Hispanic."

Ryan rubbed his forehead, appraising his best friend. Shawn had never been good at apologies. Even when he was clearly in the wrong. But the fact that he was trying meant he at least understood all the bigotry he'd spewed a few weeks back was irrefutably reprehensible.

"You don't have to agree with everything I do, Shawn. God knows I don't agree with most of the shit you say and do. But you do have to accept it."

Shawn blew out a heavy breath, raking a hand through his short brown hair. "It's going to take time all right. Zika being gay isn't what I have a problem with. It's all the other shit. The fact that he sells dope and walks around like he's some fucking gift from God."

"Kinda sounds like someone else I know," Ryan teased, raising a brow at him.

"I am not that bad."

"You're right. You're worse."

Shawn lifted a hand to his heart, feigning offense. "Et tu, Brutus? And here I thought you were my best friend."

"I am. And because of that, it's my job to tell you when you're wrong. And most of the time, you are."

Shawn snorted, grinning. "Would it kill you to let me win one for once?"

"Don't know. It's never happened. But I'll let you know when it does." Knocking shoulders with Shawn, Ryan exhaled a breath he hadn't realized he'd been holding. He resented what Shawn had said and how he'd handled himself. But he'd missed his best friend. He still planned on having a serious conversation with him about the latent racism and homophobia he harbored. But for now, at least they'd be able to work in the same office without wanting to tear each other's heads off.

By the end of his shift, Ryan knew almost every line of Eden's file by heart. Yet he still hadn't found anything that he could use to circumvent their current situation. What he had been able to find had only reaffirmed what he'd already concluded regarding Eden and his arrangement with Trevor.

Trevor Gills was smart, vigilant, and above all, ruthless. He clearly possessed a thorough understanding of the law and had used it to take advantage of every legal loophole known to man—including making patsies of all the men who worked under him. Aside from a couple of narcotics charges back in his twenties, Gills didn't have so much as a speeding ticket on his record in the last twenty years.

Yet Eden's rap sheet was longer than his arm.

If Ryan had to guess, Gills managed to maintain control through a combination of fear and blackmail. His inner circle were all men he'd grown up with—or rather, men who had grown up with him. People he knew enough about to know their weaknesses. People like Eden, with family members they'd do anything to protect. People who'd grown up under precarious circumstances, with few choices but to rely on someone like him for safety and protection. People who would likely do anything he asked, be it out of fear or some fucked-up sense of loyalty men like Gills had a talent for engendering.

Leaning back in his seat, Ryan pinched the bridge of his nose, sighing heavily.

The only thought that brought him any reprieve was the fact that it was Friday. Which meant Eden would be down at Club Zero, selling his usual wares.

After leaving the precinct, Ryan swung by the local coffee shop on his way to Club Zero. He'd need the caffeine to make it to 3:00 a.m. without being semicomatose. He'd just placed his order when a familiar voice sounded to his right.

"Ryan!"

Ryan turned and smiled as Amelia pulled him into a hug. "Hey, Amelia."

"It's so nice to see you. Did you just get off work?" she asked.

"Yeah. I heard you're finally finished with your finals."

"Thank God. I've done so much cramming these last couple weeks. It's too bad you couldn't join Eden and me for coffee this morning."

Ryan shrugged, noting the way her eyes narrowed slightly. "Yeah, but I'm sure it's nice for you two to have some one-on-one time every now and then."

Amelia gestured for Ryan to join her at her table. Taking a seat across from her, Ryan steeled himself against what he knew was coming.

"So did he tell you?"

"Tell me what?"

Amelia shook her head. "God, he's so stubborn. I told him you'd understand if he just explained it to you."

Ryan shifted in his seat. "I'm not quite sure I follow."

"I know why he didn't invite you this morning. Listen...." Leaning in slightly, Amelia lowered her voice. "I can't tell you everything because it's not my place to tell. But Eden went through some stuff when he was a kid. It makes it... difficult for him sometimes."

Ryan stared at her. A static hum settled somewhere in the back of his mind, white noise pulsing through his ear drums. Tugging at his collar, he tried to breathe. The air was hot. Too hot to manage anything more than shallow breaths. He wondered if maybe he'd somehow wandered into a crematorium.

She'd said something to him. He was sure of it. But her words didn't make sense. Standing, Ryan headed for the door, leaving without his order. He could hear Amelia call out to him, but he didn't stop.

He couldn't.

The drive over to Club Zero was a blank. His mind bent. Twisted. Contorted. Till the sun burned and the air stilled and the silence screamed.

He had to be missing something. He was sure of it. Because Eden was strong and never took shit from anyone. Because Eden was his, and no one else could touch him. Because Eden felt broken. And if he ever found out who'd made him feel that way, he was going to fucking kill them.

Empty his gun into their body till they stopped moving and stopped breathing. Till they were nothing more than bones and flesh and bullet holes. Till someone either pulled him away, locked him up, or shot him down.

And it would be worth it.

Eden

EDEN THREW back the rest of the scotch in his cup, his throat burning. He'd never been one for liquid courage, but this was a special occasion. Ryan had come here like he always did every Friday night. Looking for him. Waiting for him. But eventually he was going to get tired of waiting.

Staring at Ryan from across the dance floor, Eden set down his drink and pushed his way through the crowd.

By the time he'd reached him, the shots he'd taken earlier were finally having their intended effect. Eden's shoulder's relaxed as he leaned against the counter, flashing Ryan his usual smirk. "Hey, detective. You looking for some company tonight?"

Ryan turned toward him, his handsome features uncharacteristically taut. After a moment, though, he smiled. "Yeah. I'm waiting for someone, actually. This guy I kind of have a thing for. He's about six feet, one hundred fifty, black hair, gray eyes. And he has these perfect lips. So perfect you wouldn't believe half the shit that comes out of them."

"He sounds like a dick."

Ryan shrugged, his eyes lingering on Eden's lips for a moment. "He is sometimes. But there's a lot more to him than that. He just doesn't show it. He's really sweet, actually. He even cooked me breakfast this morning."

Eden captured Ryan's cup and drank from it. Bud Light. Of course. "What a fucking mark. You should definitely dump him."

"I would, but he's the only one I can get it up for lately. So no can do."

Eden grinned like an idiot. Sexual domination had never been a kink he'd particularly enjoyed, but knowing Ryan couldn't get hard for anyone except him scratched an itch he never knew he had. And maybe before Ryan, he hadn't.

"If you're lucky, maybe it's just early-onset erectile dysfunction."

Ryan chuckled. "If I'm lucky, maybe he'll forgive me for acting like such an ass and come sleep in my bed tonight."

Eden inclined his head toward the empty billiard room to their left. "Does it have to be a bed?"

That was all it took for Ryan to polish off his drink and follow Eden through the crowd.

Chapter Twenty-Two:
The Fault Is Not in Our Stars,
but in Ourselves

Eden

MUSIC VIBRATED through the small billiard room. The wooden floor creaked beneath Eden's feet. Yellow light cast lazy shadows into every corner. One dim lamp hung above the pool table in the center of the room, another above the bar to Eden's right. The rich mahogany-paneled walls vibrated with the muffled bass of techno music, adding a rhythmic hum to the singing in Eden's veins.

Eden took a moment to jam the door handle with a barstool before turning toward Ryan and pinning him to the wall. There was no thought. Only movement as he pushed his lips against Ryan's, forcing his mouth open and sliding their tongues together. One hand slid behind Ryan's head, holding him in place. The other slipped under Ryan's shirt, groping at his muscled chest. Sighing, Ryan dropped his hands to Eden's ass and pulled him closer till he could feel the stiffness in Eden's pants against his thigh.

Eden smirked into their kiss. He bit down on Ryan's lower lip and drug his teeth along the soft, wet skin. Shivering, Ryan groaned, his hips flexing as he rutted against Eden. The way that Ryan clung to him was enough to make Eden dizzy. He pulled back just long enough to tug Ryan's shirt off before removing his own.

He'd slept with plenty of men. He couldn't remember most of their names or faces. Half the time he hadn't bothered to ask. But *this*—the nervous anticipation that made his skin vibrate like a tuning fork—it had never felt like this before. Eden would have remembered. He'd never been to oblivion before with both feet on the ground.

Eden dropped his hands to Ryan's ass and slid inside the waistband of his jeans. His shaking fingers wrapped around Ryan's cock, already slick with precum. Ryan's nails dug into Eden's back as he leaned into his touch. The needy, desperate sound he made shot a jolt of heat straight to Eden's dick. Eden spun them around, walking Ryan backward till they hit the pool table. With fumbling hands, Ryan reached for Eden's zipper. It took him a couple of tries to unzip Eden's pants and push his jeans off before he followed suit.

The second Ryan's jeans hit the ground, Eden was on him. He dropped his hands to the back of Ryan's thighs, lifting Ryan onto the pool table. Grinning, Ryan wrapped his legs around Eden's waist, pulling Eden to him as their lips molded together. Knotting one hand in Ryan's hair, Eden stroked Ryan's dick from base to head with the other. With hungry eyes, Ryan slid his hips forward, pumping into Eden's hand.

After a couple of strokes, Eden bent down and fished a bottle of lube and a condom from his jeans. Before he could pop off the cap, Ryan's hands were on his.

"Eden, we don't have to." Ryan's words were raspy and slurred, a slight tremor to his touch as he held Eden's gaze.

"No, I want to." And fuck, did he. His dick throbbed, the adrenaline of anticipation creating a Molotov cocktail with the liquid courage in his veins. He'd fantasized about it. Jacked off to it. Told himself he shouldn't, and then done it anyway.

He'd made up his mind. He was fucking Ryan. Regardless of whether it was the "right" thing to do.

Ryan nodded and leaned back, his elbows propped against the green felt of the pool table. His legs shook around Eden. His chest heaving as Eden jerked him off with one hand.

With a couple of deep breaths to try to temper the shaking in his hands, Eden leaned forward. He gently probed Ryan's hole with the other, one lubed finger sliding in and out—first just the tip, and then down to his knuckle. Ryan's back arched, sweat prickling on his skin as he tightened around Eden's finger.

"Fuck. You look so hot like this," Eden murmured. His eyes raked over Ryan's trembling frame as Ryan stared up at him. Adding a second finger, Eden bent his wrist slightly till he rubbed against Ryan's prostate.

Cursing loudly, Ryan turned his head and bit his shoulder to keep from screaming.

"Christ," Ryan rasped, white-knuckling a pool ball with one hand. The other dug into the green felt, and Eden laughed, letting out a choked breath. He could feel Ryan contract around him, gripping at his fingers. He had to remove his hand from Ryan's dick and squeeze down hard on his own just to keep from cumming.

Eden slid his fingers out and pulled back. His arms shook as he slipped on a condom and lubed his dick thoroughly. Then he moved up Ryan's body, bracing his hands on either side of Ryan. Releasing the pool ball in his hand, Ryan wrapped his arms around Eden, his eyes burning.

"Let me know if it hurts." The words were jagged and hoarse on Eden's lips as he aligned his dick with Ryan's hole. Nodding, Ryan slid his hands down to Eden's ass, pulling him forward. Urging him on.

Eden gasped as the head of his erection slid inside of Ryan. A jolt of electricity slithered up his spine at the tight, smoldering heat. Ryan groaned, bowing his head and biting down on Eden's neck. Moaning, Eden rocked his hips back and forth, slowly easing into him. It took every ounce of his self-control not to bury himself in Ryan as deep as he could and fuck him till his legs gave out. To take what was being offered till he'd sated the burning heat in his gut. But he wanted to do this right. Make this moment as good for Ryan as it was for him. Ryan's nails dug into his back as he adjusted to the sensation, every muscle in his body straining, telling Eden he was lost somewhere between the pleasure and pain pulsing through him.

In response, Eden adjusted his angle till he hit Ryan's prostate, slowly thrusting into him. Ryan moaned into Eden's neck, and the tension drained from his body as the mixed sensations gave way to pure pleasure. Rocking into Eden, Ryan began to move in time with his thrusts. Eden cursed, his fingers digging into the green felt beneath them as he started fucking Ryan in earnest. His hips pumped frantically as he chased the heated friction. His arms shook; his hair stuck to his forehead. Dropping down to his elbows, Eden held Ryan to him, his face against Ryan's sweat-slicked hair.

Ryan's dick jerked, trapped between their sweaty, writhing bodies as Eden's hips rolled into him. He had to bite down hard on Eden's shoulder to keep from screaming when he came. His body shook violently as he tightened around Eden, cum coating both his and Eden's chests. Breathing heavily, Ryan finally went limp, falling back against the pool table. Eden came a moment later, moaning into the crick of Ryan's neck. His dick pulsed inside of Ryan before he collapsed on top of him.

Both men lay there for several moments, breathing heavily. After a while, Eden stood, his knees wobbling. He retrieved a bar towel from the counter to his right and wiped the cum from Ryan's chest and then cleaned himself off. Ryan glanced up at him, his eyes slightly unfocused as he flashed him a lopsided grin.

"Holy fuck." Ryan's voice was husky, his words garbled. Laughing, Eden helped Ryan up, handing him his clothes.

"I guess we did just christen the pool table." Pulling his clothes back on, Eden gave Ryan a subtle once-over. "Are you sore?"

"Yes. No. I mean, I am. But in a good way."

Eden smirked. "Maybe if you're not too raw, we can do it again later when we get home."

Ryan flushed as he dressed. "Yes. Hell yes."

Inclining his head toward the door, Eden took Ryan's hand and led him out. "C'mon. I wanna show you something."

Ryan raised a brow at him, twining their hands together. Leading the way out of Club Zero's back door, Eden covered the three blocks between the club and his destination hand in hand with Ryan. It was an odd feeling, displaying their bond so publicly. But he couldn't bring himself to let Ryan go. Not yet.

They reached the six-story apartment complex after a ten-minute walk. Eden led Ryan around the side and scaled the fire escape. The old railing was rusted and rickety, creaking with every step they took. Eden glanced over his shoulder occasionally to make sure Ryan was keeping up with him.

When the two finally reached the top, Eden tilted his head back, pointing out toward the horizon. Millions of stars dotted the skyline, yellow sparks of bright light hanging over the city below. Breathing in deeply, Eden smiled.

The stars looked alive. Vibrant. Beautiful even. Crickets chirped. A strong breeze drifted over them, still warmed by the sun that had set hours ago. Unlike most areas of the city, there weren't any commercial shops in the area. It was one of the few quiet neighborhoods on the south side. A beautiful night, Eden mused warmly.

"It's beautiful up here," Ryan murmured, taking Eden's hand in his once more.

"Yeah. Quiet too. Used to come here all the time as a kid."

"To clear your mind?"

"Yeah, and to sleep when we were homeless. Before we met Trevor, Amelia and Noah hated sleeping on the streets. They were scared of the dark like most kids that age. Of all the monsters in the shadows. So I'd take them up here, where they could be closer to the light of the stars and the moon. And I'd tell them stories about the stars."

"About what?" Ryan asked, sliding his hand around Eden's shoulder and pulling him closer.

"Stupid shit, really. Heroes and villains, elves and dragons. Mainly stuff I knew they liked. I'd give the stars names. Tell them each one was a person, a fallen hero that had died and become a star so they could stay on earth and watch over us. It made them feel better. Like someone was looking out for us. Like someone cared. Eventually I stopped."

"Why?"

Eden smiled a smile that didn't quite reach his eyes. "Life's always been pretty fucked-up. I kept telling them it would get better. But for a long time, it didn't. After a while, I didn't have it in me to look them in the eyes and keep telling them someone was up there watching over them while they were eating out of trash cans and using public bathroom sinks to clean themselves. It seemed crueler, I guess. The idea that someone was watching and just letting it happen, compared to the thought that there was no one there at all."

Ryan pulled him closer, sharing his warmth. "You still look up at the sky a lot. Why, if that's how you feel?"

Eden shrugged, a small laugh escaping his lips. "'Cause I'm a fucking idiot. I guess even if I couldn't say it, a part of me still needed to believe it."

"You're not an idiot. You're human. Everyone wants to believe in something."

Eden smiled. Because he'd finally found something he actually believed in. And not out of desperation, like before. But because he genuinely felt it.

The two stood there in silence for several beats, eyes upturned toward the sky.

"My brother overdosed. Coke. That's how he died." Ryan didn't look over at him when he spoke. He was still smiling, but his eyes held a sadness that made Eden hold him a little tighter. "That's why I joined the narcotics unit. Was never a good fit for me. I would've been better working something like violent crimes, where it's clear who the good guys and bad guys are. But after my brother died, I felt like I owed it to him. To change the world in a way that would help people like him."

Ryan cleared his throat. "I always blamed the drug dealers. Like if he hadn't been able to get the dope, he might still be alive. But… if it wasn't coke, it would've been something else. Alcohol. Pills. Whatever he could get his hands on. It's funny. Before you, I always felt like drug dealers were the ones taking advantage of drug addicts. Profiting off their pain. I didn't realize that they might be hurting just as much."

Eden stared at Ryan. "It's still wrong."

"It's all wrong. Stories like this don't have any heroes or villains. Only people doing the best they can with what they have." Ryan kissed Eden's forehead, running his hand up and down Eden's arm.

Eden stiffened, unaccustomed to the unexpectedly intimate gesture. After a moment, he smiled and rested his head on Ryan's shoulder.

Ryan was right. And so was he. Heroes weren't always good, and villains weren't always bad. Which meant they weren't heroes or villains at all. Just people.

People that did great and horrible things in this fucked-up, beautiful world.

Chapter Twenty-Three:
My Tongue Will Tell My Anger or
My Heart Concealing It Will Break

Eden

A CALM QUIET hung in the air as Eden walked with Ryan, their footfalls the only sound to fill the silence of the night. Eden smiled at the feel of Ryan's arm around his shoulder as they traversed the dimly lit walkway. Streetlamps overhead dotted the darkness with pockets of yellow warmth. Ryan's breaths were slow and even beside him, barely audible on the wind as the gentle spring breeze listed through the vacant street.

Barely a sound, and yet Eden clung to it. Held on to the way Ryan leaned against him, lending him his warmth when a gust whipped at the collar of his leather jacket. Or the way Ryan's footfalls fell into pace with his own, adjusting his gait to match his. Or the smell of Ryan's aftershave as he bowed his head when he spoke. Because these things were his. And Ryan was letting Eden keep them. Each and every one.

How fucking idealistic, Eden mused, leaning into Ryan's touch as he smirked at himself. If he got any worse, he was going to start quoting lines from *The Notebook* or *Titanic*. He'd never been the type to fall head over heels for anyone. Hell, he'd never even been the type to bother with remembering names or faces.

Which, admittedly, might be the reason he'd taken a couple more drinks to the face than your average Joe. He'd never lied, though. Never promised anything more. Because he'd always preferred to keep things simple. Attachment was a tricky thing, better left to people who worked a regular nine-to-five and didn't carry around a Glock as part of their job requirement.

Yet here he was, clinging to Ryan like some star-struck teenager. X was right. He was so whipped. Not that he was worried. He was already planning his revenge for that insightful little observation. Some additions to the dick tattoo were clearly in order. Maybe a voice bubble that said You're The (W)hole to My Better Half. He was still fleshing out the details, but it was in the works.

"Where'd you park?" Eden asked, skimming the street for Ryan's black Chevy Impala.

"Over there," Ryan said, pointing halfway down the block with his free hand.

"Jesus Christ," Eden snickered, raising a brow. "Where'd you learn to drive. You parked like—" Eden stilled as he spotted the silhouette of a figure leaning against Ryan's car. He didn't have to see the face to know who it was. Pausing a couple feet from Ryan's car, Eden stuck out his hand, bringing Ryan to a stop next to him.

"Stay behind me," Eden ordered, stepping in front of Ryan as Trevor pushed himself off the hood of Ryan's car and approached.

"No, Eden—"

"Just can't stay the fuck away from him, can you?" Trevor's voice broke through the calm of the night, his tone thick and gravelly. He pegged Eden with a hard glare, his arms crossed in front of him as he appraised the two.

"We were just talking," Eden replied evenly.

"Does it look like I give a fuck? Doesn't matter to me whether you were shooting the shit or sticking your dick in him. I told you to stay away from the pigs."

"Don't." Eden's jaw tightened, his voice sharp.

"What was that?"

"I said, don't talk about him like that. This is between you and me." He'd never checked Trevor before, not outright. Not like this. But Ryan was his. And as long as Ryan would allow Eden to have him, he planned on taking good fucking care of him.

Trevor laughed, the sound tinted with a mixture of disbelief and amusement. "You must've lost your fucking mind. Who do you think you're talking to?" Pulling his gun from his waistband, Trevor gestured down the street with his Glock. "C'mon. You and I are gonna have a little fucking talk."

"He's not going anywhere with you." Moving to stand next to him, Ryan leveled his gaze at Trevor.

"Oh yeah? And what the fuck are you gonna do about it?"

Ryan lowered his hand, flashing his own gun. He didn't point it at Trevor, but he made his intentions clear. "Eden, wait in the car. I'll be there in a minute."

Eden blinked at Ryan, his stomach dropping. "Ryan—"

"Wouldn't do that if I were you, blondie. You think that badge is going to protect you?" Trevor sneered.

"I can protect myself. Get in the car, Eden."

"That's right," Trevor mocked. "Get in the car, Eden. I'll just have a chat with your sister instead. Always staying up late, studying alone at the library. This city's a dangerous place for a pretty young girl like her. And you know how finicky my trigger finger gets when you piss me the fuck off."

Ryan eyes flared. "That a threat?"

"No. It's a promise. And before you grow a set, you'd better remember what the fuck you're doing here too. You really think your boss is going to believe a single fucking thing you say after I show him a video of you getting cozy with my boy in your hot tub? Shit, I could probably shoot you right now and get off without so much as a slap on the wrist. Stay in your lane, keep filing those bullshit reports, and I'll keep this between us."

Eden's fingers flexed, nausea rolling in his gut. It made him sick to think of Trevor watching them that night. Made him sicker to realize Trevor had video footage of it—something he could finally use to blackmail Ryan, make him play along with his twisted little fucking game of cat and mouse.

"I told you to leave him out of it," Eden said.

"And I told you not to fuck a pig. You did this to yourself, Eden. And to him."

Eden turned to Ryan, his movements stiff. He didn't want to leave. But what other choice did he have. If he didn't, it would only make things worse for Ryan—and for Amelia. "I'm sorry," Eden muttered to Ryan, starting toward Trevor.

"Wait." Ryan wrapped his hand around Eden's wrist, holding him in place. "Trevor, the night you came to my apartment, you told me you wanted to make a deal. You have something I want, and you know it. Tell me what you want."

Ryan

"YOU CAN'T do this." Eden's voice shook. His breaths were shallow and frantic, almost hyperventilating as he paced back and forth in Ryan's living room, gun in hand. "I can't let you.

"Eden—"

"You can't. The shit he's going to ask you to do, it'll change you. It'll break you. It'll fuck with your mind till everything bleeds black and blue. Till you'll do anything to escape."

"Eden—"

"He'll make you do horrible things, Ryan. Horrible fucking things. Things that'll never wash off. Things that'll scar you. Leave you so fucked-up you won't even recognize yourself. You won't even recognize the sun and the stars or why you even tried—"

"Eden." Ryan stood, blocking Eden's path. Stepping forward, he placed his hands on either side of Eden's shoulders. Eden's pupils dilated as his eyes shifted around anxiously. "Look at me."

"I can't." Eden shook his head, drawing in a sharp breath.

"Yes, you can."

"No I can't. Not until I shoot something. Or you tell me the last half an hour was just some fucked-up dream."

"Listen to me. I'm here with you. I know that you're scared, but this is what he wants. He wants us to be scared. Because dreams are about fear, remember? But this isn't his dream. Not anymore. It's ours. So you don't have to be scared. You don't have to let him make you feel this way."

"But I do. I do." Eden shivered, his diaphragm expanding and contracting violently. "Because he can hurt you. He can take you away. Make you leave when you finally realize that I'm not worth this shit."

Ryan shook his head, his eyes softening as he ran his thumb across Eden's cheek. "No one can make me realize that. You know why? 'Cause it's a lie."

"No, it's not—"

"Yes, it is." Ryan exhaled slowly, his hands sliding down Eden's arms and twining with his fingers. He didn't know the right words to make this better. Because honestly, he understood why Eden was scared. Any sane person would be. "It's okay. I'm okay. You're okay. I promise."

Eden stiffened, his eyes flashing. "And what if he takes even that away from you, Ryan? What if, when all this shit's done, you're not even okay anymore?"

"Then I'm still better off than I was. Because even if it hurts, it's worth it for the chance to feel all those other things. For the chance to feel you."

Ryan pulled Eden close and hugged him tightly. Because Eden wasn't the only one who was scared.

He was scared. Again. But for a completely different reason.

He'd never seen Eden like this. Never seen him so shaken. Trevor, he could handle. But he couldn't force Eden to stay with him. Couldn't tie him up and demand that he never leave his side. All he had to tether him here were his words. Words that had failed him before.

So instead, he held him, running his hands up and down Eden's back. Feeling him. He didn't let Eden go till he'd stopped shaking. Till his breathing had slowed and the rigidness ebbed from his frame.

Pulling back, Eden looked down. Looked away. Wouldn't meet his gaze.

"This tattoo on my chest, you know what it means?"

Ryan shook his head, an odd sense of foreboding settling in the pit of his stomach.

"It's Latin. *Vehementes Delectationes Vehementes Fines*. These violent delights have violent ends. I got it so I wouldn't forget. Forget the next time someone like you came along. You don't get out of this shit, Ryan. Not unless it's in a body bag. You think I would've chosen this shit for myself if I'd had better alternatives?"

"Of course not."

"Then why the fuck are you?"

"You know it's not that simple."

Eden shook his head. "Then let me simplify things for you." Walking into the guest bedroom, Eden grabbed his bag and began throwing his stuff into the small satchel.

"Eden."

No response.

"Eden." Ryan grabbed the bag, forcing Eden to meet his gaze. "You're not leaving. We're going to work through this. We'll find a compromise. Some middle ground—"

"There's no such thing as middle ground in my world. There's black, and there's white. You're a fucking cop. Isn't it time you started acting like one?"

Ryan recoiled like he'd been slapped. "And what the hell is that supposed to mean?"

"Means you need to stop acting like this shit will work. 'Cause it won't. I'm a dope dealer. You should be trying to get dirt on me. Not asking me to stay. You joined narcotics for your brother, right?"

"Yeah, but—"

"Then think of him."

Ryan took a step back, digging his nails into his palms. Red-hot anger squared his jaw. His spine straightened as he met Eden's gaze.

"He would be proud of who you are. Don't let that change because of me." Clearing his throat, Eden turned toward the door. His hands were shaking, his words rough and throaty when he spoke again. "Hate me if you want to. But stay away from Trevor. I'll let him know the deal's off."

Eden walked out the front door. Without his bag.

Ryan cursed, pacing the length of his apartment. Eden would be back. He had to be. With another curse, Ryan threw Eden's bag to the side. That was when he saw it. A pile of letters, bundled together with a plastic band.

Ryan picked them up and skimmed over the heading. They were all addressed to one person.

Lazarus.

His fingers curled around them. Was this why Eden didn't want to be with him? Because he had someone else?

He slipped the first letter out, a slight tremor to his hands as he unfolded the crumpled paper and began reading.

Ryan

RYAN MET Trevor's gaze with a practiced calm. The apartment they'd arranged to meet at was high-end, if not impersonal. The chair he sat on was black leather, the marble desk separating himself from Trevor decorated with gold accessories and a marble ashtray. Gold-framed abstracts hung on every wall. Undoubtedly the finest that money could buy. Then again, Trevor Gills was the highest-grossing drug lord in the city, so the all-leather interior was well within his paygrade.

The entire apartment smelled of cherry cigars, though that wasn't the cause of the nausea rolling in Ryan's gut. He watched Trevor light his cigar with a patience he didn't feel, a thick plume of smoke drifting in his direction as Trevor regarded him with a predatory smile.

"Well, isn't this a surprise." Trevor's voice was rough and gravelly, his eyes flashing with amusement.

"I'm not here to make small talk." And he wasn't. The fact that he was here in the first place, behind Eden's back, was already eating him up inside. Turner, standing behind Trevor like some fucking guard dog, did nothing to brighten his mood.

"No, of course not. You're here for him." Trevor drank slowly from the dark liquor in his glass, his eyes never leaving Ryan. "Humor me. We should be celebrating, after all. It's a rare occasion I sit down to share a drink with a cop. At least without a gun pointed to his head."

Ryan's lips formed a thin line as he pushed the glass Trevor had set in front of him away. "I'm not here to be your friend. Just because I'm agreeing to this doesn't mean you and I are anything other than business partners."

"Yet you're still here. In my apartment. Alone." Snickering, Trevor took a hard drag from his cigar. "You don't strike me as the gambling type, Ryan."

Ryan didn't bother answering, glaring Trevor down. He intended to get this over with as quickly as possible. If Trevor wanted to play mind games, he'd have to do it alone. Turner shifted his weight from one foot to another behind Trevor, his gaze drifting between the two.

"Which can only mean one of two things. You're either desperate. Or in love."

Ryan gritted his teeth, resisting the urge to jump across the desk and pummel Trevor to within an inch of his pathetic life. They'd taken his guns and checked him for wires at the door, but the golden paperweight on Trevor's desk would do the job just fine. "My reasons for doing this are none of your business. What you get out of it will be the same regardless."

Trevor's eyes flashed, like he'd spotted something shiny. "For once, you're not straightforward. That answers my question well enough."

Ryan didn't move to confirm or deny Trevor's implications. It wasn't that he was ashamed of how he felt for Eden. It was the fact that he knew how men like Trevor operated. He would play every angle he had ruthlessly, including Ryan's feelings for Eden.

Trevor reached into his drawer, pulled out a simple black cell phone, and handed it to Ryan. "We'll start you off with something small. For now, all I want from you is eyes and ears. Next time you boys in blue decide to swing by my place unannounced, I want to know about it beforehand. I'll call you once I need anything more."

"Fine," Ryan muttered through gritted teeth. Then he stood and walked out. He knew this wasn't the real reason Trevor had propositioned him. This was the experimental stage. He was testing him. Trying to see if he could trust him with whatever the real reason was.

And as much as Ryan hated it, he'd have to play along until Trevor deemed him trustworthy. Once Ryan reached his car, he was about to pull out when a knock on the passenger window startled him. Rolling down the window, he tensed, reaching for his gun.

"Calm the fuck down. I'm here to help."

Ryan narrowed his eyes at Turner and reached for his gun anyway. He didn't level it at him, but he kept it in his hand.

"What do you want?" Ryan growled.

"Does he know?"

"What?"

"Does Eden know you're doing this?"

Ryan bit down on his tongue, turning away from Turner. He was silent for a moment. "No."

Turner cursed under his breath, shaking his head. Reaching into his pocket, he pulled out a piece of paper and extended it toward him.

"What's that?" Ryan asked, his words laced with suspicion.

"My number. In case you run into trouble."

Ryan raised a brow, his expression incredulous. "And what the hell makes you think I would ever fucking call you?"

"It's not for you," Turner bit back. "It's for Eden. He would kill me if he ever found out I knew about this and something happened to you."

Hesitating for a moment, Ryan took the piece of paper from Turner. Not for him. For Eden. He doubted he'd ever use it. But if it came down to it, if Eden was ever really in trouble, he'd do what he had to do to keep him safe. Even if it did mean a lethal blow to his pride.

"YOU'RE SHITTING me."

Ryan held his boss's gaze, McNeil's eyes wide as he leaned across his desk, bracing his arms on the wooden surface.

"No."

"How the fuck did you get this guy to trust you? Trevor Gills won't even fucking touch his own product. We've had our best men on him for years, and they haven't even been able to catch the guy taking a shit." McNeil's expression was a cross between astonishment and downright glee as he appraised Ryan.

Ryan hadn't told him everything. But he'd told him enough. Enough to serve his purpose.

"Guess you could say he realized we have something in common," Ryan replied carefully.

"Well, shit. This was the break we fucking needed. The guys up top are gonna lose their fucking heads when I tell them about this. I knew that time off would do you good," McNeil praised, clapping Ryan on the shoulder. "I'm fucking proud of you, kid. Our most senior detectives haven't even gotten close to landing this slippery fucker. We're taking you off the Zika case and immediately putting you on Gills. Whatever you fucking need, let me know. You've got it. This son of a bitch is at the very top. We take him down, we've got it made."

Ryan shifted in his seat, bracing himself. "I have one request, sir."

"Anything."

"You drop Zika's case. Cite lack of evidence or whatever you have to, but that's the only way I'm taking this on."

McNeil stilled across from him, stroking his beard as he appraised Ryan with a pensive stare. The Irishman's green eyes crinkled, wrinkles forming between his brows. "Your in with Gills, was that through Zika?"

"Yes."

Silence engulfed the small office, McNeil chewing on his cheek. After a moment, he leaned back in his chair, letting out a heavy sigh. "Fine," McNeil relented. "Whatever it is, I don't want to fucking know about it. But we can't risk that slick son of a bitch flipping on us when we've got Gills in our crosshairs. Let Zika know the deal's off if we catch him back working his corner after this—"

"You won't," Ryan answered confidently, exhaling a sigh of relief. He sat up a little straighter in his seat before continuing, "Thank you."

McNeil nodded, flashing him a toothy grin. "I'm proud of you, Ryan. And I'm sure your father will be too, once Gills is behind bars. This is big for our unit. The closest we've come so far to really putting a dent in this shit."

Nodding, Ryan turned and left McNeil's office. Even if, for Eden's sake, he hadn't told his boss everything, he'd told him all the details essential to making his plan work. He could only pray it would be enough.

WHEN RYAN got home, Eden was waiting for him at the door. His shoulders were stiff, his eyes narrow as he pushed himself up off the wall.

"What the fuck did you do?"

Ryan swallowed hard, stilling under Eden's gaze. He'd been expecting as much. But he still hated it. Hated the fact that he'd had to go behind Eden's back. "What I had to."

"Did you not hear a single fucking word I said to you yesterday?" Eden's words were sharp, his pupils dilated. He'd been using again. Of course he had.

"I did."

Eden shook his head. A hollow laugh escaped his lips. "Nah. I don't think you did." He lowered his voice and stepped forward into Ryan's space.

"You need to fucking listen to me. And listen good, you understand? What the fuck do you think Trevor's gonna do if he finds out you're not actually dirty? He'll put a hit on your head, Ryan. Might even make me be the one to do it, just to teach me a lesson. And what the fuck am I supposed to do if he makes me choose between you or Amelia and Noah, huh?"

"You'll do what you know is right."

"What I know is right?" Eden echoed incredulously. "You know what I know? That nothing's going to be fucking right about the choices we'll have if he finds out. You see how easy that was for me, how easily I could've pulled a knife? You wouldn't even have time to draw your fucking gun. I could've slit your throat. And you wouldn't even have time to scream. That's why. That's why you can't fucking do this. Do you fucking get it now? Even if I refuse, even if I can't do it myself, he'll just send someone else. And you're not ready. You're not."

Ryan shook his head. He knew what Eden was doing. And he understood why. But it didn't change anything. Not for him.

"That's exactly why I'm doing this, Eden. So that one day the choices you're able to make will be different. You're right. It could come down to that. And if it does, we'll do what we have to do. But we have to try. You can't just resign yourself to living this half existence where all you ever do is what you have to in order to survive."

"That's what life is about for people like me, Ryan. Survival. This isn't a fucking fairy tale where the prince saves the day and the good guys get their happily ever after. This is real fucking life. All it takes is one bullet. One flick of the wrist, and it's game over. Pull out now, while you still can. Tell Trev you changed your mind."

"Eden, listen to me."

"Not until you agree," Eden demanded through gritted teeth."Promise me you will. On your brother."

"No." Ryan's tone was calm as he held Eden's gaze.

He'd turned his back on someone he'd loved once. And the guilt of losing Luca had almost killed him. He couldn't live through it again. Not with Eden.

Eden cursed and stalked down the hallway. Ryan's eyes tracked his movements till he disappeared from view. Everything in him screamed to follow, to find a way to make this better.

But Eden was in a dark place. A place Ryan couldn't follow. Because he didn't know the way. Because they had different monsters lurking in the dark.

Eden thought he didn't understand. But he did. He just knew from experience that there were some things worse than death. Some risks worth taking, no matter how great the consequence.

Eden

EDEN LET his head fall back against the headboard of his bed. He blinked at the ceiling as the room spun. He couldn't remember what day it was. Whether it was noon or night. How long it had been since he'd last slept.

He'd lost his phone somewhere between his apartment and the crack house. How he'd gotten home was anyone's guess.

His veins were humming and his head was spinning and the silence was so fucking loud he wanted to scream just to blot out the sound. So much fucking static, and he still couldn't escape the aching in his chest. Or the fact that he still saw Ryan's face every time he closed his eyes.

His movements were clumsy and uncoordinated as he clawed at the half-empty bag of white on the table. All this blow and he still couldn't forget. He'd been to hell and back. Forgotten his own name. Stumbled through the darkness till he thought he'd never find his way back.

Yet here he was. Shaking like a motherfucker. Fighting the urge to break in to Ryan's apartment to see his face and smell his scent and convince himself he hadn't dreamt him up in some drug-induced fantasy.

As a kid, he hadn't understood. He did now. Got how you could miss someone so much you felt like blowing your brains out just to stop the hurt.

Chapter Twenty-Four:
Life's but a Walking Shadow

Ryan

"DON'T LOOK at me like that. I already know I fucked up." Ryan glared at Butch, sighing heavily as he paced back and forth in his living room. Checking his phone for the hundredth time in the last hour, he cursed under his breath, glancing over at the clock.

When Eden had stormed out, the sun had been setting, right around 7:00 p.m. It was 5:00 a.m. now.

"What the fuck is he doing?" Ryan muttered, raking a hand through his hair. Eden hadn't called. Hadn't texted. Hadn't even answered his phone. If he wasn't back by eight, Ryan resolved to go out looking for him. He'd even contemplated texting Turner before thinking better of it.

Ryan jolted when his phone buzzed in his hand. Glancing down, his heart dropped.

Check your phone. Your other phone. -Unknown

Cursing, Ryan stormed into his bedroom and pulled out the burner phone Trevor had given him. An unread message from about an hour ago popped up on the screen.

Be at 5890 52nd street in an hour. -Trevor

"Fuck," Ryan muttered. He grabbed his jacket and headed out. He sent Eden a quick text letting him know where he'd be before sending McNeil one letting him know he'd be out following a lead today. He hit the highway going ninety and made it to his destination in fifteen minutes.

The building Trevor had texted him the address to looked ordinary enough, if not a little economical given the fact that Trevor's annual salary was in the seven figures. Boarded-up windows, graffiti on the exterior walls, a double door out front and then a single around back. It looked as if it may have been a bar once, now in various states of disrepair. A tattoo shop flanked the left side, the building on the right vacant with a tattered For Sale sign in the window.

Sure as hell desolate enough to be the perfect meeting spot for the top narcotics kingpin of the city. The building was on the south side, at the far end of town. An area that didn't see much traffic, primarily because everything else in the vicinity mirrored the building's crumbling, decrepit state.

Hand on his Glock, Ryan pushed through the front doors. An empty bar counter stood in front of him, a large round wooden table to his right. There were already five men seated around it, most of whom he recognized. Eden sat in the far corner, an empty chair to his right and Xavier on his other side. Trevor stood at the head. The men on either side of him were unfamiliar, though both looked to be young, no more than a couple of years older than Eden at best.

"Nice of you to finally fucking join us," Trevor growled, inclining his head toward the empty chair. Taking the cue, Ryan took a seat next to Eden, his movements stiff.

At least he knew where the hell Eden was now. He wanted to grill him, ask him where he'd been for the last ten hours, but the charged static in the room stopped him. The tension radiating off the five men was almost palpable, like a live wire over water. Every man sat stock-still in his seat, aside from Trevor, who appeared to be as unconcerned and aloof as usual.

"All right, let's get this shit started. Boys, we've got a new addition. Name's Ryan. He'll be our eyes and ears at the precinct. You have any concerns about the pigs, you go to him." Trevor narrowed his eyes at the dirty-blond to his right. "Robby, you haven't been making shit since I moved you over to Freddie's. What's the fucking problem?"

"D's men," Robby growled. "They've got the market locked down over there. None of their customers will even try our product. Say D has the purest shit. Heard three people OD'd on it last week. The man knows how to fucking advertise."

Trevor cursed, fishing a cigar from his pocket and lighting up. "Yeah, well, if we stop cutting our product to compete, we'll start hemorrhaging profits. And that greasy Russian fuck's already been fucking with my profits enough." Rapping his hand on the table, Trevor glanced around, his eyes landing on Ryan. "Might as well kill two birds with one stone. Ryan, sounds like we've finally got a real fucking job for you. Robby, how many of his men does he have in that shithole?"

"Three. But there's only one that really moves any weight. Alek Ivanov."

Trevor nodded, his gnarled features twisting into a wicked grin. "Good. Ryan, get his info from Robby. You take care of him."

Ryan nodded, cursing inwardly. He'd hoped Trevor would hold off on ordering anything that involved serious bodily injury till they had some real dirt on him. Looks like his luck had already run out.

He knew police recourse for this sort of situation. Get the target to flip, provide Trevor with some fake pictures, make it look real with the help of lighting and a good makeup artist. But he had a feeling Trevor would want a lot more than a picture, given the precarious nature of their relationship.

"And for proof?" Ryan asked, shifting slightly in his seat.

"I want to see the aftermath. In person," Trevor responded, his eyes flashing.

Of course he did. That was exactly what Ryan had been afraid of. Even if this guy did end up having the acting skills of an Emmy nominee—which he highly doubted he would—the likelihood of them gaining his compliance to that end was, well, nonexistent. Especially seeing as Trevor could just decide to pop a couple extra rounds off in "the body" once he saw him to make sure things were authentic.

Ryan nodded, his mind racing.

"You don't need to start him out with the full monty, Trev. Ease him into this shit." Eden's words were colored with annoyance as he glared at Trevor.

"Shut the fuck up before I add your name to my shit list, Eden. The way your fucking sales have been lately, I wouldn't be losing much if I did."

"Yeah, 'cause you haven't been saying that shit for years. Maybe if you grew some fucking balls instead of having everyone else do your dirty work, D's men wouldn't think they could fuck you like some loose-legged whorehouse cunt—"

"Eden," Turner cut Eden off, clearing his throat. The entire room fell silent.

Trevor stared at Eden for a moment. His lip twitched, his eyes flashing black as he cracked his neck. "Side room. Now."

Eden's lips stretched into a thin line. His eyes flashed like he wanted to say something more. Standing, he knocked his chair back and stormed past Trevor into a room to one side.

Ryan's hair stood on end. None of the men met Trevor's gaze, all eyes focused on the round wooden table. Ryan's fingers curled into fists beneath the shallow surface. He wanted to follow. Make sure Eden was all right. But part of him worried it would only make things worse. The warning glare he caught from Turner confirmed his suspicions.

"Don't," Turner muttered.

Hesitantly, Ryan shifted in his seat, eyes locked on the door Eden had disappeared behind.

The rest of the meeting passed by without incidence. Trevor was, at the very least, an equal opportunist. He lit into the other four men one by one, the majority of his complaints concerning their recent dip in profits. In fact, it wasn't all that different than what he'd imagined a regular sales meeting might be like, aside from the recurrent threats of bodily harm up to and including lethal measures.

When the hour finally drew to an end, Ryan made for the side door. He wanted to apologize. And to make sure Eden was okay. He still remembered the look in Trevor's eyes when he'd sent Eden away. Not quite murderous, but damn close.

Turner stood in his way, blocking him from following.

"Move." Ryan stepped into Turner's space. He was in no mood for Turner's bullshit. And to be honest, the prospect of a fight—especially with him—sounded pretty fucking good right about now.

"He needs time."

"And you need to get the fuck out of my way—"

"You want him to keep running his mouth around Trev just because he's pissed about whatever the fuck he has going on with you? 'Cause in case you haven't fucking noticed, Trev doesn't take kindly to that shit."

Ryan swallowed hard, biting back his response. He hated Turner, but he was right. Eden talking back to Trevor in front of the rest of his men was not a smart move. Eden's public display of insubordination had already gotten him in trouble. If he was still mad, Ryan didn't want his presence to make things worse.

"Fine." Ryan pushed past Turner and stalked out to his car. He sat there in silence for a moment before slamming his fist down on the dash. Eden had looked sick again. And there wasn't shit Ryan could do to make it better.

God knows how long he'd continue to push Ryan away. Maybe this would be their new normal. Ryan's stomach churned at the thought.

A part of him wanted to run someone down at the sheer thought. To destroy something till the frustration coursing through his veins wasn't eroding a hole in his chest. But he couldn't. Because Turner was right. He needed to focus on what Eden needed. Not what he wanted.

In the meantime, he had to figure out what the hell he was going to do about Trevor's new assignment.

Because right now, pulling out looked to be the only viable option. And there was no way in hell he was doing that—not knowing what it would likely mean for both himself and Eden.

Eden

"I TOLD YOU, didn't I?"

"Yes."

"I warned you, Eden."

"You did."

"Yet you still had to go and run your mouth."

"Got the itch. You know how I am."

"Shut up."

Eden didn't struggle as Bobby and Zane held him down. It wasn't their fault—it was either him or them. He probably would've done the same if the situation were reversed. That didn't make the sight of Trevor stepping forward with the butcher knife any less disconcerting.

At least Ryan wasn't here. That was probably about the only saving grace in all this. That Ryan wouldn't be here to hear him cry like a little bitch. Because when Trevor cut into him, he would.

Kneeling down, Trevor pushed Eden's face to the side, his scarred, calloused hand large enough to cover the majority of Eden's profile.

"You know this hurts me more than it hurts you." There was a lilt to Trevor's gravelly voice.

Eden didn't reply. Not even he could sell that one as a yes.

"But if you're not going to listen, you don't fucking need this."

Brushing a strand of hair behind Eden's ear, Trevor aligned the knife from his ear lobe to the top of his ear where it branched from his face and curved up.

White-hot pain shot through Eden as Trevor cut through the cartilage of his upper ear. A pain that made his nerve endings scream.

Racked through his entire body, from his ear all the way down to his toes. The top of his ear burned so bad he thought Trevor might have set it on fire instead of cutting it off.

His vision blurred; tears rolled down his cheek. A scream filled the small apartment, and it took Eden a moment to realize that it was his. That familiar, pungent, slightly bitter metallic scent filled his nostrils, a wave of nausea rolling through his gut. For a moment, he thought he might pass out. Or bite through his tongue.

Unclenching his teeth, he took one breath. Then another, forcing himself to breathe through the pain. He didn't want to black out. Not here. Or Trevor might take his other ear just for the hell of it. Slowly, his body acclimated to the searing burn where his right ear used to be. Eden was unsteady on his feet as he stood, slid on his jacket, and left Trevor's apartment. Once in his car, he glanced at himself in the rearview mirror.

A trail of blood stretched from his ear down to his neck, disappearing below his collar. His hair was long enough to hide most of the damage since his earlobe was still intact. But he had business to take care of in light of Trevor's recent request. Drawing in a shaky breath, Eden started his car and pulled onto the street. His arms shook. His hands were wrapped so tight around the steering wheel that his fingers went numb.

If this was the worst of Trevor's punishment, he was thankful. Most people didn't get off this easy.

Eden

EDEN TOOK a hard drag from his cigarette, exhaling slowly. His eyes drifted from Freddie's glass doors to the sky overhead. The stars were out, but they were dimmed, like a sunrise blanketed in a thick morning mist. Hoots and hollers from inebriated partygoers drifted through the open windows nearby, interspersed with the occasional hum of a car engine. The night was beginning to wind down. For everyone. Which meant his newest mark would be closing up shop soon.

Not five minutes later, he spotted Alek Ivanov, a tall, lanky brunet towering over a crowd of rowdy twentysomethings, stumbling out of the club. He was drunk. Good. That would make this shit a whole lot easier for both of them.

Eden waited till Mr. Tall, Dark, and Shitfaced had separated from the crowd and started the trek back to his car. After stubbing out his cigarette, Eden pulled on his gloves and fell into step a few feet behind the man. Ivanov was too tall for Eden's usual chloroform routine. But there was more than one way to skin a cat. Palming the taser in his jacket pocket, Eden waited till the man began fumbling with his car keys to step forward. He covered Ivanov's mouth with one gloved hand and held his taser to his neck with the other.

Between the alcohol and the electric shock, Ivanov was out cold within a matter of seconds. Eden eased him onto the ground, then dragged the man backward into the darkness.

"Fuck," Eden muttered, surveying the piss stain around Ivanov's zipper. This was why he always preferred chloroform. Less likely he'd have to deal with bodily fluids. "Your piss, your car," he grumbled, retrieving Ivanov's keys from the sidewalk. It took him a good five minutes to tie his hands, gag him, and haul him into the back seat of his car. After a half-hour drive past the city limits, Eden pulled up in front of a small farmhouse.

Ivanov would be waking up soon. He had no intentions of being around when he did, if for no other reason than recognition would complicate his catch-and-release plans. He moved quickly, ignoring the pain in his arms and back as he hauled Ivanov's body into the nearby cellar. Ungagging him, he made sure Ivanov was still out cold before untying his hands.

He'd already placed some food and water on the ground nearby. He'd have to come back every couple of days to make sure Ivanov didn't starve, but this was the only solution he'd been able to come up with in the limited amount of time he had.

He knew the shit Ryan would likely pull, and that wouldn't work. Not with Trevor. His new captive was sloppy, would likely slip up and use his credit card or get cabin fever and decide to make a run for it if the cops put him in some sort of witness protection program.

And Eden wasn't willing to risk that. Not when it would mean Ryan's life. Exhaling heavily, Eden padlocked the cellar from the outside before lighting up and pulling the captive's car into the farm's empty barn.

The walk back to the city would be a long one. He'd use it to figure out exactly how he was going to pull off keeping this fucker alive for however long it took Ryan to get the dirt he needed on Trevor. This situation wasn't ideal. Killing Ivanov would've been easier and less of a hassle in the long run. But he'd never had much of a stomach for that sort of shit.

That, and now he was officially working with the cops through his association with Ryan. Which meant going rogue was no longer an option. He'd never been much good at nuance. Never had the patience for it. But if he didn't manage to pull this off, someone—and likely more than one of them—would end up in a body bag. It was just a matter of who.

"IT'S FOUR in the morning, X. You better be dying, 'cause that's the only legitimate excuse for you calling me at the asscrack of dawn." Mumbling into his phone, Eden pushed himself up out of bed. He hadn't been sleeping, but he was in no mood to shoot the shit over whatever Xavier had called him about.

"Come outside."

"Don't feel like it."

"Don't care. Now, get your ass out here. We need to talk."

Sighing heavily, Eden shoved his phone into his pocket before shrugging on his leather jacket and heading for the front door. He spotted Xavier propped up against a wall a few feet away, cigarette in mouth.

"What?" Eden growled, stalking up to his best friend.

"I know what you did."

Eden bit down on his cheek, fishing his cigarettes from his pocket and joining Xavier against the wall. That fucker. Of course he'd followed him.

"What are you? My new fucking babysitter now?" Eden growled, lighting his smoke and staring out into the darkness.

"You know that's not it." Xavier's voice was strained, almost angry. Eden could feel his gaze burning a hole in the side of his head. "You have to fucking stop this shit, Eden."

"Stop what?"

"You know what."

Eden shifted against the wall. "If you expect me to just bend over and take Trev's shit—"

"There's a difference between not taking his shit and asking for it. You're the one who told me that, remember?" Xavier let out a tired sigh beside him. "I've got your back. You know I do. But this shit is getting ridiculous. You know Trev's going to lose his shit if he finds out. Lying up with a fucking cop was bad enough. But going behind Trev's back and keeping that fucker alive just so Quinn won't have to get his hands dirty? For fuck's sake, Eden. He's gonna think you've fucking flipped."

Both men stood there in silence for several moments. Crickets chirped. Leaves rustled softly in the breeze. A dog barked somewhere in the distance. Eden smiled.

"You remember when we were kids, X? Back when we'd always sneak into that community pool off of Broadway and 4th Street? Trev would beat our asses every time he caught us. Got to the point where every time we went, the chlorine stung our welts so bad it almost wasn't worth it."

Xavier stilled beside him, his lips stretching into a thin line as he took a hard drag from his cigarette. "Yeah. I remember."

"You remember that time I asked you not to go anymore? Begged you to just drop it. But you couldn't. Even knowing what he'd do when he caught us. And he almost always did." Eden smiled softly, glancing over at Xavier. "You said it was the only way you ever felt clean. That it was something about the smell of the chlorine. And so we kept going. Went every fucking night till that son of a bitch started handcuffing us to the goddamn heater."

Xavier's mouth twitched. "Even back then, you never listened to shit. Started bringing home milk jugs full of fucking pool water, just so I could have the scent."

Eden knocked his shoulder against Xavier's. "Had to. Was the only way I could keep you from scratching sores into your skin."

Xavier cleared his throat, coughing as he kicked at the ground. Something flashed in his eyes. And Eden hated Trevor for it. "Eden, I know what you're getting at. I do. But we're not kids anymore. He won't just beat you with his fucking belt this time if he finds out."

Eden exhaled slowly, white smoke escaping his lips in willowy wisps. "We never had nice things growing up, X. All we ever had was each other. But you're right. We're not kids anymore. As adults, shit doesn't have to be the same. We don't have to sit by while he does whatever the fuck he wants...."

"Yes, we do, Eden. We do if we don't want to end up like Vlad."

Eden shrugged because he loved his friend. And because he didn't honestly have the heart to tell him that there wasn't much of a difference if it meant letting something happen to Ryan.

Instead he looked up at the sky, his eyes tracing long-forgotten patterns in the yellow shards. "He makes me believe in the stars again, X. The fucking stars. I can't let Trev take that away. I won't."

And he meant it. With every single fiber of his being.

Chapter Twenty-Five:
Look Like the Innocent Flower,
but Be the Serpent Under It

Ryan

RYAN WATCHED as the last of the officers on shift filtered out the precinct doors. He waited ten minutes for good measure before picking the lock to McNeil's office and rifling through the files in his desk drawer.

It had to be here. How else would he have known about Eden's mother?

Ryan's fingers stilled as he spotted what he was looking for. Adrenaline coursed through his veins as he flipped open the file and began reading its contents. There had to be something here—something he could use to end this shit with Trevor and make things right between him and Eden.

"I THINK NEW England's going to win again this year."

Ryan stared blankly at Shawn from across his desk. He was droning on about something. What it was, he wasn't sure. Didn't care. Probably women or football or one of the usual trivial topics he dedicated what little brainpower he had to obsessing over.

Was that what he'd been like twelve hours ago? Preoccupied with a million little things that meant nothing at all.

"I mean, they haven't done all that well these last couple games, but—"

"You ever think you knew someone? Only to realize you never knew the first fucking thing about them. That they were the exact opposite of what you thought they were."

Shawn cocked a brow in his direction, looking extremely put-upon by the sudden change in topic. "What?"

"Have you ever felt like you knew how the world worked, where the lines were. Then something happens and you realize you had it so fucking wrong it's almost laughable."

"What the hell are you talking about, Ryan? What's with the sour face?" Leaning forward, Shawn patted him on the shoulder and froze. "Did you—are you fucking drunk?"

Ryan shrugged. "Probably." He hadn't bothered going back to his apartment last night. But he had stopped by the liquor store. If he hadn't, he'd probably be in jail right now for double homicide.

Shawn narrowed his eyes, pulling Ryan into a nearby hallway. "What the hell, man? At work? What the fuck is going on with you?"

Ryan choked out a strained laugh. "With me? Nothing. Not a damn fucking thing—" The rest of the words were lost on his lips as Ryan spotted McNeil entering his office. "I'll talk to you later."

He pushed past Shawn, grabbed the file from his desk, and made a beeline for McNeil. Didn't bother knocking as he pushed open his office door.

"You ever heard of fucking knocking, Quinn—"

"Shut up." Ryan threw the file onto McNeil's desk.

The Irishman stilled, the tension lines in his shoulders visible as his eyes drifted from the file to Ryan. "How the hell did you find that?"

"Not the question you should be asking." Ryan's voice was hard as he glared at McNeil. "Why didn't you fucking tell me?"

McNeil scratched at his beard, swallowing hard. "There was no point—"

"Bullshit!" Ryan slammed his fists onto the desk, leaning in till he and McNeil were nose-to-nose. "That's fucking bullshit, and you know it. I had a right to know."

"And what good did it fucking do," McNeil barked. "It's 8:00 a.m. on a Wednesday morning and you're in my office drunk."

"That's not the fucking point, and you know it." Ryan dug his fingernails into the cold, hard wood. He wanted to strangle McNeil. His hands were shaking, his breaths labored as he willed himself not to act on the fantasies he'd been having for the better half of the morning.

"That why you put me on his case? Because of this shit? Because you knew when Eden found out, it would fuck with his head?"

McNeil's eyes wavered. His lips tightened, but he didn't say anything.

Shaking his head, Ryan drew his arm back and punched McNeil as hard as he could. His boss stumbled back a couple of steps, bringing his hands up to his broken nose. "That's what I fucking thought, you sick son of a bitch."

"You only get one of those, Quinn. You fucking understand?"

"Don't fucking talk to me about what I do and don't get. Like you have any fucking right. Not when you couldn't even give me the truth. I've known you since I was seven fucking years old."

"Exactly. You've known me almost your whole life, Ryan. So you should know I wouldn't have kept this from you if it hadn't been in your best interest."

"And that's for you to decide?" Ryan kicked over the chair at his side, slamming it against the wall. The chair he'd sat in so many times, hanging on McNeil's words. Never thinking to question a thing. "Fuck you and your self-righteous justification. What about him, huh? What about Eden's best interest?"

"He closed that door when he decided to peddle dope. You know that—"

"No, I don't. Not when everything I thought I knew was a lie."

"Not all of it was a lie, Ryan. Luca was a good kid. You know that. You know he wasn't the same after what he went through."

Ryan laughed dryly. "Oh, I see. So my brother gets to do whatever the fuck he wants because of what he went through. Yet Eden deserves whatever fucked-up version of reality you or Luca choose for him just because he sells dope."

"It's different. Your brother wasn't like that before everything happened."

"And Eden was?"

McNeil blew out a frustrated breath. "Zika was never a fucking kid—"

"Because he never had the fucking chance to be one. Luca had all the chances in the fucking world. Every fucking opportunity to turn his shit around. Or at the very least, not become the monster that made him what he was in the first place."

"He was your brother."

"Yeah, and apparently he was a lot of other things too." Ryan didn't bother looking back as he stormed out of McNeil's office, pushed through the precinct doors, and made for his Impala.

Eden

EDEN JUMPED when a knock sounded at his front door. Probably another one of his lovely customers pissed he hadn't been out on his corner for the past week. Ignoring the unwanted visitor, Eden lowered his head and snorted another line. When the knock came again, annoyance drew his features taut.

"Fuck off," Eden yelled.

"It's me."

Eden stilled, recognizing the voice on the other side of the door. After brushing his face off to make sure he didn't have any white on his nose, he hastily wiped the remaining blow on the table into a baggie and shoved it into one of his hidey holes. Hoping he didn't look as bad as he felt, he unceremoniously combed a hand through his ink-black hair before opening the front door.

"What are you doing here, Ryan?"

Eden's eyes narrowed. Ryan stood in front of him, swaying slightly. The whites of his eyes were red, darkly shadowed. His features were strained—frayed—like he'd been walking a tightwire for the last twenty-four hours.

"Hey." Something flashed in Ryan's eyes as he held Eden's stare. "Can I come in?"

He should say no, maintain the boundaries he'd put in place. But Ryan was right in front of him. Close enough to smell, to see his smile and hear his laugh. And there was nothing he wanted more in this world than to just exist near him.

Even if he couldn't have him.

"Okay." Eden held open the door and let Ryan inside.

"Haven't seen you in a couple of days."

"Yeah, been busy."

"With what?"

Eden cleared his throat, shoving his hands into his pockets. "Work. The usual."

Ryan tilted his head to the side. "That's funny. 'Cause I've been to Club Zero every night this week, and I haven't seen you there."

Eden chewed on the inside of his cheek. Even draped in dark circles, Ryan's glacial blue eyes shone brilliantly. Tearing his gaze away, he rifled through his cabinet, retrieving a coffee filter and some grounds.

"Other work."

"Right."

The static silence that filled the room made Eden's gut churn. Eden shifted under Ryan's gaze. His eyes burned a hole in the side of Eden's head as he started the brew.

Something was off. Wrong.

"Who gave you that scar on your cheek?"

Eden's movements stuttered. He'd been asked that question plenty of times. But never from Ryan. "Someone I used to know."

"Yeah? How'd you know him?"

"He was a friend."

"A friend?" Ryan echoed, raising a brow.

"Yeah." Eden didn't look at him as he responded.

"The same friend you wrote those letters to?"

Eden stilled. So he'd found the letters. Still. They were vague enough for him to write them off as something else.

Anything else.

He should've thrown them away. Had tried to so many times. Every time he did, he always ended up digging them back up. It wasn't as if there was any point to keeping them. Not when the person he'd written them to had died over a decade ago. But six feet of dirt and asphalt could only hold so much. It was all the things he couldn't bury that had made Eden write them in the first place, to a pile of bones and a broken crown that would never read the words.

"It's complicated."

"It shouldn't be."

Slowly, Eden turned his back to Ryan and grabbed some eggs and milk from the fridge. "I'll make you some breakfast, sober you up."

"Why?"

"Because you're drunk. And you're going to have one hell of a fucking hangover if you don't eat."

"You think you know me, Eden. But you don't."

What the fuck was this? Some sort of bad trip? He was high. Ryan was drunk. They were alone in his apartment, dancing around something Ryan couldn't possibly know.

Eden turned back toward Ryan. Stray strands of his hair stuck out like he'd been raking his hands through it. His skin was pale and flushed. There was a hard set to his jaw, and a sharp edge to his eyes.

"I know everything that's important."

"Do you?"

Eden scratched at his arms. He did. But there was no way to make Ryan understand. Not without destroying everything he believed in in the process.

"If I asked you who hurt you, would you tell me the name of the person that gave you that scar?"

"No."

"Why?"

"Because. It would hurt you."

Ryan laughed, and Eden's chest hurt. Because he recognized the sound. That hollow, empty sound. "Like you should give a fuck how I feel."

"You think I'm that much of an asshole?"

"I think you're deflecting. Like you always do."

"The truth doesn't always set you free, Ryan. Sometimes it chains you to things you never knew were there."

"Is that why you keep pushing me away? Because you're afraid I'll hurt you like he did?"

"He didn't hurt me. I hurt him."

Ryan's hands curled into fists at his sides. "Don't. Don't defend him. You should hate him." He choked the words out, every syllable laced with disgust.

Eden looked down, then away. "It wasn't like that. He was nice."

"He was seventeen, and you were ten." Ryan spit the words out through clenched teeth. "My brother wasn't nice. He was a fucking pedophile."

Eden recoiled. Took a step back. Ryan knew.

How, he had no clue. But he knew. Drawing in a shaky breath, Eden forced himself to speak past the tightness in his chest. "And if I had told him to stop, he would have."

"That doesn't change shit!" Ryan closed his eyes and took a few deep breaths. "That doesn't change anything, Eden. He knew better. Better than anyone. It was wrong. He was wrong. And maybe you can't tell the difference because everything looks the same when you've lived your whole life in the dark, but it was."

"I know that, Ryan."

"Then why are you talking like you don't?" The words were raw and torn as Ryan white-knuckled the kitchen counter.

"Because. Maybe I didn't back then." Sometimes he still didn't. He'd never been quite sure whether the memories were dreams or nightmares. "Maybe it was what I needed. What you need. Maybe in life sometimes we tell ourselves lies we need to believe about the stars in the sky and the people that we meet. And about our little brothers."

"You shouldn't give a fuck about him. Or about me—"

"I should, and I always will."

Eden wrapped his arms around him as Ryan clung to him, rocking back and forth. His tears pooled on Eden's neck as Ryan's lips moved against his skin.

"I would never hurt you like he did."

"I know."

"I would never choose myself over you."

"I know."

"No, you don't. Or you wouldn't be so scared of letting me love you. Love doesn't hurt you. It doesn't cut you or take advantage. My brother died because he chose dope over everything else. Because he chose himself. Not because of you."

Eden shook his head. "I could have helped him. I should have done more. He was hurting—"

"He was the adult in that fucking situation. If life were any sort of fair, you would've never had to make that choice in the first place."

"Well, it's not. And he's dead because of me—"

"He's dead because he was a sick fuck that wanted something he never had any right to."

"Like me, with you."

Ryan cracked. Lost what little composure he had left as he pulled back and kissed Eden hard.

Eden could taste vodka on him as Ryan's soft, warm lips melded against his. Could feel the hurt and the pain and the urgency in his touch as Ryan held him, fisting the front of Eden's shirt.

"It's not the same. I'm not the same. I promise I'm not."

There were some things in life Eden would never understand. And that was okay.

Things like why, no matter how much blow he did, Luca always haunted his dreams. A constant reminder of the boy that he'd loved. The boy that he'd lost. The boy he'd been too much of a coward to save.

Or why, even knowing how things had ended—even knowing what it would likely mean for him and for Ryan—he'd turned around and done the same exact thing. Attached to someone he couldn't possibly protect from what he was and how he lived.

Or why he'd been able to walk away from Luca. To hold him at a distance even when he'd begged him not to. Even when Eden had watched it destroy him. Yet he couldn't do the same thing with Ryan. Couldn't let go of him, even in oblivion. He could travel to the edge, hold the whole world in his hands, and all he'd ever want was him. He knew because he'd tried.

He'd done so much blow in the last week that he'd burned through all his product and pawned half his living room to buy what he didn't have.

And even when he'd forgotten the world—the sun and the stars and why he even tried—he remembered Ryan. He remembered the one thing more important than a name or a face or a past that never should have been.

There were many things he would never understand. Because when it came down to it, he was just a simple boy with a sharp tongue who had fallen in love with a king.

Thirteen Years ago

Eden

"WHY DO *you call yourself Lazarus?"*

The Prince looked at me and smiled. A secret, mischievous smile, like he held all the answers to the world. He let me stand on his feet and spun me around to the slow quartet of Mozart playing over the hotel room speakers.

His sapphire eyes glistened, and his smile shone with a brightness that reminded me of the stars. He was the most beautiful thing I'd ever seen.

I wondered if he knew.

"Because, Jessie, not everyone will understand. And the ones who don't—the bad men that don't want us to be together—will use my real name to track me down and keep us apart."

"You mean the cops?"

Luca nodded. "Yes. Some people won't understand our love, Jessie. Besides, Lazarus suits me better when I'm with you."

"Why?" I asked.

"Because, when I met you, I was reborn. Just like Lazarus of Bethany. Before I met you, I felt lost. Empty. But you were so bright, you chased away my darkness. You gave me purpose again."

I smiled, because he was a Prince. And I wasn't. And he always said such sweet, impossible things to me.

"I want a code name too, then. Don't you think I should? That way they can't track me either."

Luca tilted his head to the side. "Maybe, but they don't know about you, right? You should be undocumented since your mother was an illegal."

I shrugged, not really understanding what he meant. "I don't know."

Luca bent down and kissed me on the forehead. "Sure. We'll give you a code name too. How about Eden?"

"Eden?" I echoed, sampling the way it sounded on my lips.

"Yes, Eden. Because you're my Garden of Eden when the darkness closes in."

I nodded, chewing on my cheek. I didn't know a lot. Especially about religion. My mother had been religious. But she died. So I couldn't ask her.

"Okay. I kind of like Eden."

"That's good. Because I love Eden." I giggled as he lifted me up in his arms and carried me to the bed.

Chapter Twenty-Six:
Be Great in Act as You
Have Been in Thought

Ryan

RYAN SAT next to Eden as he slept. His eyes clung to Eden's face—his strong jaw, the way it only softened when he slept. The single freckle that dotted the bridge of his nose.

He'd done the same thing so many times for Luca. Sat at his bedside to chase away his demons. To make him feel safe.

While his brother had been Eden's demon.

Bile rose up in the back of Ryan's throat. His hands shook, and he had to bite down on his tongue just to keep from screaming.

He needed to fix this. Needed to make this right.

But nothing would ever be the same as it was. He couldn't just hold Eden and tell him everything was going to be okay.

Because everything wasn't okay. And it probably never would be.

Lifting his hand, Ryan brushed his fingertips along Eden's cheek. He wanted to hold him. To pull him close and breathe in his scent and feel his warmth. He wanted it so bad his bones ached. A pain that radiated through him down to his very core.

Eden would let him if he asked. But how could he? No matter how much he loved Eden, his existence would always hurt him. Serve as a reminder of a past full of pain and scars. One that still kept him up at night, tossing and turning.

Luca haunted him when he slept. Did Ryan do the same thing when he was awake? Make it so that Eden could never truly escape his past?

Ryan cursed. His hands curled into fists, his nails biting into his palms. The helpless rage he felt tugged at his mind like a noose around his neck.

He never thought he would be glad that his brother was dead. But for the first time in his life, he was. Because if he'd still been alive, Ryan would have killed him himself.

After a few moments, Eden stirred, rolled over, and slowly blinked himself awake.

"Hey," Eden muttered groggily.

"Hi."

"Can't sleep?"

Ryan shook his head. "No. Didn't try."

"Why not?" Eden propped himself up on his elbows, batting at his eyes with the back of his hands.

"Had a lot on my mind."

Eden studied him for a moment. "Don't overthink it. If your head gets much bigger, I might have to start scaling down my God complex. And that shit's definitely not happening now that I know I'm the only one you can get it up for."

"Should've never told you." A begrudging smile tugged at Ryan's lips as he rolled his eyes.

"Damn straight. Too late for that now, though." Eden licked his lips, sliding on top of Ryan and groping his dick. "I own you here." Ryan shivered as Eden squeezed his half-hard arousal. "And here." Eden placed his other hand on top of Ryan's chest. "And I plan on keeping it that way."

"Oh yeah?" Ryan asked, resting his hands on the small of Eden's back as Eden hovered over him.

"Yeah. 'Cause you've seen me. And you're still here. You were right."

"About what?"

"When you told me I don't have to hide."

Ryan swallowed hard, holding Eden a little tighter. When he spoke again, his voice held a hoarseness it hadn't before.

"When did you know?"

"That he was your brother?"

"Yeah."

Eden's features betrayed no signs of discomfort. He visibly relaxed as Ryan ran his hands up and down his back. "I wasn't sure for a while. But I've known since the cop bar."

"How did you meet him?"

Eden stilled, something flickering across his face. It was only for a second, but it made Ryan's chest ache. He shouldn't ask. He shouldn't speak of it at all. But he had to know. He needed to know why and how and where. Wanted to know everything he'd said, everywhere he'd touched, every excruciating detail.

Because Ryan was breaking. And Eden felt broken. And he had no idea how to make any of it better.

"You don't have to tell me if you don't want to."

"Nah. It's fine. He used to buy blow from Trev. That's how we met initially."

"Is that what you dream about? Him?"

Eden was silent for a moment. "Sometimes. On a good night. He's the one that showed me the stars. Taught me to tell stories, go to a different place. Somewhere to escape."

Ryan's jaw tightened. "He wouldn't have had to if he'd just kept you safe in the first place." The words came out harder than he'd meant for them to. Not for Luca's sake, but for Eden's.

"He tried. In his own way."

Ryan closed his eyes, clamping down on the anger that threatened beneath the surface. "I hate him."

"I know."

"And I always will."

Eden frowned, shifting in his arms. "I wish you wouldn't."

"Why?"

"Because he's a part of you, just like my father will always be a part of me. Regardless of how much we hate what they did."

Ryan's body went rigid as he railed against the thought. He closed his eyes and held Eden until he began to feel himself relax again. Eden's slow, even breaths brushed over Ryan's face soothingly, and Eden nestled into the crook of Ryan's neck. For a moment, Ryan wished they could stay like this forever. Wished they could freeze this moment in time.

But for so long, he'd only seen in gray. Shades of black and white.

Eden was his color. And Luca was his blood. He had to make things right. For the sake of everything he used to believe in. And some things he still believed in.

Slipping out from under Eden, Ryan kissed him once, barely a touch.

"Sweet dreams, Eden."

Turning, Ryan left and willed himself not to look back.

He stopped by the precinct and left his badge on his desk. He wouldn't need it anymore. Not after this.

Thirty minutes at the twenty-four-hour tattoo shop on the south side of town, and he was ready. There was no hesitation in Ryan's stride as he made his way up to Trevor's penthouse. After a couple of knocks, the door swung open, Trevor's familiar gnarled face contorted with more malice than usual.

"Did you do it?"

Trevor batted at his face with the back of his hands, rubbing the sleep from his eyes. "You're going to have to be a little more specific, given your day job. I've done a lot of shit recently that might warrant whatever stick up your ass has you beating down my door uninvited."

Ryan made no attempt to hide the rage in his voice. He was sure it was already written all over his face. "His ear. Did you cut it off?"

Trevor appraised him, a mixture of curiosity and amusement flashing in his eyes. After a moment's silence, he pushed open the door and motioned Ryan inside. Ryan followed, taking a seat on a black leather couch opposite Trevor. Gills took his time responding, lighting a cigar and blowing a couple of smoke rings before he turned his attention back to Ryan.

"You know how to turn a trick out, Ryan?"

"I'm not here for a lesson in whatever fucked-up shit you're running on the side. Just answer the fucking question."

Trevor flicked the ash at the end of his cigar into a nearby ashtray. "You get 'em while they're young. Get 'em hooked. Strung out till they need what you've got. Till you're their mother. Their father. Their motherfucking God. You do that, and they'll do whatever you fucking tell them. That sort of power, it's like a fucking high. Better than any trip you can get from coke or meth."

Ryan's lips curled back in disgust.

"Problem is, eventually, they grow up. Start wanting more. A stronger high. Something that lasts." Trevor laughed. The empty sound made Ryan's skin crawl. Made his stomach bottom out, like he was standing at the top of a fifty-foot cliff. "Like love. And love is a motherfucker. Dumbs people down. Makes 'em do stupid shit they'd usually be too smart for."

Trevor leaned forward as he took a slow drag from his cigar. "Turning you dirty was never about you, Ryan. I never gave a fuck about keeping an eye on your precinct. Already got men for that. It was about testing my trick."

"He's not your trick."

"No? How do you think he met your brother? Luca was one of Eden's best customers before your brother lost his shit, thinking he could turn a warm hole into a home. That boy's been run through so many times—"

A gunshot rang out. One after another. And another. Till Ryan had emptied his gun into Trevor's lifeless body. And after he was done, he took the cigar from Trevor's hand and shoved it down his throat.

"You should really watch your mouth," Ryan muttered. Standing over Trevor's dead body, he smiled. The cops would be here soon, if Trevor's men didn't make it here first.

But he didn't care. He'd done what he'd come here to do. Done what his brother should've done twelve years ago when all this had started.

Ryan knew he would never be able to be that safe place for Eden. Somewhere that could protect him from all the horrors of the world. Because his brother was that horror. And as Eden had said, his brother would always be a part of him. There was nothing he could do to change that. Or the fact that he'd spent countless nights consoling Luca while he'd been doing what he'd done.

But he would do everything in his power to create it for him. Give him what little he had left to give. Even if it meant giving up his own.

Eden might hate him. He might not understand.

But for the first time in his life, he would be free to feel however he wanted. To be whoever he wanted.

And that alone would always be worth it.

"What the hell did you do?"

Ryan turned. Xavier stood behind him, his gaze drifting from Ryan to Trevor's bullet-riddled body.

"I killed him," Ryan answered simply, setting his gun on the glass table.

Xavier cursed. His face went pale as he bent down and checked Trevor's pulse. "He told you, didn't he?"

Ryan took a seat on the black leather couch instead of responding.

"Get out."

"I can't. The cops will be here soon."

"Exactly, Xavier snapped, grabbing Ryan's gun from the table and disappearing into a back room. When he came back out, the gun was gone, in its place a large black duffel bag.

"What are you doing?"

"Cleaning up your fucking mess. Now go."

"What?"

"You heard me. Get the fuck out. The body's gonna be hard enough to hide without me having to make up some bullshit story about why you're here."

Ryan frowned, standing slowly. Either he'd lost what little was left of his sanity, or Xavier was actually trying to help. "Why are you helping me?"

"For Eden. He needs you. And I won't be able to deal with his bitching if you get locked up on my watch. So leave through the back and keep your mouth shut about this."

Ryan blinked. Xavier, of all people, was offering to cover for him. "Thank you."

"Don't thank me. I'm not doing it for you."

Nodding, Ryan left. By the time he reached his apartment, the sun hung low in the sky. He wasn't sure how long he'd been gone. Maybe a couple of hours. But it felt like years.

He had blood splatter on his shirt and pants. Probably his face too. Hopefully Eden was still asleep. Quietly, Ryan crept up the stairs and opened the door to his apartment. He only made it a couple of steps before the lights in his living room flickered on.

"Where were you?" Eden's voice was sharp. His eyes held a hardness that answered every question on the tip of Ryan's tongue.

"Trevor's."

Eden's eyes narrowed. He took a couple steps forward till they were nose-to-nose. "Why?"

"Because I had to. To make things right."

"And did it?"

"No."

Eden's eyes skimmed across his face. After a moment, his expression fell.

"You can't change the past, Ryan."

"I know. I know that. But I have to try."

"Why are you punishing yourself?"

"I'm not."

"You think I can't tell the difference? Or did you forget how you found me?"

Ryan shook, and he closed his eyes for a moment. "I'm sorry."

"You should be. I could lose you forever on that shit. Now sit down."

Ryan acquiesced, taking a seat in the nearby chair. He didn't fight when Eden pulled a pair of handcuffs from his pocket and bound his hands behind his back.

"You remember you're mine, right?"

A thrill ran up Ryan's spine when Eden reached forward and placed his hand on his chest.

"Yes."

"You don't touch what's mine. You don't hurt it."

"But he hurt you. And I can't fucking take it. I can't take what he did."

"Then let me take it from you." Eden reached out and slid his fingertips along Ryan's jawline.

Ryan nodded. He lifted his hips as Eden pulled his pants off and palmed his dick, stroking him from base to head. His body tensed under Eden's touch, because he didn't deserve it. Didn't deserve his kindness.

But he was Eden's. Irrevocably so. And he would take whatever Eden gave him.

Eden

EDEN STROKED Ryan slowly, till his dick was hard and heavy in his hands. Eden's chest swelled at the look in Ryan's eyes as he watched him. The way he leaned back, offering himself to him. Reaching for him through the darkness.

Eden pushed off his own pants and spit into his hands. He made quick work of lubing himself up before climbing on top of Ryan and wrapping his hands around Ryan's neck.

"What are you doing?"

"Making you feel real." Eden reached back and lined Ryan's arousal up, slowly easing down onto him. Ryan groaned as he slid inside, shuddering as Eden's heat surrounded him. Eden's body tightened around Ryan's erection, railing against the intrusion.

"God, you're so fucking tight." Ryan's words were hoarse and strained as he looked up at Eden through half-lidded eyes.

Eden let out a choked laugh, forcing himself to breathe past the pain. He never bottomed. Not anymore. He'd never wanted to before. But Ryan made him want things he'd never dreamt of with anyone else. Not even Luca.

Flexing his hips, Eden rocked into Ryan as Ryan's hips lifted upward in time with his movements. It was a slow rhythm.

Like they had all the time in the world. Like nothing else existed. And for a moment, maybe it didn't. Eden rode him, slowly drawing out Ryan's orgasm till all the tension had drained from his body. Till every ounce of Ryan's attention was focused on him. On them and this single moment in time.

And when Ryan came, Eden held on to him. Took in the way his eyes clung to him, his lips swollen, his cheeks flushed, strands of sweat-slicked hair clinging to his face.

Eden smiled. Because Ryan was finally smiling again.

In this world full of great and horrible things, Eden finally understood. There was no such thing as a world where nothing was beautiful. Only people who couldn't see the beauty through the pain.

But pain was the flip side to a coin filled with so many other things. Full of life and love and happiness. Pain didn't mean it wasn't beautiful. It was what made it beautiful. Wanting everything else in spite of the pain.

And he did.

He wanted to be here.

So that he could make Ryan smile. So that he could exist near him and feel his warmth and hear his laugh. He wanted to give him the world, even if it wasn't his to give. Even if it meant hurting sometimes. Even if there would be pain.

Maybe hoping for something like that was just another pipe dream. But some dreams weren't meant to be a reality. They were meant to lead us down another path.

A path through oblivion, beneath the stars. A path to a truth he'd spent his entire life running from. Ryan had a bleeding heart. And maybe so did he. Because he'd finally found something precious and beautiful that he could call his own. And all he wanted to do was keep it safe from the darkness and watch as it shone. To protect this delicate, fragile light.

In this fucked-up, beautiful world, all he wanted to do was hold it close and feel.

All he wanted to do was *be*.

Author's Note

Homelessness, drug use, and sexual abuse are prevalent in the LGBTQ+ community, especially among teens. If you or someone you love needs help, there are resources available. Please reach out or consider volunteering.

Trevor Project - Reach a Counselor
We're here for you 24/7.
Chat With Us
Call Us: 1-866-488-7386
Text Us: 678-678

Anti-Violence Project
CALL/TEXT 212-714-1141
https://avp.org/get-help/

SAMHSA National Helpline
Confidential free help, from public health agencies,
to find substance use treatment and information.
1-800-662-4357

988 Suicide and Crisis Lifeline
Hours: Available 24 hours.
Languages: English, Spanish.
Text or call: 988

Keep Reading for an Excerpt from
Under Cover
by Amy Lane.
Available Now!

Prologue

CROSBY TRIED to slide out of bed stealthily, but he must have failed. When Garcia wrapped an arm around his middle, he mumbled something about going to the bathroom.

Shit.

He used the facilities, but he also put his socks on while he was in there because that got tricky when you put them on after you put on your jeans. He was trying for casual here. No big deal. Two colleagues who'd hooked up after a drink or two when the workday was over.

Happened all the time.

They were professionals, right? And it had been a sucktastic case.

Crosby made the mistake of looking at himself in the mirror when he was washing his face in the bathroom, and unbidden came that moment when the nine-year-old girl had been in his sights as he'd aimed at the murderer behind her.

"Don't take it if it's not good," his AIC had said in his earpiece, but the guy had a knife in his hand. They'd been hunting him, one crime scene after another. So much blood.

And here he was, knife dripping, holding it to her throat, and Crosby wondered which one would make him feel worse—if the killer got her or if Crosby got her, aiming for the killer.

And that hadn't been the worst of it. Garcia... he'd been so close. In Crosby's sights. If Crosby had been just a hair off....

He shuddered then and tried not to retch and splashed more water on his face. Garcia had toothpaste and a fresh toothbrush in the cupboard; Crosby took advantage of it. What was raiding the guy's cupboard when he'd had your cock in his mouth the night before, right?

The memory of the moment overwhelmed him.

Garcia, slighter body moving quickly down the street, Crosby's big blondness lumbering behind him. Crosby had never felt clumsy before in spite of the breadth of his chest, the muscular thickness of his thighs, but Garcia was so tightly wrought.

"Naw, man, I should go home," Crosby had said halfheartedly in response to Garcia's suggestion that Crosby not go back to his uncomfortable living sitch.

"You said she's not your girlfriend!" Garcia laughed. "Besides, you're just crashing at my place!"

From behind Crosby could see the slenderness of his hips, the wiry refinement of his ass and thighs. Garcia wore his black jeans tight—Crosby liked that.

"She's not my girlfriend," he defended. "I knew that from the beginning. We haven't been together since I got hurt."

It would have been awkward to hit her up after nearly six months of not so much as a text. And he didn't want to be needy, although God, tonight he needed somebody.

And Garcia hit him that way. Some girls did, some guys did—just hit.

Even in the spring chill, sweat dotted Crosby's chest under his fleece jacket. He wanted to take off his watch cap, but it was still in the thirties at night, and he knew his ears would be bright purple by the time they got to Calix Garcia's neat little house in Queens.

Sometimes, guy or girl, they hit *hard.*

Garcia had been hitting him pretty hard since he'd shown up in their unit six months ago. Small, quick, compassionate, and with zero ego, the guy was a dream agent. Crosby had looked forward to working with him every day.

And as he followed his fellow agent, and friend to the door so he didn't have to drive crosstown to the place where he roomed with his old college buddy who was throwing a constant party, he thought hungrily about *working* Garcia, from toes to nipples, from mouth to cock to ass.

Working him. So hard.

Garcia let Crosby in first. Crosby had paused in the doorway, letting his eyes adjust so he could find the light, when Garcia closed the door behind him and came up hard against Crosby's back.

"Tell me to turn on the light," Garcia murmured in his ear, and Crosby's heart pounded. Oh wow. Oh *wow*.

His mouth went so dry he had to clear his throat twice to speak. "No."

Garcia let out a breath, hot and violent, into his ear. They were both still wearing jackets and hats, but Garcia's hands came to rest on his hips, then snuck under the hem of his jacket, and Crosby quaked at the chill of his fingers near his flat, molded abdomen.

"Tell me to back off," Garcia murmured.

Crosby's entire body shuddered violently, and he turned in Garcia's arms and shoved him back against the door. For a moment, they stared into each other's eyes in the darkness, Garcia's gleaming black and excited, before Crosby lowered his head enough to whisper in Garcia's ear for a change.

"No."

"No what?" Garcia baited.

Crosby ground their groins together through their jeans. "Not backing off."

"Good," Garcia breathed and nipped his lower lip.

Crosby nipped his in return, and then Garcia teased the seam of his pursed mouth with his tongue. Crosby shuddered again, and Garcia thrust his package against the placket of Crosby's jeans.

"You gonna tell me it was an accident in the morning?" Garcia taunted him. "You tripped in the dark and fell on my ass with your dick?"

"No," Crosby said, tracing Garcia's jawline with his nose, bumping along his temple, working his hands into Garcia's jacket so he could feel the tight, wiry muscles underneath.

"Gonna tell me you got a girlfriend?"

"I *had* a hookup," Crosby told him, thinking it was honest.

"Now you got two." Garcia grinned and dropped to his knees, dragging Crosby's jeans and briefs down his ass.

Crosby's cock flopped out, mostly hard, and the twinkle in Garcia's eyes as he looked into Crosby's face, mouth open, and engulfed him to the root, almost made Crosby come before the first touch.

It didn't get any worse after that.

NOW CROSBY looked at himself in the mirror and remembered those sparkling eyes, and his cheeks heated.

He couldn't betray those eyes.

With a sigh he wet-combed his hair and used a cloth on his pits and all points south. He was going to be wearing the same outfit back to work that morning; he didn't want to smell bad.

Then he returned to Garcia's bedroom, taking in the redwood floors, the cream-colored area rug, and the gray-blue and brown bedding, all of it masculine and inviting and clean. He'd been to Garcia's flat before, a couple of times. Spent Christmas in the spare room, which had a bed and everything. Had shared the occasional late-night takeout when Garcia had taken pity on him and rescued him from his living sitch. Garcia had even had the team over a couple of times—once to celebrate his birthday and once to celebrate Crosby's.

This guy had his life together. His room was a little messy but not a pit. He had solid modern furniture in the small living room and even a dinette table in the kitchen/dining room.

Garcia could bring people to his place because his place was *his* place.

Crosby took turns rooming with his old college buddy or with his bestie in the unit, Gail, because he had no place in the city.

He admired someone who could make their mark in a little New York house, and he admired anyone who could work Special Crimes Task Force.

And he really liked Garcia.

With a sigh he went back to the bed and thrust his stockinged feet into one leg of his jeans and then the other. He left the placket open before grabbing his T-shirt and sitting down on the edge of the bed.

Garcia was watching him, head propped on one hand, the covers sliding down his bare chest, revealing a scattering of dark hair between the nipples.

"You going to go back to work and pretend this never happened?" he asked, and his eyes were bright—but not twinkling.

With a sad shock, Crosby realized he could hurt Garcia—hurt his friend, his partner, his colleague—if he played this wrong.

"No," he said, sliding the T-shirt on. It was chilly in the room, although he'd heard the thermostat click on. Probably on a timer.

"Then this was a onetime thing, and we still respect each other in the morning, and I see you with your girl hookup and you see me with other guys and we think, 'Yeah, I'm glad he's happy'?"

There was an edge to Garcia's voice, and Crosby's chest grew tight, his throat swelling as he tried to imagine that exact scenario. He'd never seen Garcia with other guys—had really only intuited that Garcia might be gay… until he'd closed the door last night. But the thought of that, of *his* partner, *his* guy, on the arm of another man was like a big, ugly beast in his stomach.

What came out next was more like a growl.

"No."

"Then wh—"

Crosby turned on the bed and took Garcia's mouth, not wanting any more scenarios, not wanting any "What are we now?" questions. He just wanted the taste of Garcia, and as he swept his tongue inside that warm, willing cavern, he tasted his own come and remembered that last slow, painful orgasm, the final of three, because Garcia had wanted to taste him before they fell back asleep.

Crosby's cock strained against his briefs, the whole works threatening to bubble out of the unbuttoned fly, and he pulled back, breath laboring in his chest.

"I haven't hooked up with Gail's roommate since you started at SCTF," he blurted as he pulled away.

Garcia tilted his head. "Yeah?"

"Yeah." Crosby nodded. He held his hand up because they'd done this quietly, under the table the night before, surrounded by colleagues. It was where they'd started.

Garcia gave him a guarded look and threaded their fingers together. "So what do we do?"

Crosby looked at his sex-swollen mouth, remembered his head tilted back, his eyes closed, as Crosby had pounded into his body and Garcia had begged so sweetly.

"We can't come out to the squad yet," Crosby said, wanting to do that again. Wanting to feel Garcia's come spurting between their bodies. Wanting to hold Garcia's cock, his home, in his mouth again.

Garcia started to withdraw his hand, but Crosby captured it.

"We couldn't even if one of us was a girl," he said, knowing he sounded like a meatloaf and not caring. "'Cause protocol. 'Cause it's dangerous. 'Cause we'd worry every time we had to draw our weapons."

Garcia's eyes, black-brown infinity pools, sharper than daggers. "I already worry about you every time we have to draw our weapons," he said, the brutal honesty stripping Crosby to the skin. He remembered the week before, Garcia catching a shelf to the back of the head, being sent sprawling, and how Crosby had needed to run right past him while Harding checked to make sure Garcia was okay because Crosby had point and there was an asshole with a gun and a death wish who wanted to make everybody else die first.

"But we still do our jobs," Crosby said soberly. The job—it meant everything.

Garcia nodded, and they were on the same page.

"But you don't hook up with Gail's roommate anymore," he reiterated.

Crosby nodded, not bothering to speak the truth one more time. Gail's roommate hadn't been a thing since Calix Garcia had walked in the door at the SCTF six months before. "And you don't hook up with—"

"Nobody," Garcia whispered. "I haven't hooked up with anybody, not for a really long time."

Crosby remembered the sweet yielding of his body, the way he'd devoured Crosby's cock, like he'd been starving for it. Apparently only Crosby's cock.

"Only me," Crosby said, feeling possessive.

"Yeah."

"You only hook up with me."

"Yeah."

They stared into each other's eyes for a moment, and Crosby took his mouth again, holding Garcia's hands over his head and ravaging, claiming, knowing his short beard would leave marks, stubble burns, proof that he'd been there.

But Garcia submitted, took the kiss, made it more, until the buzzing of both their phones from the charger on Garcia's dresser shocked them apart.

"We have work," Garcia murmured.

"Yeah."

"We can do this. Only hook up with each other."

"Yeah."

"Get dressed, *papi*. We can get coffee and bagels on the way in."

That got Crosby to move. He stood and buttoned his jeans, then gathered his sweater, his fleece, his boots. Garcia ran to the bathroom, probably to give himself the same sort of regimen Crosby had, and Crosby picked up his phone and texted Harding, their Agent In Charge, that Garcia would pick him up on the way.

Nobody would ask, he knew. Buddies coming to work together. Like him sleeping on Gail's couch before the roommate complication. Nothing to see here, folks; no mind-blowing sex, no uncomfortable emotional attachment.

But even as he thought about that, thought about making it clear he wouldn't be sleeping with the roommate again, he fought off the obvious, the thing neither of them had said.

If they only hooked up with each other....

If they worried when weapons were drawn....

If they pretended they weren't doing the thing....

If Crosby marked Garcia like Garcia marked his home, making the man his and fuck anyone else who looked at him....

If these were the truths they were living with now....

It wasn't a hookup anymore. It had never been one in the first place.

Covert—Backing Up to the Beginning

Six Months Earlier

JUDSON CROSBY woke up on his best friend's couch and groaned.

"You awake?" Gail Pearson had long blond pigtail braids and cornflower blue eyes—and some of the keenest knife skills Crosby had ever seen. Unfortunately those knife skills hadn't saved her from a kick from a perp that had caved her knee in exactly the wrong direction knees should go, and she'd been laid up for the last two months, acting as their team's backup hacker because Kylie, their regular hacker, had just gotten married and taken a year's leave of absence.

Gail was going nuts, and she was driving her roommate nuts, and Crosby had been called in to mediate a week into her "incarceration" at home. Crosby had shown up to be Gail's legs and her ride to work, and had stayed—on and off—for the sex with Iliana, her roommate. Iliana, who was as tall and dusky as Gail was tiny and blond, worked as a commander in Active Crimes in a precinct next door to the precinct that patrolled their street. To say Iliana's sex life was a closely guarded secret was to say Fort Knox was closely guarded. Crosby knew he was a means to an end, a flesh-covered dildo, as it were, because Iliana was straight with him—and that was fine.

But it meant that on the nights they weren't doing the quick and dirty, he was out here on the couch, because Iliana's room was Iliana's room, and he wasn't welcome, and he knew it.

It was a good thing their couch was a sweet, sweet ride to dreamland, or he'd be forced back into his own apartment, where his roommate's other guests had probably had sex on every surface, including the ceilings, with every gender known to or yet to be discovered by humans.

Toby Trotter was a great guy, but he was not—*not*—an ideal roommate.

Crosby's days often turned into weeks in the Special Crimes Task Force. A collaboration that borrowed officers from the police, the FBI, NCIS,

ATF, and probably a few other alphabets as well, the SCTF was funded by the military but under the management of Lieutenant Commander Clint Harding. Clint—formerly covert ops, though some speculated CIA while others speculated black ops, deep—answered to no other master than the Attorney General of the United States, and sometimes they had words. His job—his only job—was to track down felons who had eluded capture in their particular jurisdiction, often felons who were in the middle of a crime spree.

Clint's unit's job was, in his words, to keep the blood from spilling and to bring the bad guy in. He preferred alive, and he made that plain, but he also preferred his guys alive to the bad guy if it came down to that, and his unit was grateful.

Crosby had been tapped for SCTF as a homicide cop in Chicago, but he'd lived in New York for a year to be part of the unit. He'd managed to find a roommate—his old college roommate, actually—who was making a lot of money as a DJ and was happy to let Crosby stay in his spare room. Toby was a great guy, and he'd stayed true to his offer of showing Crosby around the city. The deal had seemed too good to be true when it had first been offered.

After a year and a half of dragging his bloody, bruised, exhausted ass into the apartment to find the party he'd left two days ago still going strong, Crosby had recognized that seeming too good to be true was often *being* too good to be true. He'd jumped at a chance to help Gail out and get some sleep, and then he'd awakened one night to Iliana taking off her robe in the middle of the living room and saying, "I don't want strings, I just want dick. You in?"

Well, if nothing else he'd needed to work off some stress.

With a moan he turned his head now to see Gail holding out a mug of coffee. He whimpered and sat up, taking it from her hands. "We got a call?" he asked.

"Yeah. I told Clint it would take us half an hour. You showered last night, because you're considerate as fuck, and I just need to change." She shook her head. "You know, if you weren't banging my roommate, I'd be afraid you'd perv out on me when you had to help me change, but you seem to be a perfect gentleman."

Crosby sipped his coffee—hot, with cream—and smiled a little. "She make it back last night?"

"Yeah. Late, though. Does she really only let you sleep in the bed when you're having sex?"

He grimaced. "She actually asks me to leave if we don't fall asleep. Don't worry. I have no illusions as to intimacy or monogamy. I know what I'm here for."

Gail sighed, the breath stirring the fine strands of gold hair that curled from her tight braids. "You have to forgive her. I mean, I was super excited when you guys started hooking up—after Danny…." She trailed off. Iliana's boyfriend, Danny Aramis, had been killed in a train derailment up in Pennsylvania on a business trip. Apparently it had been true love for them, and according to Gail, Crosby was Iliana's first step into the land of the living in over two years. Her job at the Forty-Third Precinct—she was in charge of the Active Crimes Division—kept her too busy to have much of a social life, and here, neatly delivered, was a person who got law enforcement hours and was pretty decent (if Crosby dared say so) in bed.

It was starting to dawn on them both that Crosby was a means to scratch an itch—he was most assuredly not an emotional act of bravery.

"Yeah, well…." He shrugged. "I was willing. But the good news is I can get up now and get us dressed, and I don't need to kiss anybody goodbye."

Gail didn't answer back. They both knew Iliana didn't care where he went when they weren't fucking, and that was not going to change.

But the thought gnawed at Crosby. He sat through the briefing with Clint and looked over their little unit: Natalia Denison, Clint's second in command, a former ADA with a lawyer's sharp mind and hand-to-hand fighting skills the likes of which Crosby had never seen, who wore a little silver goddess pendant that looked like something from an assassin's catalog; Joey Carlyle, former Marine with the speed and stamina of a gazelle and the patience to stalk a perpetrator through miles of woodland in the snow without a single word of either complaint or victory in case he gave away his position; Gideon Chadwick, Navy covert ops, weapons expert, and psychology major; and Clint Harding, their boss, former top secret badass, who had an uncanny way of looking at evidence and figuring out what their suspect would want, where they would go, and what they would need.

Then there was Gail, who was small, sneaky, and uncanny when it came to judging what a suspect would do in the heat of a confrontation, and Crosby, who, as far as he knew, was only there because he'd run down a serial killer in the middle of a drug war and brought the guy in alive. Doing so had also stopped the war. It had started because two neighborhoods had been losing their young people at a terrible rate, and Crosby had figured out that they hadn't been lost to gang violence, but to Cordell Brandeis, who was currently rotting in a supermax prison with over two hundred kills to his name.

It was either that or the thing that had made his entire department in Chicago want to kill him. Okay—maybe there were two reasons Crosby was in the SCTF.

These were good people, he thought seriously. They had families and kids and spouses or parents who worried about them and a special set of skills he could understand would work in the situations they'd been thrown into.

He'd been with the unit for a year and a half, and he still didn't know—really—what the hell he was doing there.

And that right there was about what he'd been thinking when trouble walked through the door.

LAURA DECOSTA grew up just outside the Mile High City. She attributes the altitude, and the friends she made along the way, to why she tends toward spending most of her time with her head in the clouds. The amalgamation of big city and granola culture left her with an appreciation for functional chaos and unpredictable weather patterns. When she's not lost in her head, grasping at the threads of another story, she likes to spend her days in the mountains, hiking or mountain biking.

For her, stories are an exploration of people and how they love (and, on occasion, of herself). If you see her around town on the few occasions she doesn't have her nose buried in a book or a video game, she'll probably be wearing a beanie and sipping something highly caffeinated. Despite her love for The Matrix (Neo was her first fictional crush), she never quite took to social media like the rest of her more well-adjusted peers.But she does have Twitter and a Goodreads account created for the sole purposeof gushing over literary (and sometimes 2D) romances. Her Goodreads account is under the profile LauraDecosta.

Links:
Twitter: https://twitter.com/LauraNDeCosta

COVERT ★ BOOK 1

UNDER COVER

AMY LANE

Covert: Book One

For Judson Crosby, the transfer to the elite law enforcement branch of the SCTF is a great escape from the death sentence he earned as a whistle-blowing patrol officer. Calix Garcia, the fierce new guy, makes a perfect partner, catching bad guys while minimizing collateral damage. Crosby loves working with him.

Of course, he'd also love to work him over in a totally different way.

Garcia has waited his whole career for a solid, dependable partner like Crosby. But after six months fighting crime together, he's done fighting their attraction.

Their coming together promises to be everything they need… until a threat from Crosby's past comes back to haunt not just him, but their entire team.

When Crosby goes undercover to keep them safe, Garcia is frantic with worry. One false move could get Crosby killed and Garcia exposed. But they have to fight their way clear, because hiding your lover under the cover of darkness is no way to live. Crosby and Garcia will risk everything for the chance to live their lives in the light.

www.dreamspinnerpress.com

A LONG CON ADVENTURE

The Mastermind

AMY LANE

"Delicious fun." — Booklist

A Long Con Adventure

Once upon a time in Rome, Felix Salinger got caught picking his first pocket and Danny Mitchell saved his bacon. The two of them were inseparable… until they weren't.

Twenty years after that first meeting, Danny returns to Chicago, the city he shared with Felix and their perfect, secret family, to save him again. Felix's news network—the business that broke them apart—is under fire from an unscrupulous employee pointing the finger at Felix. An official investigation could topple their house of cards. The only way to prove Felix is innocent is to pull off their biggest con yet.

But though Felix still has the gift of grift, his reunion with Danny is bittersweet. Their ten-year separation left holes in their hearts that no amount of stolen property can fill. A green crew of young thieves looks to them for guidance as they negotiate old jewels and new threats to pull off the perfect heist—but the hardest job is proving that love is the only thing of value they've ever had.

www.dreamspinnerpress.com

A Black Dragons Inc. Novel

Hot SEAL. Hot spy. Hot reunion. Can they work together to find a notorious terrorist without killing each other first?

When SEAL Spencer Newman accepts a dangerous mission to bring in CIA agent Drago Thorpe—the only man he's ever loved—he expects things to get FUBAR. He doesn't expect Drago to convince him to go rogue too.

Drago regrets ending their torrid affair by pressuring Spencer to acknowledge their relationship publicly, and he wants a second chance. It's always been a challenge to get the uptight SEAL to break the rules, but to eliminate a supposedly dead terrorist, they'll need to operate outside the law. Tension heats up as they track their target, but can they find him before their attraction explodes out of control?

www.dreamspinnerpress.com

PREY FOR LOVE

Best-Selling Author

DIRK GREYSON

The last three guys Phillip dated are dead. Is he next?

When successful businessman Phillip Barone attends a lover's funeral and discovers he was just the latest of Phillip's partners to die, Phillip knows he's in trouble.

He also knows just the man he needs.

Former Marine Barry Malone would love a second chance with Phillip—he just wishes the romance could be rekindled under better circumstances. But Phillip's stalker is escalating, and if Barry cannot solve the mystery of who wants Phillip dead and why, he might lose him for good. Barry's determined, but the investigation struggles against the wit of a crafty killer—one who is closer to Phillip than they could have realized.

Luckily Barry is even closer, and he'll do whatever it takes to protect the man he's falling in love with all over again.

www.dreamspinnerpress.com

COLE McGINNIS MYSTERY ROMANCE: ONE

RHYS FORD

DIRTY
KISS

A Cole McGinnis Mystery

Cole Kenjiro McGinnis, ex-cop and PI, is trying to get over the shooting death of his lover when a supposedly routine investigation lands in his lap. Investigating the apparent suicide of a prominent Korean businessman's son proves to be anything but ordinary, especially when it introduces Cole to the dead man's handsome cousin, Kim Jae-Min.

Jae-Min's cousin had a dirty little secret, the kind that Cole has been familiar with all his life and that Jae-Min is still hiding from his family. The investigation leads Cole from tasteful mansions to seedy lover's trysts to Dirty Kiss, the place where the rich and discreet go to indulge in desires their traditional-minded families would rather know nothing about.

It also leads Cole McGinnis into Jae-Min's arms, and that could be a problem. Jae-Min's cousin's death is looking less and less like a suicide, and Jae-Min is looking more and more like a target. Cole has already lost one lover to violence—he's not about to lose Jae-Min too.

www.dreamspinnerpress.com